The Testament of Leofric the Black

Volume One
(1040-1057)

Edward Cartwright Beard

Holt&Dean
Publishers

HOLT&DEAN PUBLISHERS

HD

This book is dedicated to my wife Susan, for all the support, encouragement and invaluable help with this novel and for putting up with my nonsense for nearly fifty years.

ACKNOWLEDGMENTS

I wish to thank Lee Grange, Rose Williams, Tony Beedie and Ted Boersma for their comments, suggestions and encouragement.

Place Names

Place names in historical novels can sometimes be contentious. Some readers feel the antiquated form adds to the sense of a different time, different place. Others dislike them, having the view it disrupts the flow of the story each time the modern-day equivalent is referred to.

I subscribe to the first view, using The Concise Oxford Dictionary of English Place Names to find the nearest to the commonly used name of the period.

Three letters modern readers may not be familiar with which do appear in old English texts are;

The ash Æ; æ, pronounced a as in sat.

The thorn; þ, Þ used for th as in the.

The eth; Ð, ð, is said as in leather.

A list of place names and their modern-day equivalents can be found at the back of the book from page 438

A list of characters follows, from page 442

A glossary on page 447

Runes page 449

The Testament
of
Leofric the Black

Volume One
(1040-1057)

One

We have lost the Isle of Elig.

After eighteen months of siege, Norman soldiers swarm over the island slaying everyone they can find. The screams of brave men still fill my nightmares. Regardless of our endeavour to resist their relentless onslaught, some despicable or misguided soul led them in through the secret ways across the perilous marshes. Much to my horror, there are those who claim it was I, Leofric the Black. I now stand accused of treachery, betrayal and collusion with William the Bastard, Duke of Normandy, hailed by the reckoning of many, King of Englaland and master of her people.

Six others and I are fleeing, not only from Norman soldiers but also from our own English warriors. It is the year AD 1071. It is the fourth day since we fled the Isle and we have taken shelter in a deserted priory near Brune, long since plundered by Normans. We will rest here until dark as it is safer to travel at night.

The land here was once a Saxon stronghold but is now governed by Norman thieves, so we slink into the shadows like the fugitives we are. Wulfgar, whom I trust with my life, stays close, his hand gripped tight on the hilt of his sword, watching through the window for anyone approaching. 'I can see nothing,' he said, 'not a living soul. We seem to have lost the Norman turds for now.' But still he watches, as in

1

the distance the sky glows red as Elig burns.

On the day we fled the Isle, William and his Norman devils came without warning out of the marshes. I managed to grab my sword, bow, war helmet and a small bag of coins, but little else.

I saw Hereward and a few of his men escaping on our flat-bottomed boats, jinking desperately between the reed beds; where they are now, I do not know.

We came across Abbot Thurstan on the edge of the marsh surrounded by Norman soldiers. One of them grabbed the abbot's arm trying to pull him with them, until Edwin hacked his axe into the Norman's neck causing blood to spray into the early morning air. We fought off the rest and dragged the reluctant abbot with us, despite him begging to remain to help his brothers. It would have been futile to leave him as he would have died with the rest.

As we fought our way out of the Isle, one of Hereward's men pointed across to us and shouted, 'Why did you betray us, why did you show them in, Leofric...?' Any other words died in his mouth as two Norman arrows thumped into his back and he fell face down into the marsh. One of his comrades took up the call shouting, 'It's Leofric, he's the one who has betrayed us, Leofric the Black,' then they were gone in the mist of the marshes before I could reply.

It is said one man's truth is another man's falsehood. I write these words to tell my truth. It is for others, with evidence and testimonies to prove otherwise. I have found old parchment scrolls in the small scriptorium which I can reuse when I scratch off the existing words. I have also discovered a small quantity of ink. This should suffice until I can find oak galls to make more. I have found crow quills, of poor quality it is true, but they will hold ink and serve my purpose. The Normans have taken everything else of value and destroyed the rest. Abbot Thurstan says God will curse them, yet the Normans will think that same God has blessed them.

We left Elig in such haste there was no time to bring provisions with us. Edwin, thinking of his stomach as always, grabbed a ham as we passed a deserted supply cart, but he dropped it as we came under a hail of Norman arrows.

I do not know how long we can remain undiscovered, so I will attempt to write each time we rest. If what I have written is found unfinished, it will be because I have been caught or am dead; unable to continue. I will write my account of what has passed and, when complete, do everything in my power to ensure it gets it into the hands of the man I am accused of betraying, Hereward the Saxon, leader of the so-called Saxon rebels, allowing him to judge for himself my innocence or guilt. It grieves me to think men could believe I would betray them and I will find out who the real culprit is or die trying.

I also write these words to leave a record for those who live after us to know how their forefathers fought with all their might to free this land we love, this land we call Englaland. It will tell how they battled to free it from the yoke of the thieving Normans, who have stolen, not only our possessions, but the dignity of free men. I trust it will explain how this great nation was vanquished by a meagre number of avaricious trespassers to our everlasting shame, and counter the lies spread by our adversaries to justify their murderous actions.

ᛒᛖᛏᚱᚨᚤᚨᛚᛚ

My story begins on the wind-swept shore at Sandwic. It was the year AD 1040, I was nine winters old. I sat on a dappled pony behind the chestnut mare of my father Renweard, Thegn of Æssefeld-Underbarroe. He appeared more ferocious than usual in his mail coat and boar-crested helmet, its nasal guard and visor framing his shaggy, unkempt beard.

I did not want to be there.

A nervous, timid child, I tried hard to play the part of a thegn's son but usually failed. I was always happier on my own with my books, quill and ink.

Two hundred of my father's men, dressed in mail shirts, stood behind us, many armed with spears which glinted in the sunlight, others with swords, axes and round, alder-wood shields. Everyone there was prepared to fight for their lord.

Though it was midsummer, a chilling wind blew dark clouds from the east, threatening to blot out the sun. The sea, calm when we arrived at first light, became agitated and flecked with spray.

We English had been preparing these last months for war. A war to defend King Harold, known as Harefoot, against his half-brother Harthacnut, who had gathered a fleet of ships on the shores of Brugge to come against us.

Just as war appeared inevitable, King Harold died. Now, that same fleet of sixty mighty, Danish warships packed with warriors lay in the bay before us, whilst we waited to greet Harthacnut as our new king.

We were part of a huge gathering of men. My father, one of many thegns come with their lords to greet and pay homage to the new sovereign.

The three great earls of Englaland, my father's lord, Godwin of Wessex; Leofric of Mercia and Siward of Norðhymbraland, were at the front. Also present were the bishops and other great men of the Church. To the left of them the northern thegns and their followers. I remember thinking at the time what a great slaughter there might have been that day, and I was glad the Danes came, and we received them, in peace.

This was the first time I had seen the sea. While most eyes watched the ships, mine looked everywhere, my ears ringing with the constant screeching of the gulls. The hissing of the water over pebbles, as it rushed in then was sucked back out again, dictated my breathing. I took deep breaths and my nostrils filled with the salty air.

'Keep your flea-bitten donkey still, boy,' rasped my father, as Flax, my pony, fidgeted and shook his head as sand, whisked up by the wind, stung his eyes.

'Yes, keep old fleabag under control, cripple, you'll be falling off it next.'

Although he was behind me, I knew it was Hakon goading me, he always did. Hakon and I, born on the same night under a lightning-lit sky in the village of Æssefeld-Underbarroe, were opposites. He was stocky, healthy, with hair as golden as the sand on that wind-swept beach. Hakon was the consequence of a few weeks of boredom.

When visiting our village with his father Earl Godwin, Sweyn Godwinson had taken up with Gode, the sister and ward of Grim, my father's right-hand man. Hakon was the result. Once it became known she was pregnant, Sweyn had no further contact with Gode. She died at the child's birth.

Ignored by Sweyn these last nine years, Hakon was raised by his uncle Grim and my father. Bastard or not, up to then Hakon was Earl Godwin's only grandchild. The earl agreed to pay Grim and my father a retainer to bring up the boy. They were to provide the best education they could until, hopefully, Sweyn would eventually accept him as his son.

Hakon has always despised me. I am the son of a thegn and he was thought of as merely another noble's bastard, and he used every opportunity to vent his anger against me.

'Mind yer manners, young Hakon, yer not an earl yet, though yer wouldn't think so to listen to yer.' Grim's comments made the men around them smirk. Hakon glared at him but said nothing.

'Harthacnut is nought more than a whelp,' said Grim, who had moved alongside my father, careful not to let his horse go ahead out of respect for his lord.

'It's true, Grim, but this whelp has power. He can give land to whom he pleases, and land is wealth and wealth is power. So, whelp or not, men will serve him, as shall we.'

Hakon had followed his uncle but stopped next to me on his pony, Arrowhead. She was taller than Flax and sleeker, yet I would never have swapped them. Where Arrowhead was fast and temperamental, Flax was steady and dependable.

Hakon glowered at me with steel-blue eyes as cold and cutting as a sword blade.

'One day, cripple, I will ride next to the king and you will bend your knee to me. As for now, I think you should get a closer look.'

Hakon slipped his foot from the stirrup and kicked Flax as hard as he could. Flax reared but stood her ground. Arrowhead shied away but as Flax came down on all fours, my leg, my twisted, useless leg, the reason for Hakon's ridicule, the reason for my father's disappointment in his only son, the bane of my life, my left leg shot out and kicked Arrowhead forcibly on the rump. Arrowhead did not stand her ground but was off to the left, across the front line of men, towards the king.

At first, there was confusion, men straining their necks to see what was happening, wondering why someone had broken rank. The king's bodyguards, thinking he was being attacked, closed around him brandishing spears. Hakon tried hard to get control of his mount, but with one foot still out of the stirrup and the speed of Arrowhead, it was all he could do to hang on. When men realised it was merely a boy on a run-a-way horse, they jeered, shouted and rattled their spears on their shields, which made Arrowhead run even faster.

Two men on the front line tried to stop him; one was knocked to the ground, the other gave up, raising his arms in defeat. This brought even more jeers and whoops from the soldiers.

For a moment, even I felt sorry for Hakon, although, thinking of the spite and torment he had heaped upon me most of our young lives, the feeling soon passed. Finally, as they drew near to the king's bodyguard, who had now put up their spears, Arrowhead swerved away from them. Hakon lost his grip and was thrown off, landing on the sand in an undignified heap. Arrowhead carried on alone up the beach where he was found later grazing on rough grassland as if nothing had happened. Hakon was unharmed, except for a few bruises to his limbs and his pride.

We were too far away to hear what they said, but we heard later the king had asked, 'Can't these English control their pups?' and, 'No wonder they only ride their horses to battle and not fight on them, if they teach them to ride in such a fashion.'

The king's entourage had laughed loudly at this. My father did not find it amusing in the slightest. He was even less amused when, later, he and Grim were summoned by Earl Godwin to be told, 'I pay you to see the boy has an education, not so he can be deemed a fool. See he learns a lesson from it, so he can at least act as if he has noble blood in him.'

Hakon walked back alone past the jeering soldiers, who whistled and stamped their feet, a few even pretending to fall off a horse, mimicking his plight. When he arrived alongside us, sore and humiliated, my father ordered him to stand with our soldiers for the rest of the day. I sensed his stare fixed on my back the whole time. I dreaded to imagine what revenge he was plotting against me.

My father had come to this gathering full of hope for the future. During the reign of Harthacnut's father, King Cnut, Renweard had been appointed as a shire-reeve, tax collector and law enforcer. When Cnut died unexpectedly, he left three sons. Two were from his concubine, Ælfgifu; Swegen the oldest, and Harold, known as Hare-foot. The other son, Harthacnut, was from his legal wife, Emma of Normandy. Swegen and his mother, Ælfgifu, ruled as co-regents in Norway and Harthacnut lingered in Denmark.

The great lords of Englaland had met at Oxenaford to decide who should rule Englaland. My father always talked proudly of being present at that illustrious council of the Witan. He relished relating the proceedings at the slightest opportunity to anyone who might listen.

'Earl Leofric and the northern thegns and even the leading men of Lundene wanted Harold to rule over the whole of Englaland. Earl Godwin and the thegns in Wessex, including myself, opposed it, as Cnut had wished Harthacnut to be king,' he would begin. 'After much argument, it was decided Harold should be made regent in his brother's absence and Harthacnut's mother, Queen Emma, should oversee Wessex until her son left Denmark. But Harthacnut,' and my father always shook his head when he told this part, 'Harthacnut dwelled too long in Denmark, fighting against King Magnus of Norway. Becoming bolder, Harold Harefoot eventually drove Emma out of Wessex and convinced the Witan to crown him king of all Englaland. A dreadful day it was, a dreadful day.'

I had heard the story scores of times and for those who supported Harold from the beginning, it was a good day, but for those who opposed him, it was indeed a dreadful day. Many were mutilated, even killed, others, including my father, had any privileges they enjoyed under Cnut's rule taken from them.

My father's revenue from being a king's tax collector had been substantial. His share of the many fines paid by the folk of his villages was even greater. The loss of this revenue forced him to sell a great deal of land, including whole villages to his wealthier neighbours. His invitations to the king's court, when it travelled around the country, ceased. His standing as an important man in the land diminished.

Yet many still feared to cross him, as he had always been a hard, demanding lord, and he could still raise enough armed men to be useful in times of war. He was grateful he still lived and hoped one day he may win back the king's favour. He now believed that day had come. With Harold Harefoot dead, he welcomed a new king, a king he had always wanted and supported.

The distraction of Hakon's ride over, the proceedings continued. The king was escorted to the canopy and joined by the magnates. His mother, Queen Emma, having travelled with him, but on a separate ship, now sat at his side. The leading men of the land talked together for hours. They discussed terms concerning who should get what land, who was to be replaced for their treasonable support of Harold Harefoot, and who would be rewarded for standing by Harthacnut and his mother. We heard raised voices, especially Earl Godwin's, nevertheless, the outcome would not become clear until the next day when the whole assembly would be informed of the Witan's decisions.

Once we were finally dismissed, we made our way to the camp prepared for us on the Sandwic grasslands which ran up from the beach beyond the dunes. In the centre were the big, billowing tents for the king and the magnates. Around them spread smaller tents erected for thegns, such as my father.

The rest of the men made do on the ground, huddled around countless fires. Sheep, pigs and goats, brought to fill the soldier's bellies, grazed on any patch they could find amongst that mass of men.

A small corral had been erected where the nobles had their hunting dogs, for, as most men of wealth, the king loved to hunt. Sometime over the next few days, they hoped to indulge him in his favourite sport.

Later that evening, Earl Godwin made a surprise visit to our tent, chastising my father and Grim concerning Hakon's behaviour. Humiliated and angry, Grim and my father set off around the camp to search for Hakon. I had been outside when I overheard their heated discussion and I managed to slip away undetected in the opposite direction.

The fires stretched for miles. The sweet aroma of roasting meat tantalized my nostrils, instilling a hunger in my belly. Ale and mead were being drunk in vast quantities as men, who hours before thought they might die on that beach, feasted, sang of past battles and would no doubt revel late into the night. Inevitably, with such a gathering of battle-hardened warriors, many of whom up to a day ago were sworn enemies, there were arguments and the odd scuffle broke out as I passed by. I could sense the slight tension as I walked amongst them but mostly the spirit was good and the hope for the future was high.

Bored with their drunken antics, I made my way across the camp and down to the sea. Except for a man attending to his boat and someone further along the beach running his hunting dogs, I was alone. I sat and listened to the waves breaking gently on the shore. The ships creaked as they rose and fell on the swell. I marvelled at the moon's reflection, lighting a silver pathway on the surface of the water. I had seen this on the River Æsc back home, but the sea was vast and the path stretched far to the horizon and I wondered where it would take you if you travelled it. I was so entranced, I was unaware I was no longer alone.

'There you are, cripple.' Hakon appeared with three older boys, each with a stout stick in their hand. 'We've been searching everywhere for you. How did you get here, crawl?'

My stomach cramped. A sour taste filled my mouth, though my lips and tongue were dry. I used my wooden crutch to help me stand, then stood defiantly before them. As scared as I was, there was no way I was going to let them know it.

'No, I walked. What did you do, ride and fall off again?' Hakon winced at the memory of the day's events.

'You made a fool of me today, cripple, and now you must pay for it.'

The four of them moved closer to me. I knew there was no escape. I glanced hopefully up towards the camp, but no one was watching and the noise from the singing and shouting was too loud for them to hear the cries of a small boy. And so, it began. I managed to clout one of them around the head with my crutch, but in doing so, I lost my balance and fell on the sand. Immediately the blows rained down on me as the four of them hit me with the sticks and kicked me as hard as they could. I tried to stand, but the blows made it impossible. I did manage to crawl a few feet, but still they kept on kicking and hitting. Pain seared through my body. I reached out for the crutch, thinking I might use it as a weapon, or at least ward off the blows, but Hakon kicked it away, laughing. Then I saw a flash of metal in Hakon's hand and realised he intended more than a beating. As the blade of the knife came towards me, trying my hardest not to cry, I stifled a scream and curled myself into a ball to protect my face and head, and squeezed my eyes shut.

'You pathetic, twisted, weak, little shit,' Hakon sneered, 'we're going to....'

The hitting and kicking stopped.

They had dropped their weapons and were running off into the grassy dunes towards the camp. Both dogs passed me together, their long, shaggy coats wet from the sea. Saliva flicked from their bared fangs as their huge paws pounded the firm sand in pursuit of their fleeing prey.

'Heel Vetch, heel Barberry,' a voice called out, and the dogs gave up the chase and returned submissively to their owner's side.

He knelt beside me, 'You all right, lad, wasn't that...'

I cut him short. 'I don't know who they were, lord, please don't tell anyone of this,' my voice shrill, my lips trembling.

'Well, I can't leave you here. How will I explain the state you are in?'

My arms and legs were cut and bruised, and my tunic was torn. I called him lord, but I guessed he was barely twenty. It was evident from his clothes he was no ceorl. He wore a cloak of thick, woven wool held by a beautifully-worked golden brooch. His face was personable, elegant, graceful even, with a reassuring smile, and he seemed genuinely concerned for my wellbeing. I looked up at him with tear-blurred eyes.

'I am the son of Renweard, Thegn of Æssefeld-Underbarroe. Please tell my father I stumbled and fell on jagged rocks. He will believe it. Please tell him, my lord.'

My father already imagined me as weak and helpless, knowing I had been beaten by other boys would only confirm this.

'I will tell him, don't fret.' He picked up the crutch and scooped me into his arms and, followed by his two dogs, carried me across the camp to find my father.

Ulla, one of my father's slave girls, bathed my cuts, wrapped me in a big, fur blanket and sat me next to the fire by our tent. My father bowed to my rescuer. He also called him lord. I found out later he was Harold Godwinson, the second son of Earl Godwin, the richest and most powerful man in the land after the king. He told my father he had been exercising his hounds when he had found me on the rocks. My father thanked him and after Harold left, I heard my father talking to Grim about me, thinking I was asleep.

11

'What am I going to do with him, Grim? How will he ever be thegn of Æssefeld, the boy is so weak?'

'He's clever, mind,' said Grim, 'Father Brihtric says he is good with his letters, quick like, and I've never seen anyone better with horses at his age, no one. He'll need to surround himself with strong men to fight his battles, that's all.'

'But will strong men serve him, or will they take advantage of his weakness?' said my father. 'God was cruel when He gave me him, Grim, he's more suited to be a priest than a thegn. Take your nephew, Hakon, born the same day, couldn't be more different. Men will serve him; he'll demand it and get it.'

'Strikes first, thinks later, same as his father,' Grim said, shaking his head, 'and with a cruelness for one so young. I had to stop him beating his pony earlier, drawing blood he was.'

Renweard agreed, 'We will need to watch him, Grim. I can't afford to vex his grandfather any further. We need Godwin's support to find favour with this king or there will be nothing left of my estate for anyone to inherit. Hakon's got spirit, for certain, and have you seen him run? As a deer from the hounds and as nimble as a cat. God forgive me for saying it, but I sometimes think I was given the wrong son.'

To this day, and I imagine until the day I draw my last breath, I will remember feeling so utterly dejected and wretched on hearing those words

I cried that night, not because of my cuts and bruises, not even because of the cruel trick fate had played by giving me a twisted foot. I cried because I was not the son my father wanted.

I vowed solemnly to myself, I would try my utmost to become the son he desired. I vowed to make him proud of me. I vowed I would become a warrior. Not just any warrior, but a warrior of great renown. A warrior, other warriors feared.

They were the vows I made that night, only I did not know how I would fulfil them.

Two

Next morning my body ached. Despite my cuts and bruises and my father telling me to stay wrapped in the fur blanket, I was determined to show him I was not weak. I persuaded Ulla to help me dress and get up onto Flax. My father scowled at me, no doubt wondering whether to chastise me for disobeying him but stayed silent. The morning air was cool and as the sun came up over the sea it burnt off any lingering mist. The wind had calmed to a breeze and the boats in the bay sat almost motionless. We made our way along the beach towards the canopy where the rest of the soldiers were assembling.

Modred, a sour-faced lump of a man and a captain of my father's soldiers, pointed to a lone ship in the distance which seemed to be heading towards us. Grim was with my father but there was no sign of Hakon. I overheard them saying no one had seen him since last night. Grim and others had searched throughout the camp, but he was nowhere to be found and they were starting to be concerned.

'We must find him, before Godwin gets wind we've lost him, Grim,' said my father. I wondered if Hakon had thought I would tell my father of his attack on me and was afraid of what might happen to him.

Grim took two others and they left to search the camp again for Hakon. The rest of us made our way back to the canopy to listen to the king. On the way, we met Earl Godwin and his housecarls.

'Renweard, ride beside me and let us talk,' said the earl. My father did as he was told and I followed him until a voice came from behind me.

'I'm glad to see you survived your fall, young Leofric. You need to take more care.'

It was Harold Godwinson. He was dressed in a mail coat, which reflected the glow of the sun, and a blue cloak trimmed with stoat's fur. A sword, with an intricately-worked silver hilt depicting the dragon of Wessex, was strapped to his side.

'I thank you, lord, it was an accident, I can take care of myself.'

'I am sure you can. In fact, I have come to ask you a favour.'

'Lord, what favour can a mere boy give to a warrior such as you.'

'I had a friend who has died recently and left a son who is not too bright. He needs someone to guide him, someone young to befriend him. I have been told you are good at your learning and it will be most pleasing to me if you will help him. What's more, if you should have another accident and fall,' he put much emphasis on accident and fall, so I understood his meaning, 'he will be there to help you.'

I did not mix with other children. My experience of them was usually unpleasant. 'As I have said, my lord, I do not need help. But if it pleases you, I will help your friend's son.'

'Good,' said Harold, 'he is here now, and he shall walk at your side. Brokk, here, lad.'

He called over to a group of men marching with him and one pushed his way through to walk next to me. He was twice my age and three times my size. His face was lopsided and his nose, wide and flat. His hair was the colour of burnt copper and so unruly, it looked as if a pile of autumn leaves had been dumped haphazardly on his head. He carried a large, round, alder-wood shield, and on his back was slung a two-handed axe, but the most striking feature about him was his wide shoulders and bulging arms.

'Young master, my name is Brokk and I am here to do your bidding.'

I turned to Harold, but he had returned to his father and it seemed I had now acquired my first follower.

Grim joined my father once again with the news Hakon was nowhere to be found and no one had seen him since last night. My father informed Grim that Earl Godwin felt he had been demanding too much to expect them to provide for all Hakon's needs. After all, they had been kept from the court and all the privileges they could gain from serving their king. So, he had told Renweard to be ready. When an opportunity arose, Godwin promised to do all in his power to bring Renweard to the king's attention and advise Harthacnut to use such a loyal subject as him to the full. What happened after that would be up to Renweard to take advantage. However, Godwin had stressed any more incidents like yesterday and they would regret it.

'We must not let that happen, Grim,' my father said, 'so as soon as we are finished here, we search everywhere until the boy is found. Now let's go and please a king.'

We pushed our way near the front. Men complained, but my father rode with new confidence, his old swagger returning, and we were allowed through. New banners fluttered around those of the king, as vows, bargains and oaths had been made overnight and those lords and thegns in favour had shown their allegiance. A large cart, covered with a waxed hemp canvas, had been brought alongside the canopy and its horses unharnessed and led away. Six armed men stood around it and there were rumours it was full of gold and treasure to be given by the king to his loyal followers. The men guarding it seemed agitated and others nearby complained of a terrible smell.

We waited until all the magnates took up their positions around the king. Eventually, the king's scribe unfurled a long roll of parchment and proceeded to read a list of charters and proclamations already decided overnight.

Clearing his throat, he read out, 'Lord Godwin, having proved his loyalty to both Harthacnut and his father, the late King Cnut, will retain the office of Earl of Wessex and will receive additional land as a token of the new King's recognition of such loyalty. If anyone objects to this, they should speak now and state why.'

All eyes roved about, seeking anyone who dared speak against Earl Godwin. The earl himself, a hand on the hilt of his sword, glared at those assembled, daring anyone to speak. As the scribe was about to continue, Aelfric Puttoc, the Archbishop of Eoforwic, rose from his chair. Slowly, several others stood up with him. Aelfric, face red and contorted, pointed his crosier towards Earl Godwin.

'That man, Sire, whom you hold in such high esteem, was responsible for the death, no, the murder of your half-brother, Prince Alfred, and,' he continued, turning his staff towards Lyfing, the Bishop of Wigraceaster, seated next to Godwin, 'this man, who claims to be a servant of Almighty God, also played a great part in the demise of the young prince.'

Bishop Lyfing leaped to his feet in protest.

'There'll be bloody trouble now,' Brokk said, 'he's a nasty bugger that Lyfing.'

'Quiet,' said Modred, 'I want to hear this.'

Most of the people present had heard the rumours before, but this was the first time it had been said in public, and by one in such high office as the Archbishop of Eoforwic.

Two years earlier, Prince Edward and his younger brother, Alfred, the two sons of King Æthelred and Emma of Normandy, Harthacnut's mother, had sailed from their exile in Normandy and made separate attacks on the coast of Englaland. Meeting resistance, Edward finally gave up and returned to where he had come from. Alfred was not as lucky and was apprehended by Godwin and his troops. Many of Alfred's men were either killed or tortured. Alfred himself was taken to Elig where he was blinded so roughly, he eventually died of his wounds. Some blamed Godwin; others said he was innocent of such crimes. Now he was being accused outright in front of the king and all the great men of Englaland. So, too, was Lyfing, who stood face to face with Aelfric his accuser.

'Bishop Aelfric lies, my lord king, he is jealous of what is mine and wants it for himself,' Lyfing protested, stepping back, the colour rising in his cheeks.

Harthacnut stood from his chair, his mother Emma mumbled something to him and he nodded back in agreement.

'Did you not take my half-brother, my kin, to Elig?'

'I did take him there, Sire, but only to...'

'Answer the question. Did you take Alfred to Elig?'

Lyfing shuffled uneasily, staring at the ground. 'Yes, I did, Sire.'

'And was he blinded so terribly, he consequently died from such action?'

'Yes, Sire, I believe that to be true.'

Aelfric raised his arms to the assembly of men, 'Condemned from his own lips. No man of God this, but a murderer, a killer of princes.'

Spears rattled against shields as the men vented their disapproval, scaring a pair of black-tailed godwits into flight from the dunes behind the canopy. Harthacnut, his face reddening, his finger wagging accusingly, moved nearer to Bishop Lyfing.

'So how do you answer such a grave charge, man of God? Speak now.'

Lyfing stood his ground which, my father said later, was a big mistake. He snapped back angrily at Harthacnut.

'Alfred came to this land with an army to take the crown from a king consecrated by God's will. It was my duty as God's servant to apprehend him and put a stop to such a thing. I acted purely in defence of this realm and its rightful king.'

It seemed Harthacnut was going to burst. He spun around and snatched a sword from the hands of one of his housecarls and thrust the deadly blade barely a goose-quill's breadth away from Lyfing's face.

'Rightful king! Rightful king!' The words erupted from Harthecnut's curled lips, spraying the bishop with spittle; his nostrils flared, his veins strained against his skin. 'He was a deceitful, usurping bastard who had no rights, except to hold this kingdom for me. By your actions and poor judgement, it is clear you are unfit to hold such high office and therefore I relieve you of your position as bishop and we will give it to the man who has exposed your heinous crime, Aelfric Puttoc. You will return to your abbey and seek forgiveness from the Most High God and praise my good nature for sparing your worthless life. Now be gone before I take your head, and have it stuck on a spike.'

Lyfing glanced pleadingly at Earl Godwin, who remained silent. Sensing his cause was lost, Lyfing withdrew from the canopy and with his few remaining supporters, slunk off into a hissing crowd.

Warming to his task, Harthacnut approached Earl Godwin, sword in hand, waving it towards the earl's face, 'And you, Godwin, do you also admit to these foul deeds, to the torture and murder of my half-brother Alfred? How do you answer, sir?'

Modred turned to my father, 'This will be good if he gets out of this one, even for Godwin.'

'He bloody will,' said Brokk 'he always bloody does. No pride, no shame, no concern for honour, only raw bloody ambition for himself and his family. That's what makes Godwin the most powerful, bloody man in the land and he'll not let anything, or anyone, take that away.'

The whole assembly became silent. Necks strained to get a closer view and loyal soldiers of both men put a hand to sword hilt in readiness to fight.

To everyone's surprise, except perhaps Brokk, Godwin prostrated himself at Harthacnut's feet. He raised himself slowly onto one knee, head still bowed and took Harthacnut's hand in his and kissed it.

'My most great lord, my king, I hereby make a solemn oath to be witnessed by all present, that I, Godwin, did neither by command or deed cause your brother Alfred to be deprived of his eyes or cause his death. I had only obeyed the command of Harold, your half-brother, who at the time was my lord, and handed Alfred over to his safe keeping. I am certain, my king, you know that up to then I had been your loyal servant, patiently waiting with your royal mother, safeguarding your interests when others had forsaken you for one less deserving a king than you. What's more, I swear to you, on oath, I and my sons and all we command commit ourselves to your cause. And, my sovereign lord, to show my words have substance, I have a gift worthy of one so great as you.'

If the mealy words of flattery were not enough to absolve him in the king's eyes, the gift most certainly was, for, as if by magic, the ship Modred had seen in the distance, slipped around a bend in the River Sture.

'I present to you, my king, a great warship to defend your kingdom from your enemies.'

We all gaped in awe as the magnificent galley glided as gracefully as a grayling through the shallow waters. Her huge, white sail fully extended fluttered with the breeze, the oars dipping rhythmically. A golden hue encompassed her, from the gold leaf painted on her brow to the gilded sword hilts and shield bosses held by the eighty soldiers who lined her deck. Their helmets were also partly gilded and they each carried a lance. The whole thing sparkled in the sun like a precious gemstone. The dignitaries under the canopy applauded, the soldiers banged their shields with their spears again, and the king embraced Godwin and called him, 'My great Earl Godwin,' stating he knew all along he was incapable of such a callous act, and such deeds would only have been carried out by a man of such base character as Harold Harefoot.

Harthacnut once again turned to the gathering in front of him. As well as the soldiers and dignitaries, there were now many local folk come in from the towns and villages to get a glimpse of their new king. They had gathered on the far bank of the river on the dunes, to the left of the main assembly.

Harthacnut moved to the edge of the canopy near the cart. He paused for a moment, waiting for the perfect time to get the most dramatic response for what was to come next. There must have been a prearranged signal, for the guards moved nearer to the cart and prepared to pull off the big hemp canvas covering it. Even from where we stood, you could see the discomfort on the men's faces, and the foul stench others had complained about had now reached us. Brokk held his nose with his fingers, 'Smells like a bloody manure heap,' he said.

'It's worse, more like a dead dog,' moaned Modred, wafting his hand in front of his face.

Harthacnut obviously smelled it as he moved slightly away before he finally spoke.

'The people of this kingdom, my kingdom, have proved to be an impatient people, preferring to have a usurper as their ruler instead of waiting for their rightful king. So, these people, you people, must be taught what happens when the rightful king of this kingdom is denied his birthright and kept from fulfilling the wishes of his dead father, your previous king, my father Cnut. The usurper you called 'king' had no right in the sight of God to take such a supreme office. As such, he did not deserve the Christian burial he was given.'

As he spoke, folk started to realize what was in the cart.

'He's had Harefoot dug up!'

The word spread like a gorse fire through the crowd. There were gasps of disbelief and shock, how anyone could do such a thing, even a king. Folk prayed, the bishops and priests made the sign of the cross. The biggest gasp of all came as, inexplicably, something on the cart, beneath the canvas, moved. Harthacnut's red face turned white. The bishops knelt in unison, lifting their arms to the heavens, wailing in Latin to their God. The guards, at first taken aback, moved cautiously towards the cart and grabbing the canvass, pulled with all their might to expose what lay beneath. Everyone there, including me, was shocked, as what was revealed was the rotting, dead body of Harold Harefoot, and a nauseous, but extremely alive, boy.

It was Hakon.

My father and Grim stared in horror. I don't know what shocked them most; the putrid corpse of the man who, up to a few weeks ago they called their king or the sight of their nine-year-old charge taking the attention away from their new king for a second time in two days.

Hakon froze, not knowing what to do next. He was grabbed by two of the guards and hauled off the cart. He told my father later, he had guessed he was in trouble so looked for somewhere to hide. He had seen the cart when it first arrived off the Lundene road and despite the awful smell, he had slipped beneath the canvas, where, overcome by the evil-stench, he passed out. When he came to, he heard talking and although the smell was overpowering, he had been too afraid to reveal himself. It was so dark under the canvas, he did not know what it contained.

Harthacnut, over his initial shock of the image of a moving corpse, walked towards Hakon and with his pitiless, unconvincing smile spoke softly, 'You are the boy who fell off your horse yesterday, are you not?'

'Yes, Sire.'

'Do you wish me harm, boy?'

'No, Sire,' Hakon's voice trembled.

'No, Sire,' mimicked Harthacnut. 'Do you think I am a cruel king, boy?'

'No, Sire.'

'No, Sire,' Harthacnut smirked once more. He turned back to face the assembly. 'Who is responsible for this boy?'

Those who knew looked towards Sweyn, who said nothing.

'Come now,' Harthacnut continued, 'someone must know who he is?'

My father placed his hand on Grim's shoulder, 'You'll have to get him, Grim.'

Grim nodded and rode slowly towards the king.

'And you are?' said Harthacnut at Grim's arrival.

'Grim Ealdwulfson, Sire, the boy's uncle.'

'The boy says I am not cruel, Grim Ealdwulfson. Do you think I am too weak, easily taken advantage of? Do you think that, Grim?'

'No, Sire.'

'No, Sire.' Harthacnut said and turned to face Hakon. 'You are both right, I am neither cruel nor weak. Let the boy go, he has no blame in this.'

The guards released Hakon and he ran through the lines of men until he stood behind the safety of my father.

Harthacnut began to walk back to the dais when, almost as an afterthought, he said, 'Have the uncle flogged twenty lashes and if I see him again in the next five years, I will have his right hand cut off and his tongue pulled out.'

Two guards led Grim away from the camp to receive his punishment. There were a few murmurs, but no one objected; not Godwin, nor my father, not even Grim himself.

'Words are powerful devices,' Harthacnut shouted, to command everyone's attention once more, 'but actions are even greater. I am told of loyalty and commitment to my cause. Now is the time to prove those words are not empty and I do have a kingdom of loyal subjects.

Earl Godwin, I need four strong men on horseback to show me this loyalty. Can you recommend such men?'

Without hesitation Godwin answered, 'Sire, I present four men who have already shown such loyalty by bringing the body of Harold Harefoot as you commanded. These men are without a doubt your loyal servants, my lord king.'

The four men rode to the dais and bowed their heads to Harthacnut. His thin smile creased his face.

'Are these the only loyal men in this kingdom?'

'Of course not, Sire, there are many loyal men eager to serve you, and none more so than this man who served your father well. Renweard, Thegn of Æssefeld-Underbarroe, come and serve your king.'

My father's moment had come, his chance to win the king's favour and try to retrieve all he had lost in the last couple of years. Without hesitation he moved his mount through the lines of soldiers to join the other thegns in front of the king.

Harthacnut gestured with his hand and the guards climbed on to the cart. In each corner was a coiled rope. Each guard took one of the ropes and tied it to various parts of the dead king's stinking body. One of them took the four loose ends together and jumping off the cart, gave them to Harthacnut. The new king once again addressed all assembled.

'This horse's turd wanted my kingdom,' he said pointing at Harefoot's dead body. 'He took what was not his and drove my mother out of this land. He does not deserve to rest peacefully in a Christian grave. It is an affront to me and Almighty God. I have been told of a stinking bog, north of this place, and it is there these loyal thegns of mine will drag the usurper so he can rot forever like the thief he was.'

Standing on the edge of the dais, Harthacnut purposefully thrust a rope in the hands of the first three mounted thegns, but as he reached my father he stopped, as Renweard had dismounted and had gone down on one knee before him.

'Sire, that I am loyal to you is beyond dispute, but do not ask of me

22

such a thing. I would risk my life for you. I will gladly do combat against any man you ask. But to defile the dead is a great sin, one I fear there could be no redemption from.'

My father was highly superstitious. He believed to disturb the corpse of any dead man, particularly a king, could only result in eternal persecution from the dead man's soul and bring nothing but bad luck on oneself and kin.

To hear my father say such things filled me with dismay. To a nine-year-old boy, it was simple. Do this task for the king and our future would be secure. I knew little and cared less about redemption or sin. Harthacnut stared disdainfully at my father without replying.

'I thought you said this man was loyal, Godwin, not a squeamish weakling who disobeys his king. Remove him from my sight.'

Turning his back on my father he repeated his request for loyal men. After a slight pause, Sweyn Godwinson rode forward and took the end of the fourth rope from the king.

'Do me the honour of letting me serve you twice in one day, my lord.'

Two of the king's men ushered Renweard away and pushed him unceremoniously into the body of men. They led his horse away as forfeit and my father was left to walk ashamedly to where we stood.

Harthecnut strode purposely to the corpse of his dead half-brother. Harold's hideous, lifeless head hung limply over the side of the cart. With one mighty swing of his sword Harthecnut sliced through the neck bone, and the maggot-riddled head, which once wore a crown, fell into the mud below. The new king kicked it, making it roll jerkily until one of the mounted men speared it with his lance and held it aloft for all to see.

Sweyn spurred his horse and with the others following, he headed off along the front line of soldiers. As the ropes tightened, the headless body of Harold Harefoot, once king of Englaland, flew from the cart and bounced unceremoniously behind the four horsemen across the sand. The hideous spectacle rode out over the dunes towards the marshlands lying to the north of Sandwic. Men say bits of the dead king's body lay scattered along the route and toes and fingers were picked up and kept as charms and keepsakes. Others tell tales of how the remains were thrown into a bog and sank from sight forever. Even others said sailors retrieved his body and once again he was given a Christian burial, this time in secret. Perhaps it is one of those things we will never know the truth of for sure, but I do remember thinking how strange it was that even men of great power and wealth can have such an ignoble end.

My father was given a new horse when he arrived back with us, but he slumped in the saddle, the expression of hope and expectation drained from his face. He at last had the king he wanted, only to realise, that king did not want him. Furthermore, the obvious look of anger on Earl Godwin's face told him all hope of future recommendation to the king had gone.

Three

On the journey back to Æssefeld we were despondent. Having displeased a second king, my father was in a worse position than before. Grim rode hunched over the front of his saddle, his back cut and bloodied from the whip's lashes.

Hakon, forced to ride next to my father, was visibly shaken by his ordeal and no doubt feared retribution from his uncle. I brooded, wondering what the future held for an unloved cripple whose inheritance was slipping away.

The weather matched the mood; black clouds shifting over a dark grey sky and the distant rumblings of thunder. Several of my father's men murmured, saying they might seek new lords with better prospects.

We followed Earninga Straete, the old Roman road, most of the way, then took a path through the great wood as the first drops of rain began to fall. In later years, I have come to see the great wood as a place of shelter, but as a child, it held countless fears. Even amongst such a company of armed men, we passed through with trepidation. Amongst the mighty oaks and the black, sinister trunks of the watery birch, I imagined every kind of disgusting creature ready to devour us. What was probably a deer darting through the hazel scrub, to me was a hob-goblin searching for man blood. A gnarled, old tree stump was a troll waiting to snare someone as a trophy. I imagined the sound of every drop of rain finding its way past the vast canopy of leaves, to be a wild thing or half-ling. To take my mind off such horrors, I talked at length to Brokk. I asked him about his family.

'My mother died when I was a child,' he said, 'can't remember much about her, my father was killed three weeks ago. There was a bloody accident.' He closed his eyes and took a deep breath before continuing, 'We're boat builders and fishermen. My father was one of the main builders of the ship Godwin gave to the new king.'

As he talked, he too scoured the under-growth for unseen danger. I learnt later, although Brokk feared few men, he was terrified of the other world, the world of spirits, ghouls and all things unearthly. He fondled the small wooden cross he wore around his thick neck and from the calf-skin pouch slung on his belt, he frequently took out an elf-bolt, kissing it for luck.

'We had recently built a boat for Lord Harold,' he continued, 'he used to visit us on a regular basis to see what progress we had made, and he and my father became good friends. It was Harold who recommended us to his father, Earl Godwin, and I think he felt responsible for me when my father was killed. He's a good man, Harold, unlike his elder brother. He was the only drawback of being around the Godwins.'

'You mean Sweyn?' I asked, directing my gaze to where I heard the crack of a fallen branch.

'Yes, bloody Sweyn. Most nobles treat you as cow dung on their boots but he's the worst of the brood, not a streak of kindness in him.'

'The boy with my father is Sweyn's son,' I said pointing in Hakon's direction.

'I know, Lord Harold told me. Said I had to watch him as I would the weather before setting out to sea and trust him as a pike with a minnow.'

Another sound came from a hazel coppice on our right and Brokk fondled his cross and kissed the elf-bolt at the same time. There were real dangers in the forest, especially for the lone traveller. Wild boar could charge out of the undergrowth without warning. Vagabonds, intent on robbing you, lurking in the shadows; and wolves hunting in packs. In this large company, those events were unlikely, but to a young boy and a superstitious fisherman, the threat was real enough.

Though we never saw any wolves, we did hear them howling at night.

Every few miles we came out of the trees and into a clearing. Several had one or two small dwellings in them, such as the conical shelters of the charcoal burner's huts, their fires clouding the air thick with sweet-smelling smoke. There were the thatched huts of bee-keepers and their straw skeps, the bees filling our ears with a humming, droning noise causing us to move a little faster, wary of their stings. In the distance, we could hear the woodsmen's axes splitting ash and beech. Then we would be back amongst the trees with their strange, twisted trunks, grotesque faces watching us pass, guarding the great wood. We camped overnight and slept in the shadow of a huge oak tree, whose branches stretched out like long, protective arms. Brokk stayed awake. He said it was to protect me, but I think he was too frightened to close his eyes in case something terrible came out of the darkness and devoured us all. Apparently, Hakon had wandered over to where I slept, carrying a large stick, but when Brokk had appeared from the shadows swinging his axe, saying, 'What do you bloody want?' he veered off and returned to where he had been sleeping.

In the morning, my father was angry when it was discovered several soldiers, including Modred, had sneaked away during the night and deserted us. 'Loyalty seems of little value these days,' he grumbled to Grim, sounding as if he was testing Grim's feelings more than anything else. Grim remained silent.

After two days, we came to the edge of the great wood on its south-west side and followed the River Æsc towards Æssefeld-Underbar-roe. Soon I would be where I felt most comfortable; at home with my books and my writing.

It was good to be back on fertile land. Swathes of golden rye and barley stretched into the distance. Lush, green grass spread towards the top of the gently rolling hills, and the River Æsc snaked effortlessly through the valley. I sensed the whole company's spirits were lifted by the sight. Alas, it was short lived.

The sheep that should be grazing on those lush hills were not there. Where were the ceorls who should be working on the land? As the timber palisade of Æssefeld came into sight, it was clear something was wrong. Outside the village raged a large fire. The smoke drifted slowly towards us, not the spicy aroma of the burning wood of the charcoal makers, but a rancid smell that clawed at the throat. As we got nearer, we saw people bringing carts filled with, what from a distance, looked like fleeces. A lone figure cavorted around the fire. As we got closer, a rider came out to meet us. It was Leafwold, my father's steward.

'Lord, thank goodness you're back,' said Leafwold, plainly relieved to see us, his face drawn through an evident lack of sleep.

'What in God's name has happened here?' quizzed Renweard, obviously finding it incredulous another disaster had entered his life.

'The morning you left, two sheep were found dead on the far bank of the river. The next day, six more and the day after, another ten. No one knew the cause. We brought many of the flock down to the folds outside the village, but still more died. Worse still, lord, the smith's wife, Ludella, became sick with fever and within a day she too died. The day after, it was the miller's young son. Two days later, four others died. Folk said it was the same disease and it was caught from the sheep. The priest said prayers and sprinkled the sheep with holy water.'

'And that didn't stop it?' asked Renweard.

'No, if anything it got worse and two days ago the priest himself died.'

At this news, our whole company crossed themselves. They were eager to see their kin but apprehensive about entering Æssefeld. It made me sad as the priest, father Brihtric, was my teacher and friend. It was him who had taught me to read and write and understand the tongue of the Wealas.

'Nairn said it was the old gods punishing us for forsaking them,' Leafwold continued. 'She has been to the stone and slept two whole nights among the barrows to consult the ancestors. She said the only way to stop the deaths was to make a great sacrifice to the gods, to Woden and Thor and Nertha, goddess of the earth. She said we should make a sacrificial fire and burn the dead carcasses to appease their wrath.'

We now realised it was Nairn who danced around the fire, a ritual to the gods of old.

'Is she the dream teller?' asked Brokk in a hushed voice.

'Yes, that's her,' I replied, not in the least surprised Brokk knew of Nairn. Folk came from afar to buy her charms and cures and hear her prophecies, most of all to have their dreams interpreted.

Even kings knew of Nairn and her dream that a king would come across the British sea with God's grace to conquer all before him. Ever since Æthelred returned from exile, successive kings had quizzed her to find out if it was them she had seen in her dream, but however much she beseeched the gods, the dream faded before the all-conquering king's identity was revealed.

We filed slowly passed the fire towards the village gates. The diminutive, twisted frame of Nairn danced around as she chanted incessantly in a low, rasping voice, 'Nertha, Nertha, earth mother, accept our invocation to bless the land to grow our crops and feed our beasts.'

Already stooped, she bent further to grab a young goat, which was held by her daughter, Mair, and slit its belly making it screech and kick wildly. She pulled out its entrails onto the grass and studied them for signs from the gods. The animal's small body twitched a while longer until finally it was still. Nairn repeated her mantra,

'Nertha, Nertha, earth mother, accept our invocation to bless the land to grow our crops and feed our beasts.'

She continued her frantic dance, her white shift and face smutted from the fire and her cheeks smeared with tears caused by the smoke. She picked up parts of the goat's innards and walked towards me. I tried not to look at her, but I felt her gaze upon me and I was compelled to turn my face in her direction. This woman evoked more feelings of fear in my young heart than anyone else I knew. Looking back across the years at all the foes and ordeals in my life, none have made me feel more vulnerable or desolate than when Nairn fixed those dark, searching eyes upon me. The sensation of being powerless infiltrated my very being and I sat motionless, transfixed, until Brokk came between us, as blood and offal, aimed at me, splattered over him. His expression was one of horror as he tried to disentangle the bloody mess from his hair.

'Curses on you, imbecile,' yelled Nairn.

'Bloody hell, I've been cursed by the dream teller,' shouted Brokk. Nairn showed no emotion as she walked slowly back to her daughter and they both continued to dance around the fire and sing to the old gods. Brokk stood shaking for a while until my father called to him.

'Brokk, bring the boy,' and with faltering steps, Brokk led Flax by the reins and followed my father's horse.

Æssefeld was a muddle of thatch and wood. The combined odour of humans and animals only partly subdued by the constant haze of wood smoke that permeated our village lives.

I expected my father would have gone to Nairn instead he ignored her, passing through the village and into our enclosed compound where we dismounted. My mother was waiting by the steps of the hall and she and my father embraced in their usual, formal manner. He, holding her at arms-length and kissing her forehead, she, giving a forced smile and curtsying stiffly.

I dismounted and started to make my way towards the hall. My mother held my arm to stop me, and pointing to my wooden crutch slung over Flax, said, 'Don't bob, it makes you appear stupid.'

I fetched the crutch and continued to our hall. Grim was taken to his quarters to have his wounds seen to and Hakon sulked off on his own.

The hall was filled with crosses and lit candles and the smell of burning incense. The first thing my father did, once he was sure there were only myself and my mother present, was to walk to the dais to his carved oak chair. Above the chair hung an ancient embroidery, which had belonged to our family for generations. The colours were faded and parts of it were threadbare. It depicted a beautiful maiden with a stricken soldier at her feet. Behind her were two shadowy figures, a man and woman, and behind them, was a knight in full armour. As a child, I was terrified by his helmet's crest, a crawling skeleton, with beaded eyes which stared and followed me wherever I stood in the hall.

Along the bottom of the embroidery was written a legend:
That which for years will wait,
yet be broken, when made whole,
will seal this family's and a nation's fate.

Its significance, like the embroidery, had faded with time, though many had deliberated over its meaning through the passing years.

My father pulled the heavy cloth aside and slid a panel of wood across to reveal a sparkling, jewelled sceptre behind it. Standing on tip-toe, he reached up at full stretch, his fingers curling around the thick shaft of gold, then ran them along part of its dazzling, jewelled shaft. In all the troubles to come upon my father, this was the one thing that sustained him. He had come to believe if the sceptre remained hung in his hall, everything would eventually come right. Satisfied the sceptre was safe, my father slid the panel back into place and covered it once again with the weeping lady embroidery.

The few times I ever felt close to my father was when we looked at the sceptre together. After bolting the hall doors, we would take it down and clean it with an oiled cloth. I marvelled at each precious stone. Two which stood out amongst all those glittering jewels, were a dazzling blue sapphire and a huge, dark red ruby.

My father had explained it was of ancient origin and that the many tiny diamonds stood for the stars, the sapphire represented the earth and the ruby the fire from which the earth came to be. I took delight staring at it for as long as it was kept out of its hiding place. The way the light of the candles and lamps flickered and danced off each jewel fascinated me.

The sceptre was one of two secrets of Æssefeld. The other was a secret passage leading from the sleeping-quarters of the great hall to the outside of the village walls. It had been dug by my father's ancestors as an escape route from Viking raiders. It was only ever known by immediate members of the thegn's family and was concealed by floorboards underneath a thick wolf-skin rug. It came out on the riverbank under an overhang of rock at the base of the palisade. My father told me it had been used once in the past when he was a child. He, his older brother and mother had been sent down there during a raid on Æssefeld, but thankfully, the raiders were defeated, and my grandfather had brought them back up. As a child, I hid in the tunnel on several occasions, away from my father's wrath and Hakon's bullying.

Since the burnings, the sheep deaths had decreased. A small number, showing signs of sickness, were separated from the rest and eventually they too were destroyed. Thankfully, no more villagers died from the disease.

My mother and Ulla, our house slave, had seen to Grim's wounds and my mother had reluctantly administered balms and salves sent from Nairn. My mother, Mirela, was a devout Christian. She hated Nairn and her pagan ways but even she did not deny the healing powers of her potions.

'Stay away from her,' she constantly told me, 'there is an evil in her. Stay away and be diligent at your prayers.'

My mother sheltered me, you might say smothered, as a mother hen would her chicks. She made me use my crutch always, even though I managed well enough without it. She frowned if I did anything too robust or hazardous. She constantly pressed home to me that my future was in the Church. Her father, Milosh, was of Romani descent, a horse breeder and trader of renown and otherwise dubious reputation and I had inherited what she called, my swarthy looks and black hair from him.

'I pray to God you have not inherited the violence within him,' she would say whilst making the sign of the cross.

'Your life is with God, Leofric, which is the reason you were born the way you were. It is written in the scriptures, the meek will inherit the land. It is also written; the lame will leap like a stag. Devote your life to Him and you will prosper in the life to come.'

I wanted to prosper in this life not the next. I wanted other children to like me, not ridicule and make fun of me. I wanted my father to be proud of me, but I knew these were merely the dreams of a lame boy and were unlikely to be a reality.

My father sent one of his men to inform the bishop of the priest's demise and to ask him if he might recommend a suitable replacement. The priest had been our tutor and his death meant Hakon and I were unable to have our lessons. It was rumoured his replacement might be Crispin, from the village of Thorneley, and I prayed it was, as I had been told he was a kind, gentle soul who was lenient with his pupils. It gave me time to show Brokk around the village.

Three days after our return, Hakon, Brokk and I were summoned to my father. Brokk and I were made to sit and witness the punishing of Hakon. Renweard lectured him on his foolishness in front of king and kin and the trouble it had caused himself and his uncle. He was made to drop his britches and bend over Renweard's chair, where my father took nine thin, birch rods and beat his backside six times. Hakon did not cry out. He winced as he pulled his britches up over the wealds on his flesh. His cheeks were tear stained and his lip bled where he had bitten into it, but he made no sound. He thanked my father for the lesson he had learned, but as he left, the look he gave me said dislike and jealousy had been replaced by hate and revenge. I was glad I had Brokk as my companion.

The next three weeks were full of questions. Brokk wanted to know everything about our village. 'Why is it called Æssefeld-Underbarroe? I understand the Æssefeld part with the river and the field, but Underbarroe?'

I took him up the hill on the east side of the village. There, in a fold between two summits, are the two barrows of Æssefeld. Although man-made, they rose from the ground as if they had been there since the world's beginning. Brokk stood in awe.

'Who built them, what are they for?'

'The smaller one was built for my ancestor by his followers when they first took this land. He was buried in the centre and still lies there now. No one knows the name of the people who built the big one. It is said it was the ancients who once ruled here and still watch over us today. They put this up too.'

I hobbled as fast as possible, despite the fact my crutch kept sinking into the soft turf. Brokk followed me a little way from the barrows and down the dip on the far side of the hill and there, on a small plateau, was a huge, dark stone that towered four times taller than Brokk. We approached it warily as if it was alive, a wild animal ready to pounce. We walked around it in silence. I pointed to the strange markings cut into the stone; spiral patterns and small hollows that looked like drinking cups. Also, a faint outline of a disc attached to a trident scratched into the surface. Brokk reached forward to touch the stone but drew his hand back quickly as if it might burn or bite him.

'What do the marks mean?' he whispered.

'No one knows,' I said. 'Nairn says they are magic symbols that foretell the past and future of the village. My mother says they are the marks of the devil and I should study harder at the scriptures.'

We both made the sign of the cross. Brokk took out his elf-bolt and kissed it. Since the incident with Nairn, he kept glancing uneasily over his shoulder and all about us.

'I'm sure we're being watched,' he whispered, 'let's go.'

Four

It was the first day of the month of November, or Blōtmonath as the old folk called it, the month of the blood sacrifice. The leaves on the big oak by the river had turned from brown to red, yellow and gold, many of them fluttering down to the ground covering the sparse grass under its shade. We had been hunting hares. I killed a brace with my bow and arrows. Brokk walked, I rode Flax. My companion asked question after question, 'What's this? Who's that?'

As we came to the old stone bridge, which the Romans built long before our Saxon forefathers had come to take this land, we heard a commotion. As we got closer, we could see scores of squealing pigs blocking the bridge. Leafwold, my father's steward, was thrashing the pig-herder around the face and body with his horse whip. A boy, a little younger than me, was struggling against two other men as he tried to stop the steward.

'Get off my father,' he screamed as he managed to kick one of the men on the leg. Leafwold swept the whip backwards catching the boy across the face. He was not deterred and struggled harder to be free.

'Keep hold of the little brat,' Leafwold said, as he continued to lash out at the boy's father who was cowering on the ground. Several of my father's soldiers were on the other side of the bridge laughing.

'Stop!' I shouted. 'Stop!'

Leafwold held back the whip for an instant. 'Ride past, boy, it is no concern of yours.'

'Why are you beating that man?' I said, ignoring his demand.

'He was blocking our way and wouldn't move his damn pigs.'

35

The boy cried out, 'We come over this bridge when the leaves fall, every year, to bring the pigs to slaughter. We were on the bridge first.'

Leafwold brought the whip down several times more on the pig-herder's head. The boy tried to head-butt one of the men holding him and lashed out with his feet.

I took the bow from off my back and put an arrow to the string, I pulled and let loose. The arrow landed inches from Leafwold's feet.

'The next one will hit you, Leafwold, now stop,' I said.

'You wouldn't dare, boy.' I noticed he was staring at the dead hares slung from my belt and knew I was capable.

I took another arrow from the makeshift quiver slung around flax's saddle pommel and started to load the bow. It was not a proper bow. It was a yew branch I had strung with a discarded, broken, full-size bowstring. I had three arrows I had found in the woods, lost after wayward shots missed their intended quarry. It would not kill a man, but it might inflict a nasty wound. It was probably not being shot at by my flimsy bow which dissuaded Leafwold, but to start a fight with his thegn's son was fraught with danger.

'Your father will hear of this, and I will watch with pleasure whilst he thrashes you,' Leafwold snarled. He gave the pig-herder one last kick. 'Leave the brat,' he shouted, and his men shoved the boy to the floor. Kicking their way through the mass of frenzied swine, they joined the soldiers on the far side of the bridge and rode off across the big meadow.

The boy scrambled to his father's side and tried to wipe the blood from his face with the sleeve of his tunic. The pig-herder was a nondescript man, neither tall nor short, slim nor stout. His face was cut and bruised, but I imagined that once those healed, he would be hard to pick out in a crowd. Hung around his neck was a necklace of vivid green and bright yellow pebbles, the size of hen's eggs, which clanked as he moved, and they made him memorable. The boy on the other hand, was a striking, handsome lad, tall and lithe with sharp lines to his jaw and nose.

'What's your name?' I asked.

'Olaf, lord.'

'You showed courage, Olaf. Here, wear this and vow that courage to me. When I am the thegn of Æssefeld I will need men like you.' I tossed him one of my arm rings.

'It would be an honour to serve you, lord, and I will wear this with pride.' He slid the ring over his wrist and, even if it did hang loose on his arm, I knew it would stay there and though we were both just boys, a bond had been set between us and Olaf would remain my man.

A number of villagers had witnessed the incident on the bridge but had been too scared to intervene. Once Leafwold and his men had gone they came and helped the pig-herder to the river to bathe his cuts. Others helped Olaf round up the pigs and drive them onward to the village for the autumn slaughter.

Brokk and I continued back to the village. 'That won't be the last bloody time we hear of that,' Brokk said, and he was right.

Although I wasn't thrashed, I was chastised by my father, who told me not to meddle in affairs I had no understanding of and that I had undermined the authority of his steward. He demanded me to hand over my bow and arrows and he snapped them into pieces and flung them on to the hall fire. This seemed to placate an irate Leafwold, although I was sure he was annoyed not to see me beaten by my father. My mother also berated me for putting myself in danger and insisted I go to our little, stone church and pray to God for guidance to live a spiritual life and not to pursue hunting and fighting and the ways of the world.

I heard later, the story was told around the villages of the little lord who saved the pig-herder and his son and made a fool of the thegn's steward. Leafwold also heard the tale and I knew he would seek reprisal.

Over the next few weeks, we continued exploring my father's local estates. People looked at us curiously as it was rare they saw the thegn's son. All these folk served my father and owed him either labour or rent or sometimes both. It was this that gave Renweard power over other men's lives and commanded their allegiance. My father owned several villages, distributed all over Wessex, although I was not allowed to travel that far without him. These brought in an income from rents and the sale of produce and fleeces. Fines levied on the villagers for all kinds of misdemeanours also boosted my father's coffers. However, they also cost a considerable amount to administer. As thegn, my father was responsible for the upkeep of roads and bridges. To keep order, he had to maintain many trained soldiers, which meant feeding and paying them. The revenue he had lost from no longer being a king's reeve was substantial. Æssefeld was not the only one of his villages to lose sheep and this loss also hit hard. A trade in fleeces was an important source of revenue to the estate, which meant we did not see much of my father as he was away, 'procuring the future and welfare of our holdings,' as he put it.

For me, that time in my life was good. Previously I had spent most of my time indoors. The other children, spurred on by Hakon, were mostly cruel to me and made fun of my limp. I was excluded from most of their games. Instead, I stayed inside with quill and ink and practised writing and copying intricate drawings from an old book of scripture the priest had given me. My father did not read or write, he relied on his steward and priest for such things. He saw them as a waste of a man's time. 'Work for priests, and men weak of spirit,' he called it and felt no pride that his son excelled in both.

Most of the summer the sun shone. Brokk taught me how to catch more fish in a day than most caught in a week. I asked him to show me how to split logs with one blow of an axe, but as I was hardly able to lift his ash-shafted weapon, he was unsuccessful.

'How will I ever be a warrior if I can't even handle an axe?'

'You don't need to worry about such things, you've got me.' I eventually realised it was not in Brokk's interest to teach me the art of war as it would reduce his usefulness.

On some evenings my only friend, Rush, joined us. He was the son of our Irish house slave, Ulla, and a year older than me. My father disapproved of my friendship with Rush. He was the son of a slave, I was the son of a thegn. He was the only boy I knew who did not make fun of my limp.

'He is trouble that lad, stay clear,' my father would say, 'stick to your own kind like Hakon, he may be a bastard, but he has noble blood in his veins.'

Hakon hated Rush. He often said, 'he should know his place and stay in it.' He called him Rust-head because of his red hair. Rush called Hakon, Bastard Boy. Rush said his place was next to me and the rest should go hang themselves.

Rush rose early each morning and worked all day on the land till late evening. On the nights he could, he would come and find me. When he first met Brokk he was jealous he had to share my friendship with another. Rush reckoned himself tough, picking fights with anyone he thought he could beat.

'How do we know Brokk can fight? He's big, no denying it, but can he fight? Simply big and stupid, if you ask me.'

'Why don't you ask him?' I said. 'I've found him honest, he will tell you if he can't.'

'I will,' said Rush, puffing out his chest, and straightening his back, attempting to appear taller.

It was a market day in nearby Wydeford and the three of us had come to catch the closing stages. Rush and I were watching the horse traders trying to sell their bedraggled leftovers, claiming, 'They may look like donkeys but looks can be deceptive and somewhere in there is a thoroughbred waiting to get out.'

No one believed a word, but someone would eventually get the price down low enough and the poor beasts would probably end up in the pot. Brokk was a little way in front watching a troupe of jugglers. Over to the right were a group of boys, a little older than Rush and me, playing fives. Rush sidled up to Brokk and tapped him on the shoulder.

'Leofric and I were wondering whether you were any good at fighting, big fella?'

Brokk looked across at me, I smiled and shrugged my shoulders.

'I can fight when I have to,' Brokk replied, turning back to watch the jugglers.

Rush was still not satisfied. 'He can say it, but how do we know?'

I knew, by the look in his eye, Rush was about to commit mischief. Turning away from us he walked slowly towards the other boys. Stooping to pick up a small stone and taking aim, he threw it at one of them, hitting him on the leg. The boy cried out and his companions stopped what they were doing and looked towards Rush. Having got their attention, Rush began a tirade of insults. 'What are you looking at, frogspawn face? Your mothers must have been the ugliest things in your village to give birth to you lot. Come on, if you think you're brave enough to fight me or are you all cowards, as soft as dog turds?'

All four boys broke into a run towards Rush who quickly spun on his heels and made towards Brokk, almost running into him.

'Right, big fella, here's your chance to show us your skills.' He turned to face his attackers with new bravado.

Brokk turned around and the boys all stopped short at the sight of the huge, older youth still with his axe slung over his back.

'Come on, slug dung, there's still only two of us,' yelled Rush, wearing a wide, triumphant grin.

'Fear me not,' Brokk said, smiling, 'I wouldn't dream of meddling in Rush's quarrels. If he's brave enough to hurl insults, he's either a great fighter or extremely stupid and I'm curious to know which,' and turning away, Brokk came over to me.

Rush's smile disappeared rapidly as he realized he was on his own. He looked towards me, but Brokk put his arm around my shoulders and ushered me towards the jugglers. I turned my head to see Rush scampering off between the stalls to evade his pursuers.

'He'll be alright,' said Brokk, chuckling, 'I've seen him run and he's bloody quick. Quick and bloody stupid, if you ask me,' and chuckled even more.

Brokk was right about Rush. He outran the other boys and evaded a beating. When we saw him the next evening, he said nothing to Brokk but complained bitterly to me out of Brokk's earshot.

'Told you he's all brawn and no guts. Damn all good he'd be if you needed him to defend you, damn all.'

Two evenings later the three of us were down by the River Æsc, a short walk from the village towards Wydeford, when three young men and a boy came over the hill. The boy, whom I recognized as one of the boys Rush had taunted, pointed towards us and said, 'It was him with the red hair.'

The three men came rushing towards us. Two of them carried stout sticks, the other a metal studded club.

'No one insults my mother and brother without punishment from me,' cried the one with the club, as they bore down on us with obvious intent to do us injury. In an instant, Brokk pushed both Rush and I behind himself and with one hand reached for his axe slung across his back. As the first man struck with his stick, Brokk parried the blow with the axe's shaft and kicked his assailant hard between the legs, sending him flying into the air and onto his back. As the second man with the stick aimed a blow at his head, Brokk ducked and swung the axe so he caught his attacker full in the stomach with the blunt end of the weapon, taking the wind right out of him, dropping him gasping to the ground. The man with the club hesitated, realizing Brokk was more than they had bargained for. The two of them glared at each other whilst Rush and I looked helplessly on.

'Go home and take your bloody friends with you,' said Brokk, lowering his axe as he spoke. The boy's elder brother, as we later found out he was, saw this as his opportunity and swung his club viciously at Brokk, only to embed it in the rising axe shaft which Brokk used to stop the blow. As he tried to move away, Brokk butted him so hard we heard his nose break and he held his face in his hands as blood gushed down his tunic and onto the grass. Brokk removed the club from the axe and hit the man across the back of the legs with it, felling him to his knees. We waited for Brokk to finish him off, but he did not. Brokk knew they were beaten, so did they. He ushered us away towards Æssefeld. I rode Flax, Brokk walked next to Rush. Not a word was spoken until we had nearly reached the village gates when Brokk said to Rush. 'Yes, I can fight when I must, but don't ever put me in such a position in the future or you will find out how good a fighter I am.'

Rush never liked Brokk, but he never questioned him again.

41

A few days later, Harold Godwinson came to Æssefeld. He had been visiting a lady nearby and decided to use the opportunity to take me to Wealtham.

In the past, when Harold and his father had visited Æssefeld, Harold and I had often walked along the banks of the River Æsc. We talked on various subjects, hawking being his favourite, and over time we became close. I looked up to him as an older brother.

However, on this journey, which took almost half a day, he was solemn. We rode in silence as we took the road to the church at Wealtham.

The white, stone church shone in the sunlight. 'Isn't it magnificent?' said Harold. 'Barrack limestone, all the way from Lincolnescire, but I haven't brought you all the way here to admire the architecture. Do you know the story of the Holy Rood?'

'No, I don't.'

'This church is on land owned by Tovi the Proud. His blacksmith had a dream telling him to dig on a hill near Glæstingabyrig. In doing so they found a large, intact, marble cross adorned with the figure of Christ; a beautiful thing to behold. They loaded the cross, or rood as it is called, onto an ox cart. They planned to take it to a nearby church, but the oxen refused to obey the command of the driver to turn around. Instead, they set off on their own journey, walking one hundred and fifty miles. Each time the driver tried to stop, the oxen refused until they reached this church here at Wealtham, where they eventually came to a halt and refused to move another inch. It was deemed this is where God wanted the cross to stay.'

We opened the black oak doors and walked down the central aisle of the church and there, over the altar, hung the rood. The black marble rippled in the flickering candlelight, making the life-size figure of the Christ seem alive. The eyes, full of pain, seemed to stare straight through me. A shiver tremored through my body.

'The sword, attached to the upright of the cross, belonged to Tovi's ancestors and his wife commissioned the crown of jewels on the Christ's head,' whispered Harold. 'When I was a child, Leofric, I was struck down with a malady which left me with no feeling below my waist. Nothing at all, not even pain. All sorts of people were brought to me, physicians, priests, even a bishop. None knew the reason for my affliction. Not one salve or potion had any effect. My father arranged for me to be taken to the Roman baths said to have healing waters, yet still my legs refused to work.'

'I did not know, lord, you seem so strong and able.'

'All thanks to the holy rood,' Harold said, crossing himself and sinking to one knee. 'My father needed to visit Tovi, and my mother insisted on accompanying him and, unusually, they brought me. I was normally left at home when they travelled, but the night before, my mother had a dream where an old, but faceless monk told her she must take me to see the rood at Wealtham. A makeshift litter was made and despite my complaining of the jarring journey, we arrived here, and I was brought to this exact place. My mother knelt next to me and we prayed out loud for God to restore me to my previous good health. Three weeks later, I regained the feeling in my legs and in a month, I was walking again, fully recovered. I vowed I would endow this church with holy relics and treasures to bring glory to God. Many pilgrims have travelled here since and many miracles have been performed. Open your heart to God, Leofric, and I am certain you too can be cured.'

I looked down at this man I so admired. His face was tear-stained and tense from the memory of a traumatic period in his life. He stood, took the crutch from under my arm and placed it gently on the ground. He grasped my hand and pulled me down to my knees.

'It is written in the scriptures,' he said, 'And all things, whatsoever you shall ask in prayer, believing, you shall receive. Do you believe, Leofric?'

I so wanted to say yes. I so wanted to believe. I so wanted to have two good legs to run and play with other children without their scorn and ridicule. I felt my insides bubbling and boiling with excitement, imagining what it would be like, yet my head was telling me it was impossible. I looked up at the face of the Christ once more, his lips appeared to move, compelling me to trust in him, as though he was saying 'Believe, Leofric, believe in me and I will make you whole.'

As I stood before the rood, the thought of being cured swirling in my head, I recalled the legend written on the weeping lady embroidery in my father's hall.

That which for years will wait,
yet be broken, when made whole,
will seal this family's and a nation's fate.

Could it mean me? Could it mean I would be cured, made whole, and be the saviour of my family and make my father proud?

The bubbling and boiling erupted like Nairn's cauldron deep in my guts, forcing the words up through my throat, out of my mouth and into the air. 'I BELIEVE! I BELIEVE IN THE FATHER AND THE SON AND THE HOLY SPIRIT. MAKE ME WHOLE!'

Harold squeezed my hand tighter. My body shook, the candle flames flickered. I prayed, this time silently, hoping God had heard me, hoping He was a loving, merciful God and would take my affliction away from me forever.

Five

Every day I examined my deformed foot for even the slightest improvement. There was none. I still limped. Other children still called me dipper and hop-a-long. Hakon still called me cripple. My father still looked at me with disdain. Harold Godwinson came to see me, convinced I would be cured as he had been. His disappointment was obvious as I hobbled towards him on my crutch. 'God must have a special purpose for you,' he said, 'one where this desire of yours to be a warrior would be an obstacle.'

'I do not want a special purpose, I only want to be like everybody else. I want two good legs. Why did God not answer my prayers?'

'It is not for us to know God's purpose, Leofric, though it is futile to work against Him. You must accept this is how He meant you to be and wait for Him to direct you on the path He wishes you to take.'

If God's purpose was for me to spend my life in misery, He must be a cruel, uncaring God. Or, He is not there, there is no God. I was simply born with a crippled foot, there is no reason and no cure. I would have to learn to live with it.

I quickly dismissed these thoughts from my mind. How could there be no God? I had been taught He made the world and everything in it. I was obviously too worthless for Him to heed my prayers. I must limp through this life and make my own way in the world. I said nothing of this to Harold or anyone else, but it made me more determined to succeed in my quest to be a warrior and nothing would stop me, not even God.

My father came home and everything changed.

I had not seen him arrive, but I was glad when I was told he wanted me and Brokk in the hall immediately. The first hint something was wrong, was when we entered the hall and saw Rush standing before my father's dais, his head bowed, and my father seated before him with an expression telling us all was not well. We stood next to Rush; my father remained silent. Shuffling our feet uneasily we stared at the ground and waited. How long we waited, I'm not sure, but it seemed an age. As our eyes became accustomed to the dark of the hall, I realized there were others present, standing in the shadows at the side. Ulla, Rush's mother, was one, looking tearful. My mother stood next to her, silent and serious. Next to her were Leafwold, Grim and, to my dismay, a smirking Hakon and next to him, the priest I knew to be Crispin from Thorneley and behind him, someone I had never seen before. The longer we waited the more aware I became of the eyes of the skeleton on the embroidery behind my father staring at me. I lowered my gaze to avoid them but each time I looked up there they were, watching. Watching no one else, just me.

The silence was broken as my father spoke, his voice harsh and angry.

'I have spent the last week with the thegn of Wydeford, he is a man of wealth and power. I spent many hours bargaining, haggling, cajoling, convincing, everything in fact short of begging, to prove we would both profit from collaboration with each other. I led him to the conclusion both our estates would prosper from combining our assets and working together in these times of need. He wanted to purchase my whole estate or part of it and I would hold it for him. I resisted and eventually convinced him two strong thegns would be better than one. After more lengthy discussions, I was pleased with what had been agreed and documents were drawn up to make a legal contract between us. The ink was on the quill ready to sign before witnesses, when,' at this my father stood, his face inflamed with anger, 'when the thegn's two sons came into the hall. The young one was shaking, the older, bloodstained and nursing an injured face, telling of insults

46

to their mother, the thegn's own dear wife, and an attack on their own person by louts from Æssefeld-Underbarroe. Two of their colleagues had been injured, one with broken ribs, one hardly able to walk. The gathering was aghast. I demanded to be given a description of their attackers so I could punish them for such conduct. Upon which the younger son Ulf replied, "One was a little taller than me with red hair, the other taller again but limped and used a crutch, and the other was a huge oaf with an axe." Do we recognize anyone from that description? I believe we do!' roared my father. Ulla sobbed uncontrollably. My mother tried to console her. Renweard glared at Rush with hard, cold eyes, 'You, boy, obviously have too much time on your hands. For the rest of this summer when you have finished your work in the fields, you will report to my steward and he will give you extra work to keep you busy. Also, you will stay away from my son and mix with your own kind. You are the son of a slave, do not forget that in future. If I have cause to speak to you again on this matter, I will punish, not only you, but your mother also, and the punishment will be severe. Do you understand me?'

I knew Rush was terrified, I also knew he was proud and defiant. As scared as he was, he looked my father in the eye and fighting the tremor in his voice said, 'If you wish it, lord, I suppose I must obey, being merely the son of a slave woman, though I am also the son of a warrior who died fighting for his freedom.'

My father moved slowly and deliberately toward him, then grabbing him roughly by the shoulder, through snarling lips and bared teeth, in a quiet, deep voice said, 'If you were a man, I would kill you for your insolence as I did your father. Give thanks to God you are only a boy, and make it two summers extra work, unless you would wish it to be three.'

Rush remained silent and my father diverted his gaze to Brokk.

'I allowed you into my household to look after my son as a favour to Lord Harold and you repay me by attacking my neighbours.'

I started to say Brokk had been protecting me, but my father thrust out his hand, knocking me to the floor. 'I will tell you when it is your turn to speak,' he thundered and turned back to Brokk. 'They wanted me to cut off your right hand to stop you using that axe of yours and if I hadn't thought it would anger Lord Harold, I would have agreed. Instead, it has been decided you will serve the thegn of Wydeford for at least a year to compensate, whilst his sons and companions recover from their injuries. You will return here each Sabbath and learn what looking after my son truly means.'

Brokk nodded at my father to acknowledge he had understood his punishment.

Next, it was my turn. Already shaken by the blow my father had given me, I dreaded what was to come.

'Leofric, Leofric, Leofric.' My name rolled from his lips like a curse. 'Some may feel I have neglected you as my son.' His eyes found those of my mother before darting back to mine. 'This will no longer be the case. We will find out if you are indeed destined to be thegn of Æssefeld or a man of the Church. Your education will be entrusted to this man.'

Crispin the priest stepped forward, his podgy, friendly face lifting my spirits, his smile renewing my hope. Alas, it was not to be, he had only moved aside to let the man behind him come forward.

The stranger walked slowly out of the shadows and stood next to my father. The cowl of his dark, woollen habit partly hid his face, although I could see, even in the half-light of my father's hall, it was the face of a man of around thirty summers. His eyes had a cruelness which made me shiver. He carried a long, thin, pointed, spindleberry stick the length of his arm, which he tapped incessantly on the side of his leg.

'I am Thurstan the monk and I will guide you to fulfil your destiny, whatever it may be, whatever it may take.' Having made this brief statement, the monk stepped back behind my father, and I knew my life would never be the same again.

My father continued to spell out exactly what would happen next.

'You will be taught in the things you need to equip you for your future. You will stay away from the boy, Rush. Ulf, the thegn of Wydeford's youngest son, will join Hakon and you for your lessons and I advise you to seek their company at other times, as they are of the same ilk as you. You will learn to act like a thegn's son or you will don the habit of a monk and apply yourself to good works and serve the Lord God. Now, leave me and let me hear of no more foolishness, I have an estate to run.'

Dismissively he waved us away. Leafwold took hold of Rush by the ear and yanked him yelling out of the hall. Brokk went with Grim who was to escort him to Wydeford. Thurstan the monk beckoned Hakon and I.

We crossed the courtyard from the hall to the outbuildings behind the stone church. Inside a long, low building, curtains hung across from wall to wall at either end, behind which lay straw mattresses; a large one at one end and three smaller at the other. In the middle of the room were three small desks with tall stools next to them, and a larger desk over by the far wall. There were no windows in the building and the only luxury were beeswax candles which burn brightly and have an aromatic, pleasant smell. It was clear this was to be our work and resting place for the foreseeable future. Two men pushed past us carrying a chest which Thurstan told them to place by the large desk. A carpenter and a young apprentice came in carrying wood with which they started to make shelves. Thurstan rooted around in the chest.

'The Lord Jesus made the ultimate sacrifice by giving up his life, so we sinners could live. For the time being, your miserable lives are now mine. You, too, will make sacrifices. Laughter is for fools. Learning is a serious matter. Do you understand, serious?'

We understood, and laughter was the last thing on our minds. Then I found out what the pointed stick was for, as he poked me vigorously in the arm through my tunic. He thrust a wax tablet he had taken from the chest onto my desk.

'Each day you will write your lesson on there and you will learn it by heart. The next morning you will wipe the tablet clean and you will repeat the lesson to me. Each mistake you make will be rewarded with this.'

Again, he poked the stick into my arm in exactly the same place as before. On the many occasions he poked me with his stick, the mark on my arm grew no bigger than a silver penny. It turned into a bloody scab, the scar of which I still have today.

This, I realised, was to be my young life. Ulf joined Hakon and I, and Thurstan taught us to understand and write in Latin, also the runic alphabet. He taught us the elementary workings of metre and astronomy. He showed us maps both locally and of the world. I marvelled at the drawings of great sea monsters in the oceans and dreamt I might go to such places and see such incredible creatures one day. We learnt to count and subtract and read countless prayers and supplications, which we repeated over and over again. We learnt about the life of the more important saints. Of all these tasks, the one I enjoyed most was reading a book Thurstan owned. It was a copy of the writings of a monk called Bede, about the history of our people since they came to this land, about kings and warriors and how land was won and lost. Written in Latin, it made me learn my letters quicker so I could go back to it time after time.

Books and learning were no strangers to me, for whilst other children played games, I had spent my time free from their bullying and name-calling, by copying from my mother's prayer book. But Bede's book was something more. The letters themselves, their form and colour, the way the gold and red shimmered on the parchment, held me in awe. It was the first time I had seen what Thurstan called Arabesque initials, with their interlacing foliage and rhythmic patterns of scrolling. I was enthralled and fascinated by the skill and love it must have taken to make such a book.

Once or twice, Thurstan discovered me copying these in secret. At first, he poked me vigorously with his stick and rapped my knuckles with it for wasting valuable parchment and ink. After the third or fourth occasion, he stopped chastising and even encouraged me to continue practising. A few weeks later, he said, 'There is someone you should meet. I shall arrange it with your father.'

And so it happened, Thurstan and I rode to the abbey at Sancte Eadmundes Byrig. The journey took us two days. We stopped overnight at a small priory. We spoke little, though on occasion Thurstan would ask me questions.

'Are you ambitious, Leofric?'

'Ambitious, brother?' I said, not fully understanding the question. He had told us to call him brother, to distinguish between him and father Crispin, who had become our new priest.

'Few boys have the learning you have, Leofric. They either farm or they fight. The Church on the other hand, offers different opportunities. For one with ambition, there is no limit to how high one might rise.'

'Oh no, I have no interest in the Church, brother, I am going to be a great warrior.'

'The boy is a deluded fool,' he said out loud to himself.

Several hours passed before we spoke again.

'Ambition is the reason I am at Æssefeld,' Thurstan said, as we looked down a long valley towards the abbey. 'Not my ambition, but the ambition of another, one who thought I would eventually take his position as prior. He brought false claims against me and wanted me driven from the Church. Bishop Lyfing, once again restored as Bishop of Wigraceaster, intervened and I was sent to Æssefeld. I tell you this so you will know, when opportunities present themselves, they must be taken, as all can be lost in an eye blink.'

The abbey buildings were spread over a vast area and monks and lay-men busied themselves with a multitude of tasks. We were shown to a large room which smelt of paint, parchment and glue.

'I need to talk to the abbot, you wait here and Spearhavoc will come to you,' said Thurstan.

I wandered around the room. There were three lecterns. Two were occupied by boys, both two or three years older than me. They ignored me and continued at their work. There were paintings and sketches and small statuettes of Jesus and the Virgin Mary and saints I did not know the names of. A door at the far end of the room opened, and a monk in a scruffy habit, hair like wind-tossed straw and a face with loose, baggy skin and small, pig-like eyes came out. He locked the door behind him and without speaking ushered me to the free lectern.

'Fetch parchment, ink and a quill,' he said to one of the boys, cuffing him around the head.

The boy scurried off and came back shortly with the objects asked for.

'Write your name on this as though it was the first letters in a book of psalms,' he said, poking the parchment with a short, fat finger. He walked back to the door he had come from, unlocked it and left us alone. I heard the key turn as he locked himself in.

The quill was of mediocre quality, crow or blackbird. The parchment too was poor, with a rough surface and no pumice to scrape it smooth. Both boys giggled. I wrote the letters **e o f r i c** first. In front of them, I drew the thin outline of a large letter **L**. I filled the centre of the letter with spirals and writhing snakes, then I drew maple leaves, entwined around the letter, and finished it off with the image of a heron on the bottom righthand corner of the **L**

After an hour, Spearhavoc came back through the door, locking it behind him once again. I could not help wondering what was in that room.

Thurstan returned moments later. Picking up the parchment, Spearhavoc squinted at it in the dim light.

'Remarkable for one so young. You are certain he is an acquaintance of Harold Godwinson, aren't you?'

'Certain,' said Thurstan.

'I'll teach him. I'll send for him when I want him to return.'

The monks gave us bread and cheese and we left the abbey and made the long journey back to Æssefeld. Our conversation was short and one-sided.

'Learn from him, Leofric, he is one of the best illuminators in Englaland. Forget the foolish notion of being a warrior and devote your life to God and Mother Church.'

On our return to Æssefeld, we passed a group of men and four monks erecting a stone cross, as tall as a man. The cross had been carved creating a large circle of stone near the top, from which the arms of the cross extended. It stood at the start of the path which branched off the main track and led to Nairn's hut. An inscription carved into the stone read, RENDER UNTO GOD THE THINGS THAT ARE GODS.

'Who has instructed this to be placed here?' asked Thurstan.

'Bishop Lyfing,' shouted a monk crossing himself.

'He is in the village waiting to see you, brother,' shouted one of the men as he rammed the soil hard around the base of the cross.

When we entered the village, we were directed to the church and were met by my father, Crispin the priest and Bishop Lyfing. Twenty black-robed monks swinging thuribles and chanting in a low murmur, like a droning war horn, were filing into the church

Thurstan knelt and kissed the ring on the bishop's finger.

Bishop Lyfing had the bearing of a weasel caught in a trap. Swaying incessantly, his flowing robes of white linen and purple silk billowing with the constant movement. A slim, pointed face held a permanent, insincere smile which appeared as a thin crack above a jutting chin, and watery eyes which flittered from side to side. His hair hung lank and greasy beneath his mitre.

'I am here to collect the tithes owed to the Church and God. Disappointed I am, disappointed. I am informed many folk visit Æssefeld, though I find the church empty and the alms accrued pitiful. It is rare I make such visits myself, however, the reports I have been receiving are alarming, alarming. There is talk of a woman, a cunning woman, who claims to cure the sick and foretell the future. I am told the people have more faith in her alleged skills than the Church and the one true God, and the alms owed to the Church are given to her. Is this true?'

'Her name is Nairn, lord bishop,' said my father, 'a harmless creature, deluded in her beliefs, though skilled in the way of herbs and charms. The local folk come to her for those skills. We collect a tenth of their wages for the church from work in the fields or produce they have grown, or things they make with their hands, but most are of little means and times are difficult.'

'They must work harder if they wish to gain God's favour. It is your duty as thegn, Renweard, to make sure they do. And yours, Crispin, as their spiritual shepherd, to lead your flock in the ways of the Lord and away from this daughter of Satan.'

'Nairn is hardly that, lord bishop. She has even been courted by kings,' said my father.

'Kings have many of the frailties of lesser men, Renweard, especially concerning their vanity,' said Lyfing, shaking his head. 'I have heard the tales of her dream of kings and the triumph of one over all others. Lies and fabrications, lies and fabrications, all of it. She must be stopped, do you hear me, stopped!'

'She is popular with many folk, lord bishop, not only in Æssefeld but many places,' said my father. 'To harm her in any way could cause unrest.'

'You must make sure the people see her for what she really is, Renweard, a charlatan and a trickster.' The bishop closed his eyes, mouthed a silent prayer and crossed himself. 'Bring my horse, there is much work to be done and so little time. Thurstan, you will walk with me to the edge of the village and we will talk.'

The bishop and Thurstan lead the way through the village gates followed by his personal troops. The monks scurried behind like a flock of startled rooks. My father and I followed on our horses.

As we approached the newly erected cross, the procession came to a stop. My father and I rode to the front to see what the hold-up was. A girl was kneeling at the base of the cross, a dead hare draped over one of the cross arms, its entrails and blood were smeared over the upright, bits of it still sliding downwards over the stone to the ground.

It was Mair.

'What in God's name have we here?' cried the bishop.

'It is a gift from my gods to your god,' said Mair. Her smile and wide, sparkling eyes contradicting the gruesome sight before them.

'Child of Satan,' yelled the bishop, 'bring, bring!'

Two of the black-robed monks ran to Mair and grabbing an arm each, forced her in front of Lyfing. The bishop hooked his crosier around Mair's neck, pulling her nearer till her face almost touched his horse's flank. Leaning over, he thrashed her about the head and across her puny back with his horse whip. My ears filled with Mair's screams, blood seeping through her thin dress as she struggled to break free.

'There is but one God, you filthy wretch,' snarled the bishop, striking Mair repeatedly.

'Enough bishop, enough,' my father protested, 'she is a mere child.'

'Silence man, your weakness allows such abominations to take place here. Too lenient, too lenient, these people must be disciplined, they must fear the one true God. Do you hear, wretch?' he said to Mair, his whip swishing through the air striking her twice again, once on her outstretched arm as she tried to ward off the blow, and on her face, leaving a red wheal across her cheek. 'One God, not many. Who taught you such blasphemous nonsense?'

'She is the dream teller's daughter,' said my father.

'Dream teller, dream teller, they are both heinous she-devils, Renweard. Take heed, if you continue to allow their loathsome practices to go unpunished, your soul will also burn in the everlasting fires of hell.'

Bishop Lyfing crossed himself vigorously, momentarily relaxing his grip on the crozier. Mair kicked the bishop's horse on the fetlock and dug her nails into the beast's side. The horse reared, almost unseating the bishop and Mair slipped from the crozier's grip. The two monks tried to grab her, but she was too nimble and ran past them up the path towards her mother's hut.

She stopped briefly, still sobbing from her beating, calling out, 'You say there is one god, well he must be a cruel, mean god and I will never follow him. I curse your god and you, and pray Jormungard, the serpent who circles the earth, devour you both, long before the days of Ragnarok.'

She spat towards the bishop and though it only landed three arms' lengths from herself, the venom intended was unmistakable. Then, like a slithering grass snake, she was gone through the tall fronds of bracken.

The bishop's face was as purple as his cassock.

'The king will hear of this, Renweard, the king, the archbishop and Earl Godwin. These are sensitive times, we cannot have crones and their feral offspring stirring up discontent. It is written in scripture; 'Those without faith, those disgusting in their filth, sorcerers and idolaters and all the liars, their portion will be in the lake that burns with fire and sulphur.'

Lyfing yanked his horse's head with a sharp pull of the reins and spun round in a circle. 'My work is finished here for now. Take heed, Renweard, Thegn of Æssefeld, take heed, bring your house in order or God's wrath will descend upon you and all who dwell in this God forsaken place.'

He spun his horse around once more and leant down to speak to Thurstan. I overheard him say, 'The thegn is weak-willed, the priest has a heart as soft as moss. I entrust you to find a way to turn folk against the she-devil and her daughter. Unless you wish to spend the rest of your life in this hovel you will find a way, Thurstan, you will find a way!'

Bishop Lyfing spurred his horse and his troops and the black-hooded monks left Æssefeld to take God's love to a more deserving place than ours, leaving behind him a malevolent Mair with a newfound hatred of the church and all it stood for.

Six

The problem was the tax. Already heavy from our last king, the Danish Harold Harefoot, his stepbrother, Harthacnut, was raising the tax yet again. Unsure of his welcome in a foreign land, he had brought a large navy with him from Denmark. Now he was firmly ensconced as the ruler of all Englaland, he needed money to pay off the ships' crews.

It was the second week of June AD 1041. My father received the first of two messages. The first came from an old friend of his, a trader and trapper by the name of Tripp. It was his first visit in three years and although my father often talked about him, my memory of him was vague. It was the children who caught sight of him as he came over the hill, on the path leading from the Roman road. He sat on an old, rickety cart which creaked, rattled and rocked from side to side on the bumpy path like a small boat on a rough sea. Two mules pulled the cart. Both looked as tired and old as their master, their coats were mangy, their legs bowed and chaffed where the harness had been rubbing. The cart was laden with all manner of useful items; pots, pans, various trinkets, polished mirrors, jute and amber beads, the occasional weapon and special rarities from exotic, far-off lands.

Tripp was huge, a great bear of a man. Not only to look at, with his tangled mass of brown hair and beard, which were now flecked with grey but even when he spoke, it was more of a deep-throated growl and when he ate, he tore at his food as if it were fresh from a kill. Of all the folk who ever passed through Æssefeld-Underbarroe, Tripp was by far the most travelled. He regularly plied his wares from coast to coast, from the far north of the kingdom to the far south. He had traded with the Irish in Ireland. He had eaten in the banquet hall of Gruffydd ap Llewelyn deep in the hills of the Wealas. He had been across the British sea and through Normandy and even to Rome itself and beyond the desert roads along which are brought silk and rich spices from the East. As a young man, he had lived in Byzantium, serving in the Varangian guard, where he had fought side-by-side with my father and struck up a friendship they had never lost. Although there were more profitable places to trade, this friendship brought Tripp to Æssefeld, though not as often as he would like.

The children ran alongside the cart shouting and cheering. One of the boys managed to cling to the back of it until a wheel bounced over a divot and he lost his grip and fell off. Tripp slowed the cart down, allowing others to climb up, as the cart lurched towards the village gates. I watched from the doorway of my room overlooking the courtyard, as Hakon and Ulf practised their sword skills with Grim. The disturbance had brought a large gathering to meet Tripp as he entered the village. There were handshakes and back-slaps from the men and hugs from the women. Someone thrust a pot of ale in his hand which he downed without a breath. Droplets of the honey-brown liquid trickled down his beard as the children tugged on his tunic, excited by this huge stranger with his cart of wondrous treasures. He reached into the front of the cart and pulled out a hemp sack from under the seat. He took out a selection of carved, wooden animals and spinning tops and tossed them into the air, causing a mad scramble, as tiny hands grabbed their share. These had taken him little time to make from scraps of wood but gave the children so much pleasure and ensured their grateful parents would be more inclined to trade with him. The craftsmen of the village gave Tripp's cart a wary glance, afraid his wares would compete with theirs, though most would trade and barter with him themselves.

My mother and father came out to meet Tripp at the manor door. Thurstan reluctantly finished our session and I was able to go and greet him. After embraces, we went inside. Tripp smiled as he gazed at the embroidery hanging above my father's chair.

'Can I take a quick look, old friend?' he asked my father.

Renweard looked towards the door to make sure we were alone and nodded his approval to Tripp.

Tripp walked over and pulled back the embroidery, sliding the panel across, revealing the glittering, bejewelled ceremonial sceptre. He ran his hand along the gold shaft with its carvings, both biblical and mythical, up to the winged spear. Around the socket, where it joined the shaft, it was encrusted in precious and semi-precious stones.

Tripp had been with Renweard the day he uncovered this wonderful prize from the vast treasure hoard in Byzantium. It had been a tradition, though not altogether a legal one, upon the death of an emperor, certain high-ranking guards were able to enter the treasury and take as much as they could carry with their bare hands.

Renweard had seen the ruby glistening in the half-light of the cavernous vault, faintly visible amongst a great mound of stolen riches. As he curled his fingers around it to claim it as his own, he was astonished to find it was only a small part of a spear-shaped sceptre, which he pulled from the mound. The keeper of the treasure house was as amazed as he was at the sight of the sceptre. He touched the long shaft and examined the golden figures and the strange writing etched into the spearhead. He told Renweard he was certain it was the sceptre of legend. It was said to have belonged to one of the wise men that visited the infant Jesus, and the sceptre was a mark of his authority. They were priests from the east, said to be astrologers and practisers of magic. Some say that the exquisite spear fell to earth fully formed by the gods. Others, that it was forged in the deep furnaces of the earth by magical beings before the time of man. It was made of solid gold and encrusted with precious stones. The legend claimed the image of the infant Jesus was captured in the large, red ruby, though only those of true heart could see it. It was also claimed the sceptre had the power to recognise rightful kings and whichever ruler possessed it would be victorious in all they set out to achieve. When the priests returned to their countries, they became devotees of Christ and gave up all their priestly possessions and the sceptre was donated to a temple, which, decades later, was sacked and looted. The sceptre was taken and thought lost, but obviously ended up in the treasure vaults of Byzantium. Tripp had grabbed gold plate, goblets, other trinkets and a jewelled cross, long since gone, on drink, women and gambling.

'I still say it wouldn't throw true, Renweard, it's top-heavy,' said Tripp.

'Never tried it,' said Renweard, 'too valuable to risk it merely to prove a point. So, don't you be getting any ideas you old rascal. Mind you, those were good days, weren't they?'

Renweard grinned as he slapped his companion on the back and took the sceptre from him and placed it back in its hiding place. He called out to Mirela for food and something hearty to drink for his tired friend.

Mirela and Ulla brought a quickly prepared meal of bread, pulses, salt-fish and ale. Renweard apologised for the paltry fare, Tripp assured him it was a banquet compared to many places he had been in these troubled times. As we ate, we eagerly listened to Tripp as he related to us the events he had witnessed or heard about on his travels. Lastly, he told us the worst news.

'I was in Wigraceaster. The king, the shit,' Tripp spat on the floor as he said it, 'sent two of his lackeys to collect the taxes, to pay off the mercenary crews that brought him to Englaland. The townsmen refused to pay and chased them both into the minster where they tried to hide in an upper room in one of the bell towers. By the time they got to them, the crowd were like wild dogs and tore them apart.'

Tripp paused for a swig of ale and ran his fingers through his beard, dislodging a few crumbs.

'Days later, Harthacnut's housecarls, led by all the earls of Englaland, came with an army and set about burning the whole surrounding area and terrorised the townsfolk, most of whom fled beyond the ravaged countryside. The men of Wigraceaster built a makeshift fort on Bevere Island in the middle of the River Sæfern and managed to defend themselves, but the king's men harried the town for five days before they withdrew. As I left Wigraceaster, the smoke was still rising into the sky and the devastation was as far as one could see. Be warned, Renweard, this king intends to act the same way whenever there is resistance to his demands.'

Renweard shook his head. 'All my villagers are almost at their limit. They can pay the tax this time, but after then, I don't know.'

Renweard sent Ulla to find Leafwold his steward, and Grindan, who was one of our two fyrd-men, to bring them to him. Leafwold arrived first and on my father's instruction, he rummaged around in a wooden chest, which sat in the corner of the hall. He came back to the table with a box containing quills, ink, parchment and other writing tools. Whilst my mother and I listened to the rest of Tripp's adventures, Renweard dictated a brief message to Leafwold, quietly, so no one else could hear. The steward copied the words on five pieces of parchment. My father rolled them up separately. Taking a stick of red wax from the box, he heated it in the flame of a candle, letting it drip in a small circle onto each scroll. Next, he pressed a big wooden seal hard on the circles of wax, leaving the impression of the family crest; an owl and an axe, denoting wisdom and power. Leafwold, directed by my father wrote a name on each sealed roll of parchment.

There was a loud thump on the manor door, making me jump. My father shouted, 'Enter.'

It was Grindan. Grindan was a tall, broad-shouldered man, whose muscles seemed to be bursting out of his clothing. His face had a florid complexion though scarred with weeping pox sores, and a blood red nose too big for his head. Grindan and his twin brother, Ealdan, were our fyrd-men, the men who went to war on behalf of our village.

'You summoned me, lord?'

'I need these delivered as quickly as possible,' my father said, passing the scrolls to him.

'I shall go at once. Have you given thought to the matter I asked you about yesterday, my lord?'

Renweard nodded. 'Yes! Your request will be granted when you return. Now make haste, those letters are important.'

Grindan smirked then left hurriedly.

'What arrangement have you made with that rogue?' asked my mother, scowling at me as I crossed the room without using my crutch which she held out for me to take.

My father looked down as he answered her. 'It's becoming harder to pay the soldiers. Those who are unattached have agreed to wait for a while if I order certain servant girls to their beds. Grindan wants Ulla.'

Ulla gasped and dropped the jug she was carrying onto the floor.

'You won't do it will you, my lord?' my mother frowned as she spoke.

'It's done all the time,' growled Renweard. 'Many a lord takes a servant girl to his bed and sells her on if she gets full with child. What difference is it if a lord gives them to his men instead? These are desperate times. A thegn needs soldiers. Soldiers need rewarding.' Renweard stood from the table abruptly, knocking over his jug of ale.

'Ulla, when Grindan returns you will warm his bed at night. You will work here in the day and you can return here to live when he tires of you.'

My mother covered my ears with her hands. 'Not in front of the boy, my lord.'

'Why not? I dread to think of it, but he will be lord of Æssefeld one day. He needs to know how a lord should conduct himself. You can't shield him from the real world all his life. Now, enough of this! You have my decision and that's the end to it! Tripp show me what you have brought on that heap of sticks you call a cart.'

Tripp followed Renweard outside and beckoned me to join them whilst my mother tried to soothe the weeping Ulla.

Once outside, Renweard delved through Tripp's merchandise, admiring many items, though only selecting what was necessary.

'Fine boy you have here, Renweard,' Tripp said, ruffling my hair with his huge fingers.

'He limps,' said my father dismissively.

'So, he limps, will that make him a lesser man?'

'He is a cripple, so, yes,' said my father, picking up an old, gold torc from the cart and examining it carefully.

'That belonged to a Celtic prince,' Tripp said, 'exceedingly rare. Like Leofric here, a one-off.'

'I am sure the price will reflect its rarity,' said my father putting it back on the cart. 'As they say, there is always a price to pay'.

'You never did tell me what happened the night he was born, Renweard,' Tripp said, pulling more trinkets to the top of the pile, trying to encourage my father to part with some money.

'He was born in a stable as God's own precious son was. The horses were so reluctant to give up such a child, one of them tried to snatch him back by his leg, causing the damage. God showed such wrath, He sent lightning and burnt the stable to the ground.'

When folk heard I had a deformed left foot, many said I was cursed. My father invented the story of the horses to infer I was something special. The story evolved over time to include my affinity with horses, that not only did I talk to them, but they spoke back to me, which I have never found a reason to refute.

Tripp looked heavenwards at Renweard's reply, his eyebrows raised. 'A miracle, Renweard, truly a miracle.'

The truth of it was, my father blamed my mother for giving him a deformed son and my mother blamed herself. Since they came to Æssefeld, Mirela had given birth to three stillborn girls. At first, she believed it was a punishment from God because she had married a man of violence. When I was born, she was thrilled she had at last presented Renweard with an heir, only to realise I would never be the healthy son he longed for.

Since Thurstan arrived, he had reasoned with her that God had made me this way because He had a purpose for me; not to become a warrior like my father, but to do God's work.

'It is why he has this ability to create such fine works with his hands,' Thurstan told my mother, 'You are not being punished, but blessed.'

She found this explanation far more palatable than her first reaction of self-chastisement and embraced this to the point of obsession, determined I would become a servant of God.

Tripp stayed for two weeks. He visited Nairn frequently. He and I walked together often. He told me about his time with my father. He said he had never seen a braver or more ferocious man except for the mighty Hardrada himself. The injuries Renweard had received in battle had taken their toll and he was only a shadow of the man he once knew.

'And you, Leofric, I hear you have a spiritual calling or so others tell me. Is that what you want, lad, to serve God?'

'No, it is not!' I said vehemently. 'I want to be a warrior.' I waited for, 'how can a cripple such as you become a warrior?' It never came.

After a few minutes silence, Tripp said, 'It won't be easy. I am told they don't let you practice at sword skills.'

'No, they don't, but I practice in secret. I watch the others training and I copy their moves, using this as a sword.'

I waved the crutch in the air, mimicking a sword stroke. Tripp smiled, whilst nodding his head in approval.

'Not as good as real training, but it's better than nothing,' he said.

The day before he left, we walked across the long meadow to the edge of Æsc wood. We came to a big, old oak which had a gap in its trunk as big as a doorway. He ducked inside, and I followed him into the darkness. As our eyes became accustomed to the dark, Tripp reached up and took something hanging in the tree. It was a yew bow. Not full size, but bigger than the one my father had broken and burnt.

'I have hidden this here for you, Leofric. I know your father does not approve, but a warrior needs skills.'

He reached up again and brought down a quiver with six arrows with goose quill flights. 'You won't need these yet, but they are here when you do.' He reached up once again and put the quiver back.

'Why don't I need them now?'

'Take the bow and pull it back as hard as you can.'

I gripped the stave with my left hand and pulled the gut string with my right using all my strength. I managed to move the string about two handbreadths, the stave hardly bending.

'That's why Leofric. Practice, practice, build up the strength in your arm and practice some more. When you can fully bend the bow, it will be time for the arrows.'

Tripp put his hands on my shoulders, peered into my eyes, and said two things I have never forgotten.

'Most warriors are strong in body but not all have strength of mind. Not all battles are won by sheer strength in numbers, but wise tactics. Use this, Leofric,' he said tapping my head, 'not always this,' and prodded my chest over my heart. He paused a while. 'Hear everything, act on little, and most importantly, be true to yourself.'

I was not sure what the last part meant at the time, but as I grew older, I came to understand its meaning.

Every morning before my lessons with Thurstan, I visited the tree and practised pulling the bowstring. At first, I could hardly pull it back, but eventually, it became easier and I managed to make the bow bend to its full extent. Now I was ready to nock the first arrow.

Three months after Tripp left Æssefeld, Renweard received the second piece of disturbing news. It came by means of a royal emissary. Twenty men, under the king's banner, rode into the village with trumpets blaring and a lone drummer boy beating a quick rhythm. Many of the villagers gathered around to see what the commotion was. The emissary wore velvets and silks, of red and green with trimmings of gold braid. On his head was a round hat of beaver pelts that sported a magnificent white stork plume. He introduced himself as Halvdan-the-Cautious, envoy to Harthacnut, King of Englaland and taking a long tube from his saddlebag he took from it a rolled piece of parchment. Unfurling it to its full length, he began to read:

'There is to be a wedding, Tovi the Proud and Gytha, daughter of Osgot Clapa, a close companion of the late King Cnut. It will be held in the great hall at Lambhyo on the eighth day of June in the year of our Lord, one thousand and forty-two. Your lord, Renweard, Thegn of Æssefeld-Underbarroe, his lady wife, son and ward will attend, along with Thurstan the monk and five servants of their choice. The people of Æssefeld will have the privilege of supplying the following

65

provisions: Two pigs, three barrels of eels, one flitch of bacon, half a sester of honey, three sacks of flour and four large goats' cheeses. These are to be delivered to Lambhyo one week before the aforementioned date.'

Halvdan paused for breath and gave a small cough to clear his throat. He continued:

'The King himself will be present, as will his heir apparent, Prince Edward, son of King Ethelred the second and Emma of Normandy; The Earl Godwin of Wessex and sons; The Earl Leofric of Mercia and son; Earl Siward of Norðhymbraland; Lords Beorn and Ralph; all their attendants and all the prominent thegns of the realm. All the aforementioned persons will attend this important event by order of Harthacnut, King of Denmark and Englaland.'

Halvdan rolled up the parchment and put it back in the tube and handing it to Renweard gave a click of his heels and bowed his head. I overheard him say quietly to my father, 'The King will speak to you privately on a matter of most importance at the wedding.'

The trumpets blew. The emissary remounted his horse and led the party out of the gates. The whole of Æssefeld was concerned by the news of the wedding, even though most of them would not be attending, they knew supplying the required foodstuffs would cause them great hardship. My father was puzzled. He was no longer one of the prominent thegns of the land. Normally he would not be invited to such an event.

'Why now, Grim? After all this time, why is the king showing an interest in me?'

He had, it was true, supported Harthacnut when they had elected his younger stepbrother, Harold-Harefoot as king, when it should rightly have been Harthacnut. However, since he had objected so strongly when Harthacnut had his dead brother's body dug up and thrown into a bog, the king had ignored him.

Grim shook his head. 'It's probably the taxes, wants someone else to do his dirty work and punish those who don't pay.'

'I won't do it, Grim, I will not attack my own estates, even for a king.'

'Won't the king send the earls to attack us, like he did at Wigraceaster?' I said.

'Not if someone stops him first,' replied my father.

'Who could do such a thing? It would be madness to even try,' said Grim.

'I wish Harthacnut had never come here,' said my father.

'Yer, not the only one to think it,' said Grim, 'but it's too late, he's here, and he is our king.

Seven

AD 1071

It is the twelfth day of our escape from Elig.

We have foraged berries, stole a couple of chickens and Scand, a shifty, dubious fellow who had fled the Isle with us, snared a hare. Without more substantial fare we will not survive, so we must move on. We need horses as I am slowing the others down. Abbot Thurstan says we should turn back and put ourselves at the mercy of William the Bastard. From what we know of him, he is somewhat selective to whom he shows mercy, and most of my companions believe they would not receive any quarter. For me, there was never any moment when surrendering or parleying with William the Bastard was ever an option.

My lands have been destroyed. We have decided therefore to head north beyond the Roman walls to where Prince Edgar, the rightful heir to the throne, is said to be. It is also where my love has fled. How welcome I will be when she learns I have killed her husband, I do not know.

We left the abbey ruins at the last gleam of daylight. Wregan complained, saying he needed more rest. As he had done nothing but complain since we had escaped Elig we simply ignored him. Our progress in the dark was slow, and though we stayed undetected we heard horsemen on two separate occasions. We have come across a deserted barn and we will rest here during the day. It gives me the opportunity to continue my writing.

ᛏᚠ ᚼᛌᚱᚱᛗᛏᚼᛗᚱ

AD 1042

The months after Tripp's visit dragged slowly. Thurstan gave no respite. What we learned one day had to be remembered and recited back to him the next. Each mistake or hesitation was accompanied by a sharp prod with his stick. Ulf struggled with most things, though he missed several lessons as Crispin the priest often asked if he could be excused to help him with various tasks. Thurstan gave no objection as he found Ulf a tiresome, stupid child with no ability or desire for learning. Hakon copied me, blatantly at times, badgering me even late into the night to go over what he had forgotten, not because he wanted to learn, but to escape Thurstan's wrath and the dreaded pointed stick. As for me, I enjoyed the learning. My mother was less than affectionate towards me, but she had always stressed the power of the written word and the wisdom knowledge can give. She would say, 'Most men equate power with physical strength and the art of war. Mark well though, the great men of the Church. They have for the most part, turned their backs on such worldly pursuits and applied themselves to acquiring knowledge through the written word and who can deny they are among the most powerful men in the land?' As I grew older, I came to learn certain men of the Church had not put aside as many worldly habits as my mother believed, and, along with knowledge, they used the weapons of fear and the accumulation of land to enhance their power. Yet there was no denying learning allowed them to pursue their goals. I vowed to harness that same power and make it work for me. I listened carefully and watched over Thurstan's shoulder as he translated from the Latin into the vernacular. I scrutinized how he formed each letter, learning the meaning of the words, listening to their sounds when he spoke them, reading whichever books he would let me borrow, absorbing all this knowledge in the belief it would eventually bring me power. Although Thurstan was harder on me than Hakon and Ulf, it was clear he was pleased with my diligence and enthusiasm. We spent many hours after they had left us, reading, writing, discussing the works of great writers. He was never warm or encouraging, simply appreciative of someone who wanted to learn what he could teach. Whenever I made a mistake or faltered in my reading, he would still thrust the stick at the same spot with pinpoint accuracy saying, 'Learning is a serious matter, Leofric, a serious matter.'

My father and Thurstan spoke on many matters. Before his spiritual demise, Thurstan had been admired in many quarters as a scholarly man, with an expansive knowledge, destined for remarkable things in the Church. Ever since Lyfing had visited Æssefeld, my father seemed a troubled man. He no longer took the sceptre down to look at, though he did slide the wood panel away and stare at the relic on many occasions, seemingly deep in thought. Eventually he decided to confide in Thurstan.

My father sent me to fetch the monk. When we arrived at the hall, the door was locked. My father answered our knocking and let us both in, locking the door behind us. Renweard beckoned Thurstan to join him at the hall's oak table and there, to the monk's astonishment, was the sceptre. My father told him of the legend and how it came to be in his possession. Thurstan stared at the precious sceptre in silence. He then laid his hands, palms downward, on its shaft and prayed in Latin.

'One of the Magi, you say?' he said after a while.

'Yes,' said my father, 'it was said to be a symbol of priestly authority and was carried by the one they called Melchior.'

'The Venerable Bede writes of the Magi,' said Thurstan, 'he calls them three wise men come from the east with gifts. Melchior brings gold to denote a king.' He paused. 'And the Christ image, you say, held in the ruby?'

'So the legend has it,' my father confirmed.

Thurstan leant closer, peering into the deep red ruby. 'I cannot see it.'

'I have never seen it either,' said Renweard, 'though I have met two men that have and heard of others who also witnessed such a thing for themselves. The legend claims it can only be seen by those at total peace with God, with true hearts, ready to stand in front of Him in the heavenly realm to come. The keeper of the imperial treasure vaults told me that it would bring good fortune to whoever possessed it, but it must never be sold or allowed to be stolen, as this would bring calamity and disaster on all involved. It can only be given freely as a gift. It is also said that whenever the validity of a king is in doubt, if the rightful heir lays their right hand upon the sceptre's shaft the ruby glows and the Christ child's face appears.

'Of course,' said Thurstan becoming increasingly enthralled by the sceptre and its legend. 'The Magi were there to bring gifts to the one who would be a king and would die to save the world.'

He ran his hand further along the shaft, then came to an abrupt halt as he reached a large, white jewel which sparkled in the candlelight and appeared to have a jewel within the jewel. He pulled his hands away swiftly and prayed.

'What is it, Thurstan?' asked my father, alarmed at the monk's reaction.

'A star stone,' he said, pointing at the white jewel. 'Pliny the Elder wrote they were used in the practice of magic, with supernatural powers and a thing to fear. He called them Astriotes.'

'Who is Pliny?' asked my father.

'He was a Roman writer and philosopher, a man with unlimited knowledge and wisdom. He wrote of the Magi as being astrologers and practisers of magic.'

'So, what do you think I should do with it, Thurstan? I am starting to wonder if it is more of a curse than a blessing. Perhaps God is angry with me. Perhaps He led me to it, so I could allow others to enjoy its beauty, yet I have kept it hidden away. Do you think I should give it to the Church, so all may benefit from such a relic?'

Thurstan hesitated with his reply, running his fingers softly once more over the full length of the sceptre, only lifting them off to miss the star stone.

'If this truly is what you believe it to be, Renweard, it could be powerful beyond our understanding. In the wrong hands, it could be used for men's glory and not God's. Continue to keep it concealed. I shall make it a matter of earnest prayer and ask for God's guidance.'

Thurstan left my father and me, though he glanced back at the sceptre more than once. When he was sure the monk had gone, my father placed the sceptre behind the embroidery and slid back the panel to hide it from the world.

The following day Thurstan took me back to Spearhavoc at Sancte Eadmundes Abbey. We were taken to the same room as before. As well as the small statues and paintings, the room was now full of life-size drawings of biblical scenes. One was of Jesus on the cross with Mary at his feet. Spearhavoc had written in a scrawl across the drawing, **wood, silver, gold**.

Once again, he sat me at the lectern, though this time the parchment was of superior quality with no blemishes. There was a selection of quills, mostly goose feather, and an array of inks and paints. There was a knife to scrape out mistakes and a pumice stone to smooth the parchment.

'So there is no misunderstanding from the outset, boy, I do not like children. Smelly, dirty, noisy little wretches in my experience. You will speak only when necessary, you will follow my instructions to the letter and you will call me Master.' Saliva flew from his flabby lips as he spoke.

For three weeks, he set me small writing tasks to complete. He showed me how to mix colours; lac, a bright scarlet made by crushing insects; vermillion, rust, ochre, China green from crushing buckthorn berries; smalt, which is blue; ultramarine from lapis lazuli; sepia from cuttlefish ink. He showed me how to draw drolleries, sometimes called grotesques, an amalgamation of human and animals or different animals joined together. He showed me drawings of cockerels with human heads and bird-like dragons with the heads of monsters he called elephants, on their backs. I eagerly absorbed all these new techniques, copying and practising at every moment I could. I barely slept. Each time he showed me something new, he would leave me and enter the other room, unlocking the door and then locking it behind him. Whenever he returned, he looked at what I had accomplished, shook his head, muttered, 'remarkable,' and gave me another task to complete.

On the fourth week of my visit he simply said, 'Follow me,' and he took me to the locked room. As he turned the key in the lock, I was full of anticipation.

I did not know what I expected to be in there, but I should have guessed.

Gold. Gold and silver and small boxes of jewels. In the centre of the room were two, life-size wooden carvings. One was of the Virgin Mary and child, the other, Jesus on the cross, from the drawings in the other room. They were both incomplete, as only small parts of the Christ were inlaid with gold and silver. I marvelled at the intricate skill involved in creating such work.

'This is my passion.'

'They are marvellous,' I said, tracing my finger over the delicately carved folds of the cloth.

'Marvellous? marvellous? they are sublime, boy. There is not another goldsmith in the whole of the land who could have made these, not one.'

'I have seen something similar in the church at Wealtham, though nowhere near as beautiful as these. When will they be finished?' I asked.

'There lies the problem. It takes much skill, much time and even more gold and silver. I am a poor monk who desires to bring glory to

God with these hands. What I need is a wealthy patron who lacks my skill but equals my desire to please Almighty God. I have enough gold for manuscripts, but these, for these I need a patron. Someone who is grateful to God for His blessings or sorrowful for his sins and wishes to adorn their church with rare beauty and bring praise to the one true God.'

'I know Harold has donated gold plate and coin to the church at Wealtham,' I said, 'and he has filled his church in Boseham with all manner of crosses and jewelled cups, though these surpass anything I have seen at either place. I will tell him of your work, Spearhavoc, and I am certain you will get your gold.'

'I am sure God will bless you, Leofric, and I, in turn, will teach you the art of writing with gold.'

And so he did.

Once I was back in Æssefeld, I continued to enjoy copying the letters in the books and old scrolls of Thurstan's. Time after time, I copied each letter noting the length of some, the thickness of others. There were books from Ireland, others from Italy and Byzantium. There was one from Armenia which, although I did not understand the words, had a distinctive type of illustration. Eventually, after experimenting with a variety of styles and fusing them together, I developed a style of my own, which Thurstan said was remarkable for one so young and if he hadn't seen it for himself, would have thought it the work of a seasoned scribe with a rare skill. That was praise indeed from Thurstan who had seen so many of the finest books, though it did not prevent him jabbing his stick into my arm whenever I made the slightest error or slip.

It was whilst I was engrossed in one of these practice sessions, I heard sobbing from behind the curtain where we slept. It was Ulf.

'Are you hurt, Ulf?' I asked.

'No, it's nothing.'

'Folk don't usually cry over nothing.'

'I can't say,' he said gulping for breath, tears streaming down his cheeks.

'Can't or won't?'

'If I tell, I will burn in the fires of hell,' he blurted out, his slight body shaking uncontrollably.

'Who told you that?'

'Can't say. Mustn't tell.'

'I will fetch Crispin, he will tell you, you won't burn in hell.'

At the mention of Crispin he became hysterical. 'No, you can't tell him!' he wailed.

I grabbed him by the shoulders and shook him.

'Now tell me now what's upset you or I will fetch the priest, I swear it.'

His eyes widened, his lip's trembled. 'He makes me do things.'

'Who makes you do what?'

'Crispin makes me touch him and he touches me.'

'Touches,' I said, not understanding why that would distress him so much.

'Down there,' he said, pointing to his groin. 'He makes me rub it and put it in his mouth. He does the same to me and I don't like it. He says I have to do it because he is a man of God and if I refuse him, I will anger God. He said if I anger God or tell others, I will burn in the fires of hell for ever.'

'No you won't, Ulf, he is lying to you. You don't have to do anything you don't want to in that way. When do you see him next?'

'Now. He will be waiting for me in the church. That's where he does it.'

'Take off your cloak,' I said,

'My cloak, why?' he asked, trying his hardest to control the sobbing.

'Just do it and wait here.'

I wrapped his cloak around my shoulders and pulled the hood over my head. I picked up the knife I used for sharpening my quills. I flicked my thumb over the point of the blade; small but sharp. I concealed it in the palm of my left hand and made my way to the church.

The interior was dark, lit only by three beeswax candles, as tall as a small child, which stood on either side of the altar. In front of the altar were four plain spindled chairs. On one of them sat Crispin, his hands clasped in prayer. As his back was towards me, he did not notice my limp, which would have given me away, as I walked across the nave through the arch and into the small chancel.

'You took your time, boy, I have been waiting,' said the priest. 'No matter, you're here now.'

His broad friendly smile greeted me as I sat next to him, my face still hidden in the darkness of the cloak's hood.

'You know what to do, Ulf, be quick about it.'

I proffered up my left hand which he grabbed by the wrist. He swung around towards me, hitched up his inner and outer cassock exposing himself and pulled my hand towards his member. I was shocked. I had wondered whether-or-not Ulf was exaggerating the priest's actions. His intentions were clear.

'Yes, I know exactly what to do,' I said. I grabbed a handful of his cassock just below his throat and pulled his face towards mine. I saw the surprise as he recognised my face, then the shock as I brought my knife hard up against his balls, cutting the skin. 'You will swear now on God's name you will never touch another child as long as you live, or I will slice you open, spill your pebbles onto the floor, cut off your prick and feed it to the church cat.'

We both knew he could overpower me. He was a grown man, I was a mere boy. But he realised the damage I could inflict on him in an instant.

'Put your hand on the altar,' I said.

He reached out his hand and touched the holy altar.

'Now, swear.'

'I swear,' he forced the words out, the colour gone from his cheeks.

'If I hear one word that you have reneged, I will tell both my father and the thegn of Wydeford and I am sure you can imagine what would happen to you.'

I reasoned that if I told them now, Crispin would be replaced and who knew if the replacement would not act in the same way? I was fairly sure; Ulf and others would be safe from Crispin from now on.

In fact, three days later, Thurstan told Ulf that the priest had no more use for him, and we would have the dubious pleasure of more of his company.

'Thank you,' was all Ulf said to me. I knew it was heart felt. He became less withdrawn and tried his best to learn his lessons, though it was clear he would never be more than an average scholar.

Whenever I had free time, which was seldom, I secretly met up with Rush after he finished his long days in the fields. We would sit in an old barn huddled in the straw and talk.

'My mother cries every night,' he said to me on one occasion, 'the ugly bastard hits her.'

I had noticed, ever since Ulla had been forced to lie with Grindan, she had become quiet and nervous, jumping at the slightest sound and cowering when anyone raised their voice.

'One day I will kill him,' he said coldly, which sent a chill right through me because I knew he meant it.

Sometimes, the two of us would slip into the trees at the edge of the forest out of sight and as time passed, we got bolder and ventured further and further on each occasion. Each Sabbath, Brokk, back from Wydeford, joined us. He disapproved of me defying my father and meeting Rush in this way. He had become sullen and withdrawn, reluctant to talk of his time at Wydeford, but I took little notice and carried on regardless.

Rush and I often played a game of hide and seek, taking turns to be the seeker. Trouble was, Rush was so tired from his day of hard, physical work, he would often fall asleep where he hid, and it would take me an age to find him.

It was on one such occasion I stumbled on a terrible secret.

It was Rush's turn to hide, and once I had opened my eyes, I set off to find him. Though it was late evening, it was still light and in the shade of the towering trees, it was dappled and hazy. I tried to be as quiet as a falling leaf, careful not to crack twigs with my feet or the crutch. After a while, I became weary of the game and was about to shout out to Rush to give himself up, when I heard voices in the distance. Cautiously, I moved towards them, thinking it may be charcoal burners or swine herders. I was always wary of forest folk. Brokk had told me they could be funny buggers; one day fine, next day almost murderous, so I kept close to a crop of boxwood scrub which gave me cover up to the edge of a glade.

Once there, I counted six horsemen gathered in a circle. They all wore woollen cloaks with the hoods pulled over their heads, making it impossible for me to see their faces, though when they spoke there was one voice there was no mistaking. It was Renweard, my father.

'So, we are agreed something must be done about this king?' The others murmured approval.

'But what can we do?' another voice uttered. There was a short silence. The rider next to my father spoke.

'There is only one solution. Death.'

'Death!'

'Death!'

'Death!'

One by one, each horseman repeated the verdict on the king's fate until only my father remained to speak. Surely, I thought, he would object to this madness, to this treason. I sensed the anxiety of the gathering, the horses became skittish and the hooded heads turned nervously, scouring the trees for eavesdroppers.

'Who's there?'

I knew that voice, too. It was the thegn of nearby Hearotford and for a moment I thought he had seen me. He pulled at the reins and took his horse out of the circle. Fortunately, he rode to the opposite side of the glade from me and skirted the edge of the trees, peering into the gloomy interior. Satisfied they were alone, he re-joined the others. I was shaking, terrified they might discover me and sank as low as possible in the undergrowth. A noise to my right made me jump. I briefly thought I saw someone moving back up through the forest. I panicked, thinking it was Rush come to find me and would reveal my hiding place. A deer leapt a fallen log and was gone behind a mass of sprawling hazel scrub. More of the horses became uneasy and tossed their manes, sensing the unease of their riders.

'Renweard, your answer!' the thegn of Hearotford insisted.

I closed my eyes, hardly daring to breathe, hoping my father would reject their aims.

'Death!'

'So, it is agreed. We will meet back here the hour before sunset in three days' time, to decide how the deed will be done and who will do it. Give it deep thought, my friends, the peace of the kingdom depends on it.'

With these words from the thegn of Hearotford still in the air, I heard them ride away. When I opened my eyes, I saw the last of them disappear into the forest and they were gone.

My heart was beating hard and my mind was full of confusion and questions. When I was certain the riders had long gone, I made my way back towards the village. As I drew near to the edge of the trees, I saw a lone figure leaning against a tall, beech tree.

'I thought you had gone off without me, I must have dozed off again.' Rush seemed unaware anything had taken place and I said nothing to make him think otherwise.

'You wouldn't have found me anyway, I'm too good for you.'

I laughed, 'Let me guess, not in the old, fallen tree trunk again?'

'Twice I've hidden there, and you didn't find me either time. Told you, too good.'

I slapped him on the back and we both set off on different tracks, so we wouldn't be seen together. It was always a risk meeting this way, but we were young and foolish and the danger of being caught made it more exciting. That night though, things had changed dramatically. My father and other thegns were plotting to kill the king, and as far as I could guess, I was the only other person to know about it.

What was I to do? If it was discovered my father was part of this conspiracy, he would be exiled or even executed. All his lands would be forfeit, and we would end up as peasants. I dared not tell anyone what I'd witnessed, not even Rush or Brokk. It flashed through my mind, I'd thought I'd seen someone moving in the trees. What if someone else did know? I thought of telling my father I'd overheard them, and he must not take any further part in the terrible scheme or I would expose them all. I imagined his rage if I did. Any hope of drawing closer to him would disappear. No, I would say nothing, I would sneak back to their next meeting and see what happened next, and only then could I decide what to do.

Those couple of days seemed to drag. My concentration was low and Thurstan took great delight in using his stick frequently, making blood trickle down my arm. Hakon poked it once or twice making me flinch. I had been worried by Hakon these last few months, as his usual venom towards me had been limited to a few, sarcastic jibes and the odd kick under our desks. It was as though he was biding his time until he thought of something horrible to do to me.

It happened as I was crossing the compound in front of the hall. Grim was training Hakon and Ulf in sword skills. My father stood nearby watching them. Hakon, pausing for breath, called over to my father.

'Lord, perhaps you should let Leofric train with us at least once. To me, it seems unfair to judge he cannot fight without giving him the chance to prove he can. He may be a natural.'

'You could be right, Hakon, but I doubt it,' my father said, looking around quickly to see if my mother was near. 'Leofric, put down that damn crutch and take a practice sword from Grim.'

I did as my father asked and Grim passed me a wooden sword. I turned to face Hakon.

'How's the arm, cripple?' Hakon taunted. He slashed the air with his weapon. 'Looks sore to me,' and he thrust the wooden sword the same way Thurstan did with his stick, right onto the scab, making it bleed again. My arm had been aching anyway and I could hardly hold the sword up.

'First blood to me, cripple,' yelled Hakon in delight. He came at me again, trying to knock me off balance, but I managed to parry the blow and pushed him to one side. He was quicker than me and moving swiftly to my right side, whack! he hit me with the sword's edge on the top of my arm. The pain shot down from my shoulder to my wrist and I lost my grip on the sword which fell to the floor. Hakon beamed with triumph.

'It's well you know your letters, cripple, because all you're fit for is the Church. A thegn, hah! hobble off back to your books, priest.'

Grim shouted across, 'Easy now, practice, practice,' but I could tell he was pleased with Hakon for showing me up in front of my father, who was shaking his head.

'There's your answer, Hakon,' said my father, and I felt stupid and weak.

Later that same week I met Rush one evening in the woods but told him I was feeling unwell and would have to miss our meetings for a few nights. He seemed disappointed and said it was because I feared getting caught, but I guessed he was glad of the rest after his arduous days in the fields.

I hardly saw my father. He was off checking fences with his steward or dealing with minor disputes between villagers. I tried to forget about what I'd overheard, but the terrible consequences kept flooding my thoughts. I also kept imagining someone was watching me constantly. I eventually decided it was only me being overly anxious.

The evening of the next arranged meeting of the thegns came, and I managed to get away from my lessons on time by being extra diligent, remembering the verses Thurstan set for me. Even though Thurstan made me read them aloud twice, I still got to the clearing before anyone else. I was going to ride Flax to the edge of the trees, but I was worried someone would recognise him, so I persevered on my crutch. I cutched down behind the fallen tree stump, pulling bracken and fallen branches over me to conceal my presence. The forest was quiet; the occasional birdsong, a dog barking far away. I heard the horses and one by one the thegns came together again, hooded, secretive and nervous.

The thegn of Hearotford spoke. He and my father had been friends a long time and I knew he was a man trusted by most. 'And so, my lords, what are we to do with this tyrant king who would bleed us dry?'

One of the thegns moved his horse towards the centre of the circle. 'Poison, a maid or servant slip a draft of hemlock or such into his drink.'

'We would need to take someone else into our confidence, too much of a risk. Besides, Harthacnut has tasters to test his food and drink. It wouldn't work,' the thegn of Hearotford replied dismissively.

My father was the next to take his horse forward. 'The only way is for one man, up close, and stab him to death.'

'He's always surrounded by his housecarles, how would someone ever get close enough?' I could not tell who spoke, but others murmured in agreement.

'All of us here have been invited to Tovi the Proud's wedding. We will all be expected to present gifts in person to the king and that will be the moment. One chance, and the one who carries out the deed will have no escape. He will be cut down as he stands, branded a traitor, but the deed will be done.' After my father had spoken, there was silence whilst they mulled this plan over in their minds.

The thegn of Hearotford was next to speak. 'Agreed, this seems the only way of success. Agreed?'

Reluctantly they all agreed to the terrible scheme. Someone said, 'How do we choose?'

'By straws,' said the thegn of Hearotford. 'We will return here in three days' time and each man will pick a straw. The one with the short straw will have the privilege of ridding this realm of evil. Any man who does not attend, or reneges on his duty, will be as nithing, and the rest of us will be beholden to put him to the sword. Agreed?'

'Agreed!' and as they replied in unison, they spun their mounts around and left the clearing.

My worst fears were coming true. My father was embroiled in a treacherous plot to kill his king. There seemed no going back and no way out and I was at a complete loss to know what to do. I could tell no one. All the way back to the village my mind was a whirl. The feeling of being watched enveloped me once again, though I saw no one.

The villagers went about their daily business unaware of the events unfolding around them. Even Hakon seemed occupied with something other than tormenting me and Ulf was his usual, timid self, content with avoiding Thurstan's barbed tongue and the dreaded stick.

On the following Sabbath, Brokk made his usual visit. He seemed a little more himself this time, although I could tell there was something troubling him. We climbed up to the barrows, much to his dismay, and sat peering down towards the village.

'I spoke to your father this morning,' Brokk said almost as an afterthought.

'Oh, what about?'

'About what I overheard in Wydeford.'

I wasn't fully listening to him, I was more interested in seeing what had caused several bleating sheep to scatter down the side of the hill.

'Overheard what, Brokk? Do get on with it.'

'That King Harthacnut has commanded the earls to burn any village refusing to pay their taxes in full. It appears the crews of all those ships he brought with him want payment. He says it is the English's bloody fault he had to bring them in the first place, so they should pay to send them away. After Wigraceaster, more of his collectors were attacked and he demands anyone who stands against him be punished.'

'Tripp told us it would get worse,' I said, clambering up the side of the barrow to get a better look down the hill.

'I bloody know, but there's more,' Brokk said, becoming agitated.

The sheep had come to a standstill at the far end of the meadow by the river. I could see no one. A huge bank of mist and low cloud was rolling swiftly towards us from the south and I thought it best if we go back down.

'What else did you hear?' I grunted, as I slid down the barrow.

'There's a rumour someone is plotting to kill the king.'

Now, Brokk had my full attention.

Eight

My heart beat swiftly, and my stomach churned.

'Who?' I managed to blurt out.

'No one knows, or they're not bloody saying if they do.' Brokk looked uneasy as the mist started to weave its way around the barrows. 'The thegn of Wydeford and his sons seem to think it wouldn't be disastrous if the king was killed. Though they say it would be impossible because he is guarded constantly. So they reason if they can find out who is plotting the deed, they can gain favour by exposing them.'

'They told you this?'

'Of course not. I overheard them.'

'What did my father say to all this?'

'Not much. He did toss me a silver penny and asked me to tell him if I heard any more. Can we go now?' Brokk was always uneasy around the barrows and the mist only made him worse. 'You never know what lurks here in this bloody stuff,' and he was gone into the mist, his fear of spirits overpowering his protective feelings for me.

I started to follow, but the mist had become thicker, its dampness wetting my garments. My descent was slow as the grass was becoming wet and slippery. I sensed I was not alone, something close by, a shape, moving across the path in front of me.

'Brokk, is it you?' No answer. 'Brokk, wait there.'

Still no reply. I stopped, peering into the gloom, but saw nothing more than a white blur. Gradually, wraith-like, at first a mere impression, an apparition formed in front of me. My young mind raced, a fairy, a sprite? Where was Brokk when I needed him?

'Leofric,' it whispered my name.

'What are you?' I managed to say through trembling lips. My skin tingled, the hairs on my neck and arms stood up, I tried to move my legs without success.

'Only a girl.' The mist swirled again, she moved closer to me. 'It's me, Leofric, don't you recognize me?'

'Mair!' The realization it was Nairn's daughter did little to quell the uneasiness within me, though I did manage to stop trembling.

As a child, Nairn had always filled me with dread. She always seemed to single me out and stare with her piercing eyes, as though she was seeing right inside of me, searching for something I did not understand. I knew of the dream she had dreamt about two boys being born on the same night in a storm; one would bring her power and wealth, the other death. I was also aware she thought one of them was me, the other, Hakon. Each boy's face was always shrouded from her sight and the dream always ended abruptly, with Nairn falling from a great height engulfed in flame. I knew little else of the woman some said was a sorceress, likewise her daughter, Mair. She was a year younger than me, though her slight frame made her look younger still. Mair was a strange child, preferring to keep her own company than play with other children. She always seemed to be detached from the world around her. She would sit for hours by the stone, naked, rocking back and forth, muttering strange words. Her eyes, unlike her mother's piercing daggers, were big, round and dark, like deep pools, where you might look for an age and see nothing at all. She stood before me, her thin garment, now wet, was clinging to her puny body, yet it was me who was shaking.

'What are you doing here, Mair?'

'Watching over you, of course.'

'Watching over me?'

'Someone has to. I can't leave it to that ox, Brokk.'

'I do not need watching over, particularly by a child.'

'You have come here because you are troubled,' she said firmly.

'I am not troubled,' I said, lying.

'The lamb said you are,' Mair said, holding out her hands, blood-stained from the animal's entrails she had dropped at her feet.

'That's why the sheep bolted,' I thought, repulsed by this gruesome sight in front of me. Mair knelt, poking the offal with her finger, then touching her tongue with the bloody finger and sliding the blooded tongue across her upper lip. She paused momentarily.

'You're troubled, and you need help.'

'I am not troubled and if I was, how on earth can you help me?'

'I can't this time, but Nairn can. You must seek her guidance, and all will be well.'

She was gone again, shrouded by the mist. I continued cautiously, edging my way down the greasy slope, the thought of approaching Nairn rattling in my head.

'I always watch over you, Leofric, you and I are fated to be one.' I heard Mair's voice but saw nothing. 'Resistance is futile, I have seen it in the runes and in my dreams and in the entrails, many times. Even the wind sings about it and the river when it agitates the pebbles in the rapids, shouts of Leofric and Mair. Our time will come, Leofric, our time will come.'

'Never!' I shouted, 'Never!' but there was no reply, and as I descended a little further, the mist thinned, and I could see Brokk sitting near the foot of the hill waiting for me. He was weaving his elf-bolt between his fingers.

'Sorry, I hate that bloody place.'

Although I was disappointed with him, I did not wish to make him feel guiltier than he already did. So, nothing more was said. We made our way back to the village, where we fished for eels off the bridge by the big oak. My thoughts were of my father and the king, of the thegn of Wydeford and what he might find out, of Mair and her wittering, and Nairn.

Could she help me to stop my father from murdering the king?

Dare I tell her?

Dare I even visit her?

My mother had strictly forbidden me to talk to, 'The wicked sor-

86

ceress, who will burn in the everlasting fires of hell!'

Thurstan was determined to drive her out of Æssefeld to win the favour of the bishop, who was jealous of the gifts she received in exchange for her potions and charms and translation of dreams. Bishop Lyfing believed they should be given to the abbey in his jurisdiction. After all, the Church offered forgiveness of sins and cures of all kinds by means of the holy relics, not the superstitious nonsense Nairn spouted. Instead folk were passing the abbey to seek help and solace from this cunning woman.

The bishop's wish was for Thurstan to expose Nairn as nothing more than an old woman with cheap tricks and no real power. I dreaded to think what punishment Thurstan would devise for me if he found out I'd been talking to her.

With all these thoughts buzzing around my head, I couldn't concentrate on the fishing at all. More surprisingly, Brokk caught nothing either, and although it was impossible to guess what his thoughts were, he did come beside me at one point and said, 'A curious thing did happen when I spoke to your father. We were in the great hall and twice, during our conversation, he walked over to where the embroidery of the weeping lady hangs and spoke to it and ran his hand tenderly down the woven thread. It was as if it was something precious, something possessing power.'

My father was a Christian, but he was still superstitious. Like many country folk he still had a glimmer of faith in the old gods. His belief in the power of the jewelled sceptre was a real one, especially because of the tale that accompanied this eastern treasure.

It was obvious, by what Brokk had told me, my father was concerned by the events unravelling around him. He was desperate to find answers or succour anywhere he could. I was helpless. I was eleven years old and terrified we were about to lose everything.

As we left the river and made our way to our beds, I looked towards the hill where the clouds still hung thickly to the top and filtered down like fingers of smoke through the twilight. I could vaguely make out the black silhouette of Nairn's dwelling. I shuddered to realize, however much I dreaded going to see the dream teller, I must go there at first light.

I had little sleep, and when I did start to doze, I was awoken by Thurstan, praying aloud in the corner of the room. His back was towards me, so I managed to leave unseen.

The grass glistened as the weak sun laid its soft light over the morning dew. Many of the villagers were already making their way to the fields for their day's work, so I kept close to the trees and made for the west side of Barroe Hill. Dogs barked, a cock crowed three times and I hoped I was not about to betray my father. I climbed halfway up the hill into the mist and used it as my cover as I skirted around towards Nairn's hut. My progress was as ever slow, the crutch sinking into soft, springy, sheep-grazed turf. Eventually, I arrived at the hut where the mist was thin and wispy.

There was no sign of Nairn or Mair, only scores of hens scratching about in the dirt. Nairn's hut was on a small ledge cut into the side of the hill. It was of the old style, round, windowless with a turf roof. Faint traces of smoke rose from a hole in the centre of the roof. There was a rickety cart propped up against the rear of the mud-daubed walls, and I ducked under it as I heard the dull thud of hooves approaching. I huddled close to the wall and put my ear to a sun-baked crack. Inside a man's voice broke the morning quiet.

'Greetings, Nairn, I come with gifts and seek the knowledge and wisdom of the old ones.'

It was my father. I froze and cowered lower pulling the hood of my woollen cloak over my head.

'Renweard, Thegn of Æssefeld-Underbarroe, you have come to the ones you have forsaken. Why should they listen to your miserable pleas? You are as dog mess to their eyes.'

I knew of no woman but Nairn who would dare speak to Renweard in such a way.

'I need their help,' my father pleaded, yet I sensed the resentment in his voice.

'We all need the gods' help, Renweard,' Nairn rasped. 'We are merely their playthings. We cannot choose our way, it is chosen for us. Give me your hands.'

The hut fell silent. I tried to peer through the crack, but it was a murky haze. Inside a hen screeched its last, and I imagined Nairn peering into its entrails after dispatching it to the other world. A low, deep, groaning sound gradually building into a piercing wail seeped through the walls. I knew it came from my father.

'The gods have revealed their will. You will be spared from the task you so dread, without losing face with other mortals.' Nairn's voice seemed thin and distant and rattled around the dwelling. 'Though there must be trust by you and the gods, Renweard. They need to see you are steadfast and worthy in your dealings with them. They will not be brought to ridicule.'

'Never by me, I swear it,' cried Renweard.

'They want you to proclaim your allegiance to them in full view of the whole of Æssefeld,' said Nairn. 'On the night after the morrow I shall call you, and you will come and kneel before the gods and they shall show their power and they will grant your plea. Though heed this, Renweard, there is always a price to pay.' She mumbled something in a tongue I did not understand, before saying simply, 'Now go.'

I heard the thud of hooves trail off down the track and he was gone.

My relief was immense. The king's assassin would not be my father. The gods would protect him. He may still be implicated but surely, we could find a way around that. You can always deny implication or buy a pardon, but to kill one's king would only result in death and ruination for one's family. And relief upon relief, I would not need to face Nairn. I could slip away, unnoticed and trust in the gods. I moved to come from beneath the cart when a face swung down from above, stopping a hair's breadth from mine.

'Nairn will see you now.'

It was Mair.

She jumped off the cart and beckoned me to follow her, as though her thin, tiny finger had a compelling power to draw me along.

The hut was dark, the only light filtered in through the few cracks in the mud walls and from a small, tallow lamp. A smell of poultry, blood, smoke, damp, and a fusion of herbs engulfed me as my eyes strained to adjust. Nairn stood over a huge, copper cauldron into which she stirred fluxwort, hedge-berry, cowslip, vervain and mistletoe berries, mixed with water from the sea. The embers under the great pot made its contents simmer and with a ram's horn ladle she scooped some of the liquid from the cauldron and poured it into what appeared to be a pale, leather cup, which I found out later, was made from the skin of one of my stillborn sisters. She hobbled towards me and thrust the vile smelling concoction into my hand and said forcefully, 'Drink!'

Mair skipped about the hut murmuring words I did not understand. Something fluttered in the roof space above our heads and a black, feral cat slunk from the shadows and hissed at a pair of hens, before disappearing into a pile of wicker baskets. As my eyes became accustomed to the dark, I saw bunches of dried plants and two dead hares hanging from a pole stretched across the full width of the hut. There was a heavy curtain, sewn with crescent moons and stars, which kept the rear of the hut hidden. In front of which was an upright staff, mounted with a human skull; a death sign. I wondered if that's where Nairn kept all the offerings she received. The fumes from the cup filled my nostrils with a burning, heady sensation.

'Drink,' she repeated. 'I call on your ancestors to reveal your fate, to show me the future the gods have prepared for you.'

I knew what she wanted was to find out how I affected her. Was I the one to bring her wealth and fame, or death? I wanted to leave. I had learnt what I had come for, my father would be spared from the terrible deed, and all would be well. I should have run away, but my feet felt as though they had taken root into the earth floor, unable to move. Besides, there was something inside me desperate to know my destiny. Would my desire to be a great warrior and win my father's love and respect come to fruition? Nairn's bony fingers cradled my hands and slowly pushed the cup towards my lips.

'Drink and be wise of the gods.'

It was the first time I had been so close to the dream teller of

Æssefeld. Even in the dim half-light, it was clear from the left side of her face she had once been a beautiful woman, but the right side was hideous, from the deep scars etched by the sword of her late, betrayed husband. Her hair was a tangled mass of black, streaked with grey which shimmered like silver thread. And those eyes; piercing, demanding, intrusive.

'Drink!'

The rim touched my lips and after a last moment of hesitation, I drank from the skin-cup. At first, the only sensation was a slight burning as the liquid slid down my throat, then a tingling, starting at my toes and rising through the whole of my body. The room started spinning. Nairn appeared to grow huge and menacing, towering over me, her spindly fingers reaching towards me like tendrils, pressing hard on my forehead. She peered into the cauldron chanting her incantations, evoking the spirits of the dead ancestors, and beseeching the gods to reveal their secrets.

'Let the cauldron speak, show me the wisdom of things to be.'

She released her grip on me momentarily, whilst she threw more herbs into the pot and something wriggled and made a sizzling sound as it hit the bubbling liquid. I felt as though I had left my body and was watching from the roof of the hut with the smoke-tinged bats hanging from the thatch. Nairn peered deeper into the concoction, searching for signs and portents only a cunning woman such as she can interpret. She sprung up with a triumphant screech.

'There are four kings. One you will kill, one you will hate, one you will love and one who will be your mortal enemy.'

Her words echoed in my head like shouting in an empty cave. One you will kill.

'Am I there, can you see me?' begged Mair, trying to peer into the cauldron.

'Away, foolish child,' screamed Nairn, hitting out to send Mair sprawling into the pile of baskets, disturbing the cat which hissed and spat. Nairn turned back to the cauldron. Undeterred Mair continued, 'What do you see? Am I there now?'

'I see nothing, the vision has gone,' said Nairn, 'there is only blackness.'

She shouted more strange words up into the air, waving her arms wildly. She looked again, muttering, cursing, 'Nothing, only black, black. Do not forsake me, oh mighty ones, reveal to me this boy's miserable future existence.'

Mair picked herself up and danced around and around me, chanting, 'Black, black, Leofric the black, even the gods from you turn back, Leofric the black, black, black.'

Nairn slipped a knife from her girdle and lunged towards me. As she grabbed a handful of my hair, which she cut roughly, I fell backwards, struggling to keep my balance and although it was only a short fall to the floor, it felt as though I was tumbling endlessly in a vast chasm, spinning, hurtling through darkness.

Nine

When I awoke, I was in my father's hall. Ulla was mopping my brow with wet cloths. After Thurstan had discovered I was missing, they searched for me until dark. When the search was resumed at first light, Mair discovered my crutch near a ditch. She said she had stumbled on it by chance. I knew it was likely she had something to do with me being there, probably aided by the big oaf Lugna. Shortly afterwards Brokk and a few of the villagers found me at the bottom of Barroe Hill.

As I lay there, the realisation of what had transpired the night before filled me with dread. It was I who was to kill the king, not my father! The rest of Nairn's prophecy was a blank. The one thought, I would kill the king, overpowered everything else.

The next day I caught glimpses of Nairn walking back and forth on the hillside below the stone. Lugna carried bundles of faggots on his back and Nairn directed where they were to be placed. My father seemed agitated, snapping at the servants. Glancing through the open doorway, whilst at my lessons, twice I saw him change direction when he saw my mother approaching, and Thurstan asked me if I had seen my father because he seemed to be avoiding him also. As the brightness of day faded into twilight, and twilight was engulfed by the black of night, the top of Barroe Hill burst into flames; a huge, circular wall of fire, licking the sky like hungry wolves' tongues. The flames spread their light over the slopes, casting strange, flickering shadows amongst the scree and saplings.

Brokk and I were returning from fishing on a bend of the River Æsc. We were the first to reach the foot of Barroe Hill. At first, a small stream of people began to join us, drawn to a glowing sky which could be seen for miles. Soon the stream became a torrent. Dogs barked, babies cried, an owl swooped over the gathering causing folk to curse and pray and fondle their charms to ward off evil.

Three witch-hazel staves mounted with human skulls and stuck in the ground were a warning to come no further. If anyone dared to ignore the death sign, Lugna stood a few paces behind, armed with a metal-tipped quarterstaff. Nairn appeared on the big rock, known as the devil's table, that jutted out of the hillside, below the fire.

Nairn was naked. Her body smeared in mud and blood. On her head was a tall, conical hat made of thin, beaten copper engraved with runes and symbols.

'Renweard Sigweardson, Thegn of Æssefeld-Underbarroe, the gods of your forefathers call upon you to do obeisance to them; Mighty Woden, Thunor and Twi; Frey, the ruler of rain and sun; Nertha our earth mother. Come before them and prostrate yourself, receive their guidance and blessing.'

The crowd parted as my father appeared behind them. Dressed in his war gear, the iron links of his mail jangling as he walked purposefully up the hill. His boar-crested helmet added to his already impressive height, and with his shield and two-handed broad axe, he was a formidable sight.

Lugna stepped aside to let Renweard pass, stepping back again, barring the way to anyone else.

'Father, let me come with you?' I pleaded.

'You will stay there, boy! Brokk, make sure he does.'

Brokk grabbed my arm to hold me back. Lugna took a step forward and prodded the staff towards my face. He grunted something unintelligible at me, though the meaning was clear.

I knew I was the only one who was aware of what my father was about to do, but I was unable to help him. Perhaps he needed to do this for the gods to take the deed from him and lay it on me. Maybe,

I thought, if he doesn't appease the gods, he will still have to murder the king and I would not. But those were the thoughts of a coward. I was desperate for my father to be proud of me. I had been given this opportunity, however terrible the consequences, to make it happen. So, I stepped back and let my father walk to the gods.

Nairn had left the rock, and Mair, who led a reluctant goat by a rope around its neck, joined her through a gap in the fire. Renweard followed them in.

What happened in the circle of flames will remain a mystery to all but those three. We heard Nairn screeching incantations. We heard the dying bleat of the goat. We heard Renweard, Thegn of Æssefeld-Underbarroe commend himself to the old gods and to trust in their wisdom in all his dealings.

My mother and Thurstan had now joined us and she gave an almighty wail on hearing the blasphemous words of her husband.

Thurstan pushed forwards. 'I must stop this insanity now,' he cried, 'in the name of the one true God, let me pass.'

As he drew level with Lugna, the big man whacked him around the back of the legs with his quarterstaff, bringing the monk to his knees.

'No one shall pass,' said Lugna and Thurstan did not try again.

Over the next hour there was more screeching from Nairn, more pledges from Renweard to Woden and Thunor. And Mair, having stripped off her white linen tunic, danced naked at the entrance of the soaring flames.

Eventually, Renweard reappeared and walked down the hill in silence. His eyes glazed, his face red from the heat of the fire. The Christians wept, the pagans sang. My father believed the old gods were on his side and I knew my fate was sealed.

Three days later, as the sun dipped behind Æsc wood, I secretly followed my father to find out who would draw the short straw.

My father was the first of the thegns to reach the glade. I hid amongst the scrub under the shade of a towering beech.

One by one the rest of the thegns appeared. The thegn of

Hearotford was the last. He dismounted, and from a cloth bag he took a hand full of straw stalks. He walked around the semi-circle the riders had formed, showing them six long straws and one short. He turned his back to them, shuffled the straws in his hands, then forming a fist, he presented the straws with the tops all equal and the ends hidden from view. He lifted them up to the first thegn, his face emotionless. The man stared at the straws for five or six breaths, as though he tried to see right through the fist to the straws inside. Hesitating, he reached down and plucked a straw. It slid teasingly past the remaining five to reveal itself as full-length. The thegn held it up in triumph, unable to disguise the relief he was obviously feeling. The second rider leant forward from his saddle, beads of sweat on his forehead, his hand shaking as he chose and pulled. Another full-length straw slid out of the fist, its picker's body shook, causing his horse to jerk its head and scuffle its hooves.

It was my father's turn to choose. He reached to take a straw with the steady hand and confidence of a man blessed by the gods. It slid from the fist quicker than the previous two straws. Even from my hiding place, it was obvious. My father had chosen the short straw. His face, one of confusion, disbelief and betrayal.

The thegn of Hearotford showed my father the remaining straws, proving they were all longer than the one he had drawn.

'Renweard, Thegn of Æssefeld-Underbarroe, it has fallen to you to rid this realm of its cruel king. The fate of the nation is in your hands and we will be in your debt.'

Each of the riders rode passed my father, tapping him on the shoulder, acknowledging he was the one who must carry out the deed none of them wanted. Moments later, my father was the last thegn in the clearing. I wanted to shout, 'Father, it's a mistake, it is not you who will kill the king, it is me.'

But I could not, and I stayed hidden until he had gone.

Alone at last, I sat and sobbed like the child I was, trying to come to terms with the fact that I must commit a heinous crime and face certain death.

Ten

The wedding at Lambhyo was to be the most important event in Englaland since the crowning of the king. All the major dignitaries would be in attendance and those who would be there would remember it for the rest of their lives. There were six days before the wedding.

Three nights before, the folk of Æssefeld had watched with awe as the hill, which rose gently from the valley floor, burst into flames and Nairn the prophetess enticed my father to her, casting spells and evoking the old gods. Several said they saw Thor on his flaming chariot soaring above them, his mighty hammer held aloft. Others said they heard Nertha herself on the night air, whispering the old words. Still others said they heard and saw nothing, except the crackle of the fire and their thegn and Nairn on the hill.

The next day their lord rode off. He refused to allow anyone else to accompany him, though he did seem in better spirits.

Renweard arrived back the next morning at daybreak. He appeared out of the mist, which hung low over the River Æsc, and ignored all who greeted him, heading straight for the stone chapel next to his manor house. Thurstan, seeing Renweard return, left our dwelling barefooted, leaving footprints in the heavily dewed grass, to join him in the chapel. I sat amongst the rough-cut crosses of the graveyard waiting for them to come out. At least three candle marks passed before the two men emerged. Thurstan stood at the entrance with the look of a victor after a battle, his thin lips drawn into a self-satisfied smirk.

Renweard headed straight for the manor house and quickly reappeared with a lit torch in one hand and his battle-axe in the other. Mounting his horse, he dug both heels into the beast's flanks and rode out of the village and up the hill. The whole village ran to see what their lord was about to do. Many gathered around the gates, others clambered onto the walkway along the walls. I lurched across to the stables as quickly as I could, got up onto Flax, and followed my father up Barroe Hill.

The morning sky was still and heavy with rain-laden clouds. The mist from the river sat motionless on the lower side of the hill, leaving the top visible as if it was floating in mid-air. Renweard disappeared as his horse galloped into the haze. I urged Flax up the slope trying to keep my father in sight. Necks craned and eyes strained, as the people of Æssefeld looked for their lord. They heard him before they saw him again, a blood-curdling war cry warriors make as they ride into battle. Nairn appeared at the entrance of her hut, startled by the noise, eyes adjusting to the pale light after the darkness of her windowless hut. Renweard came up out of the mist, brandishing a burning torch and whirling an axe. By the time Nairn realized it was Renweard, the torch was arcing through the air and landed on the roof of her hut. Hens scattered in front of the charging horse. One, clipped by the flailing hooves, died instantly, another suffered a broken leg and spun around in circles squawking in agony. Lugna appeared at the side of the burning shelter as Renweard rode straight into Nairn, sending her crashing to the ground. Dismayed at being faced by the lord of Æssefeld, yet distressed at seeing Nairn struck down, Lugna picked up a stout branch laying by the side of the hut. Before he could stand up fully enough to defend himself, Renweard kicked him solidly in the face, sending him sprawling backwards into a thicket of thorns. Renweard wheeled his mount around, coming back towards Nairn, who was staggering to her feet, and with his horse side-ways-on, pushed her into the side of the blazing hut. Nairn screamed as her garments caught fire. She tried to run from the flames, passing me as she waved her arms around, but she tripped over her own feet and rolled, like a ball, down the hill. I tried to keep up with her, but Flax was cautious of the hill's downward slope and Nairn soon vanished in the mist. I rode back up to the burning hut to see Mair, face down across the doorway, burning straw falling around her. I clambered down from Flax and crawled towards her. The heat was so intense I could feel my skin start to blister. I managed to grab her outstretched arms and pull her away from the flames. She opened her eyes, saw it was me and closed them again. I dragged her up the track, rolled her into the ferns and made my way back to Flax.

My father rode down the hill, holding his axe aloft as his horse stopped and reared on its back legs. Renweard shouted, 'The old gods are dead. I asked for protection and received none. I am brought to ruin along with this village. I forbid the worship of them in Æssefeld from this day on!'

He continued down towards the village and reaching the gates, ordered Grim to bring men and ropes back up the hill to the great stone. Once there, they tied the ropes around the ancient, towering pillar. Crispin the priest, who appeared on hearing the commotion, gleefully splashed holy water with a horsetail brush all around the sacred site, as men dug for hours around the base of the stone, and men, horses and oxen pulled on the ropes. At first, the stone refused to move despite their efforts, then inch by inch it started to lean over. As it gained momentum, the huge stone came crashing down. A woman screamed as a horse slipped in the mud and was crushed under the stone's great weight. Lightning streaked across the dark sky causing men to shudder.

The toppling of the great stone was a momentous event in Æssefeld. It had stood there from before men recorded time, like a guardian protector, a symbol to show the gods blessed our village above others, a direct intervention of the gods' power which enabled our ancestors to erect such a colossal slab, and now Renweard defied that power.

The devout Christians, of whom my mother was one, were ecstatic that their God had triumphed over those of the blasphemers. Led by Crispin, who sang in Latin and held his outstretched arms to the heavens in praise to Almighty God, they danced and cheered around the fallen slab of granite, which, even on its back, rose from the earth almost taller than a man. A few were bold enough to climb up on to it and dance the dance of the victor on the cold stone.

Others slunk away, fingering charms and amulets, wondering what Renweard meant by 'the village being brought to ruin' and doubting that the Christian God could protect them from the wrath of the old.

A number of folk looked for Nairn but found no sign of her. No trace of Mair or Lugna could be found either. Nairn's hut was reduced to ash. If it did hold any treasures, they were lost in the flames from Renweard's torch.

The following day my father seemed to have regained his senses and although subdued, was to be seen around the village acting as normal and organizing the last arrangements for the trip to Lambhyo. Two days before the wedding was due to take place, our party from Æssefeld–Underbarroe set out on the road to Lambhyo.

Among them was Brokk, who had now returned to Æssefeld. Because he had taken his punishment without complaint, my father chose him to deputize for Grim, who was banned from the king's presence, and who would stay to run the village in Renweard's absence.

My father presented Brokk with a new mail shirt of fine mesh. It had short sleeves and the lower edge hung below Brokk's waist, it shone and glittered in the sunshine, as did his helmet which had been my grandfather's. Brokk spent days rubbing and polishing it until it looked as new as the shirt. To add to these, Renweard gave him a splendid scarlet cloak, which fastened at the neck with a brooch and pin. He carried a spear, and his axe was slung over his back on a leather strap. Hakon and I were also dressed in our best clothes befitting the son and ward of a thegn.

I took a dagger from my father's armoury and concealed it in the armrest of my crutch, sliding it between the folds of cloth.

Along the way, we met up with those from nearby villages and hamlets, and by the time we neared Lambhyo, we were a bustling throng. Many among us had never ventured more than a short distance from their own village. We marvelled at the larger settlements as we passed them, but nothing could have prepared us for Lundene.

Lambhyo was situated on the far side of the River Temes. There is only one bridge spanning the river and to get to it you must enter Lundene through one of the several gates, spread throughout the length of the wall. The wall, originally built by the Romans, had fallen into disrepair. At first, our Saxon forefathers shunned the old Roman city believing it haunted, but during the Danish invasions, Danes dwelt amongst the ancient ruins. After King Alfred repelled the Danes from the town, he ordered the walls be rebuilt, to protect the city from further attacks, and eventually many flocked behind them for the protection they afforded. They now stood high and formidable as the wedding party approached. Although most people now lived behind the walls, a large community, ten times bigger than Æssefeld, had grown around it. The contrast of the lush green fields and verdant woods of Æssefeld, teaming with game and adorned with the vibrant colours of wildflowers, to this seething morass of humanity with its noise and stench and filth and sense of despair, took us by surprise. We passed through the muddle of sparse dwellings, from badly made huts to simple covers of branches and earth propped up by sticks, under which women and children sat. People reached out to us, to beg for money or a morsel to eat. The firm track we travelled on previously, became replaced by oozing mud. The air was now thick with smoke from the many cooking fires and smithies. The further we progressed, the noisier it became; children cried, dogs ran alongside and barked at the horses. One man ran up and tried to snatch one of the gifts from the packhorse. Brokk, rode up and down the line of travellers and kicked out at him, he even lunged with his spear towards the thief, but the rogue was too nimble and disappeared into the melee of locals. Our company of wedding guests weaved their way through this heaving sea of desperate people, and I thought, a king who allowed his subjects to live in such a manner, deserved to die. I felt for the dagger, concealed in the cloths wrapped around the arm piece of my crutch, and I knew what I must to do was worthy and just.

As we passed under the arch of the great gate, I looked up, marvelling at the sheer size of it. Wondrous carvings of dragons, trolls and serpents twisted around tree trunks and runic letters, etched into the wood, warded off evil spirits. Soldiers stood at the gate in full amour, holding long, wing-headed thrusting spears, which were inlaid with copper and bronze markings, denoting they were the king's men. On producing the letter of invitation, we were allowed in and made our way through Lundene proper towards the bank of the Temes, which means dark river. The town on the inside of the wall was slightly less ragged. The houses were more solidly built. Several even two floors high and bigger than the manor at Æssefeld.

Women tipped pots of piss out of windows onto the street below. Animal and human excrement mingled together with muddied straw strewn over the cobbled streets. The stench made us retch and gasp for breath. There were stalls selling all kinds of wares that most of us had never seen, even on Tripp's wagon. There was a man with an animal he called a monkey in a small wooden cage. It had the appearance of a small, hairy baby and a few of the wedding party left the group to peer more closely at the strange creature. Brokk, warming to his new role, rode into them, forcing them back onto the road so we could continue. The smoke was even thicker here, seeming to hang in the air, like the mists at Æssefeld, but this made us cough and stung our eyes. Many of the buildings had open fronts and every sort of trade imaginable was there; weavers and potters, basket makers and coopers. There were men making besoms from birch trimmings, others crafting hoops from hazel wood. There were bakers and butchers, tanners and leather workers. Carts and wagons, full of wool, others with hay for feeding livestock, trundled past flicking mud and shit haphazardly, splattering anyone not quick enough to dodge it. There were people who looked rich, being carried on bier-type contraptions by people who looked poor. Amongst all this, were pens with sheep and goats and wicker cages containing hens and ducks, though many of these lay empty due to the terrible diseases and violent storms which had ravaged Englaland in recent times.

Eventually, we reached the big, wooden bridge which crossed the River Temes. This bridge was not old, unlike the one it had replaced, which, we were told, had stood for several hundred years. The timbers were starting to discolour from the weather and the smoke, but it was still an impressive sight to most of the villagers following their thegns to Lambhyo. The river itself was full of all manner of boats, taking and bringing their goods to and from Frankia and Normandy and the Scandinavian countries. Men like my father, could remember the days when the Danes and Saxons were bitter enemies, although there were still those who kept the distinction, most saw themselves as one race, the English, and now, not only traded freely but also lived peaceably together as one people.

On the south bank of the river, the settlement once again became shambolic. The bigger, more substantial houses exchanged for carelessly built huts and hovels. Rats scavenged in open, rubbish pits and beggars became more prevalent. On leaving the bridge, we were escorted by a troop of the king's own guard, turned right, through the remainder of the dwellings, and out on to the wooden road leading through the damp marshlands towards Lambhyo.

The wedding would take place in and around the great Saxon feasting hall situated on an area of firm pasture land at the far end of the marshes. As we approached, I could see banners of all colours and sizes, flapping and snapping in the wind blowing up from the south. All the earls and the king himself were represented and foreign banners of various royals and dignitaries spread out above the mass of tents and temporary shelters surrounding the great hall. My father and his fellow thegns and all our followers were taken to a piece of land close to the edge of the wetlands where we pitched camp.

Exhausted from the journey, but excited at the coming events, the wedding guests sat around their fires in the still night air and talked of the coming events. My father, believing it was his last day on earth, made peace with Almighty God, ignoring the old gods who had abandoned him and prepared himself for his last and most terrible deed. He beckoned my mother and me, and we walked to the camp's edge where he told my mother of his love for her.

'Whatever happens, remember, I do everything for you and Æssefeld.' He stopped, put both hands on her shoulders and looked down into her eyes. 'If anything should happen to me, I have left instructions with Grim. Æssefeld will be yours and thereafter become Leofric's when he is of age, if he is capable.'

'What is this, lord, why do you talk of such things?' The concern was visible on my mother's face.

'We live in uncertain times, my lady, a thegn can have many enemies.' Renweard released his hold on her and they carried on walking.

My mother did not continue to voice her concerns. She had been pleased when my father ordered the pulling down of the stone in Æssefeld. He had been acting strangely these last few weeks, secretive and elusive. She shared Crispin's fear, that he spent little time in the church and even less time at prayer and was slipping back to the old ways, the ways of his ancestors. She had been distressed when Renweard stood in the ring of fire with Nairn before riding off into the night. However, since the stone was felled, he seemed more himself, if not a little subdued. Yet now, as they walked together this fine summer evening, he spoke in a way, I could sense, that troubled her. She must have been thinking, 'what could possibly happen at a wedding that would put his life in peril?'

Oh, how I longed to say, 'don't worry, it is my fate, not my father's,' but I could not. Our walk continued in silence, eventually returning to our tent at the edge of the big meadow. My mother went inside, and my father stayed outside with me.

'Leofric,' he said in his usual, cold matter-of-fact-way, 'I have something I need to give you.' Out of the leather pouch, which hung from his belt, he took out an amulet. Pointed at one end and long and flat at the other, it was made of pewter and strung on a red leather thong. Strange symbols, one like a lightning bolt, were cut into its surface and a deep cut groove ran around its edge.

'This belonged to your grandmother,' he said, 'passed from generation to generation. She told me it contained powerful magic, but its meaning has faded from memory. She told me I must pass it on to my living firstborn son. Now seems the right time to fulfil her wish.'

He placed the thong around my neck. 'I hope it brings you more luck than it has me.'

I wanted to tell him to keep it, that he may have more children. My life was soon to be over. I hoped what I was about to do would make him feel fonder towards me, but I couldn't say any of these things and I thanked him for such a fine gift. He tucked it inside the top of my tunic.

'It will be best if your mother knows nothing of this, as she will say it is pagan and unfit for a Christian to wear.'

I cared not whether it was Christian or pagan. I knew he was only giving it to me now because he thought the chance of more children had gone. I did not care; it was the first thing my father had given me, and I would wear it with pride.

He left me to re-join my mother and they retired to their bed with troubled minds and I doubt either of them slept, unlike me, sure in my mind of the path I must follow and determined to be fresh for the day ahead.

The sun rose in a cloudless sky. Folk said it was a perfect day for a wedding.

I wondered if it was a perfect day for a murder.

Eleven

AD 1042

The wedding ceremony was held outside on a large strip of grass land in front of the great hall. A pathway of fresh bulrushes led to the centre of a bower, adorned with honeysuckle and lily of the valley.

The groom, Tovi the Proud, waited outside the bower with his best man, so-called because, on occasion, an ardent, spurned suitor would steal a young woman away and force her to marry him against her will. Obviously, her family would try to prevent this from happening, so the groom would choose an able warrior, the best man available, to keep him at bay. Happily, on this occasion, Gytha came willingly and her family were all in joyful attendance. Her father, Osgot Clapa, had been a close companion of King Cnut. He walked proudly at his daughter's side as they made their way to the bower, where Archbishop Eadsige married her to Tovi in the sight of God. The gathering cheered. Gytha took off her sandals and passed them to her father, who, tapping her lightly on the head with one of them, threw them both at Tovi, to symbolize the change of ownership of the bride from father to husband. Three men with hunting horns gave a series of sharp blasts as a grand finale to the ceremony. Next, it was time for the serious part of the wedding to take place; the feasting.

The King and his entourage walked from the bower into the great hall followed by the rest of the gathering. The guests formed into two lines either side of the doors. As we passed through, each of us washed our hands in the large bowls of water provided. The doorkeepers watched out for and turned away unwelcome guests.

They took any weapons and stacked them on tables to be collected at the end of the feast. Brokk reluctantly gave up his axe, which usually never left his side.

All the men were searched. Two men ran their hands up and down my father's tunic searching for hidden weapons. My father stared up into the roof, his arms hung loosely by his side, showing no sign of alarm, unlike Lord Holden, who watched with concern, shifting his feet uneasily, expecting the men to expose Renweard, but they found nothing and Renweard filed through with the others. I was about to panic at the thought of them finding my dagger, but I was a mere boy with a crutch and the attendant ruffled my hair with his hand and I passed through with my father. Lord Holden gave my father a puzzled look, but there was no chance for explanation and we continued into the great hall proper.

Once inside we marvelled at the sight spread out before us. Wooden trestles lined the hall, each one straining under the weight of the finest fare most had ever seen. Meat from specially fattened bullocks, kid, pig, wild boar, hare, pheasant, and a bewildering array of cheeses of all smells and sizes were laid out. Bread of the best quality, fish, some of which even my father and Lord Holden said they had never seen, were delicately arranged. There were mussels and oysters, crayfish, jellied eels and huge bowls of fruit and nuts of every description. A sweet, sumptuous aroma of roasting meat and herbs drifted from the corners of the hall, where bare-chested servants, the heat of the fire causing their bodies to glisten with sweat, turned whole deer on spits.

Smoke from the fires and countless candles and birch torches, which, with their flickering flames, lit up an otherwise dark hall, wafted through the air and lent an ethereal feel to the whole proceedings. Hung on the walls were huge embroideries and tapestries, interwoven with gold which shimmered as it caught the light. Above them, under the eaves, painted shields, both round and kite-shaped, lined the whole hall like a small army ready for battle. In the far corner, a group of musicians played flutes and lyres whilst a young, slender girl tapped her fingers lightly on a tambourine and danced in front of the top tables where the king, the bride and groom and the rest of the important guests sat. Directly behind the king stood several of his bodyguards in full armour with swords, axes and spears.

'One chance before they kill me.' My father meant only to think those words, but the words slipped softly from his lips, making my mother turn towards him.

'Forgive me, my lord, I did not hear what you said.'

'Nothing, my dear, only my guts rumbling at the sight of all that food,' replied Renweard.

'It is splendid, isn't?' My mother replied, amazed at the amount and quality of the food set before her. 'I can't help thinking of all those poor wretches that have starved to death and those, even now, who scour the land for sustenance. What would they say to see us here gorging on this banquet? And what pray, would our Lord Jesus make of such gluttony?'

As she spoke these last words, my mother made the sign of the cross on her chest and said a silent prayer.

'Many here today have themselves been near to starving, my Lady Mirela, and I have no doubt if the Christ is watching, which I'm sure he is, he would be glad they at least have some relief, however fleeting it may be and however sinful you or I think it is.' Lord Holden smiled at Mirela as he spoke. 'Do you not agree, Renweard?'

But I did not hear my father's reply.

Hakon came next to me and said softly in my ear, 'You and your father should be more careful when you're out in the forest on traitor's work.'

My breathing became shallow as I gasped for air, the beat of my heart quickened, my skin blanched ashen. There had been someone else in the forest; Hakon. I tried to grab his arm, but before I could react, he walked across the hall to where Earl Godwin and his sons stood, and I watched in horror as we were about to be exposed. Much to my surprise and relief, Godwin patted Hakon on the head and continued with his conversation. Undeterred, Hakon tried to grab the earl's attention once more.

'Not now, boy, be off,' the earl waved him away and two of Godwin's attendants stepped in between Hakon and their lord. Hakon glared across at me, the smug smile of victory gone from his face. He took a deep breath of courage and turned towards Sweyn, the father he had never known.

Sweyn was with a group of men, including his brothers, Harold, Gyth, Tostig and their cousin Beorn. These were the men who aspired to leadership and power. Most other men were of less consequence in their eyes, merely chattels to do their bidding, work in their fields and even die for them in their squabbles with others. Sweyn was the tallest of the group. His arms were adorned with gold and silver rings, his hair long, the colour of dried hay, and whereas Harold had the vestige of a moustache, Sweyn had a full beard in the old Viking style, giving him the demeanour of a wild, unruly man. In fact, for some while, Sweyn had claimed to be a Dane and that his real father was King Cnut.

I watched as Hakon hesitated. Finding his courage once more he approached the noisy group. Each man drank ale from a horn flask and they all raised their voices vying to be heard above each other.

'My lord Sweyn, I need to speak with you.'

The men continued arguing, oblivious to the small boy trying to get their attention. Hakon became bolder and walked up behind Sweyn and pulled hard on his woollen tunic.

'Lord, I have something I need to tell you.'

Sweyn turned around slowly, deliberately. The men stopped talking and they all stared at Hakon. Sweyn glared at him as if a fly had landed on his arm and he was about to swat it.

'And who are you, brat?'

'Hakon Sweynson, lord,' said Hakon proudly.

One of the men spat his ale into the air, even Harold winced at what might come next.

'Hakon Sweynson?' When Sweyn repeated the name it sounded derogatory, sullied. He stepped nearer to Hakon, towering over him, threatening, ominous.

'I have no son.' He spoke the words with contempt, then holding his horn flask above the boy, he emptied its contents over his head.

Most of Sweyn's companions roared with laughter. Sweyn rejoined the group and calling for a servant to replenish his flask, continued as if nothing had happened. Hakon stood for a while motionless. Ale, staining his blond hair dirty brown, trickled down onto his best tunic.

I couldn't help but smile, though at times I have reflected on how wretched he must have felt, rejected and humiliated by the father he revered from afar. As usual, he showed no emotion. If there were tears, the ale masked them. Without uttering another word, he made his way through the guests to the top end of the hall. Though relieved, he had been thwarted once more in his purpose of exposing my father, I did not think for one moment he would give up so easily. I was torn between completing my task and following him to see what he did next.

The majority of the guests had now entered the hall. Most stood around the edges, in front of the tables, leaving a clear area in the centre for the entertainment and dancing that would follow. First, there were the toasts which accompanied any feast, but particularly a wedding. Each toast, in turn, was celebrated with a goblet of wine or an earthen pot of mead or ale.

Renweard joined in with the first few toasts, gaining courage from the drink. After the first few sips, he only raised the goblet to his lips without drinking. He was obviously determined to keep a clear head, so he could succeed in the task ahead of him. I think he was tempted to get drunk with the rest and become incapable of the sordid deed, though his shame would be worse than death.

After the toasts came the entertainment. Acrobats threw themselves, and each other, around the hall. A tall, thin man juggled with three balls and three knives, one of which he used to cut himself a piece of venison to prove the sharpness of the blade. When he had finished, dancers, three men and three women from Normandy, took to the floor and accompanied by a fiddle they trotted and pranced and flounced their way around the hall. The women watching, sighed and smiled appreciatively. The men mumbled disparagingly amongst themselves and the warriors smirked to see these baedings cavort in such a fashion.

Meanwhile, I was still watching Hakon, who, having been rebuffed by his grandfather and humiliated by his father, had moved across to where Earl Leofric of Mercia was sitting and was talking to him. The earl sat expressionless, sipping his wine. I could see his eyes, scanning every face, every corner, searching for something, somebody, until the earl's gaze was distracted as an attendant poured more wine into his goblet before moving swiftly to the king, as he called for, 'More wine, more wine.'

Renweard took the opportunity to take my mother by the hand and led her to the side of the hall to a place less conspicuous. I slipped into the shadows and felt for the blade concealed in the arm piece of my crutch to make sure it was still there.

Once the dancers left the floor, the king's bard appeared from a small door at the side of the great hall. His name was Lamont. His white linen robes and long white hair and beard gave him the appearance of one who was learned and wise. Loud applause greeted his arrival and he bowed to each side of the hall to acknowledge their admiration. Two men followed him carrying a small byre on which was a large, beaver skin bag. They took from this a beautiful, twelve stringed harp, with gilded fittings and carvings of angels' faces and cherubs on its frame. A third man brought out a tall stool on which Lamont half-sat, half-stood. The hall fell silent as he slowly turned the keys and plucked the strings to bring the instrument into tune. Once ready, he turned to King Harthacnut.

'Your pleasure, Sire?' His voice seemed to float on the air, filling all present with a calm, serene feeling. Even my father seemed less on edge as if the bard was bringing a spiritual significance to the unfolding events. The king, mouth full of wine, stood, and shouted, 'Beowulf, tell us of the mighty Beowulf!'

Everybody cheered at the king's choice. As he sat back down, the red liquid trickled down his chin onto his tunic. 'More wine,' he yelled, 'more wine,' and thrust his goblet out at full arm's stretch as an attendant scurried with a flagon to fill it up. As the servant went to move to the next guest, the king restrained him by his arm. Harthacnut drank the contents of the goblet without stopping for breath. He thrust the empty vessel under the lip of the flagon, demanding more wine and the servant quickly obeyed, pouring until the king released his grip.

The bard plucked the strings of his harp and sang of Hrothgar. He told of Grendel and men murdered in their hall. He sang of battle runes and magnificent, ancient swords. He sang of valour and courage and loyalty. Finishing the poem of Beowulf, Lamont stood from the stool and walked slowly around the hall, stopping momentarily as he played and sang, before moving on again, his audience enthralled. He sang about the battles of Brunaburh and Finnsburh and of the mighty Offa at the battle of Maldon. He related the tales of Unferth, son of Ecglaf. and monsters from the deep seas. He told of Arthur and Alfred, the great King of Wessex. The guests laughed and groaned and gasped and applauded. The bard warmed to his task, his facial expressions becoming increasingly contorted. His voice, almost a whisper, then, rising to a sound like thunder causing even hardened warriors to jump.

I was brought back to the present with a jolt, knowing it would soon be time for me to assassinate the young king who was now rocking drunkenly on his wooden throne. No bard would sing of a hero of this deed but cast me as a villain in a lament to a dead king.

Lamont returned to his stool. Once the applause had died down, he struck the strings of the harp in a dramatic fashion and said, 'For my finale, I will sing of a warrior who lives now, a man, mighty both in stature and deed, a man who leads by example and is followed willingly by others. I sing of a man of guile and daring, a maker of widows, yet a composer of delicate verse. His name is Harald Sigurdsson, the one called, Hardrada!'

The gathering gasped at the name. Some men spat and cursed, others made the sign of the cross, still others nodded respectfully. The earlier stories were classics, of past heroes, ones they had heard many times; Harald Hardrada lived now. Though most people there would never have even seen him, never mind met him, he was of their time. Some of their thegns had either fought with or against him. Love or loathe him, hearing these songs and sagas of his exploits brought them nearer to a world they knew little of, but held a fascination and sense of wonderment. They listened intently as Lamont related, how as a boy of fifteen, Harald fought in the army of his half-brother, Olaf Haraldson, against the might of the Norwegian aristocracy, some five thousand soldiers led by famous generals such as Tore Hund and Havrek of Tjotta. Olaf, his army outnumbered by at least two to one, was killed. Harald was gravely wounded but managed to crawl into a ditch where he hid until found by Rognald Brusisson, who dragged him from the battlefield and took him to a peasant family who nursed him back to health.

Lamont plucked the strings of his harp, softly and slowly, quickening the pace to heighten the drama of his words, his audience captivated by his tale. A lone drummer rapped a slow, steady beat on a Celtic drum, adding to the suspense.

Lamont told them of Harald's recovery and eventual journey to Sweden under cover of darkness to avoid detection. He also quoted from one of Harald's own early verses: 'From copse to copse I creep now, worthless. Who knows how highly I'll be heralded one day?'

Although many had listened to these stories before, they were still fascinated each time they heard them and keen to learn anything new about Hardrada's exploits. So, when Lamont continued with accounts of him killing scores of men single-handed or defeating a city by tying lit straw to bird's feet and sending them to set the city's thatched roofs on fire, or about the Byzantium Empress Zoe falling in love with him, only for Harald to spurn her advances, no one cared whether they were true or not.

They heard how Harald joined the Varangian guard at Byzantium and after many adventures and successful battles, rose to the important office of a Manglavite. This entitled him to wear a sword with a gold hilt and to walk in front of the emperor in processions with a jewelled whip with which to restrain the crowds. 'Not only that,' Lamont continued, 'he was also made a Spatharocendidatus,' The word rolled around his tongue as he emphasized each syllable separately.

The guests all applauded rapturously at this, although no one knew what it meant, but knew with a name like that it must be something grand.

'Not only that,' cried Lamont, 'the emperor had a gold coin struck in Harald's honour.' As he spoke these words, he approached a young girl sat on the floor, and reaching behind her ear, as if by magic, the bard produced one of those very coins for all to see.

'Harald Hardrada gained wealth and power, but all men who crave for such things take heed. His fate should be a warning to all, because he also gained many enemies who were jealous of his success, particularly one called Maniakes, the greatest Byzantine commander of his time. Seeing Hardrada as his main rival, he accused him of embezzlement, keeping war booty he was not entitled to, insulting Empress Zoe by refusing to give a lock of his hair when requested to do so, and not least, of murdering a man.'

Lamont stuck the harp strings with a heavy blow, making the instrument vibrate. 'Now Harald Sigurdsson, the one known as Hardrada, lies in the dark, cold depths of a Byzantium prison, left to rot until he dies.'

There was a loud groan from the audience, some muttered good riddance. Lamont sprang from his stool and made a sweeping bow, first in the direction of the king, then to all sides of the hall. Everyone clapped loudly, some cheered and whistled. The king, tossing a bag of coins in Lamont's direction, called for more wine.

As Lamont left the hall, the majority were still applauding. My father though, I could see, was preparing himself, knowing his moment was nearly upon him. I knew I had to make my move before him. I thought of praying but did not know whom to pray to. Surely the Christian God would not hear the prayers of a boy about to kill a king put in place by his own bishops. And my father believed the old gods had deserted him and mocked him by letting him believe he would be spared this fate, and yet, here he was, about to commit this terrible act.

The whole hall went silent as Archbishop Eadsige made his way into the centre. A boy of about twelve walked behind him holding a tall, bejewelled cross, adorned with a golden figure of the crucified Christ. The archbishop carried a piece of bread he had taken from the feasting tables. Crossing himself, he broke the bread and kneeling before the cross, blessed the food they were all about to eat. When he had finished, servants scurried about the tables filling great terracotta chargers with food, which they distributed amongst the guests at the top table. The king's steward ate first to test the food was safe for the king. After which Harthacnut greedily stuffed venison, wild boar meat, and anything else near to hand into his mouth, only pausing, to swill it down with more wine. Once the king had begun, everyone else joined in. The feasting now began in earnest. As food was devoured, more was brought to the tables from marquees outside the great hall. Music played, dancers weaved their way around the guests, jugglers and acrobats performed, largely ignored, and the king's hunting dogs scuttled under the trestles, feeding on the dropped scraps, snapping at each other for the best bits.

Renweard did not eat. Instead, he went to the corner of the hall where all the wedding gifts had been stored until it was time to present them. He took from the pile two bundles; one square and flat, covered in waxed parchment, the other long and slender, wrapped in green-dyed linen and bound with strips of leather. I still had no idea what presents he had brought. He made his way to the front of the hall and joined the group of local thegns waiting to come before Tovi and the king.

I made my way to the end of the centre table which stretched on up to the top table where the king sat. Around him were Tovi, the groom, a slender, long-faced man who was a wealthy landowner and who now pawed at his new bride as she leant over him and fed him slithers of venison with her fingers. Next to him was King Harthacnut himself, only recently in his twenty-fourth year. His fleshy, rotund face and ruddy complexion did not conceal a cruel crease at the corner of his mouth. A crown, a thin band of gold, sat precariously on his large head and I was amazed it was not dislodged as he teetered drunkenly on the edge of his seat. Beside the king sat Earl Godwin, the most powerful man after the king in the whole of the realm. His face, weathered and creased like old, crumpled parchment, sported a long moustache, which spread out on both sides as though a small bird in full flight had perched above his upper lip. His fair, silver-flecked hair hung to his shoulders, while around his neck on leather thongs and gold chains, he wore his private seal and badges of office. Next to him sat Leofric, the Earl of Mercia, Godwin's greatest rival. It seemed to me Earl Leofric was still searching with his eyes for some danger lurking within the hall, and I averted my gaze quickly to the next man along the table, Prince Edward, the son of the late King Æthelred the Unræd, who shared the same mother as his half-brother Harthacnut. Harthacnut, being childless, had recently brought him back from exile and had him sworn in as his heir. The fact Edward was some fifteen years older than the youthful Harthacnut, it seemed to most, highly unlikely he would ever be king.

I though, knew different. Soon Edward's life would change for-ever. I wondered how this man with the pallid face, egg white hair and pinkish, runny eyes would cope with being king. The contrast between the man I was about to kill and the man who would take his place could not be greater. One was a rough Dane, adept with a sword and happy in the company of his warriors, the other a quiet, studious man raised in the courts of Normandy. A group of Norman clerks stood behind Edward, who was more at ease with these men than his natural countrymen. To his right sat Emma of Normandy, the mother of both king and prince. Next to her, Robert Champart, Edward's friend and adviser, who was, until recently, the Abbot of Jumièges. To the left of Tovi sat the father of his new wife, Osgot Clapa. Next to him was Siward, the Earl of Norðhymbraland, a giant, ferocious man, and next to him Archbishop Eadsige, dressed in purple with his mitre making him seem taller than he was.

Behind each man stood a small retinue of their personal bodyguards and attendants. One of these stood out from all the others, a mountain of a man called Gudbrand. He was the king's champion. Any argument or difference of opinion which could not be settled by discussion was settled by Gudbrand. He was as tall as a horse, as wide as two men and had not a glimmer of compassion in the whole of his body. He wore a scar from his forehead, through his left cheek, to his jaw. His eyes were black and soulless, his nose was flat and crushed, his mouth almost toothless, except for a few, decaying stumps clinging to inflamed gums, which could have been the cause of his perpetual bad temper, and the reason he was always eager to inflict pain on others. Unfortunately, his head was as empty as his mouth, but what he lacked in brains was compensated by loyalty. I knew as soon as I attacked the king, Gudbrand would be upon me in an instant, stabbing with his great, ash-shafted spear whose razor-sharp point had spilt many a man's guts.

My father stood to the left of the main table waiting his turn to present his gifts. I knew how he must be feeling as he still believed he would be the king's killer. I took a deep breath, tried to stop my hands from shaking and prepared myself for the task ahead.

'And your gift is?' an attendant addressed the thegn directly in front of Renweard and led him up to the top table. Renweard was next. No going back now.

Most of the wedding gifts had been loaded on carts ready to take them to Tovi and Gytha's estate. However, each thegn brought two special items, one for the bride and groom and one for the king. The thegn to present his gift next had brought a stand, the top covered by a hessian sack. This was for the newlyweds, and he proudly pulled off the sack to reveal a magnificent, hooded, hunting hawk. To the king, he presented a fine, leather saddle, intricately etched with scenes from the saga of Beowulf. Harthacnut waved his hand in acceptance, though I could detect he preferred the beautiful hawk.

Words none could understand, came from the king's lips as he slurred drunkenly and poured more wine down his throat.

Now it was my father's turn. He picked up the two bundles and made his way slowly to stand in front of the king. Placing each gift carefully on the floor in front of him he bowed low to Harthacnut. I was still at a loss as to how my father planned to kill the king. As far as I knew he had no weapon. The table where the king sat was far too wide for a man to reach across and execute the deed.

'Sire, Lord Tovi, I bring humble gifts from Æssefeld-Underbarroe to mark this special occasion and to wish you abundant happiness for all your days, however long or short they may be.'

Lord Tovi nodded, a thin, insincere smile wrinkling his face.

Harthacnut pulled himself up holding onto the arm of his chair to steady himself. 'Yes, yes, get on with it,' he attempted to say a name, hesitated, asked his steward, who peered at a scroll he was holding.

'Renweard, from Æssefeld-Underbarroe, Sire,' said the steward softly.

'Æssefeld-under where? never heard of it,' said the king slurring some of the words, squinting to get a clearer glimpse of Renweard. The steward attempted to explain where Æssefeld was but was stopped abruptly by the king.

'Renweard, Renweard, aren't you the squeamish little turd who objected to me throwing the usurping half-bastard Harefoot into a bog? Not a wise move, Renweard, no wonder you live in a place I've never heard of. You shouldn't go around upsetting kings.' He gave a little laugh which others around him copied, though all could see the sternness on his face.

My mouth became dry and my heart pounded. The moment was near. I must make my move. Renweard started to answer but Harthacnut, having gulped down another goblet of wine, interrupted him.

'Save your excuses for tomorrow, old man, when I will talk to you and those other lick-spittle's about separate matters. Now get on with it and show us what you've brought.'

Renweard bowed his head. 'Sire,' he knelt and taking the flat package, unwrapped the wax parchment to reveal a folded embroidery which he spread out in front of them. 'For the newlyweds,' he said, 'we pray it pleases.'

'It's charming,' said Gytha, trying her best to sound sincere, yet not even bothering to look at it, as she continued to stroke Tovi's hair. Tovi responded by squeezing her backside and a terse, 'Put it with the rest,' to one of his servants.

Whilst everyone concentrated on these events, I leant my crutch against the wall, slid the hidden dagger out of the armrest and concealed it in the sleeve of my tunic. I slipped unnoticed under the end table and, with my heart pounding in my chest, began to crawl up the middle with the guest's feet on either side.

Sitting down, Harthacnut gestured to Renweard to continue. I could just about see the king's face through a forest of legs and his expression was of someone bored with the whole proceedings. He lifted his goblet as though to drink more wine but replaced it on the table. My father seemed to be struggling to combat his nerves and to conceal the shaking of his hands as he bent to open the second gift. He undid the leather thongs on the long, linen bundle and lifted the present for all to see.

'And this is for you, Sire.'

Everyone gasped as the ceremonial sceptre shone and glittered in the torchlight of the hall. Harthacnut pulled himself up once more, though this time even more unsteadily, having to grip the table to balance himself, his interest now fully engaged by the beautiful object before him. 'This once belonged to an emperor, Sire,' said Renweard, 'it is surely fit for a king, is it not?'

'It is,' replied Harthacnut, stretching out his hands and leaning forward to receive the gift. Renweard pulled the sceptre back slightly keeping it from the kings reach

'Even more astonishing, Sire, it is said to have been in the presence of our Lord Jesus when he was a child, and his likeness was captured in this large ruby, only visible by men acceptable to face God.'

My father shuffled his feet, changing his stance, putting the weight on to his right leg. I saw his hand twist on the shaft. At that moment I knew my father was going to use the sceptre itself as his weapon, hoping the ceremonial treasure did throw like a normal spear.

I knew I had to strike now. I would only get one chance. If I didn't act soon this would be my father's last action on earth. Any gods, whichever ones, are listening, please let me be successful.

Twelve

I gripped the dagger tightly and crawled quickly towards the king and certain death. I kept to the centre of the trestles threading my way through the dangling, constantly shifting legs. The conversations of guests turning to a babble as the sound of my thumping heart filled my head.

I was close to the top table when someone dropped a large meat bone ahead of me, and with a flurry of saliva and bared teeth, two snarling butcher-hounds came from the left and right. The dog from the left snapped its teeth into the meat, the dog from the right into the other's neck. They grappled viciously until they saw me, then releasing their grip, turned to face me, daring me to come nearer. Panic set in, I moved forward pointing the knife towards the dogs. Bred to herd and pin cows down, it is said they have the bite of three greyhounds. They both lowered their heads close to the floor, their rears stuck upright. One of them gave a low, guttural growl from deep in its stomach. Even if I managed to stab one, the other would rip me apart with its big, jagged teeth. I started to realise my task was hopeless. I could not help my father.

He was right: I was useless. I closed my eyes and swallowed.

I must try.

My hands shook. I gripped the knife tighter still. I moved forward once again. One of the dogs suddenly pounced and grabbed the meat, the other bit him again. I saw my chance and tried to squeeze past them. The dog nearest me swivelled his neck and snapped his teeth into my hand. I stifled a scream as the pain shot up my arm. The knife dropped from my hand. The dog came again, snapping, snarling. I backed off, blood trickling from my hand.

A boot swung out and kicked one of the dogs; a man cursed as it went for his boot. I peered out from under the table to where my father stood, he started to raise the spear into a throwing position. I wanted to shout, 'No, stop!' but the words stuck in my throat.

Renweard hesitated as the king's expression changed. Harthacnut's eyes bulged, his face turned purple, his hands clenched into fists, his mouth opened and closed like a distressed fish on dry land. His legs buckled. He tried to speak, but no words came, only gurgling, as he collapsed, head first, on to the table, scattering food and drink before him.

At first, those around him thought it was merely the effects of too much drink, then realized it was something far more serious. The king lay there, his arms and legs twitching, wine and foam seeping from his mouth. Gytha screamed, everyone stopped dancing and whatever other activity they were engaged in. Godwin and Tovi both went to his aid. Someone shouted, 'Murder, someone's killed the king!'

Earl Godwin called for a physician to come quickly. Gudbrand leapt towards his master, flaying his spear in all directions, catching one of the stewards in the face and sending him sprawling across the floor.

In all this commotion, my father stood motionless, the ceremonial sceptre still at his side. People ran in all directions shouting orders. Soldiers gathered around Prince Edward in case he was in danger of imminent attack. Physicians came. Servants cleared a table and laid the stricken king upon it, his body twitching, his tongue protruding from his mouth.

The physicians poked and prodded. They rubbed salves into his skin. They unsuccessfully tried to give him a slimy concoction to drink but could not make him swallow. Slowly the hall emptied as guests were ushered away to their tents. Two men fetched a bier and carried the king to his own quarters, the physicians still at his side, though at a loss at what to do.

Thurstan, Lord Holden and the other thegns gathered around the still stunned Renweard and proceeded to lead him from the hall. The dogs had gone back to fighting each other over bones and scraps. I picked up my knife as I backed off towards the end of the table. No one noticed as I slipped out from beneath the table, grabbed the crutch, replaced the knife, and joined my father and the other thegns. At the doorway, guards thrust out spears to bar our way.

Lord Holden challenged them, 'By whose authority do you prevent us from leaving?'

'By my authority as a member of the Witan and as Earl of Mercia.' Earl Leofric approached them and walking straight past Holden he came face to face with my father.

The realization that something beyond our knowledge of this world had taken away the burden thrust upon my father, had barely dawned on me when it seemed it would come to nothing. Were the gods so cruel? One moment I was expecting one of us to meet our end, the next, life beckoned once more, only now to be confronted by the Earl of Mercia. My father might die anyway. The thought reverberated inside my aching head. My hand was still painful and bleeding, as I tucked it into my tunic.

'I believe that belongs to the king or, in the event of his untimely demise, his successor,' said the earl, stretching out his hand towards Renweard.

Renweard stood speechless not understanding.

'The sceptre, it was a gift, was it not?'

Renweard blinked, 'Yes, my lord, a gift from Æssefeld.'

'On behalf of the king, we thank Æssefeld for its generosity for such a fine treasure.'

Renweard passed him the sceptre and the earl, with a slight nod of his head, turned and left. I noticed Thurstan's dismay as he saw the sceptre he had come to revere taken from my father.

The guards no longer barred the way. In fact, no one paid any attention to us at all and we were free to leave.

That night, as we sat around the campfires, each group talked of the day's events, still not sure of the fate of Harthecnut. The latest news was the king had not uttered a word since collapsing. The physicians had administered leaches and salves of various kinds, but they did not expect him to last another full day. Renweard, Holden and the other thegns said nothing of what had occurred, frightened they may be overheard. All they knew was, it seemed Harthecnut would soon be dead and none of them was responsible for his death. Thurstan spent most of the night standing in the shadows talking intently to Bishop Lyfing, away from the hearing of others.

My father seemed calm and bewildered at the same time. My mind and emotions were awash, and I suspected he felt the same. Both of us had not expected to see this night through, yet in the morning we would leave for Æssefeld. There would soon be a new, hopefully, just king and all of us at Æssefeld could prosper. It was as though we had been reborn, given a whole new lease of life. My father tossed a small log on to the fire and pulled his cloak around his shoulders. He could sleep soundly for the first time in weeks and as he closed his eyes, I dwelt on the good times ahead.

'Wake up! Wake up!' I opened my eyes as Gudbrand, loomed over my father and kicked him in the side. 'Wake up! You're to come with us.'

Two men dressed in the gold and brown livery of the Earl of Mercia hauled him up. 'The boy also,' Gudbrand said, and bleary-eyed we were escorted across the camp.

Dawn was breaking, my tunic felt damp from the morning dew. Most people still slept, though the odd few were moving around the camp, preparing to head back to their villages, others nursing bad heads from the night before. Gudbrand kicked one or two drunken villeins out of the way, as we picked our path through the maze of smouldering embers from last night's fires. We passed Harthecnut's marquee, where two armed guards stood at the entrance. Burning incense wafted through the opening and the low drone of a priest chanting a canticle disturbed the still, morning air. It puzzled me where we were going and why, but the guards said nothing and eventually we came to the entrance of the great hall. Gudbrand rapped on the huge, oak doors with the shaft of his spear. A small door to the left of us creaked open and a short man with a hunched back beckoned Gudbrand, my father and I inside; the others were to wait outside.

'I have angered the gods, this is their revenge,' my father muttered.

Although torches lit the hall, it was still dim and I blinked to adjust my eyes. Several men sat around a table placed in front of a wooden screen which separated this part of the hall from the rest. Many of them I did not know, though I could see Earl Leofric. On his left side sat Archbishop Eadsige and on his right, was Lyfing, the Bishop of Wigraceaster. Next to them sat four priests, each with a quill and rolls of parchment set out before them. Other men stood between the screen and the table, but I couldn't make out their faces. Someone sat in a chair off to the right, almost concealed in the shadows, flanked by whom I presumed to be a priest and four spear-wielding soldiers. To their right stood another group of men, also flanked by men at arms. These I did recognize as my father's fellow thegns and their faces were the faces of troubled men. I was surprised there were no Godwins present.

'You are Renweard of Æssefeld-Underbarroe, are you not?' Earl Leofric said sternly.

'I am, lord,' my father said.

My mouth felt dry, I guessed they had discovered the plot to kill the king.

'Terrible events took place here yesterday, Renweard, and a king now lies dying in his tent.' As each person spoke one of the priests wrote each word onto the parchment in front of him. 'We have information that you and others planned to take the king's life. How do you answer such charges, Renweard of Æssefeld?'

'Who would say such a thing, my lord, for it is most certainly a terrible deed?' my father spluttered.

'Who is not important, Renweard, but remember you speak in front of witnesses, men of honour, who will note your words. I will be more direct if it helps you, did you plan to kill the king?'

My father was in an impossible position. If he answered 'no' his word in the future would mean nothing to his fellow thegns. If he answered 'yes,' he and the other thegns could be condemned to death.

'If I knew who accused me of such a thing, I could ask them what proof they had against me, my lord.'

My mind was racing. If they knew of my father's plan to kill the king, why did they not try to stop him? I reasoned because they also wanted the king dead. Harthacnut was a Dane. Edward was of Saxon blood. Many had been appalled at the murder of Earl Eadwulf of Bernicia, who had been promised safe conduct to plead his innocence of a crime he had been accused of against the king, only to be hacked to death on the king's orders. This made Harthecnut an oath breaker, a despicable act in the nobles' minds. He also ruled the land ignoring their advice. There were many who could prosper from his death.

Earl Leofric stroked his moustache, 'There's always proof if you search hard enough for it, Renweard.'

'Indeed, my lord,' said my father, obviously realizing the implication of such a statement. 'How, may I ask, was I supposed to kill the king, as we were all searched before entering the hall? I had no weapon, my lord.'

The earl stood up from his chair. 'You had this, Renweard.' A soldier stepped from behind the screen carrying the ceremonial sceptre.

'That, as my lord is surely aware, is only for show, a thing of beauty, not a weapon. It would not throw true, it is far too cumbersome,' my father said.

'Indeed,' answered Earl Leofric, and as he spoke nodded in the soldier's direction. Raising the sceptre above his head he hurled it with all his strength and it flew across the hall, narrowly missing both Renweard and Gudbrand as it soared between them, and finally embedded itself in the wooden wall with a mighty thud.

Earl Leofric once again addressed the men assembled. 'As this gathering can now bear witness, Renweard stood before the king with a deadly weapon.'

My heart sank to my stomach, frantically hoping my father would think of something in his defence.

'This may be so, my lord, but the fact is, the king was not pierced by a thrown spear, yet, as you have said, he lies dying in his tent. By what means was he brought to that state?' asked my father.

Earl Leofric paused for a moment. 'It is true, having such a thing does not prove it would have been used to harm the king, but no doubt further investigation could find the truth of the matter. However, we are not here to blame someone for this unhappy incident but to ensure in future the king will be free from such dangers. We have here a document,' as he said the words, he pointed to one of the rolls in front of the priest to his left, which the priest duly unfurled. 'It pledges all those who sign it will give their total allegiance to the king and support him against all others. Failure for any to honour such an undertaking will result in them forfeiting all their lands and become nithing before men and God and banished from this land. Once it is signed, the incident with the sceptre can be forgotten. Renweard of Æssefeld-Underbarroe, will you be first?'

I knew my father had no choice. What he was being asked was to give up something he held dear. Most thegns held their lands from the king and consequently were legally bound to support him always. A few thegns, though, still owned land, passed down from pioneering ancestors who had won the land in battle. These thegns could choose whoever they wanted to support in times of conflict. Although in most cases, they would of course support their king, but they were proud they had the freedom of choice. To give it up was no small thing. Renweard looked towards the other thegns who had stayed silent throughout the proceedings. Then, Holden nodded in acceptance, and one by one, the thegns followed Renweard to the table and signed the document, witnessed by Earl Leofric of Mercia, Earl Siward of Norðhymbraland and Bishop Eadsige. When all concerned had finished signing, one of the priests rolled up the document, sealed it with wax, and placed it in a tube and locked it away in a large chest containing many other documents. Four men carried the chest outside, followed by the man who had been sitting on the chair by the screen. It was, in fact, Prince Edward, soon to be King Edward. The man who had been standing beside him was Robert of Jumièges, Edward's chaplain and adviser. He approached Earl Leofric and pointed towards the sceptre.

'That is now royal property. If, after investigation, it is deemed to be a holy relic, it will be presented to the Holy Father, the Pope. It must be kept safe.'

'I will see to it immediately, lord,' said Bishop Lyfing, and as quick as a snake, leaving Robert protesting to the earl, Lyfing commandeered four soldiers and they took the sceptre and carried it away. As the gathering dispersed, I became aware Earl Leofric had stopped and was talking to someone else who had been standing in the shadows. It was Hakon.

The following day, as we prepared to head back to Æssefeld, an iron-banded, covered cart drew up to one of the large tents nearby. Eight mounted soldiers flanked it. Six heavily-armed guards came out of the back of the cart and proceeded to enter the tent. They returned moments later carrying a long, hessian-wrapped object we guessed was the sceptre, followed by a smiling Robert of Jumièges and a rejected Lyfing.

'If Prince Edward insists the treasure is presented to the Pope, who am I to object?' said Lyfing, spreading his arms admitting defeat.

'You're bloody Lyfing, the lying, cheating, murdering Bishop of Wigraceaster, that's who,' muttered Brokk.

'Quiet, you fool,' said Lord Holden, kicking him in the leg. 'You'll have us all killed.'

The soldiers loaded the sceptre on to the cart and, accompanied by Robert of Jumièges, they left the camp.

We departed an hour later, with the news King Harthacnut had died and Edward, his half-brother was to be Englaland's next king.

Two days after returning to Æssefeld my father sent for me to join me in his hall. Hakon was with him.

'Do you hate me, Leofric?' my father snarled, his eyes ablaze with rage.

'No, father, I do not. Why would you think such a thing?'

'Do not treat me like a fool. I know what you did. Though only because Hakon had the courage to tell me. Even though he feels disloyal to you that he had to be the one that told me of such a betrayal.'

Hakon must have confessed to my father of his treachery believing it would be better coming from him than hearing it from me. My father must be angry I had not told him I knew all along of the plan to kill the king.

'I am sorry I did not tell you, father. I thought you would be angry that I overheard your plans, but then I was told I was to take your place and ...'

'What are you blathering on about boy? Whatever you think you heard is irrelevant. To go and tell Earl Leofric I was plotting to kill the king is the lowest, most despicable act imaginable.'

I could not believe even Hakon would have said such a thing to save himself. I was horrified my father had believed his lies so easily.

'Father, that was not me, it was Hakon!'

'Exactly what I thought you would say. Even now you behave as a coward and a liar. Hakon even tried to make excuses for you saying you thought you were trying to help me, and you reward him by trying to pass the blame on to him. How accusing me of treason to the Earl of Mercia could possibly help me, only you could know. I want no more lies or excuses, Leofric. I want no more talk of killing kings or imaginary plots. I am fortunate that Hakon confided in me and the earl believed in my innocence. For a son to behave in such a way towards his father is unnatural and beyond my reasoning. Get out of my sight and pray to God for forgiveness.'

Any explanation or attempt to tell him the truth would have only enraged him further. I was willing to give my life for this man I loved, and all he felt for me was contempt and loathing. I left the hall dejected, despairing, despondent, yet more determined than ever to prove myself to him and expose Hakon as the loathsome liar he was.

Thirteen

AD 1043

It is strange when you think back on your life. Some things dim in your mind. Life changing events hardly register in your thoughts. Yet, trivial things, insignificant to others, sometime shape your life, make you the person you are. So it was for me. Seasons came and went. The grass sprung up, the sun shone, the leaves fell. Snow-shrouded the land in quiet and stillness. The sun reappeared at last and the earth sprang back to life once again.

I was diligent at my lessons, Thurstan ever efficient with the point of his stick. We again visited Spearhafoc at the Abbey of Sancte Eadmundes. However, this time, as I followed Spearhafoc to the gold room, he stopped me doing so abruptly.

'I have set your lectern and the materials you need over in the corner, you will stay out of here at all times, do you understand? At all times!' The door slammed in my face and I was never allowed into the room again.

I learnt many skills from Spearhafoc, mostly concerning the application of gold leaf and the drawing of figures and beasts, though we never became close. He did seem genuinely grateful I had introduced his talents to Earl Harold, but now he had his patronage, I seemed to have become an unnecessary irritation and my visits became less frequent.

Six months later, my father received a letter from his friend in St.

Omer with whom he did business on a regular basis. Since he received the letter, he decided I should still be given the opportunity to become a thegn. So, I was instructed on the workings of the estates. My mother and Thurstan objected, but my father insisted, though he agreed I would not train in the arts of war despite my protests. Hakon had become sulky and withdrawn since the wedding. The realization his father would never accept him as his son seemed to be taking its toll and the frustration came out whenever he trained. Ulf received the worst of it, many times ending up with a bloody nose.

Leafwold reluctantly escorted me around the estate. We watched men repair boundary walls and bridges, I observed as they tilled the ground, planted seeds, tended the plants and harvested the crops. I helped with the horses, grooming and shoeing. I sat in the sweltering, smoky, smithy as the smith and his helpers turned cold metal into living swords and axes. Leafwold gave no encouragement, 'You will always be a faint shadow of your father, you're not fit to polish his mail, never mind be his heir,' was his daily refrain. Despite him, I learned the duties of a thegn, and unknown to me, my mother and Thurstan schemed to make me a priest.

Prince Edward was crowned King of Englaland, at Wintanceaster, on the first day of Easter AD 1043. My father, Grim and I were present.

'At last, a king with Saxon blood,' my father said to Grim, 'even if he does dress and speak like a Norman.'

Edward wore a white cloak trimmed with ermine. Eadsige, the Archbishop of Contwaraburg and Ælfric Puttoc, the Archbishop of Eoforwic, performed the ceremony. The king was presented with a spectacular set of royal regalia.

Firstly, Ælfric stepped forward with a golden ampulla in the shape of an eagle and poured holy oil from its beak into a silver-gilt spoon, set with four pearls. This was held by Eadsige who sprinkled it gently in the form of the cross on Edward's head, hands and heart.

'With this oil, I anoint you in the eyes of God, King of all Englaland.'

Then he was handed a spectacular, jewelled sword called the Sword of Offering. It had a tapering blade of blued and gilt steel, decorated with strapwork scrolls, and its hilt was made from gold with rubies and diamonds. Eadsige made the sign of the cross over the sword. 'I bless this sword which should be used to protect the good and punish evil.'

Ælfric took the sword and placed it on the altar. Next, he placed a large, golden orb studded with precious jewels and topped with a jewelled cross, standing for the rule of Jesus over the world, into Edward's right hand. That too was placed on the altar next to the sword. Eadsige then knelt before Edward and placed a ring on his fourth finger, 'This is a symbol of your marriage to the nation.'

Finally, a tall, slim, golden staff was placed in his left hand and a shorter golden rod, adorned with hundreds of diamonds, some fifteen emeralds, twice as many rubies, and seven sapphires, topped with a jewelled cross, was placed in his right hand. Again, Eadsige spoke, 'Take this rod of fairness and impartiality and carry out justice, taking care not to forget mercy. Punish the wicked, protect those that are just and lead your subjects on the path of righteousness. I pray that Almighty God will bless you with the gift of children to continue your house's noble reign.'

The Archbishop placed a plain gold pointed crown upon Edward's head and pronounced him, 'King of all Englaland.'

The bishops bowed before him and prayed to God for him to be a just and merciful king. The whole gathering cheered and accepted Edward as their rightful sovereign. Many people marvelled at the majesty of the magnificent, jewelled regalia that denoted God's approval of their king. Others questioned where the money for such splendour had come from when many in the kingdom struggled daily to feed their families. Yet, they quickly became silent as thegns and churchmen gave them disapproving looks. It made me think of the value of my father's sceptre and how many mouths that could have fed. It was three times the size of these, yet he had locked it away out of sight for years and now it was lost to him.

Later, the king enquired who had made the exquisite jewelled items. It was Spearhafoc. Later that year, Spearhafoc became the official goldsmith to the king. The bishops and leading men of the Church agreed, the regalia would be used in every future coronation of Englaland's monarchs, symbolising the unbreakable bond between God, His Holy Church and the Sovereign who ruled with His divine blessing.

All the lords who had pledged their loyalty to Harthacnut now knelt to Edward. Even Earl Godwin, accused of killing Edward's brother, was reluctantly accepted into the company of his leading nobles. No doubt the fact he gave the new king an even bigger warship than he had given Harthacnut helped to heal some wounds.

The following year Godwin's two eldest sons, Sweyn and Harold, were appointed as earls and the year after, on the twenty-third day of January 1045 their sister, Edith, married the king and became queen of all Englaland, binding the Godwin family to the royal household.

Ordinary folk rarely got sight of an earl, so we were more than curious when, in the spring of the year 1046, Earl Sweyn and his men rode unannounced into Æssefeld. They wore leather and mail and were more like a war band than men of peace, though their swords were kept sheathed, and their shields remained slung over their backs. The horses were lathered white with sweat, their breath misting the early morning air.

Hakon and Ulf were practising their sword skills with wooden weapons under the watchful eye of Grim. I was walking across the square. I had been dismissed early from my lessons, as Thurstan had received news that Bishop Lyfing had died and he spent the day praying for his soul. I thought a year of prayer would be insufficient to save that man's soul.

Earl Sweyn swung down from his mount and his companions followed. Four open wagons and a large, covered cart accompanied them. The cart was reinforced with iron bands and studs and its door was fastened with a huge padlock. I recognized the man seated next to the driver as Gudbrand, now obviously in Sweyn's pay. His huge frame was covered in mail and a sword was sheathed at his waist. He wore a fine helmet with silver face guards and a vicious spike on the top. He cradled a two-handed war axe and hanging around his neck on a chain was a large key. It was clear, whatever was in the cart could only be reached through him.

'Where is Thegn Renweard? Tell him we have come to collect weapons, food and coin to help push the Wealas back into their God-forsaken mountains,' said Sweyn taking off his helmet, which he passed to a boy in exchange for a flask of ale. 'Carry on fighting boys, never let it be said I ever hindered the progress of warriors.' He gulped greedily at the ale, and with a wave of his hand, several of his men went throughout the village to collect what they wanted.

Hakon and Ulf carried on their practice, though I noticed Hakon, out to impress his estranged father, had increased the intensity in his pursuit of Ulf. He swung his wooden sword at Ulf's head with force, which Ulf luckily managed to block. Hakon came at him again and managed to poke Ulf hard in the chest, twice.

'Impressive,' said Sweyn. 'This is the boy who says he is the son of Sweyn, is it not, boy?'

'Yes, my lord,' replied Hakon, as he stabbed repeatedly at Ulf, making him stumble backwards.

'Could you do it for real though?'

'For real, lord?' queried Hakon, stopping for a moment to catch a breath.

'Real blades, not wooden toys!' said Sweyn. As he walked up to the two lads, two of his men, pulled their seax from their belts and handed them to Sweyn. The earl handed one blade to Hakon and the other to Ulf. Ulf's face turned ashen, his hand shook violently as he took the blade.

'Lord, they're only boys,' said Grim, alarmed at what might happen to either boy in his charge.

'This is not play, Grim, they must learn. It is one thing to use wood and get your knuckles rapped, completely another to use steel with a sharp edge and draw blood.'

At that moment, my father appeared in the square leading his horse from the stables. I would like to think it was out of compassion for Ulf that I snatched the seax from the frightened Wydeford boy, but truthfully, just as Hakon wanted to impress Sweyn, I wanted to impress my father.

'As the son of the thegn of Æssefeld, I think it only right I should fight Hakon, not one of our guests,' I said to Sweyn.

'Makes no difference to me who the boy beats,' he replied, swigging more ale and wiping spilt drops from his beard.

Hakon seemed less confident than he had been when he faced Ulf and by contrast, the relief on Ulf's face was palpable. My father quickly worked out what was happening, and I imagine, not wanting to offend the earl by objecting or having the humiliation of seeing his son severely injured, suggested we use shields. They were made of lime wood and covered in leather with a metal boss at the centre, identical in every way to a regular shield, only smaller.

A group gathered around us; villagers who had been about their work, some of my father's men and a few of Sweyn's, who weren't gathering booty. Gudbrand climbed down off the cart but stayed close to it and Brokk left his wood-chopping and seemed concerned at what I was about to do. I am sure he would have volunteered in my place, but Hakon was much younger and smaller than him, so it would not seem brave on his part, and would make me seem weak and cowardly, so he kept quiet.

Both Hakon and I moved cautiously at first, shields held high, blades aloft. I questioned my wisdom in acting rashly and felt ashamed at the feeling of fear now we were facing each other. My mouth was dry, and I could hear my heart pounding.

I know now, fear is not a bad trait for a warrior, for without it we can make reckless decisions which can be our downfall. I tried to concentrate and remember all the moves I had watched Grim and my father's soldiers make in training. I also remembered the words of, Tripp. 'The strongest don't always win the battle and use your head, not your heart.'

It was Hakon who struck first, surging forward, slamming his shield into mine. The force sent a shudder through my arm into my shoulder, and as he thrust his blade towards me, I blocked it with mine and the metals rang and made sparks. I pushed him away with my shield and stepped back to regain some space. We both knew Hakon was quicker and stronger than me, and in an instant, he was back at me, desperate to get his seax beyond my shield. I fended him off several times but each time he spun this way and that, trying to find a way through. Each time, his blade came close to striking me, each time I managed to evade him. I could sense his frustration and knew his swings were getting wilder and wilder. Still, I waited. My left foot fixed, acting as a pivot, allowed me to move in a circle to counter his attacks. Someone shouted Hakon's name and I assumed it was Sweyn. I should have realized defeating Hakon might not be the best outcome for our village.

To humiliate an earl's son, even a bastard one, in front of his father and his men could bring unwanted consequences, but I was young, impetuous. I smelt victory, and Hakon had tried to expose my father as a king's assassin and put the blame on me.

One more wild swing from Hakon was the moment I had been waiting for. I dropped my shield low, inviting Hakon to lunge at my unguarded chest. He did so with such fervour, as I leant away from his blow, his momentum carried him forward and whilst he was off balance, I clattered him with my shield. As he fell, I brought my seax down hard cutting into the flesh of his arm. He yelled with pain and dropped his blade. Blood trickled on to the ground and I stood over him victorious. I placed the point of the seax on Hakon's throat. His warm piss soaked his britches. My father shouted, 'No, Leofric, stop!' My body shook, not with fear or nerves but with excitement. I, Leofric of Æssefeld, had won my first, real fight. I withdrew the blade, dropped it onto the ground and walked away.

No one said well done, although I knew many were glad I had beaten Hakon. The anger on Sweyn's face made sure no one dared.

Sweyn strode towards his men, who were returning with coin and plate, food and weapons from the smithy. Some of the villagers ran alongside them complaining about the stealing of their property. One was knocked to the ground for his trouble. Gudbrand unlocked the wagon and took from it several, empty, wooden chests, which the men began to fill. Others brought food which they piled on to the open carts.

Sweyn yelled at them, 'Is that all? Search harder, fools.'

My father stood defiantly in front of him. 'Lord, we have only recently paid the tax to your father. He said nothing about additional payments. Is this done with his knowledge?'

'It's the earl's command to me, direct from King Edward, the Wealas must be subdued. Wars don't pay for themselves, Renweard.'

'That is true, lord, but we have little else. Godspeed to you and may He bless your campaign.'

Sweyn spat on the floor at my father's feet. He made a motion with his hand and Gudbrand ordered the chests to be loaded back on to the wagon. He secured the padlock and clambered on to the driving seat. Sweyn grabbed Grim around the throat. 'Next time I come here, see the brat can fight properly. Otherwise, it will be you against me.'

'Renweard,' he said, 'I want your two fyrd-men for thirty days. And a word of advice, I was led to believe your son had a godly calling. I would make sure it happens, next time he mightn't be so lucky.'

He threw the empty ale horn to the floor and mounted his horse. His two men retrieved their seax. Gudbrand cracked the reigns of the wagon and they were gone from Æssefeld.

My father never praised me for beating Hakon. From that day on, I was banned from using all weapons. Instead, whilst Ulf and Hakon learnt the arts of war, I had extra lessons with Thurstan. We studied the scriptures repeatedly. I learnt prayers by rote and Thurstan taught me ten canticles which I can still sing right the way through, even to this day.

Hakon's arm soon healed, though he bore a long scar and his hatred of me grew keener than before, but he no longer tried to bully me openly.

When our two fyrd-men, Ealdan and Grindan Idenson, returned, they brought with them shocking news. On reaching Wealas, Sweyn had formed an alliance with Englaland's sworn enemy, Gruffydd-Ap-

Llywelyn, King of Gwynedd and Powys in North Wealas, and fought against Gruffydd ap Rhydderch of South Wealas. Sweyn had only a degree of success, losing several men, and antagonising Earl Leofric of Mercia, Llywelyn's and Godwin's main rival. Worse still, on their way back, Sweyn became involved with, some say abducted, the Abbess of Lemster and took her from the abbey to do with her as he wished. As far as Ealdan and Grindan knew, he still held her. The Church was horrified and called for him to be exiled.

Six months later, two more earls came to Æssefeld; Harold Godwinson and his cousin, Beorn Estrithson. My father ordered hurried preparations be made and although all we had was meagre fare, we welcomed our guests unreservedly. Once their soldiers and servants had been billeted in our storehouses, which would be their temporary living quarters, the earls and their immediate attendants were escorted to a part of the manor house reserved for such guests. I noticed Beorn was not wearing a sword, but he had three bodyguards who were never far from his side. They were dressed in full mail, helmets with boar crests and long cheek guards leaving only their eyes and mouth visible. They each wore a sword and carried a seax in their belt and held a spear. They watched over him like hawks in the day, and at night took turns in guarding the door to his sleeping quarters. No one ever spoke their names and they did not seem to mix with the other soldiers but remained aloof.

It would be hard to imagine two men least like Sweyn, than Earl Harold Godwinson and his cousin, Earl Beorn Estrithson. They were both affable, good-natured men and close friends. Unlike Harold, Beorn's parents were both Danish, but he was every inch an English earl.

As good a feast Æssefeld could manage was served to our guests, their soldiers and the leading men of our village.

'My brother Sweyn has been exiled,' Harold said, as we ate in my father's hall. 'He still has the Abbess Eadgifu and no amount of reasoning will convince him to release her. Obviously, the Church is outraged. Also, he claims our father Godwin is not his. He says he is the son of the late King Cnut, who, he alleges, lay with our mother. She is naturally distraught at the claim and denies it vehemently and has produced witnesses to verify her innocence.'

I watched Hakon, his face was sullen, the thought of his one slim chance of rising above the rabble and becoming an earl was disappearing with his father's folly. He had taken to being with the Idenson brothers since they returned from serving Sweyn. They sat either side of him and glanced at each other at this news.

'Sweyn's estates and earldom have been forfeited and divided up and Harold and I have been given them by the king, which is partly why we were passing this way, as Æssefeld is in part of my portion,' said Beorn, as he paused from demolishing a duck leg which had been cooked in honey and herbs.

'I, of course, pledge my allegiance to you, my Lord Beorn,' said my father.

'I, in turn, value your service, Renweard, and your enemies will be mine also.' Beorn lifted his goblet of mead and they drank to the bond. 'I believe Sweyn burdened you with payment before he left. We can't reimburse you but will not impose a further burden on you now.'

'You are gracious, my lord,' said my father, though I could tell he would have sooner had his property returned than fine words.

'Also, my father was concerned about your charge, Hakon,' said Harold. 'Some men may attempt to take advantage now his father no longer has the influence he once held. They should be reminded he is still the grandson of the Earl of Wessex. Whatever calamity my brother brings on our family, he is still his father's eldest son and it seems he can be forgiven many things. So, make sure the boy is treated well and made ready for whatever may be asked of him in the future. I believe he was injured by your son.'

'In a fair encounter, encouraged by Sweyn, my lord,' my father said anxiously.

'I have no doubt of it, Renweard, but an earl's offspring should be winning, not losing. I am told your son is becoming something of a scholar. You should encourage it. It is true we will always need men who can fight for our land, but truly, I believe in men who can reason and negotiate, men of letters and learning. Fighting is not always the answer.'

'Sweyn wouldn't agree with you,' said Beorn.

'There are many things my brother and I disagree on, as you well know. You indulge him too much, Beorn, as does my father.'

Beorn shrugged his shoulders, grimaced and gazed upwards towards the rafters.

'Nevertheless, Renweard,' Harold continued, 'heed my words. Make sure Leofric is taught in all matters spiritual and shuns the worldly pursuits of the warrior. The latter can only bring pain and sorrow to you both. And now, enough of this talk, I hear you have several new falcons, Renweard, I have acquired two new ones and I am fascinated by the breeding aspects. Can I see them?'

The two men stood up from the table and my father took Harold to the mews.

It had grieved me to hear the words of Harold concerning me and I was not sure whether they were said out of genuine concern for me or as a threat. He was the one man I thought would understand my yearning to be a warrior, yet even he was encouraging my father to make me a priest. Disdain must have shown on my face as Beorn moved along the bench to sit beside me.

'Take no heed, my cousin told me all about your little skirmish. He laughed about it and said, 'I'm sure revenge is sweet." Beorn laughed, 'was it sweet?'

'A little,' I replied.

'Only a little?' and he laughed again.

One of Harold's men had coerced a girl from the village, who had been helping to serve wine, to jump up on a table and begin to dance. All the men started clapping in time to her movements, and the whole gathering got louder and louder as they clapped and shouted, and ale was drunk and spilt as men tried to clamber onto the table with her. Most of them fell off because of their drunkenness or were pushed off by the girl, fearful things were getting out of hand. It was too noisy to talk anymore, so I left.

I wandered down by the River Æsc when a voice called out to me. It was Beorn.

'Wait for me, Leofric, you move quickly for someone....'

'Someone who's a cripple,' I said.

'I was going to say, someone with an infirmity.'

'The words don't matter my lord; infirm, disabled, lame, cripple. People look at me and all they see is my limp. My father despairs of me, the villagers snigger behind my back, Hakon thinks I am weak, even though I beat him, and now even Earl Harold sees me as useless, fit for nothing but a scribe. Even Brokk is lurking over there in the shadows because no one believes I can take care of myself.'

Beorn glanced quickly to the right and for a moment glimpsed Brokk who stepped smartly under the cover of the Roman bridge.

'Even I have those who watch out for me, Leofric.'

Over to the right by the big oak and to the left on the edge of a small copse and trailing some distance behind, I could see Beorn's three guards tracking our movements.

'This world is a hard place, Leofric, even God can seem cruel at times, but I believe we all have a purpose, some to till the fields, some to forge metal, some to fight for our lives and some to fight for our immortal soul. There are those who lead and those that are led. Each one has a vital role and one is weakened by the loss of the other. Take someone like Gudbrand, do you know of him, Leofric?'

'Yes, he was with Sweyn when they came here.'

'Built to fight, has not a merciful bone in his body. Nor has he the smallest scrap of brain in his head. He cannot think or make decisions for himself, he needs someone to direct him and give him purpose, but, in a shield wall, I could not think of anyone else I would rather stand next to. You though, I am told, have a sharp mind and are a quick learner. Perhaps God gave you your twisted foot so you could be spared from the rigours of battle and serve Him and men by acquiring knowledge.'

'That's what my mother believes,' I said, 'perhaps you're right, my lord, I should be content with my lot and concentrate on my learning.'

I knew Beorn was trying to be helpful and kind and I did appreciate him for it, but I knew it was not what I believed, and I was more determined than ever to achieve my vows.

Beorn stared straight into my eyes, his face serious and enquiring. 'It is, in fact, your knowledge I wish to make use of now, if I may?'

'Of course, my lord."

'It is a delicate matter, not to be shared with others. You might know the king is a dreamer. Visions come to him in his sleep and he sees things other men do not.'

'What sort of things, my lord?'

'Future events, things not yet come to fruition. He has heard the stories about the woman Nairn and her dream of kings. Such things fascinate him, Leofric, and he wishes to talk to her. I asked Brokk earlier and he told me she had gone, but you might know how to find her. Could you take me to her?'

'I am sorry, lord, but my father banished her from the village some years ago because of her pagan practices. He is a devout Christian,' I lied. 'I don't know where she is,' which was true. 'Would not the Church frown on our king talking with such a woman?'

'No doubt they would, Leofric, as would my cousin, Harold, which is why you must be discreet.'

'I will tell no one, lord, but I do not know where she, or her daughter, is.'

'No matter, we have men searching for her and no doubt her whereabouts will become known. I am sure if you hear anything you will find a way to let me know.'

'I will, my lord.'

Truly, I did not care if I never saw Nairn again. She always filled me with dread whenever she was near me and her prophecy that I would kill the king had proven to be false. Also, the absence of Nairn meant no Mair either, and that, as far as I was concerned, could only be a good thing.

'Can I ask you something, lord?'

'Of course, Leofric.'

'The sceptre my father gave to the king, what became of it?'

Beorn, satisfied no one else could hear, spoke quietly.

'It was deemed to be a holy relic. The monk, Thurstan, explained the legend behind it. Robert of Jumièges proposed it should be taken to Rome and given to the Pope. Edward reluctantly agreed. It was wrapped up in hessian and sent to Robert's quarters in Wintanceaster. When they opened the bundle, it contained five ordinary spears and no sceptre. The men who carried it to Wintanceaster were questioned so vigorously two of them died. The sceptre has never been seen since. King Edward has set a large reward for its discovery and the culprits, if found, will be executed. He has men scouring the country for its whereabouts. Why do you ask, Leofric, have you news of it?'

'No, lord, simply curious as to how such a thing of splendour could go missing. Surely none would dare sell it or even display it?'

'Unless they are keeping it hidden, as your father did for all those years, believing it will bring God's blessing upon them,' Beorn said. 'If they are, it is an act fraught with danger. There are those, other than the king, keen to know the sceptre's whereabouts. Robert of Jumièges, who has now been appointed as Bishop of Lundene, still wants it for the Pope. Stigand, Bishop of Ælmham, has sent men to seek it and Eadsige, the Archbishop of Contwaraburg, believes it should be in his church and nowhere else. These are all determined men with power in the land so, whoever has it will eventually be flushed out.'

We walked back to the hall and re-joined the festivities. Beorn sought out Harold, and I sat wondering if I could ever discover where the sceptre was and get it back for my father. Surely that would make him proud to have me as a son, but little did I know, it was already too late.

Fourteen

AD 1071
October

We have taken shelter on the banks of the River Widme. The sound of splitting stone fills the air as another of William the Bastard's castles starts to tower above the town of Lindon. They are using the stones from the ruined Roman wall, which used to surround the town, to replace the wooden keep which stood on the steep hill and has commanding views across the surrounding land.

A thin mist, weaving its way along the Widme, gives us a little shelter, but the sun will soon burn it off, so we cannot linger. Thurstan peered across the water and crossed himself, thanking God the little church of Saint Mary still stands. I asked him why it should not be standing, but he refused to answer, saying instead, 'It is futile to resist King William. We must accept he has conquered our land, to resist will only result in death. God has allowed it, so to oppose William, is to oppose God. You should lay down your arms and beg for His forgiveness and mercy.'

Without hesitation, I grabbed him by the throat, making him splutter and gasp for air.

'Whilst I have breath, I will never bend my knee to that usurping murderer, William the Bastard. He has the blood of our people on his hands and his cruelty is beyond redemption. If your God has allowed such things to take place, He is culpable, and the peoples' prayers are mere words in the wind.'

I released my grip and the abbot staggered backwards, coughing and panting, his face red and eyes bulging. I have left him on his knees and taken parchment and ink from my saddlebag and now sit, under the shelter of a group of alder trees, where I will continue my writing.

ᚠ ᚾᚾᛐᚲᚠᛒᛐᛗ ᚷᚠᚻ

AD 1048-49

My father sat in our hall at his ornately carved, oak table. He was holding a letter. Leafwold the steward was just leaving, and I presumed he had read the contents to my father. Waving the piece of parchment at me Renweard said, 'We are going to St. Omer.'

'St. Omer, why?' I asked.

'We're going to meet your future wife if she will have you.'

I stared at him open-mouthed. 'A wife?'

'You know, a woman, tend your hall, give you heirs,' he spat sarcastically.

I was seventeen winters old. The only women I had any dealings with were my mother, Nairn and Mair. None of those encounters had made me wish to make a woman a permanent part of my life.

Most of the girls in the village made fun of me. One or two pretended to limp as they passed by, their giggles adding to my discomfort. I was known to some as Leofric the Unlucky. I have been told I am a handsome man, but what woman would want an unlucky husband with a deformed foot and a pronounced limp? Perhaps a desperate one, I thought.

'I don't want a wife,' I said.

'You will have this woman as your wife. Our two families will be joined together and Æssefeld will prosper,' my father said, thumping his fist on the table.

'Does she have a choice?' I asked hopefully.

'Unfortunately, yes. Her father has promised her he will not force her into a marriage she does not want. There have been other suitors, but she has turned them down.'

Good, I thought, I will make sure she turns me down too.

My father stood. 'Leofric, it is no secret you are a disappointment to me. I always imagined I would have a strong, capable son to carry on my name after I depart this world. Everyone, it seems, thinks you are suited only for the Church; your mother, Thurstan, even Earl Harold. Leafwold tells me men make jokes at your expense. They mimic you behind your back. He feels no one will take you seriously as their master. Maybe, they are right. You will never be the son I want you to be. I should abandon my yearning and leave you to God.'

Hearing my father speak of me again in this way, I felt broken inside, and had to choke down the sob I felt welling up inside me. Tears collected in the corners of my eyes, which I brushed away with the sleeve of my tunic. Trying to stop my lips from trembling, I stuttered, 'I do not want to be part of the Church. It is not my fault you never let me learn the art of war. Did I not show I can fight when I beat Hakon?'

'You were fortunate, Hakon slipped. On any other day, you would have lost. Not only that, you made Sweyn Godwinson an enemy of this family. No man wants to see his son, even a bastard son, beaten by a half-man.'

'Half-man? By a cripple, you mean.'

'Yes, by a cripple,' my father snapped. 'It brings shame on a man to lose to a cripple.'

'Then they should make sure they don't lose,' I said angrily, feeling a single tear roll down my cheek.

My father was calm for a moment. I thought I noticed pity in his face. Whether it was for me or himself I do not know. But I did not want his pity, I wanted his love and I could sense no trace of that at all.

'I don't doubt your determination, Leofric, but if I allow you to train as a warrior, I fear you would lose your life in your first combat. If that should happen, your mother would never forgive me. The truth is, I am struggling to keep hold of our estates. This marriage will bring a substantial dowry and combine our holdings, making us stronger. So, we will go to St. Omer. You will try your utmost to impress this Agatha. You will have sons, and our name will live on through them.'

Accordingly, arrangements were made for my father, Grim, Brokk and me, with a crew of twenty men, to take fleeces to St. Omer.

My mother refused to bid us farewell and Thurstan told my father it was fool-hardy and a waste of time. We rode to Doferum where a ship had been prepared for us.

'I have never sailed on the sea,' I said to Brokk, looking out across the bay.

'Nothing to it, young lord. See, it's as flat as a bloody cow pat.'

I was helped aboard by a red-faced man with white whiskers. He wore a blue woollen cap and his hands felt rough when he grabbed mine. I passed him my crutch, which my mother had insisted I took with me, instructing Grim and Brokk to make sure I used it always.

The boat was exquisite. 'Clinker built,' Brokk told me, 'with a prow either end and a removable rudder so it does not need to turn in narrow rivers.'

Built of English oak, she had deep sides and a wide berth. She had a crew of twenty-six men on the oars and her skipper was a large man with a red beard, called Alflunn the Red. He held a long, wooden rod, and, once the fleeces were loaded, he bellowed out the order to cast off and used it to beat a steady rhythm on the side of the ship.

At first, I believed Brokk was right, this sailing on the sea was easy. As we left the bay, the flatness turned to slightly choppy and my stomach acquired little flutters as the smell of the sea filled my throat and lungs. The rowers made guttural noises each time they pulled the oars back and Wave-cutter, as she was named, slid effortlessly through the water. Slightly choppy turned to white-topped waves and Wave-cutter pitched each time she hit one. My stomach began to churn and I started retching. The bread and cheese I had eaten that morning spewed out into the British Sea. My stomach felt like it was being dragged up into my mouth. I retched and retched but there was nothing but bile and a stinging, burning sensation in my throat. I crawled from the side of the ship to the centre, to a big block of oak. It was six-foot-long and held the mast. The sailors called it the Old Woman, I never did find out why. I spent the rest of the journey clinging to this oak block, and thinking, sometimes wishing, I would die.

As the wind grew stronger, the crew pulled in their oars and the big, red and white, woven wool sail was hauled up. It made a snapping and cracking sound as it filled with the blow and Wave-Cutter skimmed across the waves, rolling from side to side. The man with the white whiskers brought me fresh water from one of the two barrels which sat at each end of the oak block.

'It happens to most people the first time. Gets better as you get your sea legs,' he said. I rewarded his kindness by bringing up a mixture of water and bile over his leather boots.

We finally came off the sea into the River Aa. The river narrowed, becoming so shallow at times the boat's bottom bumped on the river bed, and the rowers used the oars as poles to keep us moving. After a while, as we turned a bend in the river at St. Omer, the pale, stone turrets of the castle towered over the River Aa. As Wave-cutter slid into her moorings, white whisker man jumped ashore and Alflunn the Red threw him a rope to make fast. The harbour was busy with ships, large and small, their cargo being loaded and unloaded. I clambered over the side, eager to get back on solid land, only to feel I was still rolling with the motion of the boat. The nauseous feeling engulfed me again and I vomited onto the cobbled quayside.

Four soldiers, each wearing a red cloak, were waiting to greet us. We walked a short distance from the quay to a gatehouse built on a stone bridge and passed through this into the castle proper. Although I still felt giddy, the formidable structure impressed me as we walked through the castle gates. Thurstan had told me it was built to protect the Abbey of Saint-Bertin from the Norsemen. The Castellan, Wulfric Rabell, met us on the steps of the great keep. He was flanked by several dignitaries, priests and men at arms.

'Greetings, old friend,' Rabell said to my father, 'I trust you had a good journey. We have quarters prepared for you and once you are refreshed, we will meet and talk.'

'Your kindness is appreciated, Wulfric, the respite will serve us well,' replied my father.

We were taken to rooms in a round tower and I slept for hours on a soft, feather-filled mattress. When I awoke, Brokk and I were alone. I dunked my head in a bowl of cold water, which made me shiver, but I felt refreshed. I shook the water from my hair then changed into the clothes Ulla had packed for me. A crimson tunic with braided cuffs, dark brown britches, soft leather boots and a bright red cloak trimmed with the fur of red squirrels. The cloak was fastened with a round brooch engraved with a writhing serpent.

Thurstan had told me the castle housed a marvellous library that was worth seeking out, so as my father and Grim were absent, I convinced Brokk we should attempt to find it. The castle was a maze of corridors and stairwells. Besom torches lit the way as the narrow, slit windows let in little natural daylight. Brokk insisted I use the crutch, resulting in a tap, tap noise on the flagstone floor. Eventually, at the far end of a particularly long corridor was an open door and peering inside, knew we had found the library. Around the edges of the room were shelves and shelves of leather-bound books. In the centre were lines of small, open-ended boxes from floor to ceiling, which contained scroll after scroll. Close to the entrance was an extremely long, trestle table with pots of ink and quills. There were books stacked at one end of the table and open books and unfurled scrolls scattered across the other. This room was lit by beeswax candles, and a huge window of small panes of coloured glass held together by leaded strips. I marvelled at this for a while, having never seen a glass window so large or so magnificent until then.

'If you want a particular book or scroll you will have to wait. Busy, busy, busy.'

We could hear a voice, though at first, we could not see its owner. In one of the aisles containing scrolls, there was a strange contraption. It was a set of steps with small, wooden wheels and a platform above. Perched precariously on the top was a tall man. He clamped scrolls between his legs and under his left arm, and held a book in his right hand, which he held so close to his face, his nose was almost touching the vellum. He had hunched shoulders, as though he had been ducking under doorways all his life, and tufts of grey hair stuck out on each side of his head. His cheeks were puffed out on both sides of a snub nose and deep-set eyes squinted out beneath bushy eyebrows.

'Can we look around?' I asked, 'I am fascinated by books.'

'I'm bloody not,' muttered Brokk, 'musty, smelly, dusty things. Fit for nothing but wiping your arse and lighting fires.'

'Yes, yes, yes,' said the stooping man, ignoring Brokk's remarks, if in fact, he had heard him.

'I have found it! My lady, my lady, I have found it.' The stooping man was so excited he almost lost balance and teetered on top of the steps.

'Who's he bloody talking to, himself?' asked Brokk.

'He is talking to me.' A young girl appeared at the end of another aisle of scrolls. She was carrying a book, so large, she barely managed to hold on to it. 'Who are you?' she inquired.

'I am Leofric of Æssefeld-Underbarroe. And you, are you the Castellan's daughter?'

'I am,' said the girl, dropping the book on to the table with a thud. She was dressed in a full length, long-sleeved dress of dark green linen with gold coloured braid on the neck and cuffs. Around her waist was loosely tied a gold and pale green cord with dark green tassels. Her head was covered by a silk cap, but her chestnut hair fell loose behind. Her face was comely, if not beautiful.

The stooping man had managed to negotiate the steps, but hindered by the scrolls between his legs, he missed the last one and I thought he would trip over his own feet. He stumbled past Brokk and I and rolled one of the scrolls across the table next to the large book. He pointed at the scroll with a long, knobbly finger and traced it along the words.

'There, my lady, the code to unlock the spell in the Grimoire.'

'What's a bloody Grimoire?' asked Brokk.

'A book of magic,' I said.

'You know of this?' asked the girl.

'I have read of them, yes,' I replied, 'is this such a book?'

'Yes, it is called the Picatrix. This is a copy.' She opened the book and turned the pages. I recognised the writing as part Arabic and part Greek though I understood neither. There were drawings and diagrams and odd symbols.

The stooping man kept watching nervously over his shoulder.

'There are those that don't approve of such books,' said the girl. 'They say they are the work of the devil and can cause evil to come into the world.'

Brokk crossed himself five times before plunging his hand into his pouch to touch his elf-bolt.

'Do you believe that?' I asked.

'Only if there is already evil in the person who uses its power,' she said.

'What do you want with such a book?'

'To make a love potion,' she said, as she copied from the book and scroll on to a scrap of parchment.

'I wouldn't have thought you would need to resort to magic to make someone fall in love with you,' I said, feeling my cheeks flush with embarrassment.

'I don't. This is to make someone fall out of love. It is said to be a terrible thing to love someone that does not love you. Though to have someone you despise pursue you relentlessly can be equally upsetting.'

I wondered if that was to warn me not to get too close to her. I also wondered why that bothered me.

'The limp, did you have an accident?'

'It's from birth,' I said.

'Does it hurt?'

'Sometimes, yes.'

'I will consult the books and find you a salve to take away the pain.' She closed the cover of the huge book, sending up a small cloud of dust.

'Can you pass that to Izambar?' she said, and as I reached for the book, our hands touched fleetingly. A tingling sensation ran up my arm, the hairs stood on end, and my heart hammered as if it was eager to break out of my chest. I felt light-headed. I shivered and thought I might be unwell, yet I felt more alive than ever before. The stooping man, whom I now knew was called Izambar, took the book from me and shuffled off to replace it on the correct shelf.

'Can we trust in his silence, my lady?' he asked as he passed the girl.

'Yes, I do believe we can,' she said.

'And the ugly one?' he asked, pointing at Brokk.

Brokk glared at him, clenching a fist.

'Do you mean the tall, strong one? Yes, I believe we can trust him too,' said the girl.

'You have my word on both our silence,' I said.

'I never doubted it,' and she smiled at me in a way that warmed me from the inside out.

'I believe you have a particular interest in illuminated books, Leofric,' she said.

'I do, my lady. I try my best to copy the style of the better scribes.'

'More than try, I am told.'

I felt myself blushing once again, amazed at how much she knew about me.

151

'If you go to the far wall, three shelves up on the right, you will find several wonderful examples.'

I thanked her and Brokk and I went to find the books. As we walked away, I glanced back quickly, in time to see she was also watching me, our eyes met momentarily, and it came to me that marrying a girl that loved books, who was caring and intelligent and pleasing to the eye, may not be as unpleasant as I first thought. When I looked again, she was gone. I found the books she had recommended, and they were indeed wonderful examples. Normally, I would have been engrossed by the craftsmanship and intricacy of the letters, but all I could think of was Agatha, the daughter of the Castellan of St. Omer, and her blue eyes, her hair tumbling over her shoulders and the sweetest smile I had ever seen.

When we arrived back at the tower my father and Grim were waiting.

'Where have you been? Wulfric is ready to receive you. I will have no arguments from you. You will do this, Leofric, and you will do your utmost to impress this girl.'

'There will be no argument, father, I have already met her, and she appeals to me and I think I appeal to her.'

My father seemed bewildered at my sudden change of heart, though he said nothing and ushered us out of the tower as quickly as he could.

Wulfric Rabell sat in a high-backed chair made of ebony and aspen, inlaid with ivory and mother-of-pearl. He was surrounded by nobles, men of the Church and scribes. Men at arms lined both sides of the hall. Sat next to him was a woman of extraordinary beauty. A face of flawless skin and jet-black hair framed her big, dark eyes, full lips and snub nose. The scarlet silk gown she wore exposed her bare shoulders and the tops of her large breasts, which rose and fell at each breath. Strings of pearls fell around her neck like droplets of morning dew, and her fingers sparkled with gold and jewelled rings.

As we approached, she and Wulfric stood.

'Welcome, Renweard Sigweardson. I present to you, Agatha, my daughter.' He took her by the hand and walked forward.

'No wonder Leofric changed his mind,' Grim whispered to my father, 'I wouldn't mind a tumble with her myself.'

My father gave him one of his disapproving stares.

I simply gaped, opened-mouthed at this woman, this voluptuous creature.

If this is Agatha, who was it I met earlier in the library and why did she lie about being the Castellan's daughter?

Fifteen

'**Go,** Leofric, present yourself to her,' my father said, prodding me in the back. I took a step forward; she raised a hand towards me.

'Stop,' she said, 'that thing under your arm, do you need it to stand?'

'No, my lady.'

'Discard the wretched device and walk without it.'

I passed the crutch to Grim, who almost dropped it as he did not take his gaze from Agatha's breasts.

'Now come,' she said, beckoning me towards her.

Knowing I was under scrutiny, I tried my hardest to walk as straight as I could. Each time I put my left foot down, I bobbed and dipped, as I knew I would, I always did.

'Father is this a jest you play on me?' Agatha said. 'Is this some lame fool they bring with them to amuse me before they produce the real Leofric to delight me?' she giggled. 'Well, father, is it? The giggling stopped, the smile went from her lips. A harshness came over her face. 'Or do you honestly expect me to marry this thing, this hobbling, shuffling, cripple? Do you think so little of me? Do you imagine he could ever defend my honour?'

She walked around me as one does when examining a horse. She pushed me several times. At first gentle, becoming harder each time, making me move my feet to regain my stance.

'I doubt if he could even defend himself.'

She raised her hand to strike me, but before she could, I grabbed

154

her arm and pulled her towards me.

'I have always dreaded the thought of becoming a priest, I vowed it would never happen, but I would sooner spend a lifetime in a remote, religious cell than one minute in your company.'

The shock that someone had dared answer back or even touch her was obvious on her face.

'Guards, remove this insolent wretch from my sight!' she screeched.

'There is no need, I am leaving and willingly. Lord Rabell, I bid you good day.' I took the crutch from Grim and left the hall. Brokk followed.

'Bloody hell, there'll be trouble now,' Brokk said.

'No doubt,' I said, 'no doubt.'

As we entered the tower, I slung the crutch across the room and kicked the wall with my left foot sending a searing pain through the whole of my leg. 'Shit, shit, shit,' I shouted at the roof of the tower, both in pain and frustration. Where was the girl from the library? It was my only thought, even when my furious father burst into the tower; red-faced, eyes bulging, his fists clenched tight.

'Can't you do anything right, you useless fool? All you had to do was be civil to the girl. But no, you must insult her and by so doing insult her father. I thought you told me you had met her, and you liked each other.'

'It was a different girl,' I said, 'I must find her, father.'

'I have no inkling of what you are talking about, and the only thing you will find is the boat the Castellan is preparing for us to leave on immediately.'

'I can't leave until I have found her,' I pleaded.

'You will do as I tell you, Leofric, and as soon as we are home, I will instruct Thurston to make arrangements for your ordination into the Church. It is clear to me now where your future lies, and it is not as the thegn of Æssefeld. Grim, you stay here and make sure he does not leave the tower. Brokk, you come with me and we will find out which boat we are to sail on.' The tower door vibrated on its hinges as he slammed it behind him.

Grim stared at me.

'What is wrong with yer, Leofric?' he said.

'Wrong?'

'What man in his right mind would reject a woman such as Agatha Rabell-daughter?'

'She rejected me, remember.'

'So, take her by force, show her yer a real man.'

'As Sweyn did to your sister, you mean?' Grim clenched his fists and moved towards me, but he restrained himself.

'She has no attraction for me, Grim, besides, I have met someone who does.'

'Who?'

'I don't know her name, I thought it was Agatha. We met in the library earlier. If you let me out, I can go and search for her.'

'And anger yer father even more. I would be a fool to do so,' said Grim placing his hand on his sword hilt. 'Besides, there will be no place for women where yer father's sending yer. Prayers and fasting are yer future.'

'And who would be heir to Æssefeld?' I said defiantly, though I guessed he could be right.

'Hakon, my nephew,' said Grim triumphantly. 'It seems increasingly unlikely he will ever be accepted by his father. Yer father looks upon him as another son. Once yer in a monastery, he will be a natural replacement. Agatha was yer last chance and yer stubborn pride has sealed yer fate.'

The thought of Hakon taking my place saddened and angered me. It is possible that is what my father always intended and he would get the son he desired. I sat on a woodworm-riddled bench in the corner of the room and tried to work out what I could do. I contemplated hitting Grim over the head with the crutch and escaping from the tower. I knew he was too strong and would overpower me with ease. Besides where would I go?

As time passed, I was wondering why my father had taken so long to return, when the door opened and in he came. I was expecting more harsh words and to face his wrath once again.

'When do we leave?' asked Grim.

'Not just yet,' said my father calmly. 'Wulfric's younger daughter, Turfrida, has requested to meet with Leofric each day for a week so they can become more acquainted with each other. It appears they met earlier and struck a bond. Wulfric is not happy with the situation as Turfrida already has a suiter he approves of. Also, it has caused a rift between the sisters. Agatha demanded Leofric whipped and sent from the city. Turfrida has threatened to retire to a nunnery and marry no one if her father lets that happen. You will visit her tomorrow, Leofric. Brokk and Turfrida's handmaiden will accompany you as chaperones. I have been informed Turfrida is Wulfric's favourite. Whatever dowry we had arranged before will be honoured, if not bettered. See this as a reprieve, Leofric. Woo this woman and we will both prosper. Fail and it will bring hardship to both of us.'

I said nothing, for I was speechless. A few moments ago, my life was spiralling into disaster. Now the future seemed bright once more. Moreover, I would see Turfrida again. I mused on her name, Turfrida, Turfrida, it suited her so well, soft, gentle, not harsh like Agatha.

Our meetings from the first were congenial. We wandered around the castle battlements, along the river bank, and we sat on the slopes above open fields. We talked about books, our childhood, our hopes for the future. At first Brokk and Turfrida's handmaiden, Sophia, were conscientious in their role as chaperones. Sophia was not blessed with beauty. Her face was plump and her features somewhat askew. She was much shorter than Brokk and they appeared an odd pair as they followed behind us. I have never heard Brokk laugh as much, or as loud, as he did when he was with Sophia. Each day they dropped further behind us and seemed more concerned with each other than Turfrida and me.

One morning soon after daybreak, we sat on the side of a grassy knoll under the walls of the castle. Brokk and Sophia walked down by the river. The views across the low-lying plain stretched for miles beyond the river to a dark outline of forest in the far distance. We could see a cloud of dust on the far bank, coming towards the town.

'Can I remove your left boot?' Turfrida asked, tenderly.

I hesitated. No one had seen my deformed foot since I was a child when many had tried to administer a cure. Everything had failed.

'I have made this for you.' Turfrida pulled a small file of salve out of a pouch hung from her waist. 'It won't cure you, but it will ease the pain.'

I nodded, and she gently eased the boot off my foot. She placed my foot on her lap and poured the ointment from the file into her hands. I use the word foot, though my left foot is more like the end of a cudgel than a normal foot. My ankle twists inward, the foot twists upwards and my toes are scrunched into a tight ball. Hard callouses had formed along the outer edge from constant walking on it. Turfrida's fingers were soothing yet penetrative, as she massaged the salve into my skin. I peered into her eyes, expecting to see pity, but seeing only understanding, the desire to relieve my pain, and dare I hope it, love.

She replaced my boot. She leant forward and kissed my cheek. Our eyes met once again. I took her face in my hands, kissed her lips softly at first and briefly. Time passed, which seemed like hours. Turfrida leant forward once more and returned the kiss, again briefly, on the lips. Another pause, our breathing became heavier, our lips touched once more, hard, passionate and long.

We talked. At times, we simply gazed longingly into each other's eyes, no words spoken. We sat, we kissed, we talked further, and I fell in love with Turfrida, the Castellan's daughter.

As we prepared to go back to the castle, I pointed over to the far side of the River Aa.

'Look, the dust, it was horses.'

The dust had settled, and a large herd of horses grazed on the meadowlands tended by their handlers.

'They are brought here for the army by Romani horse traders,' said Turfrida.

'Maybe I will get a closer look at them before I leave,' I said, not imagining my heart would drop like a lead weight at the thought of leaving Turfrida.

'When will that be?' she said, sounding as sad as I felt at the prospect of us parting.

'Soon, I imagine. My father needs to return to Englaland.'

Brokk and I escorted the two girls back to the castle. There were a group of new horses in the courtyard being wiped down and brushed after their journey. I guessed they were waiting for Wulfric's approval. A man in a round, fur hat barked orders at those carrying out the grooming who scurried hurriedly to obey him.

I kissed Turfrida's hand.

'You must talk to my father before you leave for Englaland,' she said.

'I will, I promise.'

The big, oak door closed behind them and Brokk and I walked back along the pillared arcade on the west side of the castle. Like doe-eyed puppies, we sauntered past the pillars on our left, oblivious to the danger that lurked behind them.

'When you marry the Lady Turfrida,' said Brokk, 'Sophia will accompany her as her handmaiden. You would have no objection to me pursuing her, I trust?'

'Would it stop you if I did?' I laughed.

'Not bloody likely,'

'I thought not.' I said. 'Who's that?'

A man had appeared at the end of the arcade. He stood legs apart, his sword drawn. Dressed in a hauberk that shone like polished silver and a round-rimmed, metal helmet adorned with peacock feathers. He held a shield with decorative yellow and blue leaves and swirls, with the image of a visored helmet painted in the centre. Before we could react, two men slipped from behind the pillars behind us and grabbed Brokk and put a dagger to his throat.

The man in the hauberk spoke.

'I am Bernard of Saint Valéry, grandson of the lord of Saint Valéry. You have brought disgrace upon me and my family and I demand reparation!'

'I am Leofric of Æssefeld-Underbarroe, I do not know you or how I have offended you, but if you do not tell your men to release my friend, you will regret you ever met me.' I tried to sound braver than

I felt, wondering what to do next.

Bernard spoke again. 'I have travelled many miles to propose to the Lady Turfrida, only to find you have distracted her affection away from me to yourself. You will go down on your knees, beg my forgiveness and vow never to pursue her again. Do this, and I will let your indiscretions pass without further mention.'

'And if I don't?'

'If you do not, I will kill you,' said Bernard, and, as he strode towards me, two more men appeared from behind the pillars. Bernard handed his shield to one and the other gave him a bullwhip. 'But first, I shall humiliate you and you will get on your knees.'

Getting ever closer, he flicked the whip, the long lash stopping an arm's length from my face, with a crack and a snap.

'Down,' he snarled.

I stood my ground. 'What makes you believe the Lady Turfrida has affection for you, she has never once mentioned your name,' I said.

'We have been promised since we were children,' said Bernard, 'I have loved her from afar, now I come to claim her. She will learn to love me, and no man or boy will stop me.'

He flicked the whip for a second time. The lash unfurled towards me as a fifth man stepped from behind the pillars.

He wore a dust-covered tunic with thick, woollen britches tucked into knee-length, brown leather boots. On his head was a round hat of marten fur, and his beard and hair wore the greyness of old age. His skin had a duskiness about it and his face was deep-lined from a life spent under the sun. A large, gold ring dangled from one earlobe. In his belt was a large knife, a cross between a seax and a meat cleaver, with a single-edged blade which curved slightly at its point.

In an instant, he caught the lash as it unfurled and before Bernard could release his grip on the handle, the old man yanked the whip, pulling the surprised swordsman towards him. Thrusting his forearm across Bernard's neck, he slammed him up against a pillar. Bernard dropped both the whip and his sword.

The two men holding Brokk released him instantly, one of them uttering, 'Mother of God have mercy,' and both scampered across the courtyard, closely followed by the man who had brought the whip.

The man holding Bernard's shield came at the old man defiantly, 'Let him go, you old fool,' he yelled.

The old man whisked the curved blade from his belt and with one swipe embedded it into the man's neck, half decapitating him. The body fell in a heap, a pool of blood seeping onto the stone-flagged floor.

Bernard stopped struggling. 'Who are you?' he asked, gasping for breath.

'I am Milosh, horse trader to kings and princes, once head-man of the Atsinganoi of Constantinople on the banks of the Bosphorus.'

'And my grandfather!' I blurted out.

'And his grandfather,' he repeated.

So, this was Milosh. No wonder those men had fled. My mother and father had told me little of Milosh, always changing the subject whenever I asked about him, though I knew he had other names; bandit, thief, murderer, assassin. Someone once told me that my grandfather made Sweyn Godwinson seem like a lamb.

All this commotion brought people out of the castle to see what the disturbance was. To my surprise, Turfrida reappeared at the door and hurried passed us, paying no heed to me. She went straight to Bernard and Milosh. She carried a small, stone bottle.

'Good sir, Bernard is beaten, your grandson is safe, please release him and spill no more blood today,' she pleaded.

Milosh pushed his forearm harder against Bernard's throat. 'Anything happens to my grandson, I will hold you responsible. I will find you and I will shove that blade up your miserable Flemish arse and drag your insides to the outside and piss on them.' He cast his eyes to the knife still lodged in the corpse's neck. 'Do you understand?'

Bernard tried to answer but could not, so nodded his head instead.

'Good, make sure you don't forget it.' As if to press the point, Milosh brought his knee forcibly into Bernard's groin, taking away his breath and sending him to his knees. Milosh yanked the blade from the half-severed neck and wiped the blood from it on the dead man's tunic. He tucked the knife back into his belt and beckoned me to join him.

Turfrida knelt to tend to Bernard and bid him drink from the stone bottle.

I followed Milosh across the courtyard. His men had finished grooming the horses and were taking them for Wulfric's approval. Milosh took a small bag of coins from the saddlebag off his own horse and tossed it to one of the men. 'Give it to that little shit, Bernard, for wergild, not that the useless dolt I killed was worth much. We need Wulfric's custom and can't afford to upset him. Take that red roan over there and give her to the castellan to keep him happy. Now, how is that miserable, sanctimonious daughter of mine that you call mother?' Milosh asked.

'She is well, lord.'

'Shame, and I am not your lord, I am your grandfather. Milosh is good enough for everyone else so it will have to be good enough for you. A man's name is everything, Leofric, his honour, his standing, his reputation. Those men fled because of my name, because of the tales they have heard about me in taverns and what the skalds sing about me to frighten women and children. If people believe it's true, that is where the power lies. My reputation has saved me much trouble. Most men hear my name and decide it is wise to leave me be.'

I followed him through a narrow arch in the castle wall, where a guard opened a thick, oak door with a large key. We followed a path across a bridge over the River Aa to where the great herd of horses grazed on sweet grass.

'What do you see, Leofric?' my grandfather said.

'Horses,' I said, stating the obvious.

'How many herds do you see?'

'One,' I replied.

'How many leaders do you see?'

I moved up and down the edge of the herd peering past the outliers, further into the centre. 'The big, black stallion next to the two bays.'

'There are many herds here, Leofric, a herd within a herd, within a herd. Each horse knows its place. Each herd has its leader, usually a mare. Choosing a horse is a skill. Most men look and just see a horse, but each one has its own unique personality, each one a different temperament. You need to earn their trust. A horse can be a dangerous animal if startled. One kick on the head can leave a man forever deprived of his senses or even dead. Choose any horse, Leofric, then go and stroke it.'

I picked out a chestnut, almost red, stallion and started to walk towards him. As I approached, he began swishing his tail and pawing the ground with his hooves. He backed off, swaying his head and snorting from his nostrils.

Milosh came alongside me. 'Talk to him, Leofric, let him hear your voice, soft but firm.' He steered me to the left of the stallion. 'Come from the side, not the front or back.'

As we got nearer, I spoke softly. 'Steady boy, I am a friend, I will not hurt you.'

'Good, good, now stay at his side and stroke his face, let him smell your hand.' The stallion calmed, his tail fell still. He nodded his head.

'Now we can move to his front.'

Milosh blew softly into the horse's nostrils and mouth. The earlier aggression seemed to melt away and a quietness and calmness enveloped the stallion.

'Now we can take a closer look at him. His eyes should be bright and clear. Any discharge around his nostrils shouldn't be cloudy.'

He peeled the stallion's lips back to show his teeth. 'Check for sharp points that might need rasping. Check for decay.'

Then he ran his hand across the horse's sides under the belly. 'You should be able to feel the ribs but not see them. Run your hands down his legs, each one should be free from lumps and bumps. Make sure they don't feel too hot. Make sure they're free from cuts, no swelling or that the horse winces from pain when you touch them.'

Milosh then put his hand on the stallion's neck and walked him slowly back and forth. 'Make sure he moves freely, no lameness. A man can compensate for such a thing. If a horse is lame, he is finished.'

'There are those who say a lame man is finished too,' I said, 'worthless.'

'Depends on the man,' said Milosh, 'whether it's just his leg that's lame or his spirit and his courage as well.'

He dipped his hand into the bag slung over his shoulder and offered a palm full of oats to the red stallion, who gratefully lapped them up. He then smacked it firmly on the rump and the animal trotted a short distance before continuing to graze.

'I have heard it said you talk to horses and they talk back to you,' said my grandfather.

'Stories told by fools,' I said, surprised he knew of such tales about me.

'Do you want it to be true, Leofric? Do you want to know the language of the Horsðegn? Many have desired it, few have managed to acquire it. Several have even died trying to possess it. The ability to learn it cannot be taught but must be born within you. Only those chosen can be told the words.'

'Chosen by who?' I asked.

'By the horses, of course. Have you the courage to take the test?'

'Test?'

Milosh stepped closer to the edge of the herd. He took off his fur hat and hurled it as far as he could into the herd, making it spin in the air like a sycamore seed until it dropped to the ground, disturbing a group of grazing colts.

'Get on your hands and knees and retrieve the hat. Keep crawling and meet me on the far side of the herd.'

Milosh clapped his hands several times and howled liked a wolf. The horse closest to us recoiled at the noise, and as a pebble thrown into water causes ripples, the disturbance spread throughout the herd, making them skittish and restless. I knelt on my hands and knees. A forest of horses' legs stretched out before me, a mish-mash of limb-breaking hooves constantly shifting, creating a moving barrier between me and the hat. To attempt to crawl through there was madness.

'It is no shame to reject the test, many men have done so,' said Milosh. 'Of those that try it, few succeed. If the horses don't trust you, they could kick or trample you. If you spook them, the whole herd could stampede, and it would be certain death.'

I waited.

I had found a girl I love, why should I jeopardize my life to impress the grandfather I had never known?

I waited.

I was aware of the stories my father told about my birth and the resulting affinity that created with horses. I always believed it was just an excuse my father had invented to explain away my lameness. Was it possibly true? I looked up at Milosh. I couldn't tell if he was relieved or disappointed, I hadn't yet ventured into the herd.

Still, I waited.

I was filled with self-doubt. The fear of severe injury caused my legs and arms to shake and the hairs on the nape of my neck bristle.

I was on the verge of abandoning the task, when suddenly, a gap opened ahead of me and without another thought, drawing in a deep breath, and dragging the crutch beside me I began crawling into the herd. My grandfather leaped onto the back of the big red stallion and with a whoop, he rode off around the herd to the far side of the meadow.

At first, the horses near me backed off and my progress was unhindered. As I got further into the herd, a few became bolder and inquisitive. The black stallion I had seen earlier, came right up to me and nudged my side with his head. 'Have you seen a hat?' I said, trying to quell my nerves. He snorted, shook his head causing his mane to flick from side to side.

I crawled on, pausing at times as hooves narrowly missed my hands. The smell from the dung and piss and horse sweat was overpowering, making my eyes water, catching my throat, making me retch. Flies swarmed around me making my face sting from their constant biting. I could not see Milosh's hat. I began to think I had gone too far and would have to turn back when I saw it tossed in the air some-way to the right.

I started to chant one of the canticles I had learnt from Thurstan as I crawled. This had a calming effect on the horses and I manged to get to the hat unscathed. Two fillies were taking turns in nudging it and flicking it upwards.

'That's my grandfather's hat, please can I have it?'

The fillies ignored me and tossed it into the air once more.

The surrounding horses seemed to be drawing closer, and I feared I was going to be trampled after all, but then a big grey pushed his way through as the hat landed on the ground. He lowered his head and swung his thick neck, hitting the hat with his muzzle. It slithered along the grass just in front of me. On purpose or by chance, who is to know? but I gratefully grabbed it and stuffed it in my belt. The fillies snorted, flicked their tails, and one of them stamped her feet a few times and then lost interest and went back to grazing. The grey continued slowly in the direction I was heading, and I proceeded in his wake. My hands and knees were becoming sore, my good britches torn and soiled from the mud and dung, but before long, I could see the edge of the herd where Milosh was riding up and down on the red horse looking for me. As I scrambled out, I stood unsteadily and waved the hat triumphantly.

Milosh rode to me, jumped off the red and half hugged, half thumped my back. 'You're a fool, Leofric, but a brave fool at that. I know only a handful of men who would have attempted that and most of them would have stood and walked out before the end. You have earned your reward. Come with me.'

He led me to the edge of the forest at the far side of the meadow. There was a small ring of white quartz boulders, which glistened and reflected the fading, evening light.

'I believe these were put here by the first men to occupy this land,' said Milosh, 'it was a sacred, holy place. It seems as good as anywhere to speak the words of the Horsðegn.'

We sat in the centre of the stone ring and Milosh taught me the language of the Horsðegn. He made me swear never to repeat it to other men or to write it down in any form. From that day on, I understood horses like few men ever can, and I knew they understood me.

Over the next few days, I spent my days with Turfrida and the evenings with Milosh. He taught me more about horses than most men will ever know.

Once he had concluded his business with Wulfric, Milosh and the herd moved on. There were no goodbyes, just one piece of advice from a grandfather to his grandson.

'You are a natural, Leofric. There is something about you the horses trust. Always trust them, they will never let you down.'

He took off his hat and gave a little bow from the saddle, and he rode back out of my life, and I never met him again.

Bernard never bothered Turfrida and me again, either. He said it had all been a misunderstanding. He had never loved Turfrida and he had mistaken me for someone else. Turfrida said it was because of the un-love potion she had given him on the day he had confronted me. I believed it was more to do with my grandfather and his curved knife. Whichever it was, he was gone from St. Omer the next day, and it was many years before I met him again.

I kept my promise to Turfrida and approached her father about our marriage.

'I can't say my daughter's choice pleases me,' the Castellan said. 'Your father was less than truthful to me about you. How will you protect her and our lands? I believe it was only your grandfather's intervention that saved you from injury this very week. However, Turfrida is as stubborn as her mother was and has threatened to join a convent if I forbid the match. You are both young and if your love is as strong as you both say, it will stand the test of time. I demand you wait three years. After such time, I will contact your father, and if you both feel the same as you do now, I will give my blessing. If you act against my wishes, there will be no blessing, no dowry, no alliance with your father and you will make me your enemy.'

Turfrida and I both reluctantly agreed to his terms. We said our goodbyes, I vowed to come back for her in three years, she promised to wait.

'Sophia has a brother, Otto, he is a sailor,' Turfrida told me. 'He regularly makes the trip to Doferum to collect your father's fleeces. I shall give him letters to take across the sea to you. Is there someone you trust who can collect them and bring them to you?'

I told her I would arrange it She told me she had cast a spell to make our journey safe. I suppose it worked because we arrived back in Englaland unscathed, despite a rough crossing and me emptying the contents of my guts into the British Sea once again.

We came home to good and bad news.

Sweyn had come to Æssefeld and taken Hakon away. He had told my mother it was time Hakon was brought into the Godwin fold and equipped to be his heir. He also took our two fyrd-men for the second time, giving no explanation why. He had said he was meeting his cousin Beorn, who was going to appeal to King Edward on his behalf to reclaim his earldom. Then we were told the most devastating news of all. Sweyn Godwinson had murdered his cousin Beorn. Most of his men had deserted him and he had fled to Flanders in disgrace.

The week after we returned home, a group of Godwin's soldiers brought Hakon back to Æssefeld. He was to stay here until the family sent for him again. My father asked him what took place with Sweyn and Beorn, but he gave no answer. There was no sign of the Idenson twins, though Hakon thought they may have gone with Sweyn.

I liked Beorn, he was a good man. I wondered why Sweyn would want to kill him. I guessed it was about the lands Beorn had been given when Sweyn was exiled. If Sweyn demanded them back and Beorn refused and withdrew his offer to speak to the king about Sweyn's exile, it didn't take too much to imagine Sweyn's anger and retribution.

Earl Harold had been informed of the makeshift burial place of his cousin and had retrieved the body and given him a Christian burial.

Sweyn had been named as a nithing, a man of no consequence, an oath breaker, a despicable being. Surely, there was no way back now for the former earl.

Sixteen

AD 1049

I was the first to see him. A man on a tall horse, two Saxon ponies by his side, each with a corpse dangling over their backs.

They came unhurriedly down the hill, by the time they reached the edge of the village a small crowd gathered around them. The man appeared weary, his face serious and stern. He wore a full beard, the same dusky brown as his hair which hung in a long plait. He was dressed in brown leather with a short coat of mail. A sword, with an undecorated hilt, hung from his waist in a scabbard and strapped over his shoulder was a shield. The two corpses were that of Ealdan and Grindan Idenson. There was a gasp as the rest of the villagers recognised our fyrd-men. Neither of these men was popular in the village, but to realise their warriors were dead and what that could mean for themselves was disturbing. As the stranger stopped, someone pushed to the front of the crowd shouting, 'What's happened here? Who did this?' It was Gifre, the twins younger brother.

The stranger said nothing. His horse shifted from side to side and the ponies skittered, making the corpses jiggle as if there was still life in them.

'I said, who did this?' Gifre demanded again and reached out to grab the horse's bridle. His reward was a kick in the face from the stranger, which sent him reeling backwards.

The crowd surged forward towards the horseman. In one movement, he pulled the sword from its scabbard and with the other hand reached behind him for his shield. In an instant, he was protected by his shield, his sword poised above it, ready to strike anyone who dared to venture near. His horse, a courser, reared on its hind legs, kicking out with its front hooves and snorting from its nostrils like a mad bull. Everyone except me backed off. I stood transfixed. I had seen great warriors, friends and foes of my father, but no one had stirred the feeling of awe and admiration than this sight before me. Man and beast, silhouetted against the pale, evening sky, poised like a great snake, ready to strike its prey. Although outnumbered, there was an assurance and total belief in his own prowess that emanated from this man. I knew at that moment this was the warrior I wished to emulate. His horse came crashing back down when a hand reached out from behind me and pulled me backwards. It was my father.

'I am Renweard, Thegn of Æssefeld, this is Gifre, the brother of the men you have with you.'

The stranger lowered his sword to a less threatening position and nodded in acknowledgement to my father.

'I am Wulfgar. There was a battle on the banks of the River Usk against Gruffydd, the King of the Wealas. There was great slaughter. These men died there. Before he drew his last breath, one of them told me where they were from and I promised to bring them home.'

'We thank you for that, Wulfgar,' Renweard said. 'I am sure they died a hero's death. Gifre and the village are in debt to their courage.'

Wulfgar spat on the ground. 'They died the death of cowards, running from their enemy.'

This again brought groans from the villagers hearing their fyrd-men called cowards. Gifre moved forward again, though more cautiously than before, he seemed angrier than upset at the loss of his brothers.

'There must have been money. Where's their money?' he snarled.

'What was on the mounts is untouched,' said Wulfgar, his expression one of contempt for this churlish man.

'Where is Crispin?' my father intervened.

'Here, my lord.' The priest shuffled forward, crossing himself profusely. Hakon appeared at the same time but skulked off quickly.

'Crispin take Gifre and his kin and prepare the dead for burial. The rest of you return to your work or homes.'

The villagers obeyed their thegn, though many seemed distrustful of Wulfgar. My father led Wulfgar to our hall where he was given bread and cheese. He was offered ale, which he refused and drank water instead. I remember thinking at the time that was odd for a warrior and reckless too, as water from a village well is a precarious drink. Wulfgar said little, only to answer direct questions from my father.

'Where are you from, Wulfgar?'

'North.'

'What brings you south?'

'I am the third son of a northern thegn. I am a landless man who sells his sword to the lord who pays the most.'

'And which lord pays you now?'

'My lord is dead.'

'So, you are both landless and lord less?' my father said, probing for information from this man.

Wulfgar nodded, giving nothing away. All the time he ate or spoke, his eyes scoured the shadows, his hand always near his sword hilt.

We were joined by Grim, who also tried to pick from Wulfgar what had taken place on the banks of the Usk, but the Northerner was evasive and sparing with his answers. By the time Wulfgar was shown to his sleeping quarters, we knew little more than when he first came. My father and Grim talked late into the night. I was sent back to Thurstan, who made me copy scripture until I was so tired, I could hardly hold the goose quill. Hakon and Ulf slept, having done their work earlier, though Hakon was restless and I wondered what it was that troubled him.

Early the next day, my father sent for Wulfgar and it was decided that he would stay at Æssefeld and be our fyrd-man. An armed warrior such as him would be valued twice as much as the twins, and although Wulfgar was viewed with suspicion and unease, the news was met with relief, as it meant that the rest of the men would be free to get on with their daily lives. Gifre objected, but as it transpired, he did find money in his brother's pack, and as far as he could ascertain, it was intact, so he had no real cause for complaint. Hakon said Wulfgar should not be trusted, but gave no reason, and as Hakon mistrusted most people, no heed was taken of him. Thurstan told me Wulfgar, like all men of violence, was a disciple of the devil, and I should keep my distance. To help register the point, he jabbed me with his stick. Twice more when I cried out.

Over the next couple of weeks, Wulfgar kept to his own company. He ate alone and remained in the small hut my father had given him on the edge of the village, near the main gate. Although people talked about him, it was never when he was near and except for several amorous glances from a few of the village girls, he was left alone. When he did emerge, he would either walk up the hill to the barrows and sit looking down at the village, or he would take his horse and ride out into the forest, where he would stay for hours. I became curious as to where he went, and after weeks of guessing, I decided to find out for myself and follow him discreetly. He eventually came to a clearing deep in the forest. At first glance, it seemed like any clearing strewn with fallen branches, but as he walked around, I realised it was set up in a circle with hurdles and obstacles. He took a small axe from a bag slung across his horse and began to splice hazel branches, which he stuck in the ground at equal distances apart. He placed logs in various positions. He took from the bag a coiled rope. He tied one end to a short, stout stick around its centre, and climbing up a sturdy beech, tied the other end to a branch so the stick hung an upstretched arm's length above the ground. He jumped from the tree reached up to the stick with both hands and hauled himself up until the sick was level with his chest, to see if it would hold his weight. Stripping down to his britches, he began moving around the circle. Slowly at first, swerving around the branches so none touched him, pulling himself up and down on the rope tied to the beech tree. His muscles on his chest and arms strained. He performed press ups and ran around the obstacles repeatedly, moving quicker each time. After this, he took up his sword and practised slashing and thrusting and parrying imagined blows. Each day I witnessed the same routine.

I went to his dwelling a couple of times to talk to him. The first time, as I opened his door, he kicked it shut in my face without a word, and I hobbled off like a chastened puppy. The second time, I was determined to stand up to his abruptness. I pushed open the door and through the dim haze of the smoky half-light, I could see he was sharpening his sword blade with a whetstone. His greeting was to the point. 'What?'

I gripped my wooden crutch tighter as I sought deep for some courage.

'You should remember, I am the thegn of Æssefeld's son and you should think twice before ignoring me.' Even as I spoke, I wished I hadn't.

Without even looking up from his sword Wulfgar replied. 'Perhaps you should have sent your father to do your talking. I've thought twice,' he snarled and kicked the door closed in my face. I stood, feeling foolish, but I was still determined to talk with this man however rude or reluctant he was. I stayed away for a few days, trying to think how I could win Wulfgar's trust when the opportunity came by chance.

I heard a commotion at the stables and made my way there as quickly as I could. Wulfgar's horse was raging about the yard, rising on its hind legs whenever the stable boys got near. One boy had been struck by a flailing hoof and sat by the stable nursing an injured shoulder. The others cowered, half-heartedly attempting to grab its reins. Brokk was watching with amusement whilst giving the animal a wide birth himself. I stopped next to him. 'What's happened?' I asked breathlessly.

'Wulfgar told them to make sure he was ridden to exercise him. This is their fourth attempt and as hard as they try, they can't get near him. A couple of times Wulfgar has come out himself to see what the commotion was, and he has not been well pleased. In fact, here he comes again.'

Wulfgar strode purposely across the yard, an angry scowl across his face and a whip in his hand.

'A whip is no good, it will frighten the horse even more,' I said.

'The whip's not for the horse,' Brokk laughed, 'it's for the stable boys,' and as they saw Wulfgar coming they scurried across the yard.

'Dog turds!' Wulfgar growled at them as he came nearer. 'Couldn't trust you with a dead donkey.'

Without another thought, I walked towards the startled horse. As it saw me, it lowered its head and tossed its main defiantly, snorting, twisting its neck, his eyes full of menace. My eyes locked with his. I continued resolutely forward, one hand outstretched.

'Leave him to me.'

I knew it was Wulfgar but ignored him.

All the words of my grandfather came back to me. Be at one with the horse, never taking your eyes from his until you are on its back. Show no fear, they will sense it and use it against you. Speak the old words, sing the song of the Horsðegn.

'Stille, freond, æ ð ele d ë or.'

I repeated the words over and over, interspersed with a high pitch hum as I approached. The horse, whose name was Fleet, stood his ground and swayed his head, his dark mane whipping from side to side, spittle sprayed into the air. I did the same, flicking my black hair, swaying my body, all the while singing and humming, moving closer and closer, our eyes fixed. Someone shouted behind me. Oblivious to their calls, I slowly moved to Fleet's flank, placed my flat palm to his nose and stroked his face. He bent his neck and I ruffled his forelock. The stable boys had managed to put his bridle on before he had objected and sent them sprawling, so I gently took the reins and still singing the song of the Horsðegn, led him to the stable yard gate. Except for a few snorts and a shake of the head, Fleet came calmly.

Clambering up onto the gate, I straddled his bare back, flicked the latch which swung open freely, and with a squeeze of my knees, we were off across the courtyard out into the village and through the main gates. I had ridden horses since I was a child but none like this. It was difficult without a saddle, though I managed to grip with my knees, allowing me to feel the muscles pulsate through Fleet's body. Experiencing all that power, hearing the thud of his hooves as they pounded the turf, matching the beat of my heart, I was exhilarated, oblivious to everything else as Fleet and I melted into one, singing the song of the Horsðegn.

We eventually came to a halt on the ridge above Æssefeld. I had heard tales of men who not only rode to war but fought battles on horseback as well. I now realised how this was possible. On a horse like Fleet, a man would be a formidable, terrifying foe. I imagined hundreds of mounted men bearing down on a shield wall. All those hooves and gnashing teeth, the raw power of the beasts, and weapons wielded from above, crashing down on the foot soldier. In those few moments, I formulated in my mind my future. I would become a warrior. Not only would I have a horse like Fleet, but when Æssefeld was mine and I was its thegn, I would breed horses like him for other men who would pay me well, and I would have a mounted army that would cause men to tremble and lords would envy and value me as an ally. In two years' time, I would take Turfrida as my wife and she would bear me sons to be heirs to my great estates. What's more, I now had a plan of how I could achieve these aims. What I did not know, is that my mother, Thurstan, Harold and even Hakon schemed their own plans for me and they were all in conflict to mine.

When I returned to the stables all Wulfgar said was, 'That is a rare skill. Can I leave him in your care from now on?' He tossed me a coin, which I caught.

'Of course,' I replied tossing the coin back, 'I am the thegn's son, I do not need your coin.'

Wulfgar also caught it and put it back in his pouch. 'Next time use a saddle or you might fall off.'

As I already helped in the stables, my father had no objection to me tending to Fleet. Wulfgar, though, stayed as distant as ever, avoiding any kind of prolonged conversation.

The fair at Wareham was one of the highlights of the year. People came from all over Wessex and further afield, rich and poor, old and young.

Brokk, Rush and I where enthralled watching a troupe of fire eaters as balls of fire soared from their mouths, vanishing in the air as puffs of smoke.

'It's him over there you want, Leofric, son of the thegn of Æssefeld.' It was Hakon's quavering voice drifting over the din of the fair. Hakon and six youths from our village were being pushed and harassed by a stocky blonde youth and a group of both girls and boys, who were poking and prodding them, laughing and calling our village boys names.

'Why don't they fight back?' I said to Brokk.

'Because it's bloody Hereward of Brune, that's why' said Brokk.

'Who?'

'Local thug, troublemaker, braggart. Best at everything, even better at telling people how good he is. Apparently never been beaten in a fight. Girls swoon around him, lads everywhere admire him, and grown men fear him,' said Rush, 'we should walk away.'

It was too late for that.

'Leofric of Æssefeld, I am told you are these boys' champion,' shouted Hereward, turning his attention towards me.

Brokk and Rush bravely stood in front of me protectively.

'If neither of you are the thegn's son, step aside. I believe it is him who would wish to avenge the insults I have given to these dolts,' said Hereward. 'Is that not so, thegn's boy?'

'Step aside, it's alright' I said.

Brokk and Rush reluctantly moved to the side and I walked forward in full view of Hereward.

'Oh, apologies, Leofric, I had not seen the crutch.' Hereward seemed genuinely surprised to see I was lame.

'Why, are you frightened of crutches, Hairweard?' I said, moving half an arm's length in front of him.

'The name is Hereward, and no, I am not frightened of crutches, only of seriously harming someone who needs one to walk with.'

A crowd was beginning to form. I could see armed men riding towards us, guessing they were stewards who made sure the rules of the fair were upheld. They were entrusted to see no weapons were carried onto the fair-fields, that everyone dealt fairly and honestly when selling their wares, and that no fights or disputes broke out. Hereward saw them too and it was that distraction I needed, because whilst his attention was averted, I swung my good leg as hard as I could, connecting solidly with his manhood. Unexpecting such an assault, he staggered backwards, groaning, and fell onto his backside. Those around him were so shocked, they were confused at what they should do. One youth tried to help him up, but Hereward pushed him away forcibly. Back on his feet he brushed the dust from his tunic and scowled at me.

'No one does that to me without reprisal,' he growled, his face distorted with rage.

The crowd parted as the horsemen came bustling through, swords drawn, kicking anyone in their way.

'Away with you,' one of them shouted, 'go about your business, the entertainment's finished here.'

Hereward tried to pull one of them off his horse, but the others encircled him, three of them pointing their sword blades at his throat. One of the riders was Wulfgar. He brought Fleet between the trapped Hereward and us.

'Brokk, take Leofric away before he gets himself killed,' said Wulfgar.

'It wasn't him that ended up on his arse,' said Rush defiantly.

'Just go,' Wulfgar said.

Brokk put his arm around me and ushered me away.

'This will be finished, thegn's boy, however long it takes, this will be finished. Cripple or not, I will have my revenge!' yelled Hereward.

Hereward was still screaming his vitriolic menace at me as we left the fair and made our way back to Æssefeld.

I knew at that moment, something I had known for a long time, though never let myself admit it. I could no longer rely on other people to fight my battles.

It was time to become the warrior I had dreamt of being all my young life.

The time of dreaming must end. It was time to make it happen.

177

Seventeen

On many occasions, I followed Wulfgar to his training place in the forest. I hid in the scrub and watched him go through his routine.

Eventually, I summoned the courage to reveal myself, when he moved swiftly to where I was hiding and thrust his sword into the ground in front of the bush concealing me.

'Well, do you think you could do it?'

Startled, I fell forwards from my crouching position, through the flimsy branches, and landed with my face a finger length from the blade. I felt foolish. Wulfgar loomed above me, his breathing heavy but not laboured. I was surprised how few scars he had on his upper body for a fighting man. He was not huge, like Gudbrand, but his muscles were defined and taut.

'Well, could you?' he repeated, pulling the sword from the ground and wiping the soiled blade on his britches.

I scrambled to my feet. I was nearly nineteen winters old, and although slenderer in build, was slightly taller than Wulfgar. Keeping eye contact, I paused for a moment. 'I could if you trained me.'

'Now why would I want to do that?'

I did not know the answer. I knew I wanted him to, but I hadn't thought why he would.

'Three reasons,' I blurted out before I had even thought of one, never mind three.

'Three reasons and they are?' said Wulfgar, a curious smile almost forming on his serious face.

'One day I will be thegn of Æssefeld and if you want to stay here, you will need my approval. Second, you wouldn't want to have a lord who couldn't fight, would you?'

'And third?' he asked, the smile now barely concealed.

'I would be your friend forever.' I regretted saying that as soon as the words left my lips.

'Firstly, I don't know how long I shall stay here, I have a wandering soul. Second, that's why most lords want me because they can't or no longer want to fight. Third, I don't make friends easily. Few warriors do, friends can be a burden on a battlefield. It is a lonely profession.' The smile disappeared.

'Why do you need that?' he said, touching the wooden crutch with his sword.

'Isn't it obvious?' I replied.

'No. Can you walk without it?'

'Yes, but I limp,' I said defensively.

'Then limp.' He kicked the crutch away abruptly, making me stumble. 'You must learn to conquer the problem, not let the problem conquer you.'

From that day onwards, I stopped using the crutch, unless my mother was around. I did not yet have the courage to openly defy her. Secretly I was reluctant to dispense with it entirely as it had always been part of my life.

'I will train you, Leofric, but the first sign you show of giving up, it will be over. You will never be fleet of foot, but you must become fast with your sword and faster with your mind. Besides, it is a coward who runs from a battle and a fool who runs to one. Think three steps ahead of your opponent. Know what he will do before he does. I have seen men who use two swords, one in either hand, a seax and a long sword. We will build your strength. You will practice until it hurts. Practice some more until it really hurts and practice even more till it stops hurting. At that moment, maybe, just maybe, you will be ready.'

And so, it started.

I came to that clearing in the wet, the sun, and the freezing days of winter; lifting logs, doing press ups, pulling myself up on bars till my muscles burnt and felt if they would tear apart. I practised with a sword in my right hand, cutting, slashing, thrusting. Wulfgar came at me with his sword, I blocked and parried. I learnt to move my body in ways to deceive an opponent, seeming to go one way but moving another. I practised with the seax in my left hand, close work, stabbing, jabbing. Wulfgar became harder as I progressed, punching, kicking, drawing blood more than once.

I practised with both hands, using the long sword to attack, parry and defend. Coaxing the opponent nearer to me, drawing them ever closer, until, quick as an eye blink, stabbed with the seax when he was off guard. Each time, I believed I was improving, Wulfgar would come at me faster, stronger, attempting to get on my left, weaker side, trying to throw me off balance; succeeding.

Frequently, I wanted to stop. Each time Wulfgar knocked me to the ground, putting his sword to my throat saying, 'You're dead,' I thought of the life of a monk, safe, a life of quiet contemplation. I became cut, bruised, deflated.

Perhaps others were right, I was not built to be a warrior.

But eventually, I was.

My upper body strength soared. I became so quick with both hands, it was rare when Wulfgar could find a way through.

Finally, one morning under the boughs of a great oak, my sword blade danced and sang and slipped through the air as delicate as a butterfly in flight, yet as fast as an adder's tongue, mesmerizing Wulfgar as he parried and blocked and leant and swayed to avoid being cut to pieces. Then a rapid lunge, a flick of the wrist and Wulfgar's sword arced into the air, spinning and twisting, and the point of my sword was at Wulfgar's throat.

'Now you're dead,' I said triumphantly.

Wulfgar caught the hilt of his sword as it fell back down.

'And now, you're ready,' he said grinning. 'Now you're ready for the next test whenever that might come.'

'The next test?'

'Practice is fine, but could you kill a man? After all, that's what these are for, Leofric,' he said, tapping his sword on mine. 'It is no easy matter to take another's life. One hesitation could result in you losing yours. I guess we won't know the answer until the time comes and I pray to God that is a long way off.'

On the way back to Æssefeld, I came across a woodsman's fire. I tossed the crutch into the flames and watched with delight as they devoured it, turning it to ash.

I was prepared for my mother's complaints when she saw me limping. Instead, she said nothing. I watched her stumble across the courtyard before sitting on an old bench outside the manor house.

'Mother, are you well?' I asked.

'No, I believe I am not.'

Her face was pallid, her eyes dull, her hands shook uncontrollably. A cough, emanating from deep inside her, sent a pair of doves sitting on the manor roof, soaring around the courtyard. The sound brought Ulla from the manor. Seeing my mother's distress, she went back inside, reappearing moments later with a pottery jug. She raised it to my mother's lips. Mirella sipped at the liquid between sporadic coughing, her face wincing at the taste.

'What is it?' I asked, sniffing at the concoction and recoiling slightly from the smell.

'It is brought from a woman on the outskirts of Horton. Since Nairn left, the locals use her for their charms and potions. She has a good reputation of curing,' said Ulla.

A week later my mother died. When I tried to find the woman from Horton, no one knew of her whereabouts. I was told if anyone needs a potion or salve, different girls bring it each time and they take payment in food and goods. But where they come from or go back to, no one knows or dare ask in case they offend a cunning one.

We buried my mother next to the church, and a month later my father rode into the village with a new wife.

Her name was Silfried. She was twenty-one winters young, the youngest of four daughters of a Wessex thegn. There was no dowry to speak of, which had caused other men to shy away. My father was besotted by her beauty, some folk said bewitched, spellbound. They had married at her father's chapel. When my father introduced us, she said, 'Let us pray I can give you a healthy heir to be proud of, Renweard.'

'Indeed, my dear, indeed,' my father replied.

Silfried and I hardly spoke to one another and avoided each other whenever possible.

The other change in my life was the leaving of Thurstan to continue his career in the Church. Spearhafoc had been elevated to the position of Abbot of Abingdon Abbey and he arranged for Thurstan to be installed as the Prior of Filey Priory.

Ten months later Silfried was pregnant and everything changed.

Eighteen

AD 1050

'**I** don't believe it,' said Wulfgar as he swept through the doorway of my dwelling.

'Believe what?' I said, still only half awake.

'King Edward has pardoned Sweyn Godwinson yet again. What does the man have to do to be banished forever?'

'Why has he pardoned him?' I asked.

'Only God and the king know that,' Wulfgar growled, kicking a chair across the room.

'They say Bishop Ealdred convinced the king that Sweyn is truly repentant for his many sins. The bishop has land close to that of Sweyn's. He needs a strong earl close by to protect his estates from the Wealas. Some men will forgive anything if it suits their purpose. Sweyn has sent men here and they have taken Hakon to the Godwin estate at Boseham.'

I wondered what that would mean for me. To imagine Hakon could become the heir to the vast Godwin estates and eventually Earl of Wessex filled me with dread.

Six months later, in the late summer of AD 1051, my father sent me with Wulfgar to Doferum, to take several cartloads of fleeces to the port to be sent to St. Omer. I carried a letter with me, encouraging Turfrida to remind her father the three years he'd asked us to wait had nearly expired. I would seek out Otto and hopefully, he would give me a letter in return.

The road to Doferum was like most roads, stony in places, a quagmire in others. We stopped twice to repair broken wheels on a couple of the carts, otherwise, the journey was uneventful. We passed a make-shift camp of Norman soldiers on a bend of the River Dour, but they seemed disinterested and watched us trundle past. I wondered why the Norman soldiers were either wearing their mail coats or were in the process of putting them on.

'Bloody foreigners,' Brokk muttered, 'ought to go back to where they came from.'

'I think you'll find that's exactly what they are doing, Brokk,' said Wulfgar. 'That's the banner of Eustace, Count of Boulogne,' he said, pointing towards the largest of the few tents and the red and gold standard standing stiffly in the strong wind. 'Renweard said we might encounter them on our travels. They must be on their way back to Doferum and their ships.'

'Good thing, if you ask me,' said Brokk, 'they're such arrogant bastards. Ever since Edward was king, the country's crawling with bloody Normans. Even the archbishop of Cantwareburh is a bloody Norman. What have they come to Englaland for?'

'Because King Edward invites them, that's why. He's more comfortable with them around him than he is with us English, and they're happy to accept the lands he gives them. Count Eustace was married to Goda, Edward's sister, but then she died,' Wulfgar said.

I said nothing, my mind was on other things. When we got to Doferum we would meet with the men from St. Omer and Otto should, hopefully, have a letter from Turfrida for me. She seemed to fill my mind more than anything else these days. At least a letter would make it feel as if she was nearer to me. The last one I received was nearly half a year ago and I longed to read her words once again.

The day we took our fleeces to the port, all was good in my world. My father's estates were thriving once again, and the arrangement to supply Turfrida's father with fleeces was making him even wealthier. We produced the best fleeces. St. Omer possessed the superior skill to turn them into wool. That strengthened my father's resolve to join our families together in marriage. He still had reservations as to

184

whether I would make a competent thegn, but he could see profit in the union, so he chose to ignore my shortcomings. One day I would show him my new-found prowess with a sword and he would realise his fears were unfounded. I would marry Turfrida and eventually, I would inherit Æssefeld-Underbarroe and breed great war horses. Hakon and Thurstan were out of my life and Earl Harold Godwinson was one of my friends. So, as we arrived towards the end of the valley and Doferum came into our sights, it was with a full heart and high hopes for the future.

The old Saxon hill fort, with its Roman-built lighthouse at its side and the little church next to it, were bathed in early autumn sunlight. Down below, the town buzzed with activity. The sea was frothed up white with the wind and the many boats in the harbour tossed around frantically, their masts waving from side to side like empty barley stalks. We had been glad of the wind, as the fleeces we carried were not the most aromatic of loads, but now it seemed as if it would cause problems and delay the sailings. This didn't concern us greatly as we would only be spending one night here before returning to Æssefeld. Though, the thought of one night on a straw bed under a roof appealed far more than another night in the open.

We drove the carts down to the harbour where Wulfric's man was waiting. His name was Aenoud. He was Flemish, though he spoke both English and French. His blonde hair was cut short, and his pale skin made him stand out against the dark hull of his moored ship. He was a tall man of slim build and held a straight back, making the most of his height. He greeted us warmly and once he checked the fleeces and Wulfgar counted the bag of coins he gave him, he said he would lead us to the lodgings he had found for the night. He ordered three of his men to watch the carts, and once we secured the old tent covers over the fleeces in case of rain, he led us to the town. Brokk left to visit his parent's grave and the rest of us crowded into the small tavern where we supped ale and mead. We left our weapons on a table by the entrance, as is the custom. Brokk eventually joined us and though his mood was sombre at first, he brightened up after an ale or two. He had found out Otto was still on one of the ships and we should go and find him in the morning.

Wulfgar, who had charge of the money, did not drink but sat quietly in a dark recess, although that did not deter two of the local girls from ogling him the whole time.

Aenoud made this trip many times and he introduced me to the Doferum men he had come to know. One man, Oswin, a renown smith, knew my father and we spoke for some time. He talked of the old days when my father was a young warrior, fearless, loyal and ruthless, and he talked of Tripp and battles the three of them fought together. The time passed quickly in good company.

The room was smoky from the fire the landlord kept replenished with the logs he was chopping outside. Each time he came in, someone would call for more ale and he would help his wife and daughter refill the empty flagons and horns. Once they were served, he would go back outside to carry on chopping.

Men threw dice, others arm-wrestled but try as they might no one could beat Brokk. Wealdhere, Oswin's son, an enormous man of height and girth honed in his father's smithy, reckoned he could and left our table to try his luck. The talk turned to the price of corn, the weather and mostly grumbling about one thing and another.

Even above that din, we could hear the shouting outside.

I noticed Wulfgar strain to see out of one of the small windows. He banged the money bag down on the table in front of a flaxen-haired girl, who hadn't taken her eyes off him since we entered. He took a knife, concealed in his boot, and thrust the handle into her hand.

'Anyone touches that bag, stick that in them.'

He cupped his hand around the back of her neck and pulling her to him, roughly kissed her.

'When I come back you will get your reward. You touch one silver penny of it and I'll kill you.'

With that, he was past us to the door. 'Leofric, Brokk, weapons!'

We both responded instantly. I grabbed my sword, Brokk his axe and we bundled through the door, blinking into the bright sunlight.

'Watch you don't cut yourself with that,' Brokk joked, 'if there's any trouble, get behind me.'

Norman knights surrounded the inn. Several were mounted, the rest on foot. One of them was arguing with the landlord. My new-found friend Oswin pushed to the front of the men spilling out of the inn door. With smatterings of broken English it was established that the Normans had demanded free lodgings for all their men. When it was explained that all the accommodation was full, they insisted that because they were on the king's work, all others should be thrown out on to the street. On hearing this, the Doferum men were outraged. One of them spat on the ground at the foot of a Norman.

'Not while I'm alive will we turf good, honest Englishmen out for the likes of you,' he snarled.

From that moment, events turned in a startling and sudden way. A Norman soldier came to the fore, sword unsheathed and in good English said, 'Enough of this, we will lodge where we wish,' and before anyone responded, he struck the landlord on the arm with his blade, causing blood to spill from a deep gash. This brought more shouts of anger from the Doferum men, and as the Normans went to fetch their horses and gear, the landlord grabbed his axe from the woodpile with his good arm, and with one mighty swing, planted it in the back of his attacker. The Norman fell dead to the floor.

Both sets of men drew swords and wielded their spears and axes. The mounted men pushed forward. A spear flew from the Norman side and thudded into the landlord's chest.

'Murder!' came the call from the men of Doferum.

'Treason!' shouted the Normans and fighting broke out all around us.

Wulfgar and I drew our swords and stood back to back as we had practised many times, though this was no practice. Now was the time to show what I had learnt in all those hours of sweat and pain. I imagined the surprise on Brock's face when he saw me in action.

But he never did. All he saw was a Norman horseman bearing down on the thegn's son he protected. As I prepared to parry the thrusting spear and attempt to unseat the rider, Brock, his axe whirling above his head, threw himself in front of me.

'Leofric, watch ou ...'

They were the last words Brokk spoke as the spear pierced his heart through his leather jerkin and out through his back, almost piercing me. I grabbed his shoulders and felt the life speed from my friend. His legs buckled, no longer able to hold his weight, and he fell to the floor. Blood from his wound splattered onto my face.

His killer was gone, his horse pushing through the mass of men that were now everywhere. People from the town, hearing the commotion, flocked to see what was happening. The rest of the Normans mounted their horses and joined the fray, slashing with their swords and thrusting their spears at anyone in reach, whilst the town's folk tried to pull them from their saddles and attack them with whatever they could lay their hands on.

Wulfgar brought two men down and dispatched them like cattle. In my training with Wulfgar, we talked of control, deliberation and keeping calm in a violent situation; all that was forgotten. My eyes were blurred by tears, my heart pounding with rage and grief, my head pulsing with disbelief and my body shaking from shock. I raised my sword above my head, and gripping it with both hands, I set off in a frenzy of hacking. Anything in mail armour that came within my range took the full brunt of slashing steel and iron. How many I killed or wounded that day, I do not know, but at least nineteen Normans died and many others were wounded. The Normans, in turn, killed more than twenty of the townsfolk.

Once news spread that locals had been killed, it seemed the whole town took to the streets seeking revenge. The Normans took flight, racing their horses through the cobbled streets, regardless of any obstacles in their way. A woman dashed into the street to scoop up a crying child standing in the path of a charging mounted knight. She managed to avoid being hit by him, only to step into the path of the Count of Boulogne himself. Both woman and child were trampled to death under the Count's horse and several others that followed him. Not one of them as much as glanced back to see their victim's fate. It was on that day that my hatred for all things Norman was seeded in my heart.

I helped the local priest prepare Brokk's body. We washed the blood from his wound and rubbed oil into his skin. I helped sew up his shroud. I was shocked by the scars of whip marks across his back. When we had swum in the river together, his back was unmarked. I wondered if they were the reason he seemed so sullen and quiet each time he returned from Wydeford.

We buried Brokk next to his father in the churchyard on the hill. I placed the elf-bolt he cherished in his hand and swore on my life to avenge his death. Oswin, too, died in the affray and Wealdhere was inconsolable in his grief. I imagined my father's sadness and anger when he heard the news of both deaths.

The church bells rang mournfully all the following day. Wulfgar and I said our goodbyes to Aenoud and his crew as they set sail for home on a becalmed sea. We set off back to Æssefeld with the supplies Wulfgar purchased with money he recovered from the girl in the inn. He had disappeared into a room upstairs with her, and when they reappeared hours later, he tossed her three coins and said, grinning, 'Your reward as promised.'

She grinned back and kissed him goodbye. I did not understand how he could do such a thing after what had happened and told him so on the road back home.

'We all grieve in different ways, Leofric,' was all he said, and we never spoke of it again.

A group of men were chosen to take an account of what took place to Earl Godwin and the king. They accompanied us until the road forked, and we went our separate ways. The talk was mostly about what the king would do with Eustace when he was told how he had violated the peace of his subjects.

'Banishment,'

'Compensation,'

'Hand him over to us men of Doferum,' was the majority feeling.

'I can see trouble whatever happens,' said Wulfgar.

It wasn't until we were nearly home that I remembered the letters. In the chaos that had erupted, I totally forgot the letter I intended to send to Turfrida and the one I hoped to receive from her. All sorts of questions flew into my head. Had she, in fact, sent a letter? If so, wouldn't she be expecting a reply? What would she think when she did not get one? Would she know I hadn't received hers? I must go to her. That's what I decided to do. Both our fathers would probably object, but I cared little. I would go to Turfrida and she would become my wife.

Nineteen

AD 1051

'**Brokk** and Oswin dead?' Disbelief and sadness were etched in my father's face as we related the events of Doferum.

'Unprovoked, you say?'

'Totally,' said Wulfgar, his fists clenched. 'Something must be done about Eustace and his thugs.'

'Earl Godwin will have something to say on the matter, I'm sure. We will wait until we learn his intentions,' replied my father, and we left him to grieve on his own.

We did not have to wait long for Earl Godwin's reaction. Two days later a courier came from the earl with a letter and left as soon as he placed it in my father's hand to deliver identical letters to all the thegns on Godwin's estates. My father was distraught as Leafwold read the letter, his voice faltering as he told him to read it out loud to the rest of us. It read:

"*A few days ago, unwarranted atrocities were carried out against the good folk of Doferum town by Eustace, the Count of Boulogne, and his knights. I, as earl of that domain, sought an audience with our good King Edward and asked what measures he would be taking against the count. It seems that Eustace got to the king first and related a different version of events. He claimed his men were set upon for no reason other than they were Normans and* had to flee back to the king for his protection. The king, mortified that his guests and kin were treated in such a manner, has instructed me, no, commanded me, to attack and lay waste Doferum and all that surrounds it without delay."

At those words, Leafwold paused as everyone listening gasped at what they were hearing. Wulfgar and I looked at one another, not believing the king could take the word of this Norman against his own subjects. My father told Leafwold to continue:

"I, Earl Godwin, refused to do such a thing and pleaded with the king to allow the men of Doferum to tell their side of the matter. He has rejected this out of hand and has called for a meeting of all the great men of our land to a council at Glowecestre, on the eighth day of September before the feast of Saint Mary, to charge me with acting against the king's demands. I call upon all my loyal thegns and their followers to join me at Long-trees, from where we will go to the king and show him that all freemen of this realm disapprove of such actions, and demand that Count Eustace be delivered into our hands forthwith.

Your Lord and Protector, Earl Godwin."

At first, there was a shocked silence, quickly changing to murmuring, trepidation, anger. All there knew that Renweard would obey his earl, and they would obey their thegn.

The next day Renweard, Thegn of Æssefeld-Underbarroe and a substantial body of men, including Wulfgar and me, made their way to the ancient meeting place at Long-trees to meet their earl. All the other thegns from Godwin's numerous estates met us there, and the enormity of the situation became truly evident when we were joined by Earl Sweyn and Earl Harold and all their followers. This was indeed a vast army of men and could only be interpreted one way by the king. In our camp the feeling of unease became undeniable. To seek justice from their king seemed a reasonable thing to do, but this was an obvious threat of aggression against their sovereign lord and possible treason.

News came that Edward had sent for Earls Leofric, Siward and Ralf. They, in turn, on seeing the size of Godwin's army, sent for more of their men. We listened to this news as we sat around one of the fires scattered around our camp. Godwin and Harold walked amongst the men, encouraging their thegns to stand firm in the name of justice and right. They came to where we sat and Godwin became deep in conversation with my father, whilst Harold sat by me and Wulfgar. He sipped mead and sat staring at the flames flickering in the slight breeze, watching the thin wisps of smoke curl up towards the star-bright sky. The bustling sounds of camp life were intertwined by the voices of priests chanting their supplications to God. Godwin had brought his friend Stigand, Bishop of Wintanceaster with him to give spiritual credence to the proceedings. My father swore that he himself was more a man of God than Stigand, who had bought his way into the position, being the third richest man in Englaland after the king and Earl Godwin. The bishop had set up a temporary altar complete with a jewelled cross, and his priests sang and gave absolution to those who may have to take other men's lives.

'You were there at Doferum,' Harold stared at Wulfgar as he spoke. Wulfgar stared at the ground and moved his head to avoid Harold's gaze.

'I was sorry to learn of Brokk's fate, I knew you had grown fond of him, Leofric.'

'I had, my lord, he was a loyal friend. What the Normans did that day was unforgivable,' I said.

'I was told you fought well, Leofric. Still set on being a warrior I fear?'

'Yes, my lord.'

'You too, Wulfgar. I am told your skill with a sword was impressive. Where did you learn to fight?'

'I am a fyrd-man, lord, I train daily.'

'More than simply a fyrd-man I wager from the reports I received from the Doferum men.'

Wulfgar ignored Harold and did not reply.

'You both may soon get another chance to show your prowess. It seems what occurred at Doferum may have been more contrived than we first thought,' said Harold, casting his gaze to the fire as though he would find solutions to the situation within its glowing centre.

'There are those that feel us Godwins enjoy too much power and they wish to undermine my father's standing with the king, though Edward hardly needs any encouragement in that. The new Archbishop, Robert, feels my father has cheated the Church out of land and he has the ear of the king constantly. There are others who would benefit from the demise of our family and I fear we are playing into their hands. My father is reluctant to wage war against his king and his fellow countrymen. Make no mistake, that is the way this situation is heading. Once news of this is well known, our enemies across the sea will rub their hands in glee. Englaland's finest warriors slaughtering one another will leave its riches exposed to all. Talk and reason is the only solution to this dilemma.'

'Talk and reason are for weaklings and procrastinators. We must strike now whilst we have the strength of numbers. It is futile talking to a king that does not listen.'

The harsh words of Sweyn Godwinson disturbed the night. With a swirl of his cloak and bright mail glinting in the firelight, the earl appeared behind his brother Harold. He was flanked by his newly claimed son Hakon and the giant figure of Gudbrand.

I noticed Wulfgar's expression changed to one of vexation. His hand slid beneath his cloak to the hilt of his seax.

'The news is that more men come from the north to rally behind their earls. Strike now before they arrive, and victory will be ours. Father, my men are ready to defend your honour against this feeble king.'

'And I do appreciate their loyalty and courage, Sweyn,' said Godwin, 'but Harold is right. To cause war with our own countrymen would only mean disaster for Englaland and victory for our enemies. Edward is not feeble, ill-advised and short-sighted, yes. We must try our utmost to change that. If there is no other way to resolve this than by fighting, fight we will, but talk will come first.'

'When you've finished talking, let me know. At least you can be sure you have one son who is not afraid to fight for you!' said Sweyn, looking purposely at Harold.

194

Harold said nothing and resisted retaliating against his brother. The last thing Godwin wanted was his sons at each other's throats, though by his expression, it was clear to all that Harold was seething.

Sweyn and Gudbrand left us. Hakon came and stood by me.

'Come, walk with me, Leofric. Let's talk of good times past.'

Wulfgar leant towards me, bringing his empty hand from beneath his cloak, and whispered, 'Watch the bastard; he'll be up to something.'

'I'll be fine,' I replied.

We had only walked a short distance, up onto a ridge that sloped down towards Glowecestre where the king's forces were camped when Hakon returned to his true self.

'When I say walk, I'll walk, you'll limp, won't you cripple?' I ignored him. Now he was back in the fold of the Godwins, for a mere thegn's son to strike him would bring certain punishment.

'Things have changed since last we saw each other, cripple. Power, Leofric, is a wonderful thing. Amazing what people will do to have one of the Godwins as an ally. Now I am in my rightful place at my grandfather's side, I am treated with the respect I deserve. You should remember that, you pathetic hobbler.'

'I have always thought respect was earned by one's deeds, not simply by the name one carries,' I replied. It was Hakon's turn to ignore me.

'Talking of names, Hop-along, I believe you were keen to make one for yourself at Doferum. You always were lucky when it comes to combat. Pity you were not lucky enough to save that oafish friend of yours. Still, there's always the Church. That's where you belong, Leofric, out of harm's way in a monastery somewhere. You can leave the fighting to real men. In fact, I have already taken steps to make that happen for you. No need to thank me, cripple, indeed, what are friends for?'

I could take his taunting no longer and I reached to grab him but without warning he pushed me hard, catching me off balance, sending me tumbling off the ridge and down the steep hillside. I heard him laugh as I rolled head over heels down the hill until I came to an ungainly stop in a clump of wild brambles. I tore my britches as I freed myself from their prickly grasp. My tunic was smeared with mud. Only my pride was hurt.

There was no sign of Hakon, so I decided to walk across the hill to where the ascent was less steep. I walked only a short distance when I could make out shapes moving down towards the river. As I got closer, I realised they were men, about fifty in all, slipping away in the dark. One of them noticed me and mistook me for a peasant.

'What's happening?' I asked.

'This cause is lost, friend. We will not fight against the king, it's treason, that's what. You'll go too if you've got any sense,' and they were gone, spirited away into the night. I carried on around the hillside, eventually coming back up onto the ridge on the far side of the camp. I found Wulfgar amongst the tents searching for me.

'What happened to you?' he said, seeing my dishevelled state, 'and where is that bastard, Hakon?'

'He pushed me off the ridge,' I said embarrassed that I had been caught unawares. 'Don't worry, I will get my revenge.'

'Don't tarry over it, you may not get the opportunity much longer,' said Wulfgar menacingly.

'What do you mean?' I asked, but he did not answer.

'I have seen men deserting,' I said.

'I know, it's happening all over the camp.'

In fact, the next day it was obvious our numbers had dwindled considerably. Furthermore, reports came in that many reinforcements had joined Earls Leofric and Siward from the north, and the king's nephew, Ralf of Mantes, had arrived with his men. So, when both our forces faced each other on opposite sides of the Temes, Earl Godwin was in a weakened position.

And King Edward knew it.

Later that day, as both armies waited on their leader's instructions, an emissary, flanked by twenty housecarles, rode out from the king across the bridge. The emissary, one of the king's thegns, dismounted in front of our lines and bowed in respect to Earl Godwin and his sons. He unfurled a parchment and read:

196

"The King demands that you disband this rebellious gathering of men at once and that Earl Godwin is summoned to a meeting of the King's council of high-ranking men at the autumn equinox in Lundene to answer to charges of rebellion towards the King. He also declares Sweyn Godwinson an outlaw from this moment on for crimes against the King and the realm. He also demands two hostages to make sure these conditions are adhered to, namely Wulfnoth; youngest child of Earl Godwin, and Hakon; only child of Sweyn Godwinson, the former Earl of Herefordscir."

Four of the housecarles came forward. Godwin's face coloured with rage, but he knew he must comply, or attack the king, which he realized was not an option he could now take without certain defeat.

'Tell our most noble king that we will not disband until Doferum is avenged by the handing over Eustace, the Count of Boulogne, to us to stand trial for murder. In all other things but this, we will comply. We will send word for my grandson Wulfnoth to be delivered to the king and Hakon will go with you now.' He turned and beckoned Hakon towards him.

Hakon's face was distorted with disbelief. Just as he had gained what he had always desired, it was being taken from him so soon. He moved forward slowly and as he passed in front of me said softly, 'Your fate is already sealed, you deformed cripple.'

His grandfather took Hakon's hand and grasping his shoulder said, 'It will be for a brief time only, Hakon, until we resolve this situation. Stay firm, stay loyal and watch over Wulfnoth for me.'

Hakon was led off to join the housecarles. Sweyn rode his horse up and down our front line swinging his sword in the air, cursing and shouting at anyone who would listen.

'I told you we should have attacked when we had the chance. Yellow livered, the whole, whoring lot of you.'

Godwin rode up to him and grabbed the reins of his horse. 'Sweyn, your involvement in this affair is over. You must leave it to Harold and me to talk reason with the king. Go back to Boseham and we will join you when this is over.'

'Talking, always talking, well, you have the right son with you for talking, Godwin. My real father, King Cnut, took this land by fighting, not talking. All you could sire was a chatterer.'

Harold began to draw his sword from its scabbard, angry to have to uphold his mother's and father's integrity. Godwin grabbed his wrist to prevent him.

'We've enough problems without fighting amongst ourselves. Sweyn is angry, leave him, Harold, it will wait for another day.'

Sweyn spat on the ground in front of his kin in disgust, whirled his horse around and rode off towards the family manor at Boseham.

We watched as Hakon was led away to the king's ranks, and I wondered what Earl Godwin would do next.

Twenty

Earl Godwin requested that Bishop Stigand should be allowed to return with the king's men, to act as mediator between us and the king. This was agreed, whereupon another of the king's emissaries unrolled a second parchment, and read it out:

"King Edward, Lord over all this land, calls out the general fyrd as it is his right to do so in times of national urgency. All able men who are duty bound to serve in this capacity, will gather at the King's side forthwith or forfeit their rights as freemen."

The emissary rode the full length of our forces back and forth three times repeating this command so all would hear, before joining the rest of his comrades and riding back to the king.

To disobey this command was once again an act of treason. So, men willing to serve their earl, reluctantly changed sides, as they joined the king's call for the fyrd. Earl Godwin could do nothing. He had come here to reason with the king. Might and right had been on his side, and now his forces were diminishing, the right seemed to count as nothing. Harold's fyrd-men started to drift away. I rode next to Wulfgar, officially our fyrd-man.

'Will you go?' I asked him.

'Your father is my lord, Edward is my king. I have served Godwin's kin since I was a boy, I have unfinished business with them, so I will stay for now,' he said, though there was uncertainty in his voice. He noticed my puzzled look and turned his face away from me.

'At least my father is his own man and he will stay loyal to this cause,' I said loudly, so those who were undecided on what action to take would hear. Renweard glowered at me and I could see he, too, was agitated.

'Keep your own counsel,' he snapped. That was the first time I wondered about my father's resolve in this matter. I was certain of mine and a sense of foreboding came upon me. Eldred, the Thegn of Wydeford rode up next to my father and they mumbled something to each other. Other thegns loyal to my father gathered around us and there were heated words between them. Godwin, who had been riding amongst the men encouraging them to stay firm, noticed the disturbance and rode over to join us.

'Renweard, you will remain steadfast to us in this endeavour I trust?' It was more a statement than a question.

'My lord, I think you are about to have the answer to that soon.'

As my father spoke, I became aware of more riders approaching from the king's side. One of them was Earl Leofric of Mercia. On either side of him were emissaries carrying further roles of parchment and behind them a group of armed housecarles. Godwin and Harold moved slightly in front of us ready to hear the latest demands of the king. It was Earl Leofric who spoke first.

'Earl Godwin, the king is earnest in his desire to prevent the spilling of English blood. He decrees that you should disband this rebellious force and attend a trial where you and this matter will be heard without prejudice by the Witan. Failure to comply with these demands will result in you and your kin being exiled from this realm, and you will forfeit all your land and any positions you or they hold.'

Godwin cursed, knowing he was left with little option but to agree to such terms.

'We will comply with the king's demands, but we ask for hostages and assurances that we will attend such a meeting without danger.'

Earl Leofric nodded in acknowledgement of Godwin's request. 'I shall convey your wishes to the king, Lord Godwin,' he said, but the tone of his voice conveyed he had little faith in the king complying to such demands.

As soon as Earl Leofric had finished talking, the two emissaries moved forward. One of them opened his roll of parchment and read:

"King Edward demands that all thegns in possession of land bequeathed by the King and all those bound to the King by oaths and charters, will, from this moment, leave this rebellious horde and join him and his loyal subjects."

Once he had finished reading, he rolled the parchment back up and returned to Earl Leofric. There were mumbling and murmurings amongst our number, as thegns and their men argued as to what course they should take. Godwin and Harold both rode up and down to encourage, cajole, even threaten men to stay, but, one by one, the thegns and their followers left our ranks and headed down towards the river and the king. Soon all that remained were the personal retinues of Harold and his father and those thegns who held land in their own right and not affiliated to the king. My father was one such man, the proud owner of land won by his ancestors when the Saxons first came to this island and held over many generations and passed from father to son. Several thegns came riding up to my father, all seemed troubled by this latest development. In truth, so did my father. Harold joined them.

'Renweard, nothing is amiss, I trust?'

Harold knew that many of these men respected Renweard and trusted his judgement. He knew he needed to keep him on their side. 'My father has always been a good and true lord to you, has he not?' said Harold.

'He has, my lord.'

'I trust you will stay firm?'

'I fear not,' replied my father. I could hardly believe what he was saying.

'Father remember Brokk and Oswin. We must stand against injustice,' I blurted out.

'Leofric is right, Renweard, we must stand against this king,' added Harold.

'I am afraid I have no choice, lord,' replied my father, and I noticed as he spoke, the second emissary was unfurling yet another roll of parchment.

"King Edward has instructed me to bring to the attention of Renweard, Thegn of Æssefeld-Underbarroe, this document which is a written oath signed by him and other named thegns in front of witnesses. The contents of the said document state that all those whose signature or mark appears here," at which the emissary poked a finger at the document, "will forego all other rights and charters and bestow all their allegiance and support to Edward, King of Englaland, against all others. Failure to do this, will force the King to rekindle charges most grave against all those stated here, that if proven, could result in the loss of all privileges, land, wealth and even life. The King commands all concerned to leave this band of traitors and join his forces henceforth."

Godwin had now joined his son and they both confronted my father.

'What is this, Renweard, what charges does he speak of?' raged Godwin.

'It was a long time ago, my lord, and nothing was ever proven, though no doubt they will make sure they have proof enough now.'

'Proof of what?' demanded Harold, but my father was already riding towards the king's forces and all his men and the other thegns and their followers left with him. I spurred my horse on to be next to my father.

'Father, we must stay, it is the right thing to do!' I pleaded.

'I signed an oath to the king, Leofric, I have no choice but to join him.'

'You might have signed, father, but I did not. I will not side with a king who favours lying Normans over his own loyal subjects. I will not go with you.'

'Yes, you will. You will obey your father and stop this nonsense.'

He reached out to grab the reins of my horse, but I pulled away before he could, and spun the horse around and galloped off back to Harold. Wulfgar said nothing but remained with my father.

I was in turmoil. All my young life I had striven to make my father proud of the son he despaired of. Now, I had not only disobeyed him but deserted him in front of his men and his peers to side with another. It was a question of loyalty, but what should one be loyal to? A person, out of love and duty, or what you believe to be right and just? If I was to be loyal to my father, wouldn't I be disloyal to Brokk, taking sides with the men that had caused his death? My heart was heavy, my mouth dry, I felt sick in my stomach, though my mind was resolute, and I spurred my horse on toward Earl Godwin and Harold. The remaining men cheered as I joined them, though they knew one man would make no difference at all to what was now becoming a lost cause. Harold greeted me with a slap on the back, Earl Godwin nodded. We were now hopelessly outnumbered, so much so that the king turned his army and they rode back towards Lundene, knowing that the threat of war was gone. It was now a case of whether Godwin complied with the king's demands to attend what was now to be his trial against the charge of treason.

We also left the banks of the Temes and made our way to Godwin's manor at Suþgeweorc. Two messengers were sent to the king, asking again for assurances for Godwin's safety if he attended the trial. Both men came back with the same answer; Bishop Stigand will be sent to Godwin with all terms and conditions to ensure him a safe attendance at the trial.

We stayed at Suþgeweorc for some days. I walked with Harold many times and we talked about the ordinary things of life. He spoke lovingly of Edythe, his handfast wife, and their children. Especially the pride he felt for his son Godwin and the plans he had for his future. I was jealous of that love and wished my father had felt those things for me. I wondered what he was thinking about me now and whether we could ever be reconciled.

It was on one such walk that Harold said, 'That's it, the eyes.'

'Whose eyes, my lord?' I said, not having any idea of what or who he was talking about.

'I was thinking how when I first met Edythe, it was her eyes that I first noticed about her. I suddenly realised where I had seen your friend Wulfgar before; Beorn, my cousin. Wulfgar was one of his three bodyguards, I'm sure of it. Never seen his face, always hidden behind those helmets they wore, but the eyes, never still, always searching for danger and with a steely determination about them. I knew I had seen him before.'

'Beorn's bodyguard? Are you sure, my lord? I thought they were all killed along with Beorn.'

'So did we all, Leofric, though only one body was found, the other two we presumed had been thrown into the sea. The question now is, what is Wulfgar up to? Why did he come to your village? And what part did he play in Beorn's death? As soon as this mess is sorted, I'll be having a word with Wulfgar, that is a promise.'

As he spoke his hand gripped the pommel of his sword and I understood his meaning. I, too, wondered about Wulfgar. I did not want to believe he had anything to do with Beorn's murder and I hoped I met him before Harold did.

When Harold was too occupied with his father and brothers discussing what options were left to them, I walked alone. Often my thoughts turned back to Turfrida and I vowed to myself again to go to her once this situation was resolved. It was on one such walk down by the River Temes, I saw riders coming over the bridge. I could tell from the banners they carried that it was Bishop Stigand and I took the news to the earls as quickly as I could.

Earl Godwin and his sons, Sweyn, who had come up from Boseham, Harold, Tostig, Gyrth and Leofwine, were all gathered around a table in the great hall. Godwin's wife, Gytha and Tostig's new bride, Judith of Flanders, sat behind them, in front of a smouldering log fire. As I entered Sweyn snarled, 'What does that dog's turd want?' Everyone cast their gaze at me.

'Leave him be, Sweyn, he stayed loyal to this family when many others did not,' said Harold, striding towards me. 'Ignore my churlish brother, Leofric, what is it?'

'Bishop Stigand is here,' I said.

'Perhaps he brings good news,' said Harold, unconvincingly.

Moments later, the doors flew open and Stigand and his retinue entered the hall.

'Greetings, Stigand, you bring good news from the king I hope,' said Godwin, before taking a swig of mead.

'I do indeed bring news, lord earl, but I can hardly bring myself to speak it,' said Stigand, his voice noticeably shaky. Everyone in the room knew at that moment all was lost.

'Spit it out man,' growled Godwin, all patience now gone.

Stigand continued slowly, tears rolling down his cheeks as he delivered the message to his friend.

'The king says you may only gain his peace if you deliver his brother Alfred and all those who died with him alive, and all their possessions that were taken from them, both when they were alive and dead. Only then will he grant you safe passage to your trial.'

With that Stigand fell to his knees and said, 'Forgive me, my old friend.'

Godwin stood up and pushed the table away from him, spilling mead cups and sending parchment rolls flying.

'We are finished here for now. Sweyn, Tostig, and Gyrth will come with me to Boseham and on to Flanders as planned. Harold and Leofwine will go to Ireland.'

Sweyn turned to Harold, 'I have ships waiting at Brycgstow, take them, we will discuss payment for them later.'

'As always, the generous brother,' said Harold with a shake of his head. 'Leofric, you must return to your father.'

'But, lord!' I protested.

He placed his hand on my shoulder, gripping it firmly.

'We will need all the friends we can find in this land, preparing for when we make our return.' He took both my hands and held them out in front of me. 'When we stood on the banks of the Temes, we were joined by hundreds of men skilled at warfare. Only a hand full of them had the ability you possess. Not with your sword, Leofric, but your ability to read and write. The Abbot Thurstan told me you have exceptional skill in these hands and in here,' he tapped me on the head. 'A keen eye, a steady hand and a quick mind is how he put it, though he also mentioned a rebellious streak that needed to be curbed. I see that as the exuberance of youth that needs to be pointed in the right direction. You are not built to be a great warrior, Leofric,' he said looking at my left leg. 'Besides, there is only one destiny for a warrior and that is death. I am sure you are destined for great things, but with the quill, not the sword. Go back to your father, beg his forgiveness, continue in your studies, and when we return, I will send for you. Godspeed.'

And with that, he walked from the hall, mounted the horse prepared for him, and left with his brother Leofwine for the coast.

I stood and watched them until they were out of sight. I loved Harold Godwinson like an older brother. I respected his opinion and values, but I knew he was wrong about me. Most seemed to have decided that my vocation was with the Church. Most, that is, except me and possibly Wulfgar, though I now realised I knew little about him. One thing I did know for certain, he was a skilled warrior and he had taught me well. My leg did slow me down, it was true, but I would sharpen other skills to compensate for it. I would become that warrior I craved to be, and nothing, nothing would stop me.

Twenty-one

AD 1071

Having left Linden behind us, we followed an ancient drove road which crosses the Linden Wolds. It took us high above the surrounding land and we have taken shelter in a small copse. There are one or two small villages dotted bellow us. We have been living on wild berries and the occasional hare, but yesterday we took a sheep from a shepherd-less flock. Hunger has made us bold and we have lit a fire and made a makeshift spit to turn the meat. The aroma is intoxicating and is making my lips and tongue wet in anticipation.

I need to stop writing as Wulfgar has warned us horsemen are approaching.

We had planned for such an event. I grabbed my bow and quiver and hurried to the edge of the trees. Four horsemen came thundering up the hill. They speeded up as they saw two idiots, Scand and Wregan, chasing sheep. One of the riders unsheathed his sword, the other prepared to launch his spear. I took five arrows from the quiver and stuck four of them in the ground in front of me. I nocked the fifth, aimed and waited. Wulfgar and Edwin ran out of the far end of the trees, close to the riders.

'Normans!' shouted Wulfgar. On that confirmation, I let loose the arrow. As soon as it left the bow, I grabbed another, nocked, loosed; pulled the third from the ground, nocked, loosed. All three arrows found their mark. Two of the Normans crashed onto the sheep-grazed turf. A third slumped backwards but remained in the saddle caught by his stirrups. As soon as the second rider was hit, the fourth reined his horse away from the others, and by the time I had nocked the fourth arrow, he was already out of bowshot range, heading back down the hill.

'Shit, he will raise the alarm,' said Wulfgar as he took two swords and a spear from the dead men. 'We will have to move on before they come for us.'

He was right, but we now have three horses which we eventually rounded up. Edwin and the others dislodged the dead man's feet from the stirrups and pulled him off his mount. It was decided I would ride one horse, Thurstan another and the other four men would take turns riding the third. It was not ideal, but it would make us that little bit quicker and allow us to rest our feet and legs. We cut as much meat off the sheep as possible, doused the fire and headed north towards the River Humbre.

We have made good speed and have stopped to rest in the shelter of a small copse of alder and young beech trees. As I dip the goose quill into oak gall ink, I cast my mind back to when I rode back to my father, unsure of his welcome.

ᛏᚺᚱᛗᛗ ᚷᚪᚠᚺ ᚠᚱᚱᚠᛈᚺ

AD 1051

I arrived at Æssefeld as others were drifting back from their king's duty. No one stopped me entering the village gates, though nobody greeted me either. Folk I had known for years ignored my passing. I called to one of the stable boys to take my horse, but he turned his back and entered the stable. My stepmother stood at the door of the manor house, her week-old baby snuggled in her arms.

'You're not welcome here, Leofric.'

'Perhaps not,' I replied, 'but I am still the thegn's son and I wish to speak with him.'

'So is Edgard, aren't you, my sweet?' she cooed to the child. 'Leofric, are you not pleased for your father, that at last he has a healthy son he can be proud of?' She did not wait for my answer, taking the child inside the manor.

My few possessions had been moved out of the main house and into the dwelling I used to share with Thurstan and Hakon. I guessed my stay in the village would be brief. I slept for hours, exhausted from my journey and the week's events.

It was dark when I woke. A figure stood in the doorway, a silhouette against a moon-filled night. It was Mair.

I had not seen her for a while. She was taller; the flat chest of a girl replaced with the rise and fall of a woman's breasts. A dead hare lay at her feet, its entrails spilling out onto the rush-strewn floor. She stared at me with those large, intense eyes. I wore nothing but my britches, and my amulet hung around my neck. She clutched at her chest, feeling for something under her shift.

'You must leave Æssefeld today,' she said eventually. 'The night will hold danger.'

Her breath was like smoke as it met the cold air and her voice, otherworldly and distant. The shape of her lithe body was visible through the white shift, which was speckled with the hare's blood.

'I plan to leave in a few days' time. I will go to Turfrida and we shall be married.'

'You must leave today, at first light,' she said. She stooped down and scooped bits of the entrails into her hand and poked them with the fingers of the other. 'There will be darkness and loneliness in your days, but Mair will find you. Mair is your destiny, Leofric. To fight against the fates is useless.'

I stood up from my straw bed and shouted at her, 'My life is to be with Turfrida, Mair, not with you. She knows the magic arts too, she will weave her spells and we will be together always. Now be gone before I take my sword to you.'

'Turfrida's magic is from books, words of others without soul and without power. Mair sees things that are yet to be, things that are not written with quill and ink, but have their existence in the fabric of time; things men have no power over, things that men can only marvel at and submit to their will. There will be no, you and Turfrida, Leofric, only darkness and loneliness, but I will find you, I will find you!'

She walked away. I moved to the doorway, but she had melted into the night. I glanced at the carcass of the dead hare, for any message or sign, but I could only see blood and gore, so I flung it outside for the dogs or carrion to eat at first light.

I slept little after that, wondering what I should do next and what I would say to my father. I gave little thought to Mair. Her presence had disturbed me as always, but I gave little heed to her mad ramblings. I had learnt from Turfrida that magic was an illusion, trickery, letting people believe what they wanted to, or pandering to their fears. I was more puzzled by the feeling of arousal I had experienced at the sight of Mair and how it made me loathe myself.

As I lay there, sunlight streaming through the open door, I heard voices outside. I looked out to see my father had returned. He was met by his wife and new son. After embracing, he glanced fleetingly across to where I was, then entered his hall. I dressed in my war gear and spent time cleaning my sword and mail shirt. I polished my helmet until my face looked back at me and used my bone comb to pull the knots and stray fleas and lice from my hair. Eventually, I stepped outside and strode, as purposefully as my limp allowed, to my father's hall. He was sitting on his chair in front of the embroidery of the weeping lady. The eyes of the skeleton on the warrior's helmet watching me as always. Grim and Leafwold sat either side of my father, assessing me derisively. Behind them stood several leading men of my father's estates.

'You look the part, I'll give you that,' my father said, 'Harold must be proud of you.' I sensed the sarcasm in his voice.

'Harold has gone to Ireland,' I said.

'I know. The king sent Earl Ralf and others to arrest him and his kin, but they managed to evade them. So, now I suppose you have come to beg forgiveness from your father.'

'Would you expect the son of Renweard, Thegn of Æssefeld-Underbarroe to beg anyone, my lord? I had a choice to make. I was once told always be true to yourself. It was the king I chose against, not you, father.'

'You made me appear foolish, Leofric. How can I command the respect of men when my own son disobeys me?' His eyes blazed with anger, yet I sensed we both understood each other's position, though I feared there was no way out of this situation for either of us with our honour intact. 'There are many who believe I should disown you and disinherit you from your birth-right.' Leafwold nodded in agreement. 'What do you say to that?'

'I say that you will make that decision without the help of others, and I will abide by that decision, but whoever you give it to must be prepared for me to take it back once you have departed this earth.'

'I do believe you would try,' he said nodding. I thought I detected a smile, but it might have been a grimace.

'The truth is, Leofric, the arrangement I have made with Wulfric Rabel is too good to forfeit. You will marry Turfrida and our estates will be merged, and we will grow fat on the proceeds. Cross me again and I swear I will disinherit you from all my estates and possessions, and I will make sure it is so legally binding that any attempt to get it back will brand you a criminal and a nithing in the eyes of the law.'

'I bow to Renweard's wisdom,' I said. 'You will be pleased to know that I plan to go to St. Omer tomorrow and claim Turfrida as my bride.'

Renweard sighed deeply. 'Are you telling me her father has sent for you?'

'No, but Wulfric said three years and that has passed. I have decided we have waited long enough.'

Renweard stood from his chair both fists clenched tight.

'Hell's fire,' he roared, 'is there no limit to this youth's arrogance and foolishness? Have you listened to anything I have said? Wulfric told you, he and I will decide when you can marry his daughter. To return there before we make that decision would be an insult to our authority. It would jeopardize all the hard work we have done to bring about our merger together. If you are going to be a thegn, Leofric, you must use your head to think with, not the member between your legs. You will stay here. You will learn more about the duty of a thegn and you will prove your loyalty to me. I have a letter here giving my permission for you to wed. I will place it in the safe hands of Leafwold, and when he decides your loyalty is proven, he will give it to you, and only when that happens will you be free to go to your intended, and with my blessing, seek her father's permission.'

Leafwold took the letter and grinned. 'It'll take something for you to impress me.'

'But, Father,' I protested.

Leafwold disliked me. He thought I was weak and he held a grudge of many years, he would do anything to keep that letter from me and all those present knew it.

'No buts, Leofric, you will do this, or I will wipe my hands of you. Now go.'

I knew it was pointless to argue further, so nodded in respect and left. I walked across the courtyard and headed for Wulfgar's hut. As I reached his door, Wulfgar and two other men came out. 'Leofric, you're back.'

'Yes, I'm back. I need to speak with you, Wulfgar.'

'I have been summoned to Renweard. As soon as he is finished with me, I will come to you,' he replied.

The other men carried on walking and I grabbed Wulfgar by the arm. 'Earl Harold says you were involved in Beorn's murder. Is it true?'

'Yes, Leofric, I was involved, but I did not murder him.'

'Wulfgar! come on, you know Renweard's in a foul mood. Hurry up,' one of the men shouted.

'I must go. I will explain all to you later.'

He pulled his arm free and went to my father. I returned to my dwelling, to think hard on what course to take next. Should I defy my father again and go to Turfrida as I had planned, or do I remain and do as my father bids? Do I wait and see what happens to Godwin and his kin?

After a while, the sound of horsemen riding across the courtyard took me to the doorway and I watched Wulfgar and about eight others leave through the gates. I was surprised to see someone else I had not seen for many a year. It was Lugna, Nairn's man. He carried a lamb under one arm and moved furtively between the dwellings. I wondered why he was here and if Nairn was with him or nearby. There were rumours she dwelt deep in the forest, where folk still went to her for cures and potions.

After much thought, I decided I would do as my father asked for now but would write to Turfrida and explain why I did not send a letter with Otto on his last voyage and to tell her what my plans were. As soon as the next load of fleeces were sent to Doferum, I would make sure the letter was taken. I removed my war gear and spent the rest of the day writing my thoughts down on the best parchment I could find. I used a thin wafer of animal bone to scratch out the words which did not convey my real feelings. I found it the most difficult piece of writing I had ever attempted. It sounded either too sentimental, or too matter of fact, or too forward. I scratched at it so much that I was in danger of making holes in the parchment.

As the daylight dimmed, I lit the little lamp, filled with sheep fat, and a candle. The hoot of an owl and a dog barking somewhere across the village replaced the noises of the day. My concentration was disturbed by a sound outside the open doorway.

'Is that you, Wulfgar?' I called, though I hadn't heard any horses returning. There was no reply. I returned to my writing, taking great care with each individual letter. I was desperate to impress, knowing Turfrida herself was such a competent scribe. There was the noise again. Perhaps it's Mair, I thought, returning with her warnings of despair.

'Who's there?' I shouted. Still no answer. I reached over to my sword and slipped it quietly from its fleece-lined scabbard. I reached across and snuffed out the candle with the tip of my sword and blew out the small flame from the little lamp. Moving slowly to the doorway, I cautiously stepped out, my blade ready to slash at anything untoward.

'Leofric, here.' A hooded figure beckoned me forward. It was too dark to make out the face.

'Who's that?' I challenged. I was about to move forward when something struck me on the back of the head. My legs gave way. It became dark, then dazzling white and dark again. Arms from behind me encircled my body tightly, preventing me falling or struggling, and my wrist was rapped hard by a stick or club, making me drop my sword. I tried to shout, but a rag was stuffed into my mouth. A sack was thrust over me and pulled down to my waist. I kicked out with my right leg and a man groaned as I connected with something. Thud, another blow to my head and everything turned black.

I came too, momentarily. I was lying down, the sack still over my head, the rough material of the gag cutting into my lip. My arms were bound to my sides. I heard the sound of creaking cartwheels moving along a bumpy road or track as I was tossed about from side to side. My head ached and before long I slipped back into the darkness. This happened on a couple of occasions, drifting in and out. How long we were on the road, I do not know, I think days more than hours. At one point, there were raised voices, men arguing, then silence. We finally stopped, there was a hushed conversation. Someone grabbed my legs and pulled me across the cart. I was carried by my torso and legs, men grunting and gasping as they struggled with my weight. A door opened, its hinges squeaking. On the count of three, I was swung in the air and landed on something soft, which I later found out were dry rushes.

The door slammed shut.

I lay there, the smell of my own urine was overpowering, my head felt as if it was splitting in two. I hadn't eaten or drank in days. I wondered who had done this thing to me and why. Where was I? If someone wanted rid of me, why was I not dead? There were many questions I could not answer. All I did know was that I was in total darkness and I was alone and before I lost consciousness once more, I thought of Mair.

Twenty-two

I opened my eyes and looked at the round, smiling face of a monk. He was kneeling beside me cradling my head in his arms. My hands were tied together in front of me, and my foot was shackled. I ached all over, with barely the strength to move. My head still throbbed. I touched it, feeling a rough bandage and dried, hard blood. I had been stripped of my clothes and was wearing the same type of black woollen habit as the monk. The room was dark, lit by a solitary candle.

'Where am I?'

'The priory, of course,' said the monk. 'Drink this, you will feel better.'

I bent my neck to the cup and sipped at the liquid. Water, I thought, infused with something which tasted bitter, but it did sooth my throat.

'Which priory? And why am I here?'

'Which priory is not your concern, the prior said you were delivered to us by God's power and His great wisdom. He said you will bring glory and fame to the priory, but the madness has taken you, and we must keep you free from all harm and away from the poison of worldly men.'

The monk poured more water into my mouth as he spoke. I was too weak to argue, I drank and closed my eyes. Who had done this to me? Did Hakon arrange this before he was taken as a hostage? Was it my stepmother, wanting to make sure her son was heir to my father's estates? I even thought it could be Wulfgar, now he knew I was aware he had been Beorn's bodyguard. How was he involved in Beorn's death, why had he come to Æssefeld? These questions whirled around my head as I fell back into a deep sleep.

When I awoke, the monk had gone. The candle had burnt out, but a faint streak of daylight filtered in through the only window in the room, which was set high up in a wall, making it impossible to see out. My hands had been untied but my ankle was still fettered to a chain fastened to the wall. There was a bed made of a single board with a thin blanket draped across it. In the corner was a hole, obviously the latrine. There was a small table with a jug of water and a small drinking cup. I could make out the faint sound of the monks at their prayers. I tried to get to the door to bang on it to get someone's attention, but the chain was too short.

Hours later, the round-faced monk reappeared with a bowl of a gruel-like concoction. I lay on the floor as before and waited until he bent over me. I grabbed him by the ears and tried to pull him over. I did not have the strength. He muttered 'God forgive me,' and butted me in the face. I let go and lay still.

'The prior said the madness may make you violent,' said the monk, scraping up the food dropped during our struggle, and slopping it back in the bowl. 'When you stop being violent, the prior will come and see you, but not before.'

The door slammed shut as he left, and I was on my own in the half-light again. My nose felt broken and my lip bled. I drank a little of the water and forced the vile food down me, as I knew I would have to build up my strength if I was to escape from this prison. It may have been a priory to the monk, but to me, it was a prison and I must find a way out.

Days went by and no one came to see me. There was a small flap in the bottom of the door where a bowl of the gruel and a cup of flat ale were pushed through every couple of days. But no one spoke. The only sounds I could hear were the monks singing and the bells ringing. I wondered if anyone was searching for me. For what reason did my father imagine I had left? To go to Turfrida against his wishes? Was he so angry he had wiped his hands of me as he promised he would? My days were full of thoughts such as these.

Days, weeks, possibly months passed whilst I lived in these conditions. Several times monks came into the room to swill out the latrine
and change the old straw for new. But none of them spoke, and any
questions I asked were ignored. Once I managed to grab one of them
and wrap the chain around his throat, threatening to break his neck
if they did not release me. However tight I pulled on the chain, the
others continued to come at me until I was overpowered and flung to
the floor. The monk coughed and spluttered, his face red and flushed,
he went to drink my water, but one of the others stopped him and
they led him out and slammed the door shut again.

The days were cold, the nights were bitter. I wrapped the blanket
around me, but it was so thin, it gave no warmth. I took to walking
around the room for hours on end, as much as the chain would allow,
both to get warmer and as a form of exercise. I had developed a
tingling sensation, first in my feet and hands and eventually the
whole of my body and my thinking became unclear and muddled. The
food and water continued to be pushed through the flap, and
although they tasted odd, I consumed both eagerly. More days and
weeks passed by, and now, when the monks came to clean the latrine
and rushes, I sat quietly on my bed and said nothing.

I began to look forward to the monks' singing, which was often.
Christian monks have a song and prayer for all daily occurrences,
nothing seems to be so insignificant or small not to thank God for.
Their voices and the ringing of the bells were the only sounds
breaking the relentless silence.

Eventually, the monotony was broken. When the monks came to
clean the room, they brought with them two lit candles, placing them
on the table. They left not the usual gruel and water, but a wooden
platter with fish, bread and a cup of red wine. As I devoured these like
a ravenous dog, the door opened again and in walked the prior.

It was Thurstan.

My first inclination was to grab him and beat him senseless, but
he left the door ajar, and outside I could see two burly monks armed
with cudgels ready for such an event. The prior's tall, slim outline

loomed over me. In his right hand he held his dreaded, pointed stick, which he continuously tapped into his left palm.

'Leofric, thanks to Our Lord Jesus Christ, his Holy Father and all the saints, we were able to save you.'

'Save me?' I said, rattling the chain around my leg.

'An unfortunate necessity, as much for your own well-being as that of my brothers. You have already tried to injure two of our order and no doubt you would desire to do the same to me if you could. I am certain when you discern the reason you are here, the chain can be removed.'

I said nothing in reply.

'In your relatively short life, Leofric, it seems you have made numerous enemies, those who would see you disgraced or dead or preferably both. It was thought others would be better suited to be thegn of Æssefeld than you. Yet your father still seemed to think he could benefit from an alliance with Wulfric Rabell. It seems it was decided you would be framed for a crime, alienating your father from you forever, so he would never wish to see you again. Your father's steward was murdered, and a knife and an amulet belonging to you were found by the victim's body. The perpetrators planned for you to be shipped across the sea and sold as a slave. Some of them became nervous and decided it would be best if you were dead and your body lost in a bog; this was arranged. However, one of the men hired to do the deed was a good Christian. He also happened to be a visitor to this priory. He came to me and confessed to the crime he was about to commit.'

Thurstan stood and walked up and down the cell.

'You have always been a problem to me, Leofric. Before she died, your mother, God rest her soul, made me promise I would do all in my power to bring you into the Church. She even donated a substantial sum of money to this priory to reinforce that promise. You have always resisted your destiny to serve God, so this latest development seemed too good an opportunity to ignore. By offer of money and complete absolution from his sins, future and past, the man, who cannot be named due to the sanctity of the confessional, was convinced to bring you here.'

'So, only he outside of the priory knows I am alive?' I said.

'Alas, unfortunately, there was a terrible accident involving his cart, and he was crushed to death beneath it,' said Thurstan, crossing himself as he spoke. 'No one knows you're here, except the few monks who have attended you. They think you are a madman who has been brought here for your own protection. This is partly true, for those who think you're dead, will soon want to kill you if they discover you're still alive. But you are safe here, Leofric, the priory walls are twenty feet high and there is a maze of locked doors between this room and the outside world. Our heavenly Father has work for you here, I am certain. Next time I come, we will discuss your future and how you can devote your life to the glory of God.'

He bent and made the sign of the cross on my forehead. 'Bless you, my son. Together we can bring glory to God and fame to this priory,' and before I could question him further, he snuffed both candles, the door slammed shut and once again I was alone and in the dark.

I dwelt on the things Thurstan had told me. How much I believed, I wasn't sure. The one thing I was sure of, whoever wanted me locked away for the rest of my life, whether it was Hakon, my late mother, Thurstan or Almighty God Himself, they were going to be disappointed. I did not know how, but I was determined to escape from this place. I knew I must bide my time. Let them think I was resigned to my destiny as a priest. When their guard was down, I would take my chance. Looking back, despite the fact I have seen terrible things since and been in dire situations, that time was the lowest ebb of my life. Wretched, confused, my whole body ached. I was so weary, I could hardly continue my exercises walking around my room. However, not once did I waver in my determination to fulfil the destiny I desired. I swore to myself when I had achieved my goal, all those responsible for my incarceration would be held to account.

Over the next days, a more edible potage replaced the gruel. The odd-tasting water was replaced by wine, the rushes on the floor were changed more frequently and the infirmarian came and removed my bandages and checked my injuries. I objected when they tried to cut my hair in the fashion of the tonsure. I was told, if I agreed, the chain from my leg would be removed. I stopped resisting. My hair was cut, and the chain taken off.

Thurstan came to see me again. I noticed he still had his two minders outside the door, but he brought meat and fresh bread. The monks could only eat meat when they were in the infirmary, so this was a real treat. Thurstan watched me eat for a while before he spoke.

'It is my desire, Leofric, to bring as much glory to God in my short, mortal life as I possibly can. This priory can be a part of such glory and so can you.'

He paused for a moment as if he was expecting me to inquire how, but I remained silent, so he continued.

'We have no relic here at Filey, nothing to bring pilgrims to bestow their offerings for the miracles such things deliver. However, I will soon have in my possession a precious artefact which has been in the presence of our Lord. A wondrous object, which will adorn an equally wondrous work of art and dedication; a Psalter, the like of which has never been seen in this land before. A Psalter people will flock for miles to see, to touch, to be cured and moved by. A Psalter illuminated with the finest gold and silver, scripted with the deftest of hands, all done to the glory of God, and more to the point, Leofric, scripted and illuminated by you. In all my years, I have never seen a finer scribe anywhere than you. You have a natural, no, a divine talent for this task. Why God has blessed you with this gift when you have railed against Him is a mystery. But blessed you are. There are men who have toiled for years who could never even dream of matching the images which come from your quill and vision. Now, circumstances and God's will have delivered you to us. We have the finest vellum and inks and gold and silver. We have dedicated brothers ready to aid you in this momentous undertaking, and those not so skilled in these arts will pray constantly for God's spirit to inspire your endeavours.'

I wanted to scream, 'No!' at him and throttle his scrawny neck, but I knew the only way I could escape this nightmare was to seem compliant to his wishes and wait for my chance. And so, it began.

Twenty-three

The monks moved me from that cell-like room which, I discovered, was down near the stores under the cloisters. I was given the name Brother Luke, and I was put in a room with two elderly scribes, Cedric and Quilliam, who, because of their ages, slept in a small room separate from the dormitory. Brother Cedric was a short, stout man who perspired at the least exertion. Brother Quilliam was tall, lean with blood-shot and rheumy eyes and a nose which ran constantly. Cedric was a chatterer, which surprised me, because I thought monks were supposed to be quiet, contemplative men. Not Cedric, whenever there was no one around to chastise him for it, he talked non-stop. He also passed wind relentlessly. Perhaps the two things were related, and he talked so much to distract from the smell that was always around him. Brother Quilliam spoke seldom. His mouth did not seem cut out for it, small and thin-lipped and turned down at the edges. I never once saw him smile, and whenever he did speak, it was usually to complain or criticise something or somebody.

Each day after matins, which were the first prayers of the day, the three of us were escorted to the scriptorium by Brother Siweard. We each had a small desk set in front of three tall windows, which allowed the daylight to flood through, giving us the perfect conditions for our work. We were in a small alcove, kept separate from the other scribes by an open lattice dividing wall. They busied themselves with the mundane written business of the priory; the accounts of all transactions; the copying of ancient manuscripts which were starting to fade; copying scriptures for wealthy landowners for their private chapels. Where they used parchment, we used vellum, and we had our own apprentice, a young novice called Peter, who kept us supplied with sharpened quills and mixed our ink. He helped me with the gold and silver. I was aware from the outset my fellow scribes watched me with suspicion.

'Why was a madman put to work on such a prestigious project?'

Brother Riocus, a young, well built, fresh-faced man with fat lips and a pointed, beak-like nose, sat near to our alcove and watched me constantly.

'Watch out for him,' said Cedric, 'he's one of Thurstan's favourites. He expected to be one of the chosen three with me and Quilliam.'

Cedric and Quilliam also watched me. They, too, wondered why a madman had been preferred over them to undertake the main tasks of this work and why Thurstan should consult me, not them.

At first, they peered at my letters ready to find fault. Not long after, I sensed they looked with admiration, even if they never said so. Eventually, they stopped looking altogether and concentrated more diligently on their own work. Cedric would often say, 'How wondrous are the works of the Lord. Just when Prior Thurstan decides we should have a great book written, Brother Luke turns up from nowhere. God does indeed work in mysterious ways.'

'Very strange, if you ask me,' Quilliam would mutter, 'very strange.'

Sometimes I would break from my work and stand to gaze out of the tall windows. The one on the right looked out on to the garth and cloisters, where the monks would walk and contemplate in its serenity. The window behind us was at the far end of the scriptorium and overlooked the large, outside courtyard with the almonry at its far end. The whole area was enclosed by a perimeter wall which towered above it. A covered, arched walkway ran the whole length of the wall except where it was divided by a huge, double-gated entrance, where everything and everyone that went in and out of the priory passed through. Each morning, the poor from the surrounding villages would form a queue in the courtyard to get food and clothes from the almoner.

Seeing the wretchedness of these folks, I understood why many are drawn to monastic life. Although aspects of it are austere and predominantly hard work, it is preferable to starvation and begging. Not to say all become monks for that reason. Many are third or fourth sons of landowners, who stand to inherit nothing and turn to the Church for a way to enhance their prospects by progressing through the ranks of the clerics. It is possible for any man to rise as high as a bishop, though most will attain more modest roles and be thankful. Of course, there are those who enter the order because of a love of God and a genuine desire to serve Him. I have only met a few of those in all my years. Though one such man I was about to meet.

Word was brought to Brother Quilliam, his birth brother, Bald, was coming to visit him. I was told, as it was usual on his visits for him to stay with Quilliam, I would be moving into a cell on my own, so Bald could use my bed. However, after a whispered conversation between Quilliam and the messenger, he said, 'Sorry, did I say Brother Luke? I meant Brother Cedric. Seniority I'm afraid,' he said to me and Cedric followed him happily to his new room. When they had left, Quilliam spoke without looking at me. 'My brother has a sensitive nose and my ears need a rest.'

Later that day, Brother Bald swept into my life. His huge frame filled the doorway, and he ducked as he entered. He embraced Quilliam, hugging him tightly and pounded his hands on his back. 'Brother, so good to see you, you're looking well.'

'I don't feel well and if you keep hitting me, I will feel a lot worse,' said Quilliam tetchily.

Bald ignored the remark and squeezed him even tighter.

'And who have we here?'

He grabbed my right hand and forearm with both his hands and shook them fervently.

'This is Brother Luke. He's mad. But he doesn't smell, and he can write.' replied Quilliam with no hint of a smile.

'I am most pleased to meet you, Brother Luke,' said Bald, still shaking my arm and spoke with such feeling, I sensed he meant it.

Bald certainly lived up to his name. He told me he had never had hair, not even eyebrows. His eyes were a deep pink, almost red, which gave him an eerie, demonic look, most disconcerting for a man of God. We were interrupted by one of the novices who had brought Bald's baggage. There was a bedroll, a large, leather sack and a wooden staff topped with a solid bronze head in the likeness of a man's face. It was Saint Neot, the saint whom Bald had dedicated his life to.

'I believe your scheming prior is not here,' said Bald, 'on the Lord's business to the king they tell me.'

I looked at him quizzically. 'I take it you do not approve of our prior?' I said, sensing I may have an ally at last.

'On the contrary, Brother Luke, I have a great admiration for Prior Thurstan. He has achieved good things here at the priory in such a short time. It is his methods of achieving them I disapprove of. But I am certain he has the good of the Church and our Lord in all he does.'

'What news from the outside?' asked Quilliam, changing the conversation quickly; he knew the consequences of talking against the Prior.

'The land is full of unrest, Quilliam. The queen has been banished to a nunnery. It is said the king has taken a vow of chastity It is even rumoured that William, Duke of Normandy has recently visited King Edward and the king has named him as his heir. How true that is, I'm not sure, but we certainly live in troubled times. Earl Ralf struts through his new earldom enforcing higher taxes and treating the people with disdain, and Earl Odda of Deerhurst, a kindly man it should be said, allows injustices to go unpunished. Earls Leofric and Siward look on from the north with dismay but do nothing. The Norman friends of King Edward take what they wish and exploit the common folk for their own means. Even thegns, born of this land, resort to unlawfulness. The earls are indifferent to the people's plight and allow the thegns to act as they wish, as long as it does not affect their own power or wealth.'

Quilliam shook his head at this. 'Thank the Lord we are safe from these wicked men in this sanctuary.'

'Even we are not safe, brother,' said Bald. 'Archbishop Robert has brought more of his countrymen over to fill our churches, monasteries and priories. Many are good men, it is true, but others are not, and their ways are not always our ways, and often, not God's ways.'

'What can we do about it?' asked Quilliam anxiously, crossing himself profusely.

'Nothing! But pray to God and the saints for their protection and guidance,' said Bald. 'There is talk of the Godwins recruiting men and building ships in readiness to return and win back their lands. Whether it is only gossip or true, I could not say.'

I cursed to myself. If it was true Harold and his kin were planning to return, I should be with them to help in their quest, not stuck inside this priory against my will. I was more determined than ever to escape from this prison. I did not yet think it wise to say anything of my plight to Bald until I could be sure I could trust him.

Quilliam and Bald left to explore the priory so Bald could see the new building work, completed since his last visit. I sat on my bed contemplating what could be happening on the outside. I thought of Turfrida, of how good it would be when we finally get together. This led to my thinking once more of my escape. I had been making mental notes of the daily movements of all those in the priory. In the morning, we were led to prayers and afterwards to the scriptorium by the round-faced brother who had butted me. His name was Brother Alberic. A heavy, wooden cross swung from his belt and he carried a large bunch of keys with which he opened and locked behind us each door we came to. He had an annoying habit of always drinking half my flask of watered-down wine each time he came. 'It's always nicer when its someone else's, don't you think, brother Luke?' he would say and give a throaty cackle. I tried to remember each corridor and door we went through, although it seemed like a maze to me. On two occasions, as we walked to our work, one narrow door had been left open leading to the courtyard.

In the scriptorium, there was a door we entered through and at the far eastern end there was another. An elderly brother called

Aramos sat next to it at a desk writing the daily journal for the priory. Anyone who entered or left by that way was allowed in and out by him. Each time this occurred, which was not often, he gave a long, deep sigh and wearily dragged himself from his wooden stool, and drew a small key tied to a string hung around his neck inside his habit. He would fumble around as he tried to put the key in the lock and eventually open the door. What lay behind, I did not know, but whenever Prior Thurstan appeared, it was usually from that door.

I had also kept close watch on the poor who came for food. Mostly it was different ones each day, though I noticed there were a few regulars. One was a bearded man accompanied by six children, whether they were all his, I am not sure, but they seemed to evoke sympathy from the monk ladling out the broth, who gave them a little extra each time. There was also a hunched figure in ragged clothes whose face was always swathed in bandages. I guessed he had been marked by pox or leprosy and hid his disfigurement. Also, a tall man on crutches, who had been deprived of both his ears, his right hand and his left foot. He was obviously a man who had flouted the law many times. Each person or circumstance I considered carefully, how they or it could help in my plans to escape the priory.

Over the next few days, I got to talk to Brother Bald on several occasions. Apparently, he had devoted his life, not only to God, but in spreading the teachings and wisdom of Saint Neot. Neot had been a monk at Glaestingabyrig who took up the hermit's life in Cornwealum. It was said he was only one foot tall and used a milking stool to stand on when he read his sermons. Hunted animals were said to flee to him for shelter, and many stories involving miracles and animals related to him. The most famous story concerning Saint Neot, and one Bald delighted in telling, was of an angel who gave him three fish. Neot was told by the angel, if he only ate one fish a day, there would always be three fish. Unfortunately, his servant was of the greedy kind and took out two fish, boiling one and frying the other. Saint Neot chastised the servant, brought one of the cooked fish back to life and replaced it in his well. It was because of this, and other miracles, people believed Neot had the power of God within him. His bones had lain in a monastery in Cornwealum for a hundred years until by trickery, monks from Eanulfesbyrig had removed them in secret and taken them to their own monastery which they renamed St. Neotstoc. There the bones remained until they were moved to Croyland Abbey in fear of Viking raids. It was to Croyland, Bald was heading on a pilgrimage he made once a year.

Bald was always interested in what I had been doing in the scriptorium.

'I wish I had your skill with a quill, Brother Luke. I am compiling my own book, but the text is a scrawl next to yours.'

'A book about what, brother?'

'A collection of charms, remedies and cures for all kinds of ailments and a list of the herbs and plants they can be made from. I say I am writing it, but I have copied much of it from an earlier book which is falling apart. It was owned by an ancestor of mine, also called Bald, who instructed a man named Cild to write it and it was passed on to me. I have added to it and continue to do so.'

He took from his bag a bedraggled collection of thin, worn parchment, held together by two covers of hard leather and bound with twine. The writing was basic but readable.

'I know a girl who would be most interested in reading this,' I said, thinking of Turfrida. 'She made a salve to take the pain away from my foot, though I used the last of it a while ago.'

'Did it have a sweet or sour odour to it?'

'Sweet, like honey.'

'I know what it is likely to be,' said Bald. 'I shall make it for you, as well as a sleeping draft. My brother says you are restless at night. I will give you something which will work quickly and banish the tossing and turning.'

The following day, Bald gave me a salve to ease the pain in my foot and a small file of liquid, from which I put two small drops into my wine or water before I retired to my bed. I was drowsy in seconds and asleep in minutes.

I liked Bald. He was sincere in his love for God and he never preached at me. He would give me a chastising look with those red eyes whenever I spoke against God and His son, but I found him a man slow to judge and quick to forgive.

'Tell me, Brother Luke, what causes these mad rages of yours?' asked Bald during one of our conversations.

'Being kidnapped by monks and held against my will for one,' I replied, having decided to trust Bald to help me.

'Of course,' said Bald, 'I was told you would claim to be a prisoner here. I understand, brother, I have experience with those who have a sickness of the mind. You must fight against it, Luke, and trust the brethren to care for you and nurse you back to health.'

I moved forward and, grabbing him by the shoulders, stared directly into his eyes.

'My name is Leofric Renweardson, I am from Æssefeld-Underbarroe. Someone has committed a crime and made it appear I was to blame. I have been brought here to fulfil the plans of Thurstan and am being held here against my will, and you are my last hope.'

Bald's huge hands gripped my arms and pushed me forcibly away.

'Damn the madness that has taken you, brother, but as the brother who stands behind me will bear witness, I do not believe a word of your ranting and I pray God will bless you and help you recover your senses.'

Bald stepped to the side, revealing Brother Alberic standing in the doorway.

'The prior has returned and wishes to greet you in his quarters, Brother Bald. If you will follow me, I shall take you there.' Alberic moved his hand in a sweeping gesture towards the door and Bald, without another word, left the room. A short while later Alberic and two other monks returned along with Cedric.

'Sorry, Brother Luke, seems as if I was supposed to stay here all along,' said Cedric.

'Gather your things and come with us,' said Alberic, in a manner that told me there was no choice in the matter.

I was ushered back to the room I had been held in originally, and there I stayed, back in the dark, no food, only the strange tasting water. The tingling sensation came back to my body and despair and confusion enveloped me like a damp blanket.

Back in the darkness and loneliness of that desolate room, I was once again despondent. It seemed I would never find a way out of the priory. All exits seemed barred to me. I was watched constantly. Bald was the only person I had talked to from the outside world for months. When I was allowed back to the scriptorium, he had gone. Back to his pilgrimage, convinced I was a madman.

I was visited once by Thurstan who told me of his disappointment in me. I was spurning a rare opportunity to serve God in a unique manner, and that my eternal soul would be in grave danger unless I committed myself unselfishly to the task God had undoubtedly determined for me. From now on, he would make sure I had no contact with anyone from the outside, and any further outbursts or attempts to leave the priory would result in severe punishment. He left. I was alone in the darkness once again.

Part of me said, 'give in, escape is impossible.' I should come to terms with the fact I was destined to remain a monk for the rest of my days. I should embrace the work before me, be joyful I could serve God and create something which would inspire future generations to worship Him. After all, it would not be too much of a hardship. To see those letters and illustrations take shape and form from my quill and brushes filled me with pride and satisfaction. Besides, the tingling sensation pervaded my whole body. The will to resist Thurstan was ebbing away.

Yet something from deep within me always fought back. The desire to be free, to clear my name, to be reconciled with my father, to go to Turfrida, to become the man I had vowed to be. Through all the despondency and self-doubt, these feelings clawed their way to the surface and kept me determined to escape from Thurstan's grasp.

Twenty-four

I was eventually released and brought back into the scriptorium. The days were colder and Peter lit a brazier each morning. It was never blazing, just enough to keep our hands from freezing. Armageddon, a black, feral cat which wandered the cloisters, often curled up as near to it as she dared without getting singed from the odd spark. The monks named her Armageddon because she was the end of the world for many unwary creatures. She would often bring mice or small birds into the scriptorium and drop them by the brazier. Several would still be half alive, and Peter would try to revive those he could. Riocus, never looking to assess their condition, simply tossed them onto the hot embers, seeming to smile at the sizzling sound they made. The cat was a snarling, spitting mass of black fur, yet it would often stand stroking itself on Riocus's legs. Once or twice I saw Riocus bend down to stroke her when he thought no one was looking.

Peter was keen to learn as much about illumination as he could. He watched carefully as I drew light lines across the vellum with a sharpened stick and planned where I would place images and text. He would watch as I shaped the goose quills, hardening them in a pot of sand he heated for me on the brazier. Peter watched to learn, Riocus watched to find fault. There were many supposed accidents; ink spilt over newly written texts, tears appearing in the vellum for no reason, quills broken. They always happened when Riocus was around, yet no one ever saw him do anything. He was always quick to blame Peter, and it would be Peter Thurstan chastised.

On occasion, I would become so engrossed with my work, nothing else mattered. Each morning, I would take the pieces of gold leaf Peter hammered until they were thinner than a butterfly's wing; translucent. I would mix the gold with stag's glue, add water and gently dissolve it with the warmth of my fingers. Once the gold was soft enough, I could apply it carefully to the vellum. My concentration was intense, as, if the gold touched any paint I had previously applied, it would stick to it and ruin the whole page. All the instruction I had received from Spearhavoc came into practice, and I was lost in a world of colour, silver and gold. I would burnish the gold with a small tool I had made myself, an agate tip and ash wood handle. Any mistakes I had made previously with the text, I would cautiously remove with a dog's tooth, which I had also fitted with a wooden handle. Peter watched and learnt, he became adept at mixing the paints exactly as I wanted. On occasion, Thurstan would punish Peter for causing another accident, and he would be made to stand in the chapel for a whole day and night reading out loud from a book of prayer. However much I protested, Riocus would take his place as my assistant. Riocus was not a listener. The paint he mixed was either too thick or too thin, almost runny. He was an impatient, clumsy boy and as soon as Peter was free from his penance, I insisted he was returned to me.

Thurstan often came and stood behind me watching my progress. He seldom spoke. Once or twice, he would suggest a slight change when I was sketching in the outline of an illustration with a reed pen. Some I agreed with, others I simply ignored. For the most part, I was left alone to continue my work. Once I was back working in the scriptorium, the water I was given no longer tasted strange and I became less lightheaded and the tingling sensation stopped. I concluded they had been drugging me to keep me subdued. Now, Thurstan wanted me alert and steady handed to produce my best work. It meant I was able to think straight about the predicament I was in and plan my escape from the priory. I also stopped taking the draught bald had given me deciding I could put it to better use, even though the pain in my foot increased in the cold.

I continued to watch through the large window onto the courtyard. The beggars would file out, one by one, through the big gates and into the outside world. It became evident the leper was always the last to leave in the evening. A plan started to formulate in my mind. If I could get into the courtyard as the poor were leaving, I could grab the leper, steal his cloak, join the others and simply walk out to freedom. There were many flaws with this plan, but I was desperate. I decided I would make my attempt the next evening.

Rain, pouring from a broken gutter, woke me before the first bell. I crossed the narrow corridor and, looking out into the courtyard, I saw a carriage and several pack horses loaded with bulging saddle bags. I could hear a voice I knew, but not someone from the priory. I was certain it was Spearhavoc. At last, someone to help me. After a few moments, two men stepped out from the corridor underneath the dormer. One was Thurstan, the other was Spearhavoc, who passed something to the prior.

I banged on the small glass panes with my fists.

'Spearhavoc, Spearhavoc, it's me, Leofric.'

Vision was poor in the rain, but he looked up and I knew he must have seen me. Thurstan was waving his arms frantically and pointing towards me. I saw two of the brothers, running around to where I was. 'Spearhavoc, it's me, Leofric of Æssefeld. I am here against my will, help me.'

The bishop lifted his cassock to keep it from the wet ground and made his way to the carriage. I saw the horses leaving through the courtyard gates. Peter was crossing the yard and as the horses passed him, something dropped from one of the bags. It was hard to see clearly what it was in the rain but it looked like a golden chalice. He bent down and picked it up, passed it to one of Spearhavoc's men who snatched it off him and forced it back into the bag. Spearhavoc never once glanced back as I continued to bang the windows.

Two monks came running down the corridor and dragged me from the window.

'Come away, Brother Luke, we don't want to upset the bishop now, do we?'

They pushed me back in my room and locked the door as they left.

I learnt later, that King Edward had elevated Spearhavoc to the Bishopric of Lundene. Archbishop Robert refused to consecrate him claiming that the Pope forbade it. Once Spearhavoc's patrons, the Godwins, were banished, the bishop-elect feared for his life. He consequently took countless precious items from many churches and along with jewels the king had given him to make a new crown, fled the country and had not been heard of since. I presumed Thurstan had arranged for his friend's safe passage and whatever was passed to him that night was payment for his help.

The rain persisted all day. Large puddles formed in the garth and courtyard. In the early evening, as the light faded, lightning cracked the sky, sending a flickering light across the priory. Rain made a hammering noise on the tiled roofs and water cascaded in rivulets off the thatch. I heard Alberic's nauseous cackle as he came to take us to prayer. I took the file of sleeping draught Bald had made me and poured a few drops into my flask of watered wine, making sure Quilliam and Cedric didn't notice. Alberic came in, grabbed the flask and drank all of it.

'It always tastes better when it's someone else's, don't you think, Brother Luke?' and cackled once again as he led us out.

As we made our way to Compline through the long corridor, I glanced out over the courtyard. Armageddon slinked under the covered walkway, shaking the water off her fur. Because of the rain, there were few people about. The man with the six children was leaving through the big gate and the leper was getting food from the almoner. I hoped the sleeping draught would work in time to give me my chance. There could be no holdups. Grab the leper, knock him out, put on his cloak and head for the gate. Hopefully, the driving rain would make the two monks at the gate less attentive and I could get out before the alarm was given.

We walked in silence, the bell rang calling us to prayer. The end of the corridor was where I would make my move. Alberic led our little procession as usual. Quilliam and Cedric walked behind him, after them the three brothers from the scriptorium. Peter and I were next, Brother Riocus at the rear. When we arrived at the door, Alberic would unlock it and wait as we all passed through, re-locking it behind him.

Alberic reached the door, he seemed his normal, gruff self, 'Hurry, or we will be late,' he shouted.

Shit, I mustn't have used enough of the sleeping draught. I had been cautious in case it worked too soon. Quilliam, Cedric and the three brothers all passed through the doorway. Outside the corridor window, I could see the leper coming away from the almonry carrying his bowl of pottage.

It was all going wrong.

As Peter entered the doorway, Alberic tottered forward, grabbing hold of Peter's habit, and fell to the floor.

'Are you unwell, brother?' Cedric cried.

Riocus hurried to help them. As the monks gathered around their stricken brother, my plan changed. Originally, I was going to slip away and try to get into the courtyard and hope no one noticed. I knew in my heart it could not work. It was a futile attempt by a desperate man. But now, there in front of me on the flagstones were Alberic's keys. I reached between the legs of the others, grabbed the keys, stepped back through the doorway and locked the door behind me.

'Brother Luke, what are you doing?' I heard Riocus shout.

I shuffled down the corridor unlocking and locking each door behind me, through the narrow door, out into the courtyard, and slid into the recess. I was sure the leper had not seen me. My heart was banging in my chest, my breathing heavy. I could hear the footsteps sloshing in the puddles. Riocus and the others were trapped in the corridor behind locked doors. It would give me a little more time before they could raise the alarm. The leper was feet away. I prepared to pounce, when the big gates at the end of the courtyard opened and a cart trundled through. Monks ran out to meet it. The leper looked across towards the cart and I threw my arm around his neck and dragged him into the recess. He dropped the bowl of pottage.

'I am sorry for this,' I said, as I was about to bang his head against the wall.

'Leofric, you fool, it's me.' I pulled his hood down and froze in disbelief.

It was Mair.

'What are you doing here?' I spluttered.

'Waiting for the right time to get you out of here,' she said.

'What are you doing?'

'Escaping,' I said.

'Not tonight, you fool, the augurs are not in your favour.'

Across the courtyard, three men climbed down off the cart, one of them was tall and carried a staff. They all wore monk's habits with the cowls over their heads against the rain. Another flash of lightning cracked the sky and the top of the monk's staff glinted.

'Shit, it's Bald.'

'Who's Bald?' said Mair.

The courtyard became full of monks, carrying flaming rush-lights.

'Brother Luke has gone mad again. Find him and stop him leaving,' one of the monks shouted.

Mair and I stood as still as we could. Something brushed against my leg, I instinctively kicked out. Armageddon lifted off the floor screeching and spitting as she landed on all fours.

'Over there,' came the shout. The three monks from the cart had a head-start on the rest and ran towards us.

'That's Bald, the big bugger with the staff coming right to us.'

It was too late, the big monk swept into the recess. I grabbed him by the shoulders. Mair grabbed an arm and screamed, what I presumed was a curse. The other two monks arrived seconds later.

'He's on your side, Leofric, he's the reason we're here.' The monk speaking pulled his cowl off his face, it was Wulfgar, the other was Rush. I released my grip on Bald. He quickly stepped out of the alcove to confront the approaching monks.

'It was only a cat, look.' He pushed Armageddon, hissing and spitting, her back arched, out into the rain with his foot. 'Try that way,' he called. The monks seeing the cat, scattered in all directions to find me.

'I don't understand,' I blurted out.

'Bald suspected something was not right. Said he smelled herbs in your drinking water which were not for your well-being,' said Wulfgar. 'He came to Æssefeld to check out your story. He was told a pack of lies. We found out he had been asking about you and we confirmed his suspicions. We thought if we could find you, we could sneak you out in the cart.'

'Tripp is waiting with horses further inland,' said Rush.

'So, what do we do now?' I asked. 'Have you brought weapons?'

'No, not here, Bald wouldn't allow it,' said Wulfgar.

'I have this,' said Rush, pulling a dagger from his boot.

'I said no violence and I meant no violence,' growled Bald, knocking the blade from Rush's hand.

'Just how are we going to get out of here?' quizzed Rush.

'I know a way, but we need to get into the priory,' said Bald, 'we need a distraction.'

'Leave it to me,' said Mair.

She discarded the leper's cloak, pulling her garment up over her head, becoming naked, except for an amulet around her neck and a small leather pouch on a loop around her wrist. Bending, she picked up the dagger in one hand and with the other grabbed Armageddon, who had been more intent on eating the spilt pottage than being afraid of us. Mair held the cat by the scruff as she walked brazenly into the rain to the very centre of the courtyard. She held both arms up high and screamed spells, incantations and curses on the monks and their god.

The monks still in the courtyard came to a dead stop. Others, hearing the disturbance, ran out from the cloisters and other buildings. Many had never seen a naked woman before, never mind this beautiful girl with mad eyes, dancing in a circle, with a cat held aloft, which was shrieking like a distressed baby. Mair lowered Armageddon and with one movement drew the blade across its throat. She slit it down its belly, like gutting a trout, and its innards poured out onto the floor. By this time, we were already running across the courtyard back to the door I'd come out of. I looked behind to see Mair poking the cat's entrails with her fingers. A few of the monks found their courage and started moving towards her. She took something out of the pouch on her wrist. She stood upright again, her arms stretched out before her. The encroaching monks faltered and backed away. We lost sight of her as we came to a door. I fumbled with Alberic's keys, eventually finding the right one. Once through, I realised Bald was heading for the scriptorium, why, I couldn't fathom, surely we would be trapped? We hurried through another corridor and passing a window we saw Mair once again.

'I see blood and fire and destruction. Every monk will perish, and the true gods will gloat at your pain,' she shrieked. Mair clapped her hands together, thick white smoke billowed across the courtyard and when it dispersed, Mair had gone. We continued to the scriptorium, we heard monks coming up the corridor from our left. There was a door to the right. Bald tried the latch, it was open. We bundled in and closed the door quietly.

'Search these rooms,'

We heard doors being opened and closed. I was trying keys from Alberic's bunch, turning them quietly in the lock; none worked. Someone came outside the door and the latch lifted. It was Quilliam. Bald and he exchanged looks. He must have been thinking, 'Do I expose them, or do I let them go and get rid of Luke forever?'

'Anyone there, Quilliam?' It was Riocus's voice. 'Somebody must have freed them from the corridor.'

Quilliam put his finger to his lips.

'No, nothing,' he called out behind him.

Bald whispered, 'God bless you, brother.'

'I hope He does, because the prior certainly won't,' Quilliam whispered back. He pulled the door closed and joined the rest of the search party as they carried on up the corridor. We waited until it was quiet again before leaving the room. The scriptorium was empty except for Aramos, snoozing at his desk.

'We need to get in there,' said Bald, pointing at the door behind the dozing monk.

I slipped the key from around Aramos' neck and quietly opened the door.

We bundled inside the room.

'Lock the door, and help me move this,' said Bald, grabbing one end of a heavy chest that was next to the far wall. Wulfgar and Rush helped him. It was not what it seemed. The front end was on large metal hinges attached to the floor. The whole chest leant forward exposing a hole big enough for a man to squeeze down.

'A priest hole, an escape route from Viking times,' said Bald, 'Quickly now.'

I turned the key in the lock. A solitary candle lit the room. There were books and scrolls on each wall. I went to help the others with the desk when I noticed a lectern with a leather book cover on it. It was not so much the cover which took my eye, but the huge jewel at its centre. As soon as I got a closer look, I knew, without a doubt, it was the ruby from my father's sceptre. I had gazed on that precious stone so many times I knew each facet. I took the candle and held it over the jewel, and I saw it! the face of the Christ child staring back at me through the ruby. I nearly dropped the candle with shock.

'Hurry up, Leofric, we need to go,' shouted Wulfgar.

There was banging on the door, monks shouting, 'Where's the key?'

At the other end of the room, from behind a curtain. there was more banging and shouting. 'It's another door leading to steps from the chapel,' said Bald, 'You must go now.'

'What do you mean, you?' said Wulfgar.

'I must stay here,' said Bald. 'Hit me, make it look as though I was trying to stop you. You must make it look as if you held me against my will or I will never be able to show my face in another religious house again.'

'I can't hit you after all the help you have given us,' said Wulfgar.

'I can,' said Rush, bringing his fist under Bald's jaw and hitting him again as he slumped to the floor.

'Leofric, come now,' shouted Wulfgar again. Still in shock and confused at seeing the face in the ruby, I tried to wrench the book from off the lectern, but it was held fast by a thick chain. The jewel was also unmovable, embedded in the leather. I had nothing to prize it out with. Rush grabbed me by the arm and pulled me away.

'Get down there now,' he said, pushing me into the hole and onto narrow, stone steps. Rush pulled the chest back towards him so it once again covered the hole. Wulfgar was already making his way through a dark, damp tunnel. Cobwebs brushed my face and hair. I had brought the candle with me, but it blew out as soon as we came off the steps. The floor was wet and uneven, making me stumble. I could hear Wulfgar up ahead but could not see him. Each time I stumbled, Rush bumped into me, cursing. I could no longer hear the banging or shouting from the priory. Wulfgar shouted, 'I can see the end.'

We came out onto a pebbled beach at the foot of the cliffs beneath the priory's east wall. The rain still pelted down and the occasional flash of lightning lit our way.

'There is a ruined abbey up on the point, Tripp is waiting there,' said Wulfgar.

We scrambled over big boulders and climbed up a steep, overgrown path. Nettles stung my legs and brambles ripped my habit, but I was free at last, and we could see no sign of any pursuers. When we reached the abbey ruins, Tripp was waiting with horses and a cart.

'Get into the cart and lie down,' he said to me. They threw blankets and dried seal skins over me to conceal my presence. The cart lurched forwards and we set off, away from the priory, to where, I did not know or care. I was sore, exhausted and wet through but I was free of Thurstan and before long I was fast asleep.

Twenty-five

When I awoke, the rain had stopped, though the blue sky was peppered with remnants of dark, storm clouds as a brisk wind chased them north.

We had stopped in a clearing encircled by trees. Rush sat by a fire and the sweet smell of roasting meat filled my nostrils. Wulfgar and Tripp stood talking together. They had taken off their habits and wore their own clothes. They had brought clothes for me, and I was glad to get out of my wet habit and dress normally again.

'I suggest you keep the hood of your tunic up if we have company until your hair grows back,' Tripp said.

We sat by the fire and ate, saying little, although my head was bursting with so many questions, I did not know where to begin.

'I suggest we continue northwards,' Tripp said eventually. 'I have a friend, Gilbert of Ghent, who has land near Streanæshealh. You can take refuge there until you decide what to do.'

'North? I must go south, back to Æssefeld, to prove to my father my innocence of whatever it is I am supposed to have done,' I said forcibly.

'It is said you killed your father's steward and stole something from him.'

'Never,' I shouted.

'Your amulet was found near the dead man's body,' said Wulfgar.

241

'Never,' I cried, jumping to my feet, 'it's a lie!'

'We believe you, Leofric,' said Tripp, 'that's why we're here, but your father has been convinced of your guilt and has men watching for you.'

'There is a price on your head. You cannot go back until you have the real culprits to confess their crimes,' said Rush, pulling another piece of meat from the spit. 'Besides, I can't go back. You know what they do to runaway slaves.'

'Don't think I'll be too welcome either as his fyrd-man, who's also left your father to help his wayward son,' added Wulfgar.

'Then we will go to St. Omer and to Turfrida.'

'Your father has informed Wulfric of your so-called crimes and he has banned his daughter from ever seeing you again. Even if you were to go to her and she came willingly, you would be making her defy her father. You must clear your name first, Leofric, and that won't be easy,' said Tripp, shaking his head.

'We are not even sure who it was that did this to you,' said Wulfgar. 'We think it was originally Hakon's plan, but when he was taken as a hostage, others decided to carry it out instead.'

'Is he still a hostage?' I asked. 'Bald told us the Godwins were planning to come back to their lands. Surely he is free now. I will find him and force him to tell the truth.'

'The Godwins are back, Leofric, more powerful than ever,' said Tripp, 'and the Queen has been brought back from the nunnery, but not Hakon. When they found out Godwin and his sons had returned, many of the Normans who had opposed them fled the country. One of those was Archbishop Robert. As a last gesture of defiance against the Godwins, he took Hakon and Wulfnoth with him and both are now hostages of William, Duke of Normandy.'

'In that case, we must go to Harold, he will help me,' I said, not knowing whether he would or not.

'Possibly he might,' said Tripp, 'but something else you should know. Sweyn Godwinson made a pilgrimage to Jerusalem to atone for his sins and died of pneumonia on the way home. Godwin took the death of his eldest son hard and became ill. Whilst feasting at

King Edward's court, Edward accused him once again of being complicit in his brother Alfred's death. According to cynical men, the earl supposedly answered, 'To show I had no part in your brother's death, let this morsel of food pass down my throat without causing me harm.' As he took the next bite of his bread, it choked him to death. Whatever the truth of the tale, Godwin is dead. Consequently, Harold is now Earl of Wessex and as such, he cannot deal with you as a friend, but must be seen to deal with you in a lawful manner. You must prove your innocence to him also.'

'How am I supposed to prove my innocence if I don't know who is to blame?' I said, becoming more frustrated by the hopelessness of the situation.

'That is why we should go to Streanæshealh. Gilbert may have news and we can decide the best plan of action to take next,' said Tripp.

And so, when we broke camp, we made our way secretly to Streanæshealh, hiding like the outlaws we were, staying off the main tracks and keeping to less-travelled trails Tripp had used many times.

The sky was cornflower blue and despite the fact the weak, winter sun emitted little warmth, it was still bright enough to make the white houses of Streanæshealh shine. Predominately of Danish descent, the villagers had taken to painting their houses white so they could be seen easily from the sea when they were returning from their voyages. In fact, I believe it is now no longer known by the old name Streanæshealh, but Hvitaby.

We passed the ruins of the old monastery, which the Vikings had destroyed many years since, and just before the village, on a prominent rock, was Gilbert's palisade. It was impressive, with its high, wooden walls and tall, arched, carved oak gates, flanked either side by immense dragon heads, also carved in oak. Tripp told us it was a training base for young Flemish and Norman men aspiring to be knights, and many of them watched us closely as we entered through the open gates. Rush sat on the cart next to Tripp, his sling loaded but out of sight. Wulfgar and I rode either side. Wulfgar was clothed in leather; two swords slung criss-cross on his back. His two-headed battle-axe was hooked around the pommel of his saddle. I could have been mistaken for a peasant with the hood of my rough tunic covering my tonsured head, but the bow across one shoulder and a quiver of arrows across the other, the sword and scabbard strapped to my leg and a seax hung from my belt, told otherwise. Tripp also had his battle-axe within reach.

The chief steward greeted us. A tall, well-built man called Dagfin, who had one arm and deep gouges down the side of his face and wore an eye patch of leather. He limped more severely than I did, almost dragging his left leg as he walked.

'Welcome. My lord will talk with you, Tripp, if you will follow me. You can sleep in the barracks. Your servant,' he said looking at Rush, 'can bed in the stables.'

'He's not a servant, he's our friend,' I said, 'he will stay with us in the barracks.'

The steward glanced at Tripp who nodded his agreement.

'As you wish, I trust you will find it satisfactory.'

Tripp climbed from the cart and the steward led him off to meet Lord Gilbert. We were taken to the barracks and our horses were led away to the stables. It was hard to tell the difference between the barracks and the stables. It was a wide, long, low-slung building, divided by many stalls. Each stall had a wooden bench, a straw mattress and pegs fastened on the wall to hang clothes. At the end of the building, there was a communal latrine and a large barrel of water for washing. We were each given a stall and told there was food and ale in the great hall. A tall, muscular man in a mail vest, leather britches and a dark, dowdy, woollen cloak, leant on one of the stalls and nodded as we passed. There was also a group of young men gathered by our stalls talking in French.

'More Saxon exiles, they can't control their runts, so they throw them out of their lands and inflict them on us.' The man who spoke these words was tall, slender, wiry in build and dressed in linen and fine silk.

'I suppose they also think they can fight the world and win,' said a smaller, thickset man with dark, curly hair and a condescending smirk.

'More exiles?' I asked in their tongue. 'Are there more Saxons here?' The laughter stopped, surprised I had understood them.

'The braggart Hereward, who has bewitched our lady. To her, he can do no wrong. The young maids swoon at the mere mention of his name and he delights in making a fool of us with his exploits at wrestling, spear throwing and anything else he tries his hand to,' said the man in silk. 'Do you know of him?'

'Oh, we know of him,' said Rush. 'Leofric here knocked him onto to his arse. He won't be too pleased to see us.'

One of the men pushed forward and peered at me with a look of incredulity. 'You knocked Hereward over and you're still alive?'

I said nothing. He was a short, rotund man with fat cheeks. He reminded me of one of my mother's pin cushions and I imagined pricking him a hundred times with my seax.

'Of course he's alive, he's here isn't he!' said Rush. 'We're not afraid of Hereward, he's no trouble,' which was only partly true. I was not afraid of Hereward, but a man like him does not forget someone getting the better of him, however fleeting. Soon or later he would bring trouble, I was sure of it.

The man in the silk spoke again. This time he gave a little bow, 'I am Guy Beaufort. We are here to further our skills in combat and learn the ways of the knight. What brings you here?'

'Tripp has business with your lord,' said Wulfgar.

'Tripp?' said Guy, 'he's a peddler of wares. What business does he have with our lord?'

'I would think that is between Tripp and your lord. If you're so curious, ask them,' said Wulfgar. 'Now we will take our leave of you. We are hungry and have been told there is food and ale waiting for us in the great hall.'

The three of us pushed through the group of would-be knights, each one looking at us as if we were dog shit.

It is forbidden to take weapons into the great hall, which made us feel vulnerable. The food was good and welcome. The men from the barracks arrived after us and sat at a table opposite. We could not hear what they said, but it was obvious we were the subject of their talk. I imagined only the fear of offending their lord held them back from attacking us.

After a while, Tripp re-joined us. He ripped a piece of meat off the bone and grabbed a jug of ale, which he downed in one, before speaking. 'Lord Gilbert says we are welcome to stay as long as we wish.'

He stuffed as much meat into his mouth as he could. He tried to swig more ale, but there was no room, and it spilt down his beard. Once he had managed to swallow, he continued, 'The problem is, he is aware of Leofric's plight and feels there are those here who might be tempted to claim any reward on offer for his capture. Therefore, he says he cannot guarantee our safety.'

'We can guarantee our own safety,' said Rush, loud enough for all to hear.

'That may be so whilst we're awake, but a knife to the throat whilst we're sleeping,' said Wulfgar.

'And I have no wish of being taken prisoner again,' I said.

'There will be one of us awake at all times to watch over the others and we will tarry here no longer than a couple of days,' Tripp said.

'What then?' I asked.

'We will continue north,' he replied.

'Are we going to keeping running north until we fall into the sea?' I asked, the sarcasm clear in my tone.

Tripp stared at me, considering whether to answer or ignore me when a commotion at the hall's entrance diverted everyone's attention. A group of noisy, chattering youths had entered the hall, young men and women squealing, shouting, laughing, one young girl was even weeping. Their attention, it seemed, was concentrated on one man, Hereward of Brune. The young women threw flower petals and blew kisses at him, the men fawned over him, as if they were his closest companions. Most warriors I knew would have been embarrassed at such antics. Not Hereward, he revelled in it. He wore a crimson cloak, which swirled behind him as he cavorted through the hall. His one true companion, Martin Lightfoot, kept discreetly to one side, obviously used to, but bored by, the whole charade. The tall man in leather and mail from the barracks had followed them in and stood next to the entrance, arms folded, watching the performance.

'I forgot to mention Hereward was here,' said Tripp tearing at more meat. 'Apparently, his father has tired of his escapades and beseeched the king to exile him.'

'We've already heard,' I said, 'although he's not popular with everyone here it would seem.'

'He and Gilbert have returned from an expedition to round up a band of brigands,' said Tripp. 'One of Gilbert's men got himself captured. His captors were presumably going to ransom him later. They were thwarted by Hereward, who killed three of them and set the man free. Because of this and many other deeds, Gilbert has nothing but praise for Hereward and has offered to make him a knight.'

'And will he be one?' asked Rush.

'Hereward refused, saying he has done nothing yet to merit such honour,' Tripp replied.

The commotion stopped instantly, as Hereward, pushing his admirers aside, bellowed in our direction. 'What have we here? Unfinished business if I am not mistaken.'

He strode towards us and leapt on to one of the oak tables, scattering goblets and chargers in all directions, causing men to scramble to get out of the way. Jumping off the table, he landed in front of us, fists clenched, his smile replaced by a scowl.

'So, we meet again, cripple,' he said looking straight at me. Rush started to stand, but I steadied him with my arm and he remained seated.

'It would seem so,' I replied, fixing my eyes on his. 'You seemed somewhat aggrieved.'

'As I said, unfinished business,' he snarled.

The rashness of youth urged me to jump up and trade blows with this most arrogant of men. However, my imprisonment had taught me patience and to wait for the right moment. I also knew I was not strong enough yet to fight him and a quick look around me showed men eager for two Saxons to fight each other.

'I agree, and I would be more than happy to put you on your backside again, but it would seem discourteous to Lord Gilbert's hospitality for his guests to brawl in his great hall.'

'It would,' boomed a voice from the doorway. Lord Gilbert entered, a huge grin on his face, his arms outstretched in a welcoming fashion. 'Come, Hereward, share a horn of mead with me and tell me once again how you saved my man.'

Hereward paused. He looked towards Gilbert, then me. 'The time will come,' he said softly, 'make no mistake.'

Hereward and Lord Gilbert embraced and walked to the far side of the hall to share mead.

Guy Beaufort leaned across from his table. 'It would seem there is not much regard between you and Hereward. I think he is a man who should be taught to respect others honourably.'

'And who's going to do it, you?' said Rush, sniggering.

'We could make sure that anyone that does would be victorious,' said Guy.

'Meaning what exactly?' asked Wulfgar.

'Whatever you want it to mean,' said Guy. 'We shall talk of this again.' The other young men followed him as he left the hall.

'If they are going to gang up on him, why do they need us, surely there's enough of them?' asked Rush.

'So if it goes wrong or Lord Gilbert finds out, they have someone to blame.' I said.

The next few days went by without much incident. Tripp and Rush ate and drank. Wulfgar and I practised and trained in a small, private courtyard that was out of sight of the rest of the palisade. I had lost my sharpness being cooped up in the priory, and Wulfgar gave me bloody knuckles and rapped my head a few times with the flat of his sword and made my ears ring. We saw little of Hereward, who spent most days hunting with Gilbert. I used this time to broach a subject with Wulfgar. I already knew part of the answer, I just needed the full story from him.

'Earl Harold thought you had something to do with the murder of

Beorn,' I said.

'Do you think that?' he asked me.

'No,' I answered truthfully.

'Well, you're wrong,' Wulfgar said, 'I was involved.'

I bridled at that and raised my sword. Wulfgar stepped back but kept his sword low.

'Do you remember, Beorn always had three bodyguards that shadowed him everywhere?' he said.

'Yes.'

'I was one of them,' said Wulfgar shaking his head slowly. 'I was young and naïve, even so, that is no excuse. My Lord Beorn had agreed to go with Sweyn, to plead on his behalf to King Edward, to be forgiven once again and brought in from exile. On the way to the ships at Boseham, they argued loudly, about what, I don't know. By the time we reached the ships, they seemed to have settled their differences and were at ease together. We sailed out past Porland and came ashore at Dertamuõa. We made camp on the shore. We three bodyguards, Glom, Uliric and me stayed at Beorn's tent's entrance. Sweyn retired to one of his ships. Two of Sweyn's men came with drink and dice, and we drank and played outside our lord's tent. We sensed no danger. It was a clear, moonlit night. Our fire burned bright. Our lord was safe under his cousin's protection. After a short while, I needed to relieve myself, but as I tried to stand, my legs gave way. My eyesight became blurred and my head span. Five or six men came from the shadows. They were armed with swords and their faces covered by the cheek guards of their helmets. It all happened so fast. I managed to pull my sword from its scabbard, but it was kicked from my hand. Glom had managed to stand, only to have a sword thrust into his belly. Earl Beorn was dragged, tied and gagged, out of his tent, a dagger to his throat, and taken towards the ships. I tried to retrieve my sword, but a blade sliced deep into my shoulder. Before I passed out, I saw Uliric's still body, his throat cut, lying next to me.

The sheer coldness of the sea water must have shocked me back to consciousness. I was still groggy, and my shoulder stung with the salt, but I managed to get to the surface and pulled myself up to an overhang of rocks, where I clung onto some kelp. There were two other splashes, as Uliric and Glom's bodies were thrown in to join me. They both sank to the bottom. All was quiet, except for the gentle lapping of the water against the rocks. I managed to pull myself along the edge to a place where it was shallow and hauled myself onto the beach and hid amongst the dunes. Four men came from the boats, they stopped on the shore and dug a hole, into which they unceremoniously rolled the body of Earl Beorn and hastily covered it over. Two of the men removed their helmets, wiping their brows from the exertion. It was your two fyrd-men, Leofric.'

'Ealdan and Grindan?' I said, taken aback.

'Yes, and what's more, when the third one spoke, he said, 'My father will pay you well.''

'It was Hakon!' I said, again shocked at what I was hearing.

'I am certain of it,' said Wulfgar, and he continued, 'after that, there were raised voices a little way along the beach. Several of Sweyn's boats left. I found out later that many of his men were so disgusted at the murder of his kin they deserted him. Not long after, as the sun rose slowly from the horizon, the rest of the ships left. I tried to drag myself further along the beach but passed out. When I next came to, it was days later. I was in a fisherman's cottage and his pretty daughter was mopping my brow. Apparently, they had found me when tending to their lobster pots. They had brought me back to their dwelling where Aelthwith nursed me. She had cleaned my wound and bandaged it with scraps of an old underskirt. They procured a sword and a horse for me by selling a ring I gave them. When I left, I stopped at a tavern where I came across the two men I had seen on the beach with Beorn's body. They were bragging of their exploits and the coin they received. I confronted them and I found out their names and where they were from. They died a coward's death, pleading for their lives. I gave them as much mercy as they had given to my Lord Beorn. So, I came to Æssefeld to find Hakon and hopefully, Sweyn.'

'And do what?' I asked.

'Wait for the opportunity to kill them both,' said Wulfgar, 'to avenge my lord. He died because I neglected my duty and became drunk. '

'So that's why you no longer drink ale or mead.'

'I vowed never to allow one drop to pass my lips until my lord is avenged. But now Sweyn is dead and Hakon a hostage. My lord will be avenged however long it takes, I will not rest until Hakon is dead.'

'It is no small matter to kill a member of the Godwins,' I said.

'Neither is it a small matter to plot to kill a king,' said Wulfgar.

Trying not to show I was shocked he knew anything about my involvement with Harthecnut, I said calmly, 'Meaning?'

'Meaning, before he died, I had an interesting conversation with Ealdan. Hakon had told him your father plotted to kill Harthecnut and how you tried to help him. He told me Hakon planned to disgrace you and wanted their help, though Ealdan did not yet know what the plan entailed. He also told me he and his brother were planning to blackmail your father with the information. Their plans ended with the stroke of my sword, and your secret remains safe.' Wulfgar made a slicing action with his blade as he spoke.

'What are your plans now?' I asked.

'To find a new lord until I can fulfil my vow to kill Hakon. And you, Leofric, what do you plan to do?'

I hesitated, acknowledging to myself that I believed his account of what happened with Beorn and I could trust him. I was relieved because I had come to value my friendship with Wulfgar.

'I have decided to stay here a little longer. When all my strength returns, I shall go to Turfrida. I need to show her I am alive and tell her of my innocence of the charges against me. After that, I will also seek a lord, make my name, and bring those who have defamed me to heel.'

'I shall go to St. Omer with you. We can search for a lord together.' Wulfgar extended his arm towards me and I grasped it as recognition of our pact.

He pulled me nearer to him. 'Have you noticed someone in the third window on the right watching us?' he said quietly.

'Yes, he was in the barracks and later in the great hall; a tall man in a mail shirt,' I said, having also seen him.

'We need to watch out for him and those others. I think it would be unwise for us to remain here much longer,' Wulfgar said.

I nodded. Without warning, Wulfgar released my arm and with all his strength swung his sword at my head. This time I was quicker and parried the blow, bringing my own blade down to hit him hard on the arm with the flat of the blade.

'You're getting better,' he roared with laughter.

'Just as well,' I said grimacing, 'you would have taken my head off.'

'Now, that would have been an improvement,' said Wulfgar. We both laughed and made our way back to the barracks.

Twenty-six

AD 1071
November

We reached the River Humbre at dawn. The land here and beyond is charred, black and devoid of life, the result of William's relentless devastation of the North. The stench of burning and death claws at our throats and stings our eyes. Ash, wet with morning mist, clings to our boots. It is said the destruction was so great that even now, after two winters, not a blade of grass grows between the Humbre and the River Tese. No village had escaped the ravages of fire and plunder. It is said any folk who survived the Norman slaughter resorted to eating dogs and horses. It is whispered, in dark places, some even fed on human flesh.

We have decided to wait overnight before we attempt to cross this wasteland. We have seen the odd horsemen, keeping their distance. Perhaps they had heard of the fate of the men whose horses we now rode and are waiting for reinforcements. Edwin has returned from a mill we passed. I gave him two coins and he bought bread and cheese and a flagon of ale. He said the miller started to ask questions, but when he noticed the coins, he was happy to make the trade.

We woke this morning to find Thurstan gone!

He has taken one of the horses and left a note to say he will beg William to pardon him and will plead for our lives. Edwin says the abbot is brave and selfless to do that for us, but Wulfgar and I agree, that is not the Thurstan we know.

We have gathered berries and saved some of the cheese and bread. We will set off across this black desert, travelling day and night. There is little shelter, but I doubt anyone will follow us into this hellish morass. I doubt there will be chance to write until we have reached the other side so I will continue my tale until we have to leave.

ᛏᚻᛖ ᚹᚫᛋᛏᛖᛚᚫᚾᛞ

AD 1053

The next three or four days continued much the same as the last. Wulfgar and I trained in the quad. It got harder and harder. I became faster and stronger. Rush had befriended a servant girl and had taken to 'long walks' in the nearby woods. Tripp mainly ate and drank and discussed trading opportunities with Gilbert. Hereward hunted and delighted at showing his expertise at everything he did and revelled in proving all others to be inferior in their efforts. We had also discovered, that the tall man that kept watching us was Reinald Levett, the Norman master of arms and head trainer of the garrison. Apparently, he was an accomplished knight, a seasoned warrior and deadly with most weapons, especially the sword. He had been indiscreet with the wife of one of the Norman nobility. Too good a soldier to be lost to them completely, he had been sent here until the scandal died down.

I had taken in the evenings to sit in the small arena where Gilbert kept wild animals for testing the strength and courage of the prospective knights. It was a three-quarter circle of wooden benches arranged in tiers around a sawdust-covered fighting area. In the final quarter were wooden cages, housing a variety of wild beasts, which were pitted against the best men at the end of their training. In one cage were two wild boars, sharp-tusked, heavy boned creatures, with brutish eyes and scarred from previous battles. Another cage housed six grey wolves, with thick, matted hair and bite-marked legs, where they had snapped at each other. There was a large stag with enormous antlers, that could do untold damage, and two black bulls with horns that could toss a man like a corn dolly or gore him to death, and three brown bears that walked back and forth in their cage, their claws as lethal as their teeth.

As impressive as these creatures were, there was one animal which surpassed all others, both in size and ferocity.

A massive white bear.

When it stood on its hind legs it was bigger than two tall men. It was said to be kin of the Earl of Norðhymbraland, Siward Beornson, and to have the power of speech, but only spoke to men as they were about to die. I was told only three men had ever been brave, or foolish, enough to fight it: two it had killed, the other was Dagfin, Gilbert's steward. He barely survived and his present condition was the result.

The white bear fascinated me. Even on four legs, it came level to a man's shoulder. It did not pace its cage like the brown bears but swayed from side to side and rolled its head on its thick neck. Its eyes were black and small for such a big head. Its paws were as wide as a man's foot is long, with webbed toes and long claws. It also had forty-two sharp teeth for ripping flesh. As well as being caged, the white bear was chained by its left leg to a large millstone. It reminded me of when I was chained in the priory, desperate for freedom.

'Do you believe the white bear can talk?' It was Hereward. He came and sat a few benches from me.

'I think you would have to die to find out,' I replied.

'My godfather won't let me fight him,' said Hereward, not taking his eyes off the beast. 'He thinks I am too youthful and that my father would be displeased with him if it killed me. They say it is magical, with superhuman powers. They call it the Fairy Bear.'

'It's a magnificent creature,' I said.

'Would you fight it, Leofric?'

'Only if I had to,' I answered truthfully.

'Most wise.'

We had been joined by Dagfin. As he spoke to us, his eyes never wavered from looking at the white bear.

'I was the best of my generation of young, prospective knights. All had yielded to my sword over time. I had killed boars and a huge black bull in this arena. No one surpassed me in the hunt, not even Lord Gilbert. My reward was being allowed to fight the white bear. With the exuberance of youth, I faced the Fairy Bear with spear and axe. Defeat was unimaginable. I would carve my name in Senchal's history. There was no hesitation, it came for me like a snowstorm. I threw my spear, which it brushed away as if it were kindling. Before I could swing my axe, its claws tore at my face, removing my eye from its socket. It ripped my arm from my body and shattered the bones in my leg. It took ten men with spears to drive it back into its cage. They dragged my almost dead body from this place, my days as a warrior and ambition of knighthood over. So, yes, to choose to fight the white bear would be madness.'

'Then I am mad,' said Hereward, 'for I would choose to fight the white bear, and if I should die, I could not think of a worthier opponent. Many men have tried to end my life, none have proved able yet.'

'You are fortunate my Lord Gilbert is a wise man, for he has forbidden you to fight the Fairy Bear and that will preserve your life,' said Dagfin. 'I came here to seek you out Hereward, Lord Gilbert wishes to discuss tomorrow's hunt with you.'

'Tell him I will be there presently after I have discussed a personal matter with Leofric,' said Hereward.

'Make sure it stays a discussion and not something more boisterous or my lord will be most displeased,' said Dagfin.

'Of course, we will honour Lord Gilbert's wishes, I give my word,' said Hereward. Dagfin nodded and left us alone.

As we talked, neither of us looked at the other, both of us watched the white bear as he swayed from side to side and rolled his head.

'You realise, I cannot have people knocking me over without consequence,' said Hereward eventually.

'Fully,' I said, 'you have your reputation to think of.'

'You could beg for mercy in front of others and I could show how merciful I am,' he said, without a hint of irony in his voice.

'I could, but you should understand I cannot have people calling me a cripple and getting away with it. You could beg for my mercy in front of others, and I could show how merciful I am,' I replied.

We both still never took our eyes from watching the bear.

'I will fight the bear, cripple, and after I have killed it, there will be a time and place when I will kill you.'

'I sincerely hope the bear does not end your life, Hereward, so that pleasure may be mine.'

Before either of us could say another word, the white bear gave an almighty roar and dragged one of his front paws across the bars of his cage making all the cages shake and rattle, which set off the wolves and the dogs, and the bulls bellowed loudly whilst scraping the dirt with their hooves as if they were about to charge.

Hereward stood and with his customary flick of his cloak, left.

I stayed a little longer until the noise subsided. In those few moments the madness Dagfin talked of engulfed me and I thought, what if I fought and killed the white bear, how my reputation would soar? Despite the fact the thought terrified me, I would fight it, even if I was not strong enough yet to defeat it. I decided not to mention this to the others, as I knew they would try to prevent me from doing so. I gave the Fairy Bear one last look and wondered if I would ever hear him speak.

The following week was much the same as the last. Rush

womanised, Tripp drank and negotiated, Wulfgar and I practised, practised and practised again.

In the next few days, it would be Easter.

Traditionally, Christmas, Easter and Pentecost, were the times when Lord Gilbert would choose a number of young men to fight against the animals in the arena. I felt I was ready and I would ask him if I could fight the Fairy Bear.

The fates ignore the plans of men.

The day before Long Friday, Wulfgar, Tripp and I were walking past the arena on the way to the great hall. There was a crowd of men armed with spears running from the barracks towards the hall and the lord's manor house. The gates to the arena lay in splinters on the ground. What we saw inside was a scene of bloody mayhem. One of the boars lay dead, its body smashed and ripped. The other boar cowered, whimpering in its broken cage, bloodied, with half its hind leg hanging off. The wolves were howling, and the brown bears gave deep throated growls and pawed at the bars of their cages. There were also two men on the ground at the edge of the arena both gravely injured, but seemingly still alive.

We came out of the arena and made our way towards the hall where the armed men were now gathered at the entrance to the courtyard. We pushed through to the front to find Lord Gilbert himself was there. His favourite hunting dog lay dead at his feet and further across the yard, two horse's broken bodies were spread out before us.

In the middle of the courtyard, the cause of all this chaos was the great, white bear. His mouth and claws were dripping with blood and blood was spattered over his white fur. The broken chain was still connected to his hind leg and swung behind him like a writhing serpent as he moved.

Several of the men threw their spears at him, but they either missed their target or he knocked them away effortlessly. Lord Gilbert urged caution and was resigned to the fact the bear could not be taken alive. This was my chance. I unhooked the axe from Tripp's shoulder before he had the chance to stop me and moved forward cautiously towards the Fairy Bear. I learnt that day when Hereward is involved, caution translates as slow. He appeared from the small, side entrance of the courtyard. He came quickly, his sword at the ready, his cloak swirling behind. The bear rose before me standing on its hind legs. Spittle and blood flew from its savage mouth as he shook his head violently. It gave a great roar, I readied the axe and moved a little nearer.

'Prepare to meet your end, beast,' roared Hereward.

In one movement, the bear, seeing Hereward come from the side, altered direction and crashed to the ground, its huge paws sending dust flying into the air. Without pause, he pounded towards Hereward. Gripping the hilt of his sword with both hands, Hereward held it aloft above his head, the blade pointing downwards at an angle. Most men would have sidestepped at the last moment and thrust at the bear from the side, but not Hereward. He stood his ground as the monstrous frame of the bear charged towards him. As it was almost upon him, Hereward leant forward and rammed the sword straight into the beast's head. The blade plunged through flesh and bone, killing the ferocious creature instantly. As the dead beast slid along the ground, Hereward leapt forward, over its head, on to its back, narrowly avoiding being crushed by the momentum of the mighty, blood-soaked, white-furred carcass. Still gripping the hilt of his sword and keeping his balance he rode the dead beast until it came to a sudden halt. Everyone gasped and looked on in awe.

I was relieved, but also furious that Hereward had taken my moment from me and spellbound at the ease and simplicity with which he had dispatched such a creature as the Fairy Bear.

Lord Gilbert embraced Hereward and hugged him as he jumped off the dead bear's back. Others slapped his back, shook his hand. Now the danger had gone, ladies and maids who had rushed inside when the bear had first appeared, came flocking back outside, running to kiss Hereward and shouted their undying devotion towards him. His companion, Martin Lightfoot, helped him raise the bear's head and shoulders so all could see this once mighty beast close to.

To their shame, several of the would-be knights had hidden inside with the women, afraid to face the wild creature. One by one they filed out, blinking in the sunlight, to see the bear with Hereward's sword lodged in its brain.

'That's it, you can come out now, the ladies have checked the bear is dead, you're quite safe,' said Hereward mockingly.

No one replied, but I believe it was at that moment they finally decided to kill him.

The bear was skinned and made into a magnificent fur cloak that Hereward would wear to remind him and others of a remarkable feat.

Lord Gilbert left the day after the killing of the bear to take care of a matter in Eorferwic. We said our farewells and thanked him for his hospitality, for we planned to be gone before he returned.

We made our preparations to leave in two days' time. At last, we would be going to St. Omer to see Turfrida. Tripp still thought it was a bad idea, but he was going his separate way to continue his trading. Wulfgar was happy to go wherever he might find a lord to serve and Rush did not care, as long as there were women and ale.

Reinald Levett came and sat next to me in the feast hall the day before we planned to leave. He placed a jug of ale and two drinking horns on the oak table. He filled both horns from the jug and offered one to me.

'Drink with me, Leofric.'

'I will,' I said, taking the horn.

Reinald Levett drank the horn dry and filled it again from the jug.

'Many of the young men here are good men,' he said as he gestured me to drink mine, 'men who put valour and honour before other things.' He smiled as I drained my horn of ale and proffered it for a refill. 'There are also those who have lived privileged lives who are accustomed to having things their own way. They care little of honour. They're full of pride, greed and ambition.' He drank from the horn again, this time slower and not all the contents. 'I bring you news, Leofric, that you may find good or bad. Do with it what you will. I have watched you train and have been impressed. I witnessed your bravery in front of the white bear. I believe you to be a man of honour.'

'Many would refute that,' I said downing more ale.

'Oh, I have heard the stories about you, Leofric of Æssefeld-Underbarroe, for all that, from what I have seen of you here, I suspect most are untrue.'

I supped the last of my ale and covered the horn with my hand to indicate I wanted no more. 'What news do you bring, Reinald?'

He leant closer and looked around to make sure no one else could hear. 'When Hereward returns from hunting tomorrow, as he passes through the rocky pass, he will be ambushed. Outnumbered, even he will be in grave danger. You may be willing for this to happen or you may want to prevent it. The choice is yours.'

'Why are you telling me this?' I asked, wondering if it was to trap the rest of us as well.

'I am not particularly fond of Hereward of Brune, I find him an arrogant, overbearing man. Nonetheless, I admire his courage and skills and I loathe cowards. If none of these men are brave enough to face him alone, they do not have the right to kill him. Telling him will not prevent this from happening, he will still face them believing he can win. You though could make sure it was more of an even contest if you so wish it. If not, my conscience is clear.'

Reinald Levett explained to me in detail what the assailants' plans were. Afterwards he finished the rest of the ale and left.

I told Wulfgar, Tripp and Rush what I planned to do, and they agreed to join me; Rush reluctantly.

'Let the arrogant bastard die,' were his exact words. He shrugged his shoulders, saying, 'If that's what you want to do,' and shrugged his shoulders again.

Later that day, I sought out Martin Lightfoot. I told him of the ambush. 'We will make sure the odds are fairer. All you have to do is deal with what happens in front of you.'

He looked at me suspiciously. 'This will not change Hereward's intentions towards you,' he said.

'Nor would I expect it to,' I replied.

'If that is true, I am grateful to you.' He gave a nod and left.

The next morning, before first light, we dressed in our mail shirts, gathered our weapons and horses and quietly made our way out of the compound. We told the guards we were leaving for St. Omer and none of them seemed sorry we were leaving. Tripp drove his cart left at a fork in the road, as if he was leaving us and re-joined us again a couple of miles further on.

We came to the place Reinald Levett had described and it was the perfect place for an ambush. The track was long and narrow, flanked on either side by high, sheer cliffs. Every so often there were clefts in the rock face, leading nowhere, but large enough for our concealment. We found one big enough for Tripp's cart and he and Rush put nose-bags on the horses to quieten them. Tripp had his axe and a spear. Rush had collected many decent size pebbles to launch from his sling, his seax hung from his belt. Wulfgar and I were in a smaller fissure on the opposite side of the pass, both in mail vests and armed with swords. Wulfgar also had his axe and I had slung my bow over my shoulder as a last resort. We waited there all morning. We were sheltered from the wind, though a constant trickle of water down the rock face made us damp and cold. Martins were flittering above us making mud nests in holes in the rock and occasionally we would be splattered by their falling debris, making us curse under our breath.

About midday, we were aware of armed men appearing at each end of the pass and concealing themselves amongst the rocks, oblivious to our presence.

Again, we waited. The horses were skittish but thankfully remained quiet. Rush fell asleep for a short while in the wagon. The sun came and filled the pass with bright white light before passing over, leaving us in dark, cold shadow.

We heard them before we got sight of them, Hereward's laughter being unmistakable. He and Martin Lightfoot rode slowly down the pass towards us as if there were nothing untoward. They had a carcass of a large deer slung over a spare horse; the fruit of a day's hunting. The horsemen appeared as silhouettes at the end of the pass behind them. There were six of them, wearing mail and helmets of metal plate with long nasal bars.

Hereward, never one to shirk a fight, swung his horse around to face the attackers. Martin Lightfoot did likewise. They let the horse with the deer run loose and hefted their spears in readiness to defend themselves. They were outnumbered three to one, but I would still have wagered on Hereward and Martin Lightfoot being victorious, until at our end of the pass, another eight horsemen appeared, obviously intending to trap Hereward in the middle. The first group had now dismounted and led by Durand Bourgault, the man, who only days before, had been saved by Hereward, moved deliberately towards their intended victims. Those at our end of the pass remained mounted and moved steadily towards us, unaware of our presence. Hereward realised the trap they were in and shouted to Martin to watch their backs.

Tripp gently flicked the reins of the cart and pulled out of the cleft to block the way. He and Rush stood on the cart, axe and sling at the ready. The assailants reined in their mounts to prevent colliding with the cart. One of them, giving a derisory snigger, launched his spear. It narrowly missed Tripp, thudding into the cart. Wulfgar and I rode out of our place of concealment swords drawn.

'This is not your concern, Leofric,' said Guy Beaufort, alarmed at our sudden appearance. 'Leave this place now with your lives and no more will be said of it.'

'You made it our concern when you decided it would take fourteen men to kill two,' I said, 'hardly the actions of men of honour.'

Guy Beaufort rode towards me, swinging his sword violently towards my head. I simply ducked and saw the look of surprise on his face at the speed and power of my own sword, as it pierced through mail and leather and straight through his body. Blood gushed from the wound as I pulled my blade from him and he fell, lifeless, from his saddle to the ground. At the same time Rush unleashed a pebble from his sling and another rider was sent backwards off his horse, having been struck in the centre of his forehead. The others reigned in their mounts in panic as further along the pass, Durand Bourgault, about to throw his spear at Hereward, was killed instantly by the man from Brune and another of his colleagues fell to Hereward's sword, blood spraying into the air. Death came quickly and easily in that ravine. The main instigators of the ambush both dead, the remainder fled out of the pass, as fast as they could, like the cowards they were.

Hereward seemed genuinely shocked that a man he had rescued a few days earlier would wish him dead.

Jealousy can be a powerful potion and drive men to extreme actions, especially when the fear of humiliation fuel that fervour.

Hereward rode to us. 'I believe we have all outstayed our welcome here. We bid you farewell and God speed.' Martin Lightfoot and the man from Brune spurred their mounts and left us.

'Oh, and what he meant to say was and thanks for saving our lives,' said Rush sarcastically.

Arrogant he may be, but Hereward was right about overstaying our welcome. We said our farewells to Tripp, and as he headed west, we went east to find fame and fortune and where I would marry Turfrida, the Castallan of St. Omer's youngest daughter.

Twenty-seven

AD 1054

The road to the boats that Tripp told us would take us to St. Omer, passed through a small, wooded valley, carpeted with violet-blue columbine which constantly moved in the breeze like doves in flight. We came out onto a high ridge to a sight we had not been expecting.

Stretched out below us was the camp of a large army. Tents, cooking fires, carts, horses and thousands of men, filled the valley below.

'Why the hell are they there?' said Rush, as the three of us dismounted and crouched behind a cluster of holly bushes.

'I don't know,' said Wulfgar, 'but I don't think we should stay to find out.'

'Neither do I, but we will have to find another route,' I said. As we turned to leave, at least thirty mounted men-at-arms rode towards us, no more than twenty paces away. There was nowhere to hide, and it was pointless to resist.

Three of them eased their horses towards us. One, obviously the leader, wore a jacket of black bear's fur with a mail shoulder guard and riveted conical helmet. His hair was dark and worn long in many plaits. His face was battle-scarred. The skin above his upper lip was clean shaven, though he wore a long thick beard from his chin. A sword was partially visible behind a shield slung from his saddle.

The other two men were monks and I recognised them both:

Brother Riocus and Brother Alberic. The warrior spoke first.

'Are these the men you seek?'

'Yes,' said Riocus pointing. 'The red-haired one is a runaway slave. Apparently that one,' pointing at Wulfgar, 'is sought after by Earl Harold regarding the murder of Harold's cousin Earl Beorn, and he is a madman the prior locked away in the priory for his own and others safety,' he said, pointing directly at me.

The warrior looked at each one of us for a moment, deciding if what the monk said was true.

'I have been ordered to provide you with an escort to assist you in taking them back to the monastery, but first I must question them on the orders of Earl Siward,' he said, addressing the monk.

'There's no need,' said Riocus, 'we have troubled you enough. Prior Thurstan will deal with them when we get back to the priory.'

The warrior gave Riocus a look which would have concerned braver men than the monk.

'Once we have questioned them, we will tell you what we have decided to do. Was I clearer that time, monk?'

'Perfectly,' said an indignant Riocus, 'though Prior Thurstan will be most displeased when I tell him of your hindrance.'

'You do that, monk, you do that,' said the warrior, obviously not caring what Riocus did or what a prior thought.

The warrior waved his hand and four sword-drawn men came forward.

'You will come with us,' one of them said, and we were marched down from the ridge and into the camp.

As we passed through the maze of tents, it was evident this was an army preparing for war. Forges had been erected and swords, spears and axes were being made or sharpened. There were cartloads of shields and provisions and streams of men were coming from all directions to join those already there.

The warrior rode ahead of us to a large tent which flew two banners from its central pole, one depicting a white bear, the other a raven. We were taken to a smaller tent and ten of the horsemen dismounted and encircled it to become our guards. Our hands tied behind our backs, we were pushed into the tent. Inside was a large wooden table, two chairs and nothing else.

'What do we do now?' asked Rush when we were alone.

I thought for a moment. 'We will deny everything Riocus said, we will say we are mercenaries looking for a lord to serve. We were told of the army gathering and we have come to offer our services. After a couple of days, we will simply slip away.'

'Oh, good,' said Wulfgar, 'we're wanted for thievery, murder, betrayal and now we're going to add desertion.'

'I'm already wanted for that,' said Rush, 'so makes little difference to me.'

'Have either of you got a better idea?' I snapped. The silence told me they did not.

The tent flap flung open and the warrior with the plaited hair and five other men two carrying cudgels came in.

'Take the slave,' the warrior said. Two of his men grabbed Rush.

'Get off me, you sons of turds,' he yelled and butted one of them in the face. The other responded by striking Rush in the stomach with his cudgel, taking the breath from him. The first man, wiping blood from his nose, hit Rush again, this time on the head, making his legs crumple.

'It will be a pleasure to see you hang, shit for brains,' he said through a fat lip and they dragged Rush outside. I twisted my wrists to free my hands but to no avail.

'Leave him alone, he is a free man, not a slave,' I cried.

Another man smashed his fist into my face, sending me backwards onto the ground.

'Who asked you?' he said as he kicked me in the stomach.

The warrior stood over me slowly stroking his long beard.

'My name is Keld,' he said, 'I can make men's lives good and I can make them bad.'

'An e's gonna, make yours 'orribly bad,' said the one who had hit me, and he kicked me again in the stomach, making me gasp.

'Take no heed of him, Leofric, he's a miserable bastard who likes kicking people. In fact, he likes it so much, I've seen him kick men to death, horrible way to die, Leofric, slow, painful, undignified. But don't worry, I won't let him do that to you. You're far too valuable to me. You see, I know all about you and your quiet friend here. I know who you are, where you're from and why you are on the run. Most importantly, I know what you're worth and I know people who would pay good money to get their hands on you. I also know you stole something of great value, but what it is or where it is, I don't know.' Keld paused for a moment stroking his beard again.

'Some fight in this army, Leofric, for glory and booty. We only fight for booty. So, if we can get the booty without the risk, all the better. You're going to tell me what it is you stole and where you have hidden it.'

'Piss off, you son of a whore,' I spat through bloody lips, bracing myself, expecting another kick. Instead, Keld put his arm out to stop it from happening.

'It's unfortunate for your friend here you don't want to co-operate with me. Let me introduce you properly to my other two men. This one is Regnar the Mean, and this is Asger Blood Spiller. You will be glad to hear they're both useless at kicking. Their speciality is the seax. I have seen them remove men's internal organs without hardly leaving a mark on their bodies.'

Both drew seaxes from their belts and moved towards Wulfgar.

'I stole nothing,' I rasped, 'the stories are lies.'

Keld stroked his beard and shook his head.

'Let's take his kidneys,' said Regnar.

'Where's 'is kidneys?' asked Asger.

Regnar pushed Wulfgar against the central tent pole and held his seax to his throat. 'I don't know, just stick your knife in and slide it around. They're in there somewhere.'

Asger ran the point of his blade down the front of Wulfgar's jerkin, cutting the leather, exposing his bare chest and midriff. I tried to stand, but Keld placed his foot on my shoulder and pushed me back to the ground.

The tent flap flung open again and a soldier entered.

'Can't you see I'm occupied?' Keld shouted at him.

'You're to bring your two prisoners to Earl Siward immediately,' the soldier said, before whispering something to Keld.

Keld looked upwards, 'Shit,' was all he said. He grabbed my arm and pulled me to my feet. 'Seems you have influential friends, cripple.'

We were taken outside and across the camp to the big tent with the banners. At the entrance stood two guards with spears, barring our way, on seeing Keld they let us pass.

This tent was different from the one we had been in. The floor was strewn with clean rushes and tapestries had been hung on horizontal poles. There were boxes and chests and several tables where priests and other men sat writing. In one corner, next to a huge bed covered in woollen blankets and furs, was a stand with an array of weapons, chain mail coats and war-helmets. There was a smouldering brazier to take away the chill, which tainted the air with faint, wispy smoke. In the centre, was a throne-like chair with elaborate carvings of wild beasts and birds in which was sat Earl Siward of Norðhymbraland.

The expression bear-like is given to many men huge in stature but never was it more applicable than to Earl Siward. His nick name was Digri, which means the stout. And, with his fair, almost white hair, which hung to his shoulders, his full beard, flecked with grey and small, dark eyes, it was easy to see why it was believed he was descended from a great, white bear. He ruled Norðhymbraland almost as a king. Left much alone by King Edward, Siward laid down the rules and laws of this wild region from the Humbre to the Forth.

Many men, soldiers, priests and advisers surrounded him. Two men I knew, Lord Gilbert of Ghent and Reinald Levett. Wulfgar and I, Keld and his three henchmen were ushered to stand before them.

'It seems you didn't tell me all you discovered about these men, Keld,' said Earl Siward, his voice booming around the tent.

'I have told you everything, lord,' said Keld, lying. 'I was trying to find out more when we were summoned here.'

'What did you find out about them?'

'Nothing, lord.'

'Nothing? You didn't find out they are on the run and there might

269

be a large reward for them? Or they might be aware of other booty? And if you had found these things out, you wouldn't plan to profit from them yourself would you, Keld?'

It was Keld's time to feel fear. Earl Siward considered himself a fair man, but he was known to be ruthless. No one could be seen to get the better of him either physically or mentally. Men who crossed him died. As one of his leaders, Keld must have seen this on many occasions. He bent down on one knee.

'Lord, as God is my witness, I do everything for your honour and gain. My sword is your sword and your enemies are my enemies.'

'See it remains so, or I will hang your balls from a pole for the ravens to feed on. Not that they would get fat on them. Now, wait at the back of the tent.'

As Keld and his three men skulked to the rear, the man who had kicked me said quietly, 'You will die, cripple, and soon.'

Earl Siward watched us a while before speaking.

'I remember you, boy, when you were skinnier than you are now,' Earl Siward said to me. 'You had disobeyed your father, defied a king and taken sides with that puffed up bag of wind Godwin. Now I hear stories of theft, murder, madness and fighting magical bears.' He paused, 'I like you, Leofric, I like your spirit, something missing in young men today, spirit.' He paused again. 'Trouble is, I have two monks saying you must go back with them. What do you say, Leofric, do you want to back to their monastery?'

'No, lord,' I said.

'They say you were there because you're mad.'

'I was there against my will, lord, but it's true, I would have gone mad if I was there much longer.'

'So, what do you want?' Siward asked.

'Three things, my lord,' I answered

'Only three things,' he said sarcastically, 'and what might they be?'

'First, for our friend Rush to be restored to us. Second, to go to St. Omer to marry a girl there, and third, the chance to clear my name.'

'Ah! A girl, whenever a man is in trouble there's usually a girl involved. This friend, Rush you say, is he the slave they've taken to hang?'

'Yes, my lord, but he is no slave, he is our friend.'

'I am told he is your father's slave and he has run away, is it not so?' I could detect a growing impatience in his voice.

'Yes, lord, but...' Siward held out his hand to stop me.

'He's a runaway slave. He should hang as an example to stop others doing the same thing.' He spoke to an attendant, 'Bring me the slave if he hasn't been hung already.'

'Leofric, you said you wanted three things, well there are three reasons why I am still talking to you and didn't let Keld continue to work his charm on you. One is, I know your father, he is a good man and doesn't deserve to go to his grave thinking his son is a coward. Another is these two men whom I respect,' he said looking at Gilbert and Levett, 'tell me you are courageous and a capable swordsman. I need such men. Lastly, a few weeks ago, I was visited by a sorceress who told me you would come here.'

All the priests at the tables lifted their heads and frowning, crossed themselves.

'Mair,' I thought to myself.

'She told me things, Leofric, things only one with mystic powers could possibly know.' He stood from his chair and walked to Wulfgar and me and spoke softly so only we could hear. 'She also told me you are lucky, Leofric, a charmed one and destined for great things.'

I was not feeling lucky or charmed but kept silent.

'She told me if you were to join us in this coming campaign, we would be assured of victory.'

As Siward walked back to his seat, the attendant returned accompanied by two soldiers who were holding Rush up on either side. He was cut and bruised and barely conscious.

'You have two choices, Leofric. I send you back to the priory with the monks and an armed escort. Wulfgar will be handed over to Earl Harold to answer charges of cowardice and betrayal and he,' pointing at Rush, 'will hang. Or, you will swear allegiance to me as your lord. You will come with my army to the land of the Scotti to fight the usurper Mac Bethad mac Findlaich and help put my kin Malcolm in his rightful place as King of Alba, as his father was before him. You can take a share of any booty you acquire, and when this campaign is over you can continue with your quest to prove your innocence of the charges brought against you. Wulfgar and the red-headed one can go with you, as long as they accept my terms.'

It was no choice. I either agreed or live the rest of my life as a prisoner and condemn both my friends to death. I would still have to wait to see Turfrida, and I wondered if that was behind Mair's intervention and prophecy.

Twenty-eight

My ribs and stomach ached from the kicking I received, and my spirits were low. I was in no position to object to any demands from Earl Siward. I dropped to one knee. 'I accept you, Earl Siward Beornson, Dragon Slayer, Earl of Norðhymbraland as my lord and gift bearer. I swear to maintain your laws and uphold your name, reputation and honour and bear arms for your cause.'

Siward's grin was clearly visible beneath his thick beard.

'Cut his binds,' he ordered, and the rope was taken from my wrists. The earl handed me three gold arm rings, as a tangible sign of our pact, which I slipped over my bruised wrists. Siward turned his gaze to Wulfgar.

'Earl Beorn was a friend of mine. His death saddened me. He always spoke proudly of his three heorawerod. He trusted them more than any other men. I will give you the chance to prove you deserved his trust. If I find you were in anyway responsible for Beorn's death, I will kill you myself. Leofric has accepted me as his lord. I will not send you back to Earl Harold if you accept Leofric as your lord.'

Wulfgar stared into my eyes. This man had taught me how to fight. He had rescued me from the priory. He was a warrior, I was still a young man, untried in a shield wall. He dropped to one knee.

'Leofric, son of Renweard, Thegn of Æssefeld-Underbarroe, I acknowledge you as my lord and will serve you with my life.'

The look in his eyes told me this was no idle gesture and I slipped one of the arm rings off and handed it to him.

'Although you call me lord, you will always be my friend and equal,' I said. Earl Siward pulled a seax from his belt and passed it to me. I cut the ropes on Wulfgar's wrists and we embraced.

Siward, took the seax from me and placing the flat of the blade under Rush's chin, he lifted his slumped head. Still supported by the two guards, Rush, slowly opened his swollen eyes as wide as he could.

'I do not know you, boy,' said Siward, 'but I know Leofric wants you to live and if it wasn't for him you would be dead now, hanging from your neck. You must swear to me you will serve Leofric all your days. Do this and you will live.'

I knew the look on Rush's face; resentment, frustration, rebelliousness. He knew there was only one course to take if he was to stay alive.

'I swear it, lord.'

'You were born into slavery, were you not?' asked Siward.

'Yes, lord.'

'Yet you ran away from your master. How can I be sure you won't do the same again?'

'I have sworn it, lord.'

Siward made a gesture with his hand and a man came from the brazier with an iron rod which had been placed into the base of the fire where it glowed hot. Aware of what was about to happen, Rush struggled against the two guards. The sleeve of his tunic was rolled above his elbow to expose the upper arm and the brand was pushed hard against his skin. Rush tried his hardest to stifle a scream, which resulted in a muffled groan like the last death throes of a hunted boar.

The smell of burning flesh filled my nostrils and my friend had a **W** burnt onto his arm. It was a custom that had died out in Wessex, the branding of a Wealas, the old Saxon name for a slave; obviously it was still practised here. I was ashamed I had allowed it to happen, but I was powerless to stop it and I consoled myself Rush was still alive.

'Good,' said Siward, 'now I have a war to prepare for. Leofric, you will report to my son, Osbeorn. He will teach you the ways of us from Norðhymbraland and you will guard his back.'

Most of the company around the earl laughed loudly at this. I did not know why but I was soon to find out. Our horses, weapons and meagre belongings were restored to us and we were taken to a part of the camp where a different banner flew. It carried the symbol of what seemed to me, like the instrument used to kill cattle. It turned out that's exactly what it was, but one modified for war.

Osbeorn Siwardson was nicknamed Bulax because of his favoured weapon and the skill with which he wielded it. A long pole with an axe-shaped cutting blade on one side for chopping limbs, a hammer-head on the opposite side for crushing bones and skulls, and on top a sharp spike for piercing mail and amour. It was a weapon to be feared, especially in a skilled man's hands.

We were shown to our tent which we were to share with eight, gruff northern soldiers who mumbled about soft-bellied Southern-ers and why had they been saddled with a cripple, a traitor and a runaway slave. We made Rush as comfortable as we could, bathing his wounds and leaving him to sleep.

Wulfgar and I went out into the camp to look for Osbeorn. We came to a clearing where men were wrestling, sword fighting and generally training for war.

One group, being drilled in shield wall formation, were screamed at if there was so much as a chink of light between the shields.

What caught our attention was a framework structure erected at the end of a makeshift arena, on which hung a line of pig carcasses. One by one, a group of soldiers ran along the line thrusting a spear into a dead pig, withdrawing the spear before running on to the next.

When they had finished a lone warrior stepped forward. He was about the same age as me, but taller, with long, unkempt blonde hair hanging below his shoulders. His face was unmistakeably a younger version of his father, Earl Siward. Stripped to the waist, his muscular torso glistened with sweat. He held in his hands the weapon we call a poleaxe and the Danes call a bulax. He swung it around his head a few times getting the feel of its weight and balance. While the weapon was still whirling in the air, he started running at the hanging swine. At the first one, he brought the poleaxe down vertically, severing one

275

of its legs. Without pausing he continued to the second pig and, twisting his upper body slightly, brought the blade across horizontally decapitating the dead animal in one move. At the third, he aimed the hammer-head straight between its eyes, making the distinctive sound of crushing bone. The fourth carcass, on which had been draped chain mail, he thrust the pointed blade with such force it pierced both mail and flesh and protruded out the other side. Pulling it from the carcass, he ran to the fifth and final pig and bringing the poleaxe straight and high over his head, cut the body in two from its head to its hind-quarters. From start to finish the manoeuvre had taken seconds and was rhythmic, agile and lethal.

A group of young men, who had been watching Osbeorn, banged spears on shields in admiration. Their jubilation was short-lived as they and everyone else were distracted by five horsemen making their way through the ranks. It was Keld and his three henchmen, led by a portly man riding a white horse and carrying a shield adorned with a painted heron. He also wore a dark wing feather of a grey heron in his helmet. As he rode by, he tapped certain men on the shoulder with a long staff. Regnar the Mean and Asger Blood Spiller, who had both dismounted, shoved heron wing feathers into the chosen men's belts.

'Who's he?' I asked the man who stood next to me.

'Fritjof Heironson, one of the leading thegns of Norðhymbraland and a commander of Earl Siward's forces. He knows Osbeorn has the best trained men, so he comes and helps himself.'

'And Osbeorn lets him?' I asked.

'He used to stop him. Bloodied the fat bugger's nose many times, but Fritjof complained to Earl Siward saying he was unjust allowing his son to have all the best men. Not wanting to seem to be favouring his own and alienate such a powerful ally, Earl Siward made Osbeorn vow not to attack or hinder Fritjof. Osbeorn, in turn, ordered his own men not to resist, although they all dread the touch of the staff. Thegn Fritjof is a cruel master and cowardly always leads from the back out of harm's way.'

'And does Osbeorn have the best men?' I asked.

'Yes, but only because he trains them to be the best,' replied the soldier.

Whilst this was taking place, someone had approached Osbeorn and pointed us out to him. He passed his weapon to a comrade and strode over to greet us, ignoring Fritjof and his men.

'So, you're Leofric,' he shouted as he approached. 'I have heard stories about you. Welcome to our army. Come, join me in my tent for a horn of mead.'

I stared at him unsmiling.

'I am afraid we cannot join your army, lord,' I said loudly.

He stopped short, frowning.

'We cannot join an army that harbours cowards, my lord.'

'Be careful what you say, Leofric,' said Osbeorn, bridling at the accusation.

'We cannot be brothers with men who are only brave when their opponents are bound and rendered defenceless. We cannot fight alongside or trust our own lives to those who kick men to death when they are down,' I said.

'Do you have someone in mind, Leofric, or do you besmirch this whole army?'

'Lord, Earl Siward's army is renowned as brave and as fierce as any. Your men particularly are so famed for their skill and courage, others come to steal them. But cowards tarnish such reputations.'

Keld and his three henchmen had drawn close to us. Most men had stopped what they were doing and watched us closely.

'This dog shit,' I said, pointing at the man who had kicked me, 'would slit your throat as you slept, or stick a seax between your shoulder blades from the shadows. I doubt he has ever fought a man face to face in his life.'

The man next to me shook his head. 'Shut your mouth now whilst you still can.'

My victim, because that's all he was, slid his sword from its scabbard. He looked at Thegn Fritjof. 'Lord, this little 'obbling shit has questioned my 'onour, I can't let 'im get away with that.'

Fritjof Heironson looked disinterested and irritated by the delay.

'Kill him and let's get on with it,' he said.

I drew my sword and men stood back to make room. My opponent glowered at me.

'I said you'd die soon, 'obbler, now you've given me an excuse.'

'I do not even know your name,' I said, as I exaggerated my limp and moved deliberately slowly, 'I should know it before I kill you.'

'All you need to know, 'obbler, is that for you, I'm Death.'

'Then the scops and bards will tell of the day when Leofric of Æssefeld-Underbarroe slew Death,' I said.

Without further warning he rushed at me, both hands gripped tightly around the hilt of his sword and slashed wildly at my head. His death was easier than I had anticipated. I leant backwards and spun on my good leg, I brought my sword around with such force, the edge of the blade cut into his throat and almost severed his head. A rush of blood spurted from the gash, his eyes swelled, and he fell dead to the ground.

Before I was aware, Asger Blood Spiller came behind me. He lunged at my back with his seax. Wulfgar reacted quicker. He moved between us, grabbed Asger by the throat and brought his own seax into Asger's gut. Wulfgar twisted the blade in a circular motion and the Blood Spiller's blood spilt onto the ground as the life went from his body.

For a fleeting moment, I thought Regnar the Mean would be the next to attack, but Keld brought his horse between us and waved him away.

'You will both pay for this with your own lives,' Keld said, 'a slow, lingering death and I will be there to see it.'

Thegn Fritjof rode close to Osbeorn. 'Your father will hear of this outrage. You're no leader, just a boy who cannot control your rabble of an army,' he snarled.

'Fritjof, Leofric mistakenly thinks you are welcome here. You are not! You should leave whilst you still can.'

'I am going straight to your father.'

'Before you go,' I said, 'you have forgotten something.'

I had seen Regnar the Mean slinking through a group of men, trying to get behind us. As he sprang towards Wulfgar, I stuck my foot out and tripped him sending him sprawling in front of me. He dropped the seax he had in his hand and grabbing his hair I hauled him back onto his feet and held my own seax to his throat. Pushing him forward I took him to the seven men Fritjof had touched with his staff.

'Take the feathers from their belts,' I demanded. As he reluctantly did so, I told each one to return to their fellow soldiers.

'You can't do that,' whined Fritjof.

'I just have,' I said. 'Now Regnar, put the feathers into your mouth.' Regnar looked at me in disbelief. 'Now!' I said, pushing my seax tightly to his windpipe. He pushed all seven feathers into his mouth, spluttering as he did so. 'Now swallow,' I said yanking his head back by his hair.

He gagged repeatedly as he tried to swallow, bits of feathers flying from his mouth, his face turning scarlet. Keld could contain himself no longer and started to draw his sword, but several of Osbeorn's soldiers pressed around him and he thought better of it and pushed the weapon back into its scabbard.

Purple with rage, Fritjof wheeled his horse around, kicking out at anyone until he found a way through. Keld led Regnar's horse to him and stilling retching and half choking, he hauled himself into the saddle and the three of them slowly threaded their way through a swelling body of men, many of whom were now banging spears on shields. True to their vow to Osbeorn, nobody attacked them. All the same, the atmosphere was decidedly hostile.

As they left, I shouted, 'Now we will be proud to join your brave army, Lord Osbeorn.'

Osbeorn's men cheered. Osbeorn embraced me. 'You have made many friends today, Leofric, but also dangerous enemies. Come, let's go and drink mead and talk of war.'

As we walked away, I said to Wulfgar softly, 'We already have enemies, a few more will make little difference. It was friends we needed, now we have several.'

Wulfgar nodded, 'Even so, it was a risk, he could have killed you.'

'No, he couldn't have, I had a good teacher.'

'True,' said Wulfgar, 'absolutely true.'

Neither he nor Osbeorn realised I was shaking and my insides were churning. Killing men, however abhorrent they are, is no small matter. Even though I have now killed many, it still brings me no joy.

Twenty-nine

Someone once told me there was no such thing as too much mead. I found out that day there certainly is. With a thumping head and blurred vision, I was helped back to our tent by Wulfgar. We discovered two women from the camp had been assigned to see to Rush's wounds and to care for his general wellbeing. He was much improved than when we had left him.

The mood of most of the men had changed towards us. The grumbling stopped, and it had been noted I wished to see a girl in St. Omer. Someone knew someone, who knew someone's steward who was travelling there on estate business. His name was Runolf. He was brought to me and agreed to deliver a letter to Turfrida, whom he said he knew personally. I gave him one of the coins Tripp had given me, with the promise of another when he returned and he vowed he would bring back news.

For a week we trained. Wulfgar and I took our turns in the shield wall, learning to keep the shields tight together, lunging over the top of them with spear, sword or axe, quickly ducking back behind to avoid the enemies counter thrust. A soldier with the unfortunate name of Iscariot bellowed out instructions. He was not a particularly tall man, but he was broad in the shoulders, muscular and solid, like a small oak tree. He walked back and forth in front of the wall of shields, banging his sword against any he believed were too high or too low or not touching the one next to it. Any man too slow with his spear thrust or not quick enough to back behind the shields, was met by Iscariot's contorted face spitting saliva and screaming, 'Quicker, you useless bag of shit. You would be dead now and so would the man next to you. I pray to God you're not next to me when it matters.'

No man wanted this said about them, so each one quickened until the whole shield wall worked in unison.

We found out that Malcolm Canmore was also at the camp. We were told he had been living at King Edward's court and it was Edward who had supplied most of the army and recruited Earl Siward to lead them. Malcolm was the son of Duncan, the last King of Alba, who had been killed in battle by Mac Bethad mac Findlaich. Mac Bethad now called himself king and ruled in his stead. This army was preparing to reclaim Malcolm's crown for him.

We saw little of him or Earl Siward as they talked tactics about how they should deploy the army and their fleet of warships to flush Mac Bethad out into the open. We did see a lot of Osbeorn and his cousin, who was also called Siward. Siward had the similar features of his uncle and cousin, though his hair was brown and he was clean shaven. They were more like brothers than cousins and it was obvious they were devoted to each other, yet competitive in all they did. If Osbeorn threw a spear, Siward had to throw one further. If they rode horses, one would always try to be faster than the other.

'That's the reason Osbeorn needs someone to watch his back,' said Sigeberht, who had stood on my left in the shield wall practice. 'Those two are so intent at outdoing each other they become oblivious to all else. They are always in the thick of battle. Osbeorn leads from the front and Siward is always at his side trying to kill more men than his cousin.'

'So why did men laugh when Earl Siward appointed me to watch his back?' I asked.

'Because the last three men to attempt it were all killed trying,' said Sigeberht. 'To face Osbeorn is so perilous, many opponents try to get behind him, and those trying to protect him are often so outnumbered they die in the trying. It's Earl Siward's way of testing a man's prowess. If they die, it's God's will and if they live, they are worthy to protect his son.'

The next day we broke camp. Thousands of men and weapons moved north; banners flew, the sound of drums rattled through the countryside, men sang, and skalds chanted war poems. I was on my way to my first real battle. I should have been terrified, instead, amongst that company, I was exhilarated. Wulfgar and I rode behind Osbeorn Bulax and young Siward, confident that whoever or whatever we came up against we would be victorious.

As a slave, Rush was made to walk at our side. He was allowed no weapon but his sling. I promised him once we were free from this situation, he would again be seen as our equal. He simply shrugged as if he was resigned to his fate, but I could see that darkness and resentment that always seemed to lurk around and envelop my friend.

As we rode, I was captivated by this land; dark rolling hills, thick, foreboding woodland interspersed with lush meadows and fish-filled, quick flowing rivers. There was permanence about the place, personified by harsh, granite rock, the opposite from the transience of the shifting chalk downs of Wessex. I felt at home, as though this was the place I was meant to be, a land of hard, rugged men, a land for warriors.

We marched five abreast to the beat of drum and pipe, a snaking line of men, reaching back nearly a mile. We were watched from afar by locals. They must have trembled as we passed by and sighed with relief as we eventually faded from sight. Others were not so lucky, as our raiding parties stripped their fields, took their livestock and if they resisted, took their lives. Occasionally, we would see plumes of smoke in the distance as whole villages burned in our wake.

We marched from dawn till dark, sustained by bread and cheese and water from goat's skin water bags passed from man to man. Except for Earl Siward and Canmore, who had their tents erected, we slept under the stars, our countless campfires mimicking their flickering light.

After four days, the rain came, a spattering at first making our clothes damp and the road slippery. As the wind blew harder, it came in squalls, one moment at our backs, next full in our faces. Wulfgar and I dismounted, feeling less exposed walking, as the men in front partly shielded us from the wind and rain. Visibility dropped to an arm's length. The drums and pipes had fallen silent. The only sound, the thud, thud of men's feet. Although each man's head was covered by the cowl of his cloak, our faces were stung by the rain which was now driving straight at us.

Out of the mist, a thin, pale arm appeared grabbing my wrist, pulling me out of the line and into the swirling dimness.

Wulfgar shouted, 'Leofric, where are you? Leofric?'

Other voices, 'Are we being attacked?'

'No,' yelled another, 'it's a wraith, it's taken the Killer of Death.'

It was Mair. I could have resisted, but something urged me to go with her. She pulled me deeper into the murk until I could barely hear the shouts. Something touched my face; damp fur, fresh blood. I pushed it away with my hands, but it swung back again. Peering through the mist I saw it was a bloodied, dead hare, its mouth twisted, eyes bulged. It was strung from the branch of a blackened, lightning-struck tree. On the next gnarled branch hung a dead cockerel, blood dripping from its slit throat.

Mair was dressed in a thin, grey shift of flimsy material, almost blending with the mist. Something hung from her neck that wriggled on her breast. It was a live toad, threaded through its legs onto a leather throng.

'Is this Yggdrasil?' I asked, all reason leaving me and a sense of dread clinging to me like my damp clothes.

'No, Leofric, this is not the tree where the Norms sit spinning their threads of the fates of men. Yet, this is a sacred tree, a place where things are unleashed that men cannot comprehend. I have seen things about you, Leofric, about your future. There are two paths you can take. One is to greatness, one is to death. There is no escaping that truth, but you can decide which path to take. Only you can make that decision. It is true your final fate is already spun, but there are still many choices for you to make to decide what the journey holds until you reach that final destination. I know from these signs,' she ran her fingers through the blood of the hare and the cockerel, 'that your time is not yet due. Whatever risks you take in this battle, you will not die. There will be a moment when all seems lost, but you will sense that victory is close. You alone will possess the wisdom to bring defeat to your enemy when others do not.'

'How do you know these things? Why should I believe you? Nairn said I would kill Harthacnut, I did not. You said I would never be with Turfrida, yet as we speak, she has my letter that says I will be with her soon.' Of course, I did not know if that was true, but I hoped it was.

'Your father doubted the gods, Leofric. When he drew the short straw to kill the king, he thought that they had abandoned him. But did he kill the king? '

'No, but...'

Mair moved so close I could feel the warmth of her breath on my face. She placed a finger on my lips to stop me talking. 'No, he did not. Did Nairn say which king you would kill? No, she did not.'

More shouts of, 'Leofric' came from our right and left but weak and distant.

'What do want of me, Mair?' I said, frustrated that what she said was true.

'I want much from you, Leofric. I have told you before, our lives are entwined. We need each other to achieve what we want. But the future waits hidden in the mists until it's time to be revealed. I have seen three betrayals and one deception. One has happened, one is soon to happen and the other will happen in the future.'

'Why does everything have to be in riddles? Tell me now. I could easily shout out and you would be discovered.'

'And who would dare hurt the Sorceress? Your father attacked my mother. He has lost his wife, his son, his prize possession and soon, because of his foolish vanity, he will lose his new wife, village and his life.'

These things were shocking to me, how could she know?

'None of these things are true,' I shouted, 'You are a foolish girl

285

who makes lucky guesses and kills lots of helpless animals to frighten people. Why have you brought me here, Mair?'

Mair did not retaliate. Calmly she took both my hands in hers.

'Many winters past, Nairn was in these lands when Mac Bethad mac Findlaich was Mormaer. He knew of Nairn's prophecy of kings and sought her out. She read the runes, examined the entrails of creeping things and looked deep into the dark cauldron. She told him that when King Duncan was killed, he himself would take the crown and wear it for fourteen winters until the wood of Burnham came to the castle of Dunsinane. At that time, another would take his kingdom. That time is now. When it happens, you will realize I speak the truth.' I yanked my hands from hers and backed away from the tree.

'I still don't understand why you tell me these things. Why do you need me?'

She moved towards me once more, her eyes flickered red. 'You will be given land where a young girl will become sick. She will die, and I will bring her back to life.'

'That is impossible, even you know that,' I said, shocked.

'Nothing is impossible for the true gods, Leofric. The people are desperate. Many are near starvation. They are terrified of your army and what it may do to them. They need heroes, Leofric, something to believe in. We are going to give them those heroes. Their Christian God has not returned. Many have waited for that to happen and he has not come. The time is right to return to the real gods of this land. I shall lead the people back to their spiritual home. I will give them the miracles they crave, and you will be a hero they sing of in their halls.' She paused for a moment. 'I rescued you from the abbey and softened Earl Siward towards your cause. When I call you, Leofric, you will come, you owe me that.'

Before I could refuse or object, she grabbed my arm and dragging me the way we had come, she flung me forwards through the mist and I thumped into Wulfgar and Rush.

'Where the Christ have you been?' said Wulfgar, 'You've brought the whole bloody army to a standstill.'

'It was Mair and her nonsense,' I said, realizing she was nowhere to be seen.

'Get back in line, you piece of horse shit,' spat Iscariot, as he came striding up to us, pushing men out of his way. 'I'm watching you.'

'What did she want?' asked Wulfgar through clenched teeth as he glared at Iscariot.

'Something about heroes,' I said, not certain myself I understood what she had meant and thinking it better not to mention her bringing back the dead.

'We could do with a few heroes, that's for sure,' muttered Rush.

'I think she was talking about me,' I said.

'You?' said Rush unconvincingly and looked at the brand burnt into his arm and shook his head. Wulfgar said nothing and we carried on marching.

We marched for another entire day. Sometimes I rode, sometimes I walked with the other men. The rain finally stopped and as the mist lifted, it gradually became visible ahead of us. To many of us, a thing of legend, to others, a familiar sight, but one that still struck awe in most men.

The wall.

Thirty

AD 1071

We have crossed the wastelands. The horses are barely alive. The rivers are fishless, except for the floating bodies of dead ones. The only greenery, the odd shoots of pine forcing their way through the grey ash. On sunny days, the ground is dusty and shifting like sand. On wet days, a muddy morass that clings to the feet like sticky fingers refusing to let go.

On the far side of the River Tese, the land is green, alive and beckoning. A herd of deer are drinking at the river's edge. We have allowed the horses to drink a little and shortly we will cross over the old, stone bridge that lies a short way downstream. I remember a village, two miles north of here, whether it is still there and if it is in Saxon or Norman hands, we will not know until we get there. It is a chance we must take as we need food and fresh horses.

The village is still there and held by a Saxon thegn, who now pays rent to a Norman overlord for his own land. They have fed us, and I have purchased six new horses, though I sense the thegn is keen for us to leave in fear his absent lord should hear they have harboured fugitives and administer retribution.

He has told of us of a mad, bald, red-eyed hermit who

lives close to the Roman wall who may give us succour. I trust I know who it is, and as today we had a short flurry of snow that petered out without settling, we will search him out and seek shelter for the winter. Whilst the others sleep before we set out tomorrow, I will write on, relieved we have survived the wastelands, yet recalling the bleakness of when I first ventured into this land.

ᛏᚺᛗ ᛘᚠᚺ ᛘᚠᛏᛉ

AD 1054

Looking across the crumbling ruins it was hard to imagine many men had once lived here, and even more had met their end in bloody battles. Now except for sheep and ravens, it was deserted.

'They say it stretches from the sea in the west to the sea in the east,' said Wulfgar.

Most of what was left was a ruin, but part of it still towered high above us, bleak and foreboding. Big, square cut stones set in mortar were aligned seven feet wide and as high as three tall men. Built on a natural ridge, the Romans had cut a deep ditch on the north side for extra defence.

'No wonder the Romans conquered most of the world if they could build this,' said Wulfgar.

'Makes you wonder what they were trying to keep out,' I said, clambering on to a broken section of the ruined wall and looking out to the wild country ahead.

'Wild men, head hunters, cannibals, eaters of babies,' Iscariot spat as he spoke. 'Romans called them Picti.'

'If there's any left, they dwell far north in the high mountains,' said

Wulfgar. 'It's the Scotti we will face, wild enough, but not cannibals.'

'And Normans,' added Levett who had joined us on the wall. 'Men driven out of Englaland after the Godwins came back. Mac Bethad has given them land in exchange for their services in war.'

'You would fight your own countrymen, Levett?' I asked.

'Each man must choose his own path, Leofric. You were prepared to fight against your king and your father.'

'It would never have come to that,' I said, uncomfortably.

With a faint smile Levett replied, 'And if it had, which would you have chosen?' He paused. 'Perhaps none of us knows until the moment we have to choose. I was sent to tell you we are to make camp here for the night whilst men clear a way through for the horses and carts.' He jumped from the fallen debris and disappeared into the crowd of men.

Fires sprang up around the camp as men ate, drank ale and sang songs of war and home and great deeds of warriors. Smells of roasting pig and beef and the sweet aroma of herbs masked the stench of animal and human waste, which was inevitable in a camp this size. I looked from that heaving mass through a gap in the wall into dark stillness and wondered what horrors lay in wait for us beyond that ancient barrier. My thoughts were interrupted by a lone soldier who had sought me out.

'You are summoned to Earl Siward's tent.' Wulfgar started to rise from our fire. 'Only you,' the soldier said to me. Wulfgar was about to protest but I assured him I would be fine.

'If they meant me harm, I would be dead by now. Try to rest, we have a long day tomorrow.'

Earl Siward was sat on his great, carved chair next to Malcolm Canmore and flanked by spear wielding guards. There were also two priests at a desk, but Earl Siward waved at them to leave.

He was abrupt and to the point. 'You were taken by the sorceress.'

'Yes, my lord, she came out of the mist and took me to a tree of fortune.'

'And did she tell of the battle?' Malcolm asked impatiently.

'Yes, my lord, she said we would be victorious when Burnham

Wood goes to Dunsinane. '

'How can a wood go anywhere?' asked Earl Siward.

'I do not know, lord,' I replied.

'I have heard this before,' said Malcolm, 'many years ago. '

'The sorceress said I would understand when it happened,' I said, not believing any of it.

'Did she say anything else?'

'Only that I would not die in the battle.'

They muttered something to each other, then Earl Siward beckoned me nearer. 'Many think I assigned you to guard Osbeorn's back expecting you to die, that couldn't be further from the truth.'

'I'm glad to hear it, lord.'

'What I want to know, Leofric, is, will knowing you won't die make you less alert in battle and endanger my son? '

'I like to think the reason the gods say I will not die is due to my prowess as a warrior, not because of their divine intervention. You can trust I will do all I can to protect your son, although from what I have seen over these last days, he seems less in need of protection than any other man in your entire army.'

Earl Siward laughed out loud. 'Oh, he can fight, Leofric, nearly as fierce as me, but he is reckless, almost foolhardy at times. I asked the sorceress his fate, but she could give me no assurance, only that his life, like all men, was spun in the threads of the three Norms, carved in runes on the trunk of Yggdrasil when he was a child. It was only you she was sure about, Leofric. Chosen by the gods for greatness, she said.'

I guessed this was something Mair had conjured up to perpetuate our usefulness to the Danish lord and it seemed to be working, so who I was to sow doubt in his mind?

'If I can be great in your service, lord, I will indeed be a proud man.'

'Help bring victory against Mac Bethad, Leofric, and I will reward you with land and men and you can be free to go and prove your innocence against your accusers.'

Siward placed his hand on my shoulder. His eyes peered intensely from behind the mass of hair and shaggy beard. 'Don't dismiss the sorceress lightly. We can battle against men and our chances of success can be good. With practice of our skills and courage we can prevail where others may fail, but there are things beyond our understanding, whether they are miracles or prophecies or demons from a dark, forgotten realm. There are those whose strength is not from the body, but from a place where most mortals are unable to inhabit. They have power over reason and people's thoughts. They are imbued with the insight of the gods. Whether we believe in them or not is irrelevant, most folks do and that makes them more powerful than even great armies like this. To fight against them is futile. She has seen something in you that other men don't possess. Embrace it, Leofric, use it to achieve your ambitions. If it wasn't for her, I would probably have sent you back with the priests or even had you killed. There have been many who have come to me with their charms and portents and sham promises. Many have lost their lives on the point of this,' he half drew his dagger from his belt. 'But the girl was different, Leofric, she told me things only I could know. She told me things that I would wish to be false, but I fear are not. If you are like most headstrong, young men, you will ignore her and trust in yourself. If you are wise, you will keep her close and heed her counsel. My priests would berate me if they could hear me talk this way. They say it is all superstition and delusion, and perhaps they would be right too, despite the fact they have their saint's bones that work miracles and pieces of bread and wine they say turn to flesh and blood in the mouth.

The day after tomorrow we shall be upon the enemy, we want all the gods to be with us, Leofric, not against us. Osbeorn has asked to lead the army into battle. He shall get his wish. I shall stay behind in the camp and he will lead this army to success. Canmore is leaving tonight to be with the fleet but will return to be at Osbeorn's side, as will his cousin Siward, and you will watch their backs. Now leave us and rest before the dawn breaks.'

We broke camp at first light. We crossed the wall and headed north. Wulfgar and I walked alongside Rush and the other men. Those around me smirked at first at my lilting gait, but after many miles, appreciated I could be riding but chose to be with them and share their pain.

'You should be on your horse, Leofric,' said Ingvar. 'We have a long way to travel.'

'If you can manage it, so can I, you heap of crap,' I said laughing. The men around us, including Ingvar, joined in the laughter.

After a day's march others encouraged me to get back in the saddle. 'You will need your strength for the battle,' someone shouted.

'I will still kill more men than you however tired I get,' I shouted back. In truth, my feet were sore with blisters and my left leg throbbed with pain. I knew most of these men were in as much discomfort as me and I would not let them see my affliction as a weakness. We did not make camp on that march. We stopped for short rests and were given hard cheese and weak ale and pressed on. A few men sang, others saved their breath. At times drums would bang out a steady beat to keep us marching at a constant pace.

On occasion we would see horsemen on ridges or skirting the edges of woods and copses in the distance, marking our progress. The land we were now in was undulating. Beneath our feet was thick heather, spongy and uneven, which sometimes caught around your feet, making even the nimblest of men trip. Rugged crags jutted out of small hillocks and twisted, gnarled trees leant at strange angles from decades of high winds. Each evening swarms of midges plagued us, stinging our flesh as they took our blood.

After three days, we came to what men called the other wall. It was a huge, deep cut ditch with a soil and rubble mound running along the top. A Roman named Antonine had this built to push the Picti further north, but it was unsuccessful and did not last long, resulting in them retreating to the wall the Emperor Hadrian had built. We did not stop. We swarmed over the remains of that ancient defence, knowing we were now near the enemy we sought.

Outriders along the ridges and small hills became more frequent. Our scouts reported movement of men in the north but no significant army yet. Someone rode alongside the column asking if anyone had seen Reinald Levett. Apparently, no one had since the evening before.

'Typical Norman, buggering off before the fight,' said Iscariot.

'Didn't strike me as a coward,' I said, 'there must be a reason.'

'There is, he doesn't want to fight, like many of this rabble here, but they know they will have me to face if they don't.'

Our army consisted of mostly seasoned warriors, soldiers of King Edward and his earls, Siward's northern men from Norðhymbraland, various mercenaries and Scotti who supported Canmore against Mac Bethad. Then there were the fyrd-men who had been seconded from their farms. These would stand at the back of the shield wall to give depth and strength of numbers.

After half a day, we marched up a long, gradual slope until we came to its brow, and stretching out below us was a great plain and at the far side, where it sloped upwards, were a group small hills. On one of them, called Dunsinane, sat an old fort built by the ancients before the Romans came. Our scouts had reported many men were gathering in the hills, but they were out of sight to us. To the left of the plain was Burnum Wood. We set camp on the slope, sent lookouts along the brow, and prepared for battle. We rose to find Malcolm Canmore had returned with more men from the fleet.

At first light, the following morning, we came down from the ridge and half way across the plains formed a mighty shield wall, a hundred men wide and thirty deep. In the first two lines stood battle-hardened axe men, behind them two lines of spear men, each with a throwing spear and a spear to jab with. Behind those was the body of the force, armed with axes, swords, spears, cudgels. Each man carried a round shield of lime wood and wore a helmet or a leather cap. Wulfgar and I stood in the second line in the centre, directly behind Osbeorn Bulax and his cousin Siward. At the rear were a line of bowmen and a hundred horsemen on either flank. Fritjof Heironson and Malcolm Canmore were both on horses and rode across the front of the army shouting out orders and encouragement. Iscariot walked the whole length of the front line banging his sword on each shield.

'Keep the shields tight and stand your ground until you're told different,' he barked.

We waited and waited. The waiting is the worst part for a soldier. Once the fighting begins, you think of nothing else but survival; kill or be killed. But while you wait, there is too much thinking. This could be your last battle. You could be severely wounded and die a long, lingering death. Many men think of their women folk and children, how they will survive without them. Most never think of these things when they set out from home, only as the battle is about to start.

Malcolm Canmore rode across the lines once more and addressed the men.

'My father was the rightful king in these lands and he had his crown and his life taken from him by the usurper, Mac Bethad mac Findlaich,' he cried. 'I look to you brave warriors to help me regain that crown against Mac Bethad and his rabble. Our fleet has landed at Dundee and taken much booty from merchant ships which lay in the harbour. They have sacked the city and gathered even more riches. You men will share in any booty we take when we are victorious. The skalds will sing about you and the bards will write of your deeds. Osbeorn Bulax will lead you to a great victory and your children and their children will listen in awe when you tell them of this day.'

Osbeorn walked out of the line and with his lethal poleaxe held aloft, he paraded to cheers and spears rattling against shields.

'I ask nothing of you I do not ask of myself,' he roared. He took a jewelled ring from his finger and held it aloft. 'Any man who kills more men than me shall win this ring.' More spear rattling. 'Give me the victory, so I can give it to my father who has honoured me this day, entrusting me with leading this mighty throng of men. Give me the victory!'

The men cheered, more spear rattling, falling silent once more as we waited yet again.

As the dawn finally broke, a whining sound came across the plain. It was accompanied by drums and someone told us it was the Scotti's war pipes. It sounded like a thousand pigs being castrated. Our own drummers responded with a heavy, loud beat and the blast of war horns filled our ears. We knew the waiting would soon be over. Wulfgar and I unsheathed our swords. Osbeorn and Iscariot returned to the shield wall, Canmore and Fritjof Heironson joined the horsemen, one on either side. The pipes and drums became louder, but still we could see no enemy. My mouth became dry, the shield and sword felt heavier with each passing moment. This was my first time in a shield wall. Yes, I had killed men and fought in a skirmish at Doferum, but this was the first real battle I had been involved in. Fear twisted my gut, my heart thumped, my legs shook, I took deep breaths, gripped my shield and sword harder, and focused on the empty plain in front of me. Maybe they would not come, maybe they had seen the size of our army and fled.

A huge flock of ravens whirled across the sky like a swift, black cloud. Battle carrion, soldiers called them, come to a gruesome feast; each man determined not to be part of their ghoulish meal.

Mair was nowhere to be seen, even so, I knew she would be somewhere near, splattered in blood and calling to the gods.

Siward's priests walked in front of the lines amongst the men, splashing them with horse tails of holy water and swinging bowls of incense. They chanted in Latin, which most men did not understand but knew they were seeking God's blessing on the carnage ahead of us. The drums and pipes stopped, our drums also fell silent. The only sounds, the deep breathing of thousands of men, the air rushing through a multitude of beating wings and the Kruk, Kruk, Kruk of the black flock.

I looked around me. Men said silent prayers to their Christian God, crossing themselves, their lips moving in inaudible supplications. Others prayed to Odin and Thor to guide them to victory and valour or a glorious death worthy of a warrior. Crosses on chains around men's necks were caressed, lucky charms and elf stones were kissed. I looked back across the plain, and, as though by magic, the hills became alive with men, a great horde of screaming warriors running down the hill towards us, their pipes and drums once again filling the air, drowning out the ravens' calls.

Thirty-one

Still they came, getting closer each footfall. Our Danish horsemen set off on either flank, riding on the outsides of the oncoming horde, slashing with swords, cutting down men with ease before turning back and attacking the backs of men as they ran. Norman cavalry led by a man called Osbern Pentecost, and I was told, Reinald Levett, came from the edge of Burnum Wood to intercept them. After a short but ferocious clash the Normans were overcome, with few losses to our own horsemen. The roaring engulfed us now as the Scotti were almost upon us. We locked our shields and leant forward ready to take the initial impact. Scotti spears came hurtling over our heads. The cries of stricken men as spearheads pierced flesh. There was a whoosh sound overhead, as our archers loosed their arrows.

'Stand firm,' Iscariot shouted, barely heard above the din.

'Spears, loose!' came the order and two hundred spears sped their way towards our foe. There was a loud crash as the two armies slammed into one another. It was like Thor's hammer blow, jolting the whole of my body, but we stood firm.

Our axe men started hacking over their shields. Several of the Scotti had leapt at the shield wall feet first, attempting to hurl themselves over the line. A few were successful and were hacked and stabbed by axe and spear as they landed on our side. Osbeorn's poleaxe whirled above his head before smashing into helmets, flesh and bone. Men screamed in pain, blood seeped into the grass beneath

297

our feet.

The Scotti's axes smashed into our front-line shields. Wulfgar and I tried to work in unison with Osbeorn and young Siward. As they swung and struck, we would lean forward stabbing with our swords, drawing back as they prepared to swing again. Sometimes we would strike the wood of shields, other times our blades would glance off helms or be parried by the Scotti's weapons, but mostly we struck flesh and we brought our blades back covered in blood.

Before long the ground in front of us, thick with the corpses of slaughtered Scotti, was slippery with blood making it difficult to stand. The smell of death and severed flesh attacked nose and throat; eyes stinging with sweat. A small number of our front-line men had also fallen but were replaced by those in the row behind so we maintained a solid, impenetrable wall. Many Scotti started to stumble over their dead and eventually they pulled back, out of spear throw. We too, were glad of the respite. My arm ached from stabbing with my sword and my shield arm was bruised from the constant battering of axes. Horse-drawn carts came along in front of us gathering bodies and removing them to the sides, clearing the way for the next onslaught. Those who were too gravely wounded to continue to fight were taken to tents back at the camp. Those whose shields had been smashed to pieces were given new ones. Our horsemen had returned to our flanks, only a handful having been lost. Skins of wine were passed around to wet parched lips.

A tall warrior with long, red hair came to the front of the Scotti. He wore chequered britches, a leather tunic, a metal breastplate and an ornate helmet with a large red plume. He held a long sword in one hand and a war hammer in the other. He strutted in front of his men shouting in a language I didn't understand. Apparently calling us lowland Sassenachs, whose mothers were whores and our fathers simpleton cowards. A man next to me who understood the words told me what was being said.

'Mac Bethad mac Findlaich,' cried Canmore in retaliation, 'murderer and usurper, give back your stolen crown. Let your men return to their families, let them watch their young boys grow into men. Put down your weapons and bend your knee to me, the rightful king by birth.'

Mac Bethad turned to face his men. 'You men of the highlands, have you not prospered in the last fourteen years?' A roar came from his men. 'Do you want to be ruled by lowlanders who parley with the Englaland king? Or do you want to drive these invaders back across the walls to their own lands?' More roars of approval, pipes and drums rang out.

Canmore rode along the line and cried, 'Shield wall, advance.'

As one we locked shields and started to slowly walk forward, banging axe, sword and spear on shields. We pushed forward, quickening our pace. They came again with a fury more intense than the first, intent on revenge for their fallen kin. A hundred more spears were thrown from behind us thudding into the earth or finding their target and piercing mail, leather and flesh. I waited for the crash and jolt again as our two forces came together for the second time that morning. As before, we held the shield wall tight, swords slashing and stabbing, axes chopping and hacking, Osbeorn's poleaxe crushing, breaking, cutting. Many times the enemy came upon us, fell back, came again. The dead lay thick on the ground. The slippery, blood-slickened grass replaced by the bodies of fallen foe and comrades alike. The sound of breaking bones as we stood on arms and ankles, fingers of desperate, dying men grasping, clawing at our legs. The overpowering stench of shit and blood. All the things the bards and skalds leave out of their heroic verses. War cries were now replaced by screams of pain. Men groaned and puffed and sweated and bled. The order was given for the shield wall to move forward again. Slowly, as one unit, we began to push our opponents back. It was hard work at first without much movement but as their men at the rear lost heart and deserted, we advanced quicker and quicker until their spirit broke and they turned and ran. The order was given to chase and destroy. The shield wall had done its job and we swarmed forward to pursue the fleeing rabble. Osbeorn and young Siward were the first to break, mercilessly cutting men down from behind as they fled. I realized I would never keep pace with them on foot so grabbed a loose horse encumbered by its dead rider. His foot was still stuck in a stirrup and he was being dragged unceremoniously through the corpses, becoming trapped in a mass of limbs and dropped weapons. I dislodged the foot and speaking the language of the Horsðegn, I coaxed my mount through the chaos to re-join Osbeorn and Siward, who, along with Wulfgar, were giving great slaughter to the fleeing Scotti. Ahead, a large group had rallied and turned to face and fight us and so began a host of individual battles. We were joined by Malcolm Canmore who had now dismounted and led his men into the fray. Fritjof Heironson and his men joined in on our right, although Fritjof himself hung back on the fringes of the fighting, picking off wounded, half dead men as they staggered about. I dismounted and took a position with Wulfgar behind Osbeorn Bulax who, with his cousin, waded into the thick of the struggle and slew all in their path. Men tried to get around the back of them only to be confronted by Wulfgar and me, high on battle fever. No one could withstand the four of us as we carved our way through the Scotti. I lost count of the men I killed who were trying to reach Earl Siward's son. In one skirmish to the left of us, I saw Reinald Levett dispatching two of our men. He was on foot, his visor up, his tunic smeared with blood and mud. Then he was gone;þ pushed back by a group of roaring Northumbrians.

The axe, a small, one-handed woodsman's tool, spun through the air and lodged its self in young Siward's neck. Blood spurted high from the wound and the brave nobleman fell to the ground. Osbeorn tried to reach him, shouting his name in despair, killing men to his left and right, when a spear was thrust from amongst the melee in front of us and was driven right through the body of Osbeorn Bulax. I tried to reach his assailant, but all I could see was a zig-zag scar on the forearm holding the spear which had ran him through, then he was gone, lost in the body of men. A red-haired giant of a man barred my way forward and I managed to ward of his hammer blow with my shield, the force sending me backwards on to the bloodied ground. He came again, his hammer bearing down on me. I managed to roll to the side, the hammer thudding into the earth. I lunged my sword at his middle, thrusting the blade into his gut, twisting and ripping sideways. He watched his entrails spill out before him as he crashed to the floor in a heap.

The cry rang out that the young noblemen had fallen, and it filled our men with an extra fury which eventually became too much for the remaining Scotti who turned and fled, this time not stopping, but fleeing into the hills towards the old fort on Dunsinane Hill. Our warriors pursued them up the hill towards the fort but were met with a barrage of rocks and slingshot preventing them making much headway.

We eventually turned back and returned to the camp on the brow of the low hill at the edge of the plain. Wulfgar and I insisted to be the ones to take back the bodies of Osbeorn and young Siward. We put them on makeshift wooden stretches, each one harnessed to a horse, and we rode slowly back to Earl Siward. Weapons and armour of the dead were gathered as war booty. The ravens were already enjoying their feast and the air was full of their kak, kak, kak as they fought over the juiciest morsels of what had earlier been brave warriors.

Earl Siward was at the entrance of his pavilion dressed in full battle gear. He wore a bronze helmet crowned by a tall, twisted spike. He was clad in leather and fur and his great, chainmail byrnie, which he called Emma. He had a huge, long sword in a fleece lined scabbard and carried the biggest two-handed battle axe I have ever seen. His shoulders momentarily sank as the two bodies of his young kinsmen were brought before him. He bent and kissed his son's brow and likewise his nephew. If he shed a tear, it was hidden in the mass of hair and beard. After all, he was Earl Siward, mighty warlord of Norðhymbraland. Emotion was for private moments, not in the sight of others.

'All I ask is, was he killed from the front or the rear?' he asked in a strong, steady voice.

'From the front, lord, as ever, fighting as the bravest of men,' I said, 'slain by a coward's spear thrust from the safety of a crowd of warriors.'

'And young Siward, my sister's son?'

'An axe, thrown from distance. No man able to best him in face to face combat.'

'And you, Leofric, did you do all in your power to protect my son?'

'I swear I did, lord, but it grieves me it was not enough to prevent his death.'

'I have already been told of your valour, Leofric, and I put no blame on you. I ask you to join me now in exacting bloody revenge on this Scotti rabble and the usurping upstart Mac Bethad mac Findlaich. We will drive them from their ant's nest into the sea and put King Edward's vassal Malcolm Canmore on his rightful throne.'

I bent my knee, repeated my allegiance to him, and vowed to avenge his son.

Canmore, Fritjof, and Siward's other generals followed him into the pavilion. Wulfgar and I turned to go, but we were summoned to join them. They stood around a large table strewn with maps and diagrams of the surrounding land. It was Malcolm Canmore who spoke first.

'We need to get into the fort, but we cannot get near whilst they bombard us from above. We need to get men amongst them but there is scant cover and they will see us before we reach them.'

'Starve them out,' shouted Fritjof Heironson, 'they can't stay there forever.'

'Truth is, they can probably last longer than us. Our scouts tell us most of this land has been stripped of its crops and livestock,' said Siward. 'Our supplies will only last so long.'

'We will send a small force in the cover of darkness up the steep side of the hill, they won't be expecting that,' said Gostric, one of the northern chieftains who had served Earl Siward for many years.

'The moon is full at night, they would be seen,' said Canmore, who was pacing the tent apart from the others. 'There was a prophecy about the wood and the hill, Leofric, you told us the sorceress repeated such a prophecy to you on the moors. Did she not explain further?'

'No, my lord, but I have been thinking about it, we know a wood cannot move by itself, but what if we moved the wood instead.'

'And how do we do we move a wood? The boy is mad,' mocked Fritjof.

'We don't move the whole wood,' I said ignoring his disdain. 'We cut boughs, complete with leaves, big enough for a man to conceal himself behind. In the dark, together as a shield wall, we will move slowly up the slope at the side of the hill. Even with the hay moon, we will be upon them before they realize the wood is getting nearer.'

There was silence for a while as men thought upon the plan.

'It may just work,' said Canmore. 'If we place the rest of the army around the hill, they will be too preoccupied with them to notice moving trees.'

As the sun set and the light grew dim, our army encircled Dunsinane Hill. We kept out of range of the arrows and slingshot. One or two of our men were hit by boulders, which the Scotti rolled towards us, but our losses were few.

Canmore and I took a group of men into Burnam Wood. We cut boughs from the trees and using them as cover we began our ascent of the hill. The rest of our army stayed at the foot of the hill banging shields with swords, axes and spears and shouting threats and abuse.

Our plan worked better than we could have hoped. Creeping slowly, hidden behind the leafy screen, we inched our way up towards the fort. Canmore led the way, watching for movement on the battlements, signalling with his hand to stop or move. Before the fort's defenders realized what was happening, we were at the top of the hill, then abandoning the branches, we swarmed over the fort's feeble defences forcing our way inside. That was the signal for the rest of the army to charge upwards and take the fort. Once we were in, our victory was swift and bloody. Resistance was short-lived as the remaining Scotti surrendered their weapons.

Earl Siward called out for Mac Bethad.

A small man with a wiry physique, all sinew and muscle, came before him.

'I am King Mac Bethad's man, Donal Bane. The man you seek has long gone; safe in the northern mountains to fight again.'

Siward drew his sword from its scabbard.

'Mac Bethad mac Findlaich is no longer king. He has relinquished his right by defeat and deserting his army is the act of a coward, not a king. You, Donal Bane, will bend your knee to your new king, Malcolm the third, king by birth right and battle won and vassal to King Edward of Englaland, or you will lose your head by my sword.'

Donal Bane stood defiant. 'Lord, I am oath sworn to King Mac Bethad and cannot support a vassal of an English sovereign in our own land.'

'You are a fool, Donal Bane, a loyal, courageous fool, but a fool none the less,' said Earl Siward, as he signalled to two of his soldiers who grabbed Donal Bane by the arms and forced him to his knees. They both stepped back quickly and Siward's sword swept across Donal's neck and his severed head rolled along the ground leaving a slick of blood like the trail of giant slug.

'Do we have any more fools amongst us? If not, I bid all men kneel before King Malcolm and pledge their allegiance and sword to his service.'

Every man there knelt before Malcolm, known as Canmore, and swore to be his man. Some willingly, others reluctantly. Those still loyal to Mac Bethad had fled with him. Many of the Normans who had taken refuge with him had died on the battlefield, though there was no sign of Reinald Levett. We took hostages from the leading men amongst them to ensure their loyalty. We stripped the corpses of weapons and armour, loading it all onto carts, to be shared amongst our men.

Over the next three days, Earl Siward and Malcolm met with the chief men of Alba who gave their oaths of allegiance. The land was divided out and many men joined Malcolm's army, so they could defend what had been won and repel Mac Bethad if he tried to return. Malcolm confirmed his allegiance to King Edward and swore to stay out of Norðhymbraland and to protect the borderlands against brigands and all enemies of Earl Siward.

On the third day, I was sent for and Earl Siward handed me the deeds of several small parcels of land in Norðhymbraland. Fritjof Heironson and mainly his supporters objected because I had failed in protecting Osbeorn and young Siward. Most of the men rejected this, saying I had fought bravely and did all in my power to protect the young lords. I was also given a share of the war booty, collected from the fallen Scotti and Norman knights, which I shared with Wulfgar, and put some aside until I could release Rush from slavery.

When I returned to our tent Wulfgar had news.

'When I was crossing the camp this morning, I saw Runolf. I went to speak to him but as soon as he realised it was me, he sidled off into a group of men and disappeared from sight. Apparently, he returned from St. Omer on one of the merchant ships our fleet sacked in the Forth.'

'Why would he run from you?' I said, anxious to know if he had delivered my letter to Turfrida. I now had land I could bring her to and was free to prove my innocence of the crimes I was accused of.

'It puzzled me also,' said Wulfgar, 'but I think we should find him before he leaves again.'

We scoured the camp and asked if anyone had seen him. No one had. It seemed we had lost our man, when Rush, who had re-joined us, spotted him saddling a horse, apparently planning to leave. We split up and encircled him in case he bolted again and approached him slowly.

'Runolf,' I said calmly, 'I expected you to bring me news.'

He turned, startled. 'Lord, I was going to come to you, but I feared for my life.'

'Why, what have you done, you little weasel?' snarled Rush, grabbing Runolf by the throat.

'Easy, Rush,' I said pulling his hand away. Runolf staggered backwards, falling to the ground. Instead of standing he got on his hands and knees and crawled in front of me.

'Stand man, I have no desire to harm you. I only want news of Turfrida if you have it.'

He stayed on the ground, not daring to look at me. His body shook.

'Do you have news?' I repeated.

'I do, lord, but it is not good.'

'Just tell me the truth, man, and you have nothing to fear. Did you give the letter to Turfrida?'

'No, lord, she was not there.'

'What do you mean, not there?'

'Gone, my lord.'

'You're not making any sense man, gone where?

The next words came out of his mouth as a high-pitched squeal, 'She is married, lord!'

Thirty-two

'**Married,** what do you mean married?'

I grabbed Runolf by both arms and hauled him up to look at his face.

'What do you mean married?'

'She has married another man.'

The muscles in my neck tightened, I could not swallow, my stomach churned with nausea.

'Who told you this?' I started to shake him as I spoke and the fear in his eyes increased.

'Her father, Wulfric Rabell. He appeared elated by the marriage. She had been promised to another, a man Wulfric did not approve of, though it was an arrangement between the two families.'

'Yes, our families,' I managed to say.

'No, my lord,' said Runolf, 'for they believed you to be dead or a criminal on the run. A new arrangement negotiated with a knight from Saint Walericus. Hereward came to St. Omer and fought off the knight and all men who would make a claim on the Lady Turfrida. He wooed her and she became besotted by him and when her father agreed, they were wed.'

I stood motionless. For a moment, my head spun. No words would come to my lips.

'The bastard,' was all Rush said, 'the bastard.'

'Are you certain of all this, Runolf, you know it to be true not just rumours or gossip?' said Wulfgar.

'I swear it is the truth,' whimpered Runolf.

'Hereward and Turfrida.' I said the names like a curse. 'Hereward of Brune, who slew the great white bear?'

'Yes, lord, the same.' Runolf spoke but I was no longer listening.

'Hereward and my Turfrida, wedded?' I repeated this aloud and over and over in my head.

Wulfgar told Runolf to leave without further payment as he had tried to avoid telling us. He was relieved to get away unscathed. Wulfgar and Rush took me back to our tent and poured wine down my throat.

In truth, I had not seen Turfrida for over three years, but in all that time she had rarely been out of my thoughts. All my future hopes involved her, and now they amounted to nothing. I stormed out of the tent, across the camp and up into the hills.

For three days, I sat on my own on a small outcrop above the camp. I took no food or drink. My thoughts whirled around my head. Had Hereward done this to get back at me, to humiliate me? Would Turfrida have wed him if she thought me still alive? Did Hereward not tell her I was still living? Why had I not gone to her and explained my innocence? Would she have believed me? Did she ever genuinely want me or was my mother right and she just felt pity for me? These were all questions I had no answers to.

What to do next? Everything seemed pointless knowing Turfrida would not be with me. I did not even care about clearing my name. I conjured up her face in my mind. I remembered the brown, curling hair and the green eyes, but the rest seemed vague and hazy. She must appear different now she is older. Why was I so upset about losing a girl that I found hard to remember what she looked like? I did remember our walks in the glades of her father's lands. I remembered the touch of her hand on my face, the scent of the freshly picked flowers I placed in her hair, the sweetness of the grapes she placed in my mouth.

I kicked stones across the outcrop and shouted at the empty sky in frustration. I wished I had died in the battle not knowing of her rejection. For three days and nights I revelled in self-pity.

I thought of finding Hereward and killing him in front of Turfrida but realized that would hardly endear me to her. I even thought of returning to the abbey, becoming a monk and finishing the work on Thurstan's Psalter.

On the third night, I eventually fell asleep and when I awoke dew-soaked in the morning light, Mair was standing over me.

'You're a fool, Leofric, but miraculously the gods still favour you and you can still fulfil your destiny, even though you try your hardest to spurn their will.'

'So, you've come to gloat, have you? Go on, say it, I told you so.'

'I have no interest in your hopeless, romantic notions or your feckless strumpet. You are destined to be unfortunate in love, Leofric, but destined to become a great warrior, though you must play your part. There are those who need you. Have you the metal to live up to others' expectations of you, or are you going to stay up here pondering the past and what might have been, or face the future and what can be?'

I turned away from her.

'What others need me? Wulfgar and Rush can make their own way in the world and there is no one else. Besides, I have lost faith in yours or anyone else's gods. What did any god do for the men who prayed to them in the carnage down there?' I said, pointing down to the plain. 'Tell me, Mair.'

I turned back to confront her, but she was gone. I called after her, but Wulfgar appeared instead.

'Did you see Mair?' I said, certain he could not have missed her.

'There's no one up here, Leofric, just you and me,' said Wulfgar. 'You need to come.'

'What for?'

'Just follow me,' said Wulfgar and walked off down the slope.

When we arrived at our tent, thirty shabbily dressed men stood outside. One of them stepped forward.

'Who the hell are you and what do these men want?' I asked.

'My name is Starcolf, lord, and along with these men I am here to serve you.'

309

'It seems they come with the land you've been given,' said Wulfgar.

'I don't want men,' I said, 'send them away.'

'With respect, lord, most of the men don't want you as their lord either, but it looks like we're stuck with each other. Besides, where else would we go, our farms are on your land?' said Starcolf with no sign of fear in his face.

I looked at the rabble in front of me. A couple of them were obviously bearing wounds from the battle. Only five of them, including Starcolf, wore mail, most of which seemed of inferior quality. Three of those wore swords, the other two carried axes. The rest held an assortment of scythes, bill hooks and clubs. Two or three also had a seax in their belts.

'Why would they not want me as lord?' I asked.

A tall, thick-bearded man came and stood next to Starcolf, he had weary eyes and an air of mistrust. 'My name is Ansgar, lord. The man who held the land before you was a thegn, but he was old, mean, cruel and foolish. His estates, once large, are now diminished, cheated out of most of it by his neighbours, part of it sold to pay his debts. All that remains are six small villages sitting on the banks of the River Cocwud. The only good land is where the lord lived, and the rest has fallen to wilderness as he made us work his land so often, we had no time for our own. Now he has died, we hoped for a rich lord who would bring prosperity back to our villages, one who would have land of his own.'

'And what they have is me, who they see as not much more than a boy,' I said, 'who, up to a week past, they looked upon as a fugitive, a thief and a cripple for good measure.'

Ansgar and Starcolf stayed silent but the men behind them nodded and muttered in agreement.

'And if I decide to walk away and not take up these lands?'

'We would most likely become the property of our old lord's neighbour, as he owns most of the surrounding land,' said Starcolf.

'And who is he?' asked Wulfgar

'Fritjof Heironson!' said Ansgar and spat on the ground.

I looked at Wulfgar and could tell, by the expresion on his face, he knew what was coming next.

'In that case, I will be your lord,' I said, 'though there is one matter I would like to settle first. Stay there.'

I entered our tent and took from a small chest the deeds of the lands Siward had given me. I came out and held the documents up. 'These papers say I own all your lands and everything on it. If anyone of you thinks I am unworthy or unable to be your lord, or I shouldn't expect your loyalty, or you could do it better, here is your opportunity. Wulfgar, offer your sword to any man who thinks he can defeat me and if any can, you will see to it Earl Siward changes the deeds from my name to his.'

Wulfgar drew his sword and holding it by the blade tip he offered it to the astonished men. Most shook their heads and backed off. All except one. He was tall, muscular, fair-haired and had wild, dancing eyes. As he moved forward, he drew his sword from its scabbard and pushed Wulfgar's away.

Starcolf stepped between us, 'Lord, with all respect, this is not wise!'

'Let me be the judge of that,' I said and gently moved him aside.

'I am Scalpi,' my challenger said, 'I was our old lord's right-hand man after Starcolf became too soft-bellied for the task. If anyone should be this rabble's lord, it is me.'

'Here is your chance, Scalpi, kill me and these deeds are yours.'

He passed his sword from one hand to the other a couple of times and started to move slowly from side to side. I gave him my best startled, frightened look, moved backwards exaggerating my limp and feigned as though I was going to fall. As he lunged forward for the quick kill, I came at him low bringing the flat of my sword up hard against his wrist. His sword flew into the air and he lost his balance and fell at my feet. I caught his sword by the hilt and brought both blades to rest on his throat. Staring into his eyes, I saw they were still dancing and instead of fear, I sensed astonishment. I withdrew the blades, replaced mine in its sheath and helped Scalpi to his feet. I handed him back his sword.

'You are free to go your own way, Scalpi, or will you call me lord and vow to serve me above others?'

There was a moment of hesitation before Scalpi knelt and lay his sword at my feet. 'I accept you, Leofric, as my lord and my sword will be your sword and your enemies will be my enemies.'

The rest of the men knelt before me and I swore to be their lord and to do all in my power to bring prosperity and protection to them and their kin. As the sun rose above the hills, we left the camp and made our way south to my new lands. Little did I realise what I had been given.

Thirty-three

Starcolf rode next to Wulfgar and me and told us of the land I had been given. Six villages strung out over a few miles between the two Roman walls. The largest, Horsdone, was home to eighty people and had a manor house, a church and a mill. The next largest was Trogbyrne, home to forty-four people and also had a mill, though it had been severely damaged by the old lord, so all the villages became dependant on his mill at Horsdone. The rest were small places of less than forty folk in each, namely Falostunte, Branlei, Dunstede and Fenbrige.

'When we left, lord, many were on the verge of starvation,' said Starcolf. 'We were forced to come here to fight by our old lord when Malcolm's men passed through on their way to the fleet, and demanded he joined them in the battle.'

Starcolf told us he had been the old lord's enforcer, but after objecting to the amount of force he was ordered to use, he had been replaced by Scalpi who seemed to revel in violence and was hated by the other villagers. Ansgar had been the miller at Trogbyrne until it had been wrecked and closed. Now he just tilled the lord's land with the other villeins and drank too much mead.

'Fritjof Heironson owns most of the surrounding land,' said Starcolf.

'And I guess now he will want what's mine,' I said.

'Yes, lord.'

I sensed the hesitation in his voice. 'There is something else?' I asked.

'The old lord has a daughter. She was the only thing he loved. Her name is Astrid, her beauty would be rare in heaven. She has spurned Fritjof repeatedly. Her father promised her she would be free to marry any man of her choice. Of all the worthless vows he made, that is one he stayed true to. Now he is dead, only God can protect her.'

'She has no kin?' I asked.

'Her mother died three years past. There is an uncle, Ætheric, her mother's brother, but he would cut off his own arm for coin or just for an easy life. He would not want to provoke Fritjof, nor would any man who valued his life or the life of his family,' said Starcolf.

Nothing more was said. I wondered if Hereward had forced himself on Turfrida or if she had chosen him freely. Perhaps I would never know. I vowed to myself, if I found it was by force, I would find and kill him.

The men who walked behind us were a sullen band. They neither sang nor talked much. They had fought a battle but gained little. Six men who had started out with them were now dead. They complained Rush should walk at their rear as he was a marked slave. I insisted he walked with them because as far as we were concerned, he was a free man and their equal. They were not happy but complied with their new lord.

The midges became fewer as we came further south. As the land became less hilly, we left dark clouds skittering away to the north. Thick woods, interspersed with copses of hazel and buckthorn, gave way to lush meadows. Burbling streams became strong, flowing rivers. We followed one of the rivers down through the valley between two small hills. The sun shone, but the wind made the air cool. I had taken a richly woven cloak from a fallen Scotti and I pulled it closer around my shoulders.

As we rounded a bend on the river, Starcolf pointed, 'Horsdone is a mile ahead. Your land begins at the willow tree, my lord.'

The bay willow was a majestic tree; bending slightly towards the river, its shiny, oblong leaves lightly caressing the water. As we approached, it seemed to sing a welcome to us as the wind passed through its dangling branches, which obscured our view ahead. It was Wulfgar who noticed the smoke first, billowing clouds blown away from us on the wind. The three of us set off at a gallop towards Horsdone. The men ran behind, weapons at the ready. As we approached the village, we passed a huge bed of tall reeds stretching alongside the river. From amongst them came the sound of terrified screaming. As we approached, a man, sword in hand, came out of the reedbed. Obviously startled to see us, he ducked back into the reeds.

'One of Fritjof's men,' shouted Starcolf.

'You press on,' I said, as more screams came from amongst the reeds, 'I'm going in there.'

I dismounted and pushed my way into the thick, reed bed. Although the wind blowing through the reeds made a loud hissing noise, like meat sizzling over a hot fire, I could faintly hear movement. Cautiously moving forward, I caught a quick glimpse of a figure which slipped between the waving stalks. I heard a woman's scream and a man shouting, 'There's one.'

'Never mind the others, just bring me that Astrid bitch.' I recognised the voice of Fritjof Heironson.

I pushed through to the water's edge. A moorhen nervously slipped from the reeds and scurried out across the river. I saw a shape ahead of me but distorted by the constant movement of the reeds. With my sword ready to strike, I moved forward slowly. Up to that point in my life I had seen few, naked women. Like most young men, I dreamt about them, but my most vivid dreams never prepared me for what was now in front of me. Tall, slender, skin as white as the chalk on the Southern Downs, hair the colour of the winter sun, eyes like Azurite and beautifully rounded breasts, which rose and fell with each frightened breath she took. It was how I imagine a wood nymph to look and I stood transfixed by her beauty. I was brought back to reality by the sound of a sword slashing at the reeds behind her. I removed my cloak and threw it to her.

'I will not harm you. We must get out of here now,' I said.

She wrapped my cloak around herself, hiding her nakedness, but stood without a sound as though she was rooted like the reeds themselves. A second later he was behind her; a spitting, cursing, lump of sweat and iron. The beauty shrieked and sprang away from him towards me. I pushed her behind me and nearly lost my balance as I parried his sword with my own blade.

'Over here!' he yelled, 'she's here, and that accursed cripple's with her.'

He came at me again, slashing fiercely. I could hear others coming towards us thrashing about in the shallows and pushing through the reeds. I regained my balance and began fighting back. With two hands on my sword's hilt, I swung my blade back and forth in a chopping action, forcing him backwards. I was stronger than him and eventually he could hold me back no longer and as his guard dropped, I lunged, pushing the blade between his ribs. He cried out and fell backwards into the river, his blood forming a thin slick as it washed downstream. I grabbed the girl by the hand and started to lead her out of the reeds.

'If you don't harm me, you will be well rewarded. I am the daughter of the lord of this land,' she half whispered, half whimpered. She gripped my hand tightly. Another swordsman came crashing out of the reeds towards us. I dispatched him easily with a cut to the neck.

'We need to get out of the reeds and onto the bank,' I said.

She nodded her agreement. I slashed and hacked at the reeds, no longer concerned of concealment. As we emerged from the reed bed so did three other men, two with swords, and the portly, panting, sweating, Fritjof Heironson with a seax in one hand and a woman's garment in the other. He stayed behind the two swordsmen.

'You have my property,' he snarled, 'and you are on my land.'

'If you are referring to this lady, I doubt she is anyone's property. And you, Fritjof, are on my land.'

'My father is lord of this land,' Astrid protested.

'Your father is dead,' said Fritjof. 'We had an agreement, if he died, his land would become mine and his daughter would become my wife.'

'My father would never have agreed to that, never!' sobbed Astrid, clutching my cloak tighter around her body.

'This is not your land, Fritjof. Before he died, the old lord forfeited what was left of his estate to Earl Siward, as he could no longer pay the taxes due to King Edward. Earl Siward, by the power given to him by the king, gave me the land and I have the deeds to prove it,' I said. 'There are your horses, I suggest you get on them and leave before my men arrive and put you to death for burning their village.'

Fritjof glanced over his shoulder to see horsemen coming towards us from Horsdone.

'That girl and this land will be mine, cripple, make no mistake. You will come to me and beg I take them both off your hands.' The three men mounted the horses and rode away before my men arrived.

'We killed three of his men, the rest have scattered,' said Wulfgar as he galloped up. 'They killed two of the village men and burnt the manor house and two other dwellings.'

'Welcome to your new home, lord,' said Starcolf.

We learnt later, the women had just finished bathing in the river when Fritjof attacked. Most of his men rode on to the village whilst he and five others pursued the women. They had caught Astrid, but she had fought back. Fritjof ripped her garment off, but she managed to run to the reeds. One of the other girls had been raped and it turned out to be Ansgar's daughter. It took three men to stop him going in pursuit of the attackers, which would only have led to his death. I promised him we would avenge the crime, but he just growled, 'All you lords are the same,' and lost himself in a flood of mead.

Horsdone, once a fine village, was now partly run down. Only one of its three stores were full of grain, controlled by the lord. The fields were ripe for harvest, but the lord's work demands and the men gone to war, meant it had not been gathered. The mill produced good quality bread for the lord, but substandard loaves made of maslin for the villeins. There were many hives, but few produced much honey through neglect, and the cost for allowing the swine to feed off the acorns in the lord's wood was so high it was out of most villeins' capabilities. The surrounding fields and hills were good for grazing, though there were few sheep. There were two oxen, both owned by the lord, and the river teemed with fish, but only the lord was allowed to fish it. Any surplus was taken away to market and the profit filled the lord's money chest. The other five villages were mere hovels, groups of worn thatched huts, the land about them overgrown, and the villeins too weak and hungry to care. They all walked into Horsdone each day to work the lord's land and were fed pottage and maslin bread for their labour.

The lord's manor house had been reduced to ash and part of the adjoining church had been slightly damaged. Wulfgar, Rush and I cleared an old stable out and turned it into our living quarters. Astrid's uncle had offered to take her in, but she refused and chose to live with the smith and his wife.

I appointed Starcolf as the bailiff over all the villages. He would make sure everything was done in a fair, legal way and oversee restoring the villages to a profitable, workable estate in my absence. He was instructed to use force if necessary, but I trusted him to be lenient and fair.

Rush, I appointed as steward of Horsdone. Again, the complaint was raised, he was a marked slave and couldn't hold such an office. I stood my ground and demanded he could hold whichever office I decided because I was their lord.

'Makes you no different than all those other lords who force their will on the rest of us,' came the cry.

'What do you expect from Southerners, they do not know our ways or our laws?'

I was eager to be a fair and honest lord. So, I relented and appointed a man called Bruni, a popular fellow who knew the village well. Bruni could throw a spear as good as any man and was a good organiser and able to delegate.

At the news, Rush told me I was weak for giving in to their demands, said I treated him like the slave he was and not the friend and equal I claimed him to be.

I promised Rush I would have his slave status overturned and he would become a free man finally. I believed it satisfied him and he understood the position I had found myself in.

It was a mistake I would come to regret.

Thirty-four

Astrid redefined the word beautiful, surpassing any words I knew. From the moment I saw her on the river bank, naked, swaying, blending with the slender reeds, I was lost. All grief from the news of Turfrida vanished from my mind. Freed from the restraints of her father, Astrid blossomed. She rode with me from village to village.

'I had no idea they were so hungry,' she said, as tiny, bony hands reached up to us pleading for food. 'We always ate well, and I assumed they did too. These people look so weary, Leofric, with soulless eyes. It's as if all hope has left them.'

I promised them I would change their plight, but I doubt any believed me; except Astrid.

When we returned to Horsdone, I gathered everyone from the six villages to a local moot. We organised the harvest to be gathered whilst the weather held. I sent a working party to repair the mill at Trogbyrne. I revoked the ban on fishing, though restricted the catch enough for each family's needs. We trebled the production of bread at the mill at Horsdone, until the one at Trogbyrne was up and running. Astrid and I travelled to each village with cartloads of best bread and she fed the children as if they were her own. Each time her hand brushed against my arm or her breath warmed the smallest patch of my skin, I became increasingly besotted.

She taught motherless girls how to use the spindle and sew. I organised teams of men to go to each village to rebuild the hovels into sturdy, dry dwellings, which kept the weather out and the warmth in. I reduced the working days, depending on how much land each villein was in possession of. Those with most did two days' work for the estate and those with less land worked three days. The remaining days they could develop their own small strips, which eventually would feed their families. I opened up the wood for the swine and I bought two new teams of oxen and we started to reclaim the overgrown lands in the other five villages. I used the war booty we had collected to finance the work and slowly we rebuilt my estate.

The most surprising aspect of Horsdone was the church. The only building built of stone, it was narrow but towered in height. Stone from old Roman ruins and rocks from the nearby hills had been combined to construct an impressive herringbone-effect exterior, with narrow pointed-topped windows which were covered in stretched animal skins to keep out the wind and rain but let in the light. It was, however, the inside that took the breath away with its lavish, jewelled crosses and challises. There were friezes and murals of Mary, the Blessed Virgin and the apostles painted on the walls of the nave. The chancel was reached through an arch, over which a large, stone rood stood on its beam, staring down at all beneath it. The altar was covered in a gold embroidered cloth and either side stood two golden candle holders, each the height of a man. For all his cruelty, the old lord had been an avid Christian. He believed by bringing glory to God, his sins would be forgiven and his path to heaven secure. Astrid had the same love for God but doubted all the golden crosses in the world could make amends for the injustice metered out by her father to the starving villeins.

One man who looked far from starving was Edmund the priest.

He had left in a hurry when Fritjof's men attacked and appeared three days later. I watched him fumble with a bunch of keys, trying to open the church door. After trying each key without success, he wobbled over to our converted stable.

'Some fool has changed the lock on my church!' he spluttered through a wide mouth with plump lips. His bloated cheeks were crimson, and his large eyes bulged, giving the appearance of a talking toad.

'I had the lock changed,' I said, as I ran my fingers over the blade of my sword, which I had placed on the table in front of us. 'As the new lord, I believe it is my church, not yours, priest.'

'With respect, my lord, is it not God's church?' said Astrid.

'Of course, my lady,' I said, 'it is God's church, priest,' I paused, 'God's,' I paused again, 'and mine, not yours.'

'A figure of speech, my lord, a mere figure of speech.'

'Do you believe in God, Edmund?'

'Of course, I do, lord, I am a priest!'

'In my experience, the two things don't always go together.'

'I can assure you, lord, in my case they most definitely do.' He fell to his knees, crossed himself several times, and looked up at the sky.

'Do you believe if you die as a martyr you will be taken to heaven to sit next to God?'

'Most sincerely I do.'

'If that is true, why did you run away and leave your flock to the mercy of Fritjof's wolves?' asked Wulfgar.

'Lord, I am merely a weak man of flesh and blood. I am of no use in a physical fight. I thought it wiser to make sure I lived so I could continue to help with their spiritual struggle.'

'Is that why most folk are kept out of the church, to help them with their spiritual struggle? Is that why you refused to speak on their behalf, even though the lady Astrid pleaded with you to do so on numerous occasions? Is that why the arms and tithes you collected, never found their way to the poor and starving? Did this all help with their spiritual struggle?' I stood up from the table and leaned towards the shaking priest.

'I don't care much for priests, especially ones who neglect the people they are supposed to be serving. You have grown plump on the fat of this land, whilst your flock has gone hungry. I am led to believe most men were not even allowed in the church but forced to worship at the old stone cross in the meadow in all weathers. Is this true?'

'It was the old lord's wishes. He said the holiness of the church was debased by the presence of ragged wretches and they should worship where they have done for centuries, at the old cross. As for accepting the sustenance my benefactor provided, it would have been churlish of me not to.'

I reached down under the table and pulled out a bedroll and a muslin cloth which contained a loaf of bread. I tossed them to the priest. He caught the bread but dropped the bedding.

'What is meant by this?' he cried, 'I am a man of God, you cannot treat me this way.'

'It is time you put your trust in your God and leave this place,' I said.

'And go where?'

'Wherever the Lord God leads you,' said Wulfgar, 'now go.'

'This is an outrage,' cried Edmund, 'the bishop will hear of this and the wrath of God will be brought upon you all.'

The villeins who had been watching us crossed themselves, but in truth, not one of them was sorry to see the charlatan leave the village, still cursing under his breath.

For four months, we had no priest and no honey. I had opened the church for anyone who wanted it and folk from the six villages entered to pray. Although many, without the prompting of a priest, stayed away and busied themselves with the necessities of life. Astrid had taken it upon herself to sweep the church daily and to pick wildflowers to place around the altar.

There was more concern about the lack of honey than spiritual guidance. Mead supplies were running low and many foodstuffs tasted sour without the sweetness honey gave them. The old lord had bought his needs from a local market, especially beeswax candles for the church and his hall, whilst others made do with tallow candles or tallow dipped rushes.

So, when the cry, 'The bees are back!' was heard, it was met with great glee amongst the villagers and scores of folk ran across the long meadow to see for themselves. However, it was not just the bees which took their interest, but the woman who brought them. She rode a white horse and wore a white dress under a blood red cloak, sewn with golden stars and crescent moons.

It was Mair.

A cart followed her, laden with live chickens, leather pails full of herbs, and the bees' nests. Two scruffy children, of ten or eleven years, she called Fech and Kary, ran alongside, driving a gaggle of geese with sticks.

'I shall live here next to the bees,' she said. 'You, Leofric, will build me a round, thatched dwelling and I shall have a patch of land to grow my herbs. I will curse your enemies, bless your crops and cure the sick and soon we will be renown throughout the land.'

I had learnt it was futile to argue with Mair. Astrid was horrified at the thought of such a woman near the villages. I had now come to value Astrid's company and opinion, so I promised I would double my efforts to find a new priest and explained Mair was one of the reasons I had come to own this land. Astrid was not happy but agreed she should stay if she remained out of the village.

Mair told me I was a fool. I had just escaped one foolish girl, only to fall for another. 'It will end in tragedy,' she told me. 'You will never be fulfilled in love, Leofric, the fates have spoken.'

This time I knew she was wrong, for Astrid and I were falling in love and nothing, even the fates, could stop us.

Just before Yuletide, as the first snow fell, Tripp came. He brought furs, iron and news.

'Your father is unwell, Leofric. He keeps to his bed and shakes continuously. He didn't recognise me. Grim runs the estate, and some say your stepmother is his mistress.'

'I must go to him, Tripp. I need to make my peace with my father,' I said.

'You have been deemed a wolf's-head, Leofric, you can be killed with impunity.' As he finished speaking, his whole body shook as he gave a cough, which he seemed to draw up from his boots. 'Can you remember anything about the night you were taken from Æssefeld?'

324

'All I remember is being hit on the head and when I awoke, I found I was imprisoned in the priory,' I said.

'Think, Leofric,' Tripp said, 'can you recall anything else?'

'Only, when we were escaping from the priory, there was a leather-bound book cover. In its centre was a ruby. I would swear it was the ruby from my father's sceptre.'

'Are you certain, Leofric?'

'I have seen that jewel a hundred times, I am certain Tripp, but something else!'

'What?' he asked, coughing again.

'When I looked into the ruby, I saw the face of the infant Christ.' Tripp frowned, knowing my scepticism of such things.

'Tripp, I don't know how, but in that jewel was trapped the image of a child.'

'Bald said he guessed they had been drugging you with the wine you drank.' Tripp paused for a moment. 'So Thurstan had you and the ruby?' This time the cough was prolonged, and I waited with my reply.

'It would seem so,' I said. 'Who did this to me, Tripp, and why?'

'I guessed it was Hakon's doing at the outset, but when he was sent as a hostage, I imagine Grim and your stepmother saw an opportunity for themselves and continued with the plan. With you out of the way, either disgraced or dead, your half-brother Edgard would eventually inherit Æssefeld. He is still a child, if anything should happen to your father, your stepmother and Grim would have free rein over the estate and all its income. It seems our friend the prior also recognised an opportunity and took it with both hands.'

'Thurstan kept talking about something that would come into his possession which would bring glory to the priory and God,' I said. 'When people hear of a great Psalter, with a jewel which carries a vision of the Christ child, no doubt said to have miraculous powers, they will flock from all over the world to see it. He will have his relic and his coffers will overflow.'

'But how did get his hands on the ruby after all this time?' Tripp said. He coughed again, this time wiping green phlegm and blood

325

from his beard with the back of his hand.

'I don't know, but I intend to find out,' I said. 'But how do I prove my innocence, Tripp? The man who drove the cart is dead. The only other person who possibly knows the truth, besides the perpetrators, is Thurstan and he is unlikely to help me.'

'If you returned voluntarily and finished his Psalter, he might.'

'It would take years, Tripp, besides, once it was finished, he would have me murdered in my bed. I know too much and would have outlived my use to him.'

'Then you must prove he imprisoned you against your will.' He gave another three short coughs

'And if I do, it would be my word against his?'

'I do not know the answer, Leofric, but you must find a way. Now, all this talking makes a man thirsty, I have been told your mead is worth a journey.'

'Of course, old friend, it is so good to see you.'

'And you, Leofric, I am impressed with what you have achieved here in such a short time. When I came here last, it was a sad reflection of what it once was. I would be grateful if I could stay through the winter. The years are passing me by and my bones are getting weary.'

'Stay as long as you wish, Tripp, and I will have something brought to you for your cough.'

'It's a bloody nuisance, can't seem to shake it off.'

As my new hall was still under construction, we found a dwelling near to our stables for Tripp, and I sent to Mair for a potion to help subdue his cough. Throughout the winter I would visit him frequently. We talked about times past. He told me stories of himself and my father. Each time I visited, he seemed to cough more and grow weaker. Astrid also visited him, and they grew close as he told her about me as a child. How I was different to other children, more interested in learning than playing. How I was a natural with horses and the bow, but distant with people.

I had never known anyone quite like Astrid. She listened intently to what people said and genuinely cared about how others felt. She told me of her regret at passively following her father and ignoring his cruelty and disdain for others. She went out of her way to compensate for it and spent endless hours helping those less fortunate than herself. We rode across my new lands together. I told her my innermost feelings, about my mother and father, my mistrust of most people and my waning faith in any gods. I told her about the unfinished Psalter I had worked on and she said one day I should return and finish it and maybe God in his mercy would open my eyes and help me to believe. I even told her about Turfrida, that I had always dreamt I would be with her and how that dream had been broken in an instant like an earthen pot swept from a table and dashed to pieces.

Over those weeks, that dream faded little by little, until each time I closed my eyes, it was Astrid's face I saw, not Turfrida's. And as the birds sang the song of impending spring, we made love for the first time on a carpet of crocus, under a canopy of larch and naked beech trees waiting for their fat buds to burst open. She kissed and touched the whole of my body with a tenderness I had never experienced before or since. A week later we were married at the church by the new priest. The only thing that marred my happiness was Tripp was too ill to attend.

Mair had taken scant time marking her territory, as a feral cat would. A group of local, old women had shown her an ancient tree, said to be sacred, but long fallen into disuse. She drank a potion, then urinated on the tree's gnarled trunk. She carved runes into the hazel's withering bark and sang to it in a long-forgotten tongue under a waning crescent moon to evoke the tree's spirit. Before the moon was half grown, the tree's leafless branches were festooned with ribbons and strips of garments to catch a young man's love or ease a child's birth or increase the yield of the harvest.

Astrid complained that it was a slight against the one true God, though Wulfgar was certain he had seen her tying something of her own to a branch one moonless night.

The new priest was not my choice, but that of the Bishop of

Wigraceaster, who came the week after we finished my new hall, with a retinue of armed men and a letter from Earl Harold for my arrest.

Thirty-five

The face of Ealdred, the Bishop of Wigraceaster, was worn, line etched with a florid complexion. He wore a coat of mail over his pure white alb. His red chasuble flowed from his neck and shoulders onto the rump of his chestnut stallion which was decked out in full war livery. A sword with a gold pommel swung at his side. Instead of his mitre, he wore a glittering helmet intricately engraved with crosses and biblical battle scenes.

We had three days' notice of his coming and all six villages went into a state of panic. I reluctantly moved out of my new hall and had it prepared for his needs. Thirty soldiers accompanied him; four novices who ran along the side of his horse and four clerics seated on a carved oak cart driven by a giant of a man, I recognised as Gudbrand. Another man I knew rode just behind the bishop and I feared the worst. He had replaced his monk's habit for the garb of a priest, but there was no mistaking the beaked nose and fat lips of Riocus.

One of the novices helped Ealdred from his horse, whilst another knelt on all fours to act as a step.

'I have brought you a priest, Leofric,' said the bishop.

'What if I don't want him?' I said, staring at Riocus.

'If you don't want him?' the bishop said. Rummaging in a saddle bag slung over his horse, he pulled out two scrolls. 'If you don't want him, I shall give you this.' He proffered up one of the scrolls. 'This is a warrant for your arrest, for murder, theft, and treason, signed by

King Edward.'

'And if I do want him?'

'If you do want him, Leofric, I shall give you this one,' and held the second scroll towards me. 'This is a letter from Harold, Earl of Wessex, he has word of what you have achieved here. He asks you to join him to assist in rebuilding Hereford in the war against the Wealas and to give you the opportunity to deny these charges to him in person.'

I stayed silent, continuing to stare at Riocus. The bishop placed his hand on my shoulder.

'Leofric, allow the priest to go to the church and begin his work, we have much to discuss. I am a busy man and the world moves on. Earl Harold urged me to seek you out. He remembers your loyalty when many others deserted his family. He wants to repay that loyalty.'

He looked about him gesturing with his outstretched arms. 'What you have achieved here in such a brief time is remarkable, but at what cost, Leofric? No doubt there will be more expense I am sure; livestock to buy, seed to sow, boats to build, these all take silver. Wars bring gold and booty. Join Harold and you can continue to prosper here.'

It was true. Most of the spoils from the war against the Scotti were gone. It would be some time yet before my estate would be profitable. So Riocus became the priest of Horton and I would go to Hereford to meet once again with Harold Godwinson.

The bishop's entourage camped in the big meadow and I sent carts to the port at Ambell to bolster our supplies to feed them.

Despite Mair's potions, Tripp's cough became worse and he developed a fever and the shakes. Rush spent much of his time administering cold compresses to Tripp's forehead and helping him to sip the concoctions Mair sent. Rush did little else except drink and brood, so I was glad he had found something to occupy his time. I had tried to give him some responsibility around the estate. His answer was always the same.

'I am a slave, no one takes any heed of what I say. I ran away from your father to help you. You're the lord here, you should order them to obey me.'

The other folk resented the fact that Rush did less work than them even though he was a slave. Before I left, I promised him I would speak to Harold and plead for his freedom. He promised me he would take care of Tripp and Astrid whilst I was gone.

I gave instructions to Starcolf and Scalpi concerning the estate and asked them both to watch over Rush. They reluctantly agreed. Starcolf wanted to come to Hereford with Wulfgar and me but I needed to leave someone I could trust and who the other villeins respected. Eight other men would accompany us, including Ansgar and Scalpi. I trusted neither of them, but they could both fight, and I would sooner have them near me where I could watch them.

Astrid was not happy with me leaving, but realised we needed coin to continue what we had started here. She helped Riocus in the church and he complained to her about the complacency of the flock and why I allowed Mair to stay near the village.

'If he has a problem with that, why does he not come to me?' I asked.

'I fear he is afraid of you, lord'

'So he should be,' I laughed. 'I dislike priests, particularly that priest.'

Astrid sensed I spoke only partly in jest.

'Tell him, I said if the folk are drawn to Mair more than him and his God, maybe her magic is stronger than his. If he wants them to be his flock, he needs to find a way to convince them, not come crying to me or my wife.'

'And if he does find a way, no harm will come to him?'

'Not from me, as long as Mair is not harmed. Although I would wager Mair would prosper in any conflict between them.' I circled my arms around her, kissing her forehead and lips. 'Can we stop talking about priests and concentrate on things that do interest me.'

She kissed me back, I lifted her up and carried her to our bed, all thoughts of priests and Mair forgotten.

Two nights before I left, Astrid took my hand and walked me down beside the river. The moonlight flittered through flimsy clouds and the air was still and crisp. She took my hands and placed them on her belly.

'Come back soon to us, lord. Your son will need the hand of a father to show him how to run the estate he will inherit, and I need your arms around me to keep me safe.'

'You're with child?'

'Yes, I am with child,' and I noticed the glow of her skin for the first time.

'How do you know it's a boy?'

'I spent my waters on wheat and barley seed,' she said, 'and the barley sprouted. Besides, I just know,' and I believed her.

The glow on her skin grew brighter.

'Lord, look'

'I am looking, and you grow lovelier each moment. Radiant in fact.'

'Look behind you.'

From over the top of the trees at the edge of the wood, I could see flames, sending the last of their light towards us.

'Are we under attack, lord?' Astrid cried.

'I don't think so, the alarm would have sounded. It's around where that sacred tree is, I think. What's Mair up to now?'

As we came to the clearing, most of the villagers were gathered in a circle, bathed by the firelight of the burning tree. Riocus stood, eyes closed, hands clasped in prayer. Gudbrand had positioned himself behind the priest, dressed in his armour and armed with a spear to deter any attacks on the man of God. Mair looked on expressionless.

It was evident that kindling and bundles of faggots had been lit at the sacred tree's base, and ribbons, cloth strips and corn dollies shrivelled in the searing heat as the flames devoured the ancient branches.

Riocus opened his eyes. 'I challenge you once again, Satan's whore, invoke your gods, unleash your power, save your so-called sacred tree, or is it, as I have impressed on these good folks, that your words are as the smoke from these flames, lost in the air. Your gods, nothing more than a distant memory of tales told to frighten children and old women, the remnant of a godless land. Quench the fire with your magic, save the tree. Beseech your gods for a sign.'

Riocus paused. He looked upwards, arms outstretched. 'I see no gods coming to seek vengeance against me. I see only the night sky and the myriad of stars the one true God made at the beginning of creation. Let your gods act now, or else admit you are nothing but a charlatan and a trickster who has led these people astray with your lies and cheap tricks. Save the tree or leave these people in peace to worship the one true God and his son Jesus Christ, the lamb who came to save the world.'

There were those that urged Mair to do something.

She did nothing.

The tree burned to the ground.

The gods did not come.

The priest was not struck down.

The villagers eventually returned to their homes and Mair returned meekly to her thatched hut and the bees.

The day before we left, a man from my village at Trogbyrne came banging on the door of the church. Riocus came out and the man flung himself upon him, sobbing and wailing. His name was Gustav and I knew he had a daughter who had become sick.

'You must come, father,' he cried, 'my little girl is dying. You must bless her.'

For all his faults, Riocus seemed diligent in his role as a priest and he left with Gustav immediately. When I returned to the barn, Wulfgar, Astrid and the young smith from Atheric's forge were waiting for me.

'You have been given a nekename by the villeins,' Wulfgar said.

'Have I?' I asked suspiciously. 'What?'

'Leofric the Black, Killer of Death,' said Wulfgar.

I have had worse. When I was a child the other children called me dipper because I moved liked the little river bird. Peg-leg, hop-a long, cripple were all names I had been called behind my back, so Leofric the Black was an improvement. It also seemed logical. With my jet-black hair and swarthy skin passed down from my grandfather, I stood out amongst those fair, pale Northerners with their Danish descent. But I knew it was Mair's doing.

Astrid lifted something from a wooden chest and brought to me a coat of black mail. There was also a black leather jerkin and black leather britches. The smith came forward and handed me a hessian wrapped bundle.

'You have saved our villages and transformed our lives. I made this to make sure you come back to us safely. It is made from the metal Tripp brought. I took it to the sorceress and she held it aloft to the old gods and I have inscribed the blade with the runes she wrote down for me. The gods told her its name is to be Widewe Wyrhta: Widow Maker.'

I unwrapped the hessian bundle to reveal a sword, the like of which I had never seen.

'I made it the old way,' said the smith. 'Six iron rods twisted together to form one blade, and a steel shoe on the edges and tip.'

I ran my fingers over the flat of the blade. It had a herringbone effect over its full length and it was decorated with runes and strange, snakelike symbols. The blade was supple and springy, which would make it difficult to break and the edges and tip were sharp enough to split a blade of grass. The hilt and cross guard were black with silver inlay and the pommel was of burnished bronze. It felt perfectly balanced as I swung it above my head and slashed the air in front of me.

'I also have a gift,' said Wulfgar, and he stepped outside. When he returned moments later, the stable doors were thrown open and he led in a magnificent black destrier. 'His name is Storm-bringer. He is strong, fast and has the bite of a wolf-hound.'

I approached the steed, ran my hands gently over his back and flank and each leg.

'He is perfect,' I said, 'as are all your gifts. It is truly wondrous how you all thought to make everything black to coincide with my new nekename.'

'It was Wulfgar's idea,' said Astrid. 'He said warriors follow men with a good name and stature. He said it would cause fear in folk to see a warrior in black and it would keep you safe.'

A little later, as we were making last preparations for our journey, Wulfgar and the young smith came to me and said, 'It was Mair's scheming. She said you needed a push or we would all rot in this backwater; nameless, deedless and in time forgotten to all. She said a warrior clothed in black would remain in people's minds all their and their children's lives, and in their tales and in the songs of the bards and poetry of the scops. Wulfgar told Astrid it was his idea, as she would never have agreed to it if she thought it was anything to do with Mair.'

'It is true the great warriors of legend have nekenames; Eric Blood Axe, Iva the Boneless, Swein Fork Beard and now, Leofric the Black,' said Wulfgar. "They will sing of your deeds and those who ride with you; of Wulfgar the Enforcer and Mair the Sorceress.'

I smiled. 'Wulfgar the Enforcer, is that how you want to be remembered?'

'It's better than the man who betrayed his lord,' he snapped back. 'Not long ago we were landless men, without real purpose, accused of crimes we did not commit. Now, you have land, men to follow you and soon an heir to leave it to. I have a lord to follow once again and a chance to prove my loyalty. What we need are more men to follow us, an army that earls or kings cannot do without. If you, dressing in black, helps us to achieve that, so be it. No one's asking you to swirl a gaudy cloak about your shoulders or strut around bragging of your exploits. Our deeds will be what others talk and sing about, but when they do, they will say our names and remember us.'

'I doubt they will sing of Mair, now the priest has shown she has no real power. Just a woman who is clever with herbs and plants,' I said.

'The priest is a fool,' said the young smith, 'and so is anyone who believes that.'

From that day on, I became known as Leofric the Black, Killer of Death, with Wulfgar the Enforcer.

Later that afternoon Riocus returned with news that the girl had died.

'Nothing we knew could save her. Even many prayers to the one true God failed to prevent her death,' the priest said, visibly moved by what had happened.

'And Mair, she could not prevent it either?' I asked.

'I sent the sorceress away,' said Riocus, 'there is no place for spells and blasphemy in the presence of the Most High God.'

'She left without argument?' I asked.

'She did,' he replied.

Wulfgar and I exchanged a look of incredulity.

'The people have lost faith in her. Since she could not even save her so-called sacred tree from the flames of righteousness, how could she possibly save a child.?' said Riocus.

Later that evening, over the trees down by the river, the sky glowed red once again.

Thirty-six

A boy came running to the edge of Horsdone and shouted, 'The sorceress says she will bring the dead girl back to life. Folk are flocking from all over to see this miracle, the night is ablaze with torches, the old gods have been awakened.'

It seemed the whole village poured from their dwellings and followed him down towards the river. Wulfgar and I stood watching the glowing sky, when, as if from nowhere, Fech and Kary appeared behind us.

'Mair says you must put on your clothes of black now, and take up Widewe Wyrhta,' said Fech.

'You and Wulfgar must ride down to the river, but stay out of sight until she summons you,' said Kary. 'Mair says to tell you, there is always a price to pay and this is the time to pay what you owe.'

Wulfgar and I rode in the shadows unseen by the procession of people carrying flaming torches that lit the night. Men chanted the old words to the gods of their forefathers. Women clutched their children, unaware of the man in black on a tall black stallion and his companion, armed with sword, axe and spear. As we approached the river bank, we saw Mair dressed in a shift of thin, white cotton. Her hair loose, spilling down the full length of her back. She turned to face the crowd, the limp body of the girl cradled in her outstretched arms. She looked towards the sky as the moon slipped behind a dark cloud, her eyes white and vacant as though she dream-walked. She called out in a shrill, piercing voice,

'I call upon Baldur, god of rebirth; to Freya; to Buri, the first god; to Odin, the all father; to Nertha, the earth mother; to Abnoba, goddess of river and woodland; to Arawn, the god of the otherworld. I call on you to give up this child and restore her back to our earthly realm.'

She took long, slow strides on her walk to the water. The people crowded around the edge of the river as she waded in until the water lapped above her waist. They gasped as one, as she knelt so that the water covered her and the girl completely; lost in the crow blackness of the river. Only the lapping of the water and the flicker of the torch flames broke the stillness.

A moment of doubt, suspense, uncertainty, replaced in an instant with belief and conviction, as Mair emerged from the depths, water cascading from her like liquid pearls. The girl in her arms coughed, spluttered, her dangling fingers moved. A child screamed out as the girl's eyes sprang open. Again, the onlookers gasped as Mair gently let her down into shallow water. She steadied herself, confused at where she was and why so many people were staring at her.

'Praise to Cernunnas, horned god of the forest; to Herne of the wild hunt; to Lugh, master of skills; their power is truly great,' shouted Mair. 'Praise to Cerridwen, keeper of the cauldron of the underworld, where all knowledge is brewed.'

'The girl lives,' shouted some.

'It's a miracle,' shouted others.

'How?' I asked Wulfgar. He hesitated.

'Trickery must be,' he said. But no one cared. The girl lived.

The old gods were back. They had a sorceress to look over them.

The throng stood aside as Mair and the girl walked from the water. Mair's naked body was visible through the wet linen, bathed once more by the light from the moon and torches. Yet now the light danced in her eyes and hair. She wore a look of triumph, as hands reached out to touch her. To touch Mair that night was to touch the gods themselves. People wept with joy. Reason and sense had no resting place on that night.

338

That night was Mair's night.

The girl's father threw himself at Mair's feet. 'The old gods have restored my child to me,' he sobbed. 'The old gods have proved real where the Christian God has been shown to be powerless.'

The girl, still bewildered by the events, cuddled her father and he picked her up in his arms. 'Give praise to Odin, to Baldor and all the gods of our ancestors and the ancients,' her father shouted.

'To Odin and the old gods,' went up the cry from young and old, carried by the emotion of the night.

Mair, though, had known all along that not everyone would welcome these events. That's why she had made sure I was there.

Firstly, she was confronted by a horrified Riocus. He had brought the jewelled cross from the church and held it out in front of himself.

'What unholy evil is this?' he cried. 'What deception do you bring to these people, sorceress?'

'There is no deception, priest, except by you and your false god. You yourself pronounced the girl dead and now the true gods have made her live again.'

Gustav carried the girl to Riocus. 'My daughter has been restored to me, father, how can that be evil? Does not your holy book say that the Christ brought Lazarus back from the dead? If he could do it, why not the old gods?'

'Because the old gods are not real,' yelled Riocus, 'this is the work of Lucifer, not God, you must drive this woman away from our midst, else the wrath of the one true God will be brought upon us all.'

Most there knew what they had seen, and no yelling priest would convince them otherwise. Others though, disturbed by the events and the priest's words, sided with Riocus and began cursing Mair. There was pushing and shoving, scuffles broke out. Wulfgar and I started to move our horses out of concealment to protect Mair. She glanced over towards us shaking her head. Before we could intervene, the mob began to move aside as Fritjof Heironson with at least twenty armed men pushed their way through. We had seen nothing of him since the day we came to Horsdone, though three dwellings had been destroyed by fire, half a field of wheat flattened and some newly erected fences pulled down. These were all attributed to Fritjof and his men. Two priests walked at his side, severe looking men dressed in white and purple linen with gold crosses hanging from their necks. One swung a thurible, its sweet-smelling incense permeating the night air. The other held a wooden staff topped by a cross. They bore a look of self-importance and disdain for people they deemed beneath them. Behind them were Keld and Regnar the Mean, and two other men I did not know.

'I was warned there would be dark arts abroad tonight. This woman brings shame and blasphemous practices to you all,' said Fritjof. 'She is the whore of your godless master. She must be driven from our land. As chief thegn of Earl Siward and loyal follower of King Edward, I order you to expel this wicked harlot from your midst.'

No one moved. Mair, seemingly unperturbed, stood her ground.

'Any man who attempts to harm me will evoke the wrath of the same gods who brought the child back from the dead. They and all their kin will be cursed until the world ends.'

This was enough to dissuade the majority of folk. No one wants to risk a sorceress's curse.

Fritjof Heironson believed in only one God. Like many nobles, he disregarded most of God's rules, but he believed emphatically in the consequence of disobeying them. So, he gave generously to the Church. He had donated land and commissioned an abbey to be built on it. He paid many priests to pray and supplicate God on his behalf. Now the two priests beside him started praying in Latin,

'Benedictus Deus, Benedictus nómine sancto eius. Maledictum hoc blasphemer, et eius nequitiae et misit Satanas et daemones in gehennam ignis, Amen.'

Although most there would not know these words rebuked the Devil and his wicked spirits and bid God to cast them into hell, they did know it was invoking the Christian God's power against the old gods. The priests repeated the prayer three times with Riocus joining in on the third. The priest with the staff laid it down and was passed a vessel of holy water which he flicked at Mair with a horse tail brush.

'Now that your spirits will have fled before the one true God, who will stop me from casting you out?' said a triumphant Fritjof.

Mair lifted her arms skyward. She seemed to grow as the moonlight cast a long shadow behind her. Her laughter pierced the night. 'You think archaic words and drops of water trouble Woden and Thor? They will provide the means to stop you. I summon Leofric the Black, the Killer of Death!'

As she spoke, she flicked her hand towards us and there was a flash of light, a cracking sound and thick, white smoke filled the air between us and her. I took this as her signal and Wulfgar and I rode through the smoke to appear like magic at her side. Even Fritjof took a step back, amazed at our sudden appearance.

'Mair is here at my invitation,' I said. 'I own this land, given from Earl Siward. Anyone who tries to harm her will answer to him and me as well the gods.'

I drew Widewe Wyrhta from its scabbard and Wulfgar and I rode straight at Fritjof and his priests, sending them into a heap on the ground.

His men backed off, fear on their faces. Although they outnumbered Wulfgar and I, they did want to risk inciting the whole gathering against them. They also knew something other worldly beyond their understanding had taken place that night and their courage deserted them. Mair flicked both her hands and there were two flashes and more thick smoke. Hidden from view, Mair reached out her arm for me to pull her up on to Stormbringer. I noticed a small, finger-sized tube of reed stem drop from her hand but thought nothing more of it. We rode off through a gap in the disorientated melee. By the time the smoke cleared we had disappeared into the night.

Several suspected trickery but they could not prove it and the majority would never believe it. They had witnessed Mair, the sorceress, resurrect a young girl pronounced dead by a priest. She had produced their lord from nowhere and finally disappeared in a cloud of smoke that came from her hands. A legend began that night and somehow, I was part of it.

Thirty-seven

AD 1071
Winter

After a long search we have found the mad monk. It is, as I had guessed, Bald. He has repaired several out-buildings belonging to a small, long abandoned homestead. He grows his own vegetables and herbs and has a goat for milk and chickens for eggs. He prepares salves and soothing oils and balms which he sells to the locals, or exchanges for supplies he can't make for himself.

He seemed reluctant at first to agree to our staying throughout the winter, as he has grown accustomed to a solitary life, only seeing others on rare, necessary occasions. I sense now, after our first week, he is enjoying our company and has promised to acquire a quantity of parchment for me in exchange for helping him to build a shrine he wants to dedicate to Saint Neot.

He had been surprised to see me as he had heard of the terrible events at Elig and assumed the Normans had killed us all. Bald was as sceptical as Wulfgar and I to hear of Thurstan's concerns for our wellbeing and his alleged bravery in planning to confront William the Bastard.

'I fear there is more to his actions than we might suppose,' said the big monk.

We have finished the shrine to Saint Neot just in time as

the first heavy snows of the winter fell yesterday. Bald insisted we sat and watched as he placed the worm-riddled milking stool he believed to be the original used by the saint himself, in front of a small, wooden altar we had cobbled together from pieces of old doors and broken sheep pens. He had made a large cross that stood upon the altar and he laid his staff with the saint's image at the foot of the cross. He placed a small, carved box, no longer than a man's foot and as deep and wide as a drinking pot, on the stool. He knelt and prayed to the Christian God.

'Holy Father, bless this precious relic. Allow it to be hallowed before You and men. Acknowledge its healing powers and keep it safe from greedy, grasping thieves. Priceless among glittering jewels, protect it until it has made its final journey. Make me steadfast, Lord, in spreading Your word and in the pursuit of administering to the sick and needy. Help all men to confess their sins and come to know You in all Your glory. Amen.'

He lifted the box from the altar, tucked it under his arm, picked up his staff, and after thanking us for attending, he trudged back through the snow to his small cell.

From that day on he repeated the same ritual every morning. Even on the rare days when someone came for a cure for boils or a nettle-based tincture, or just to gape at the red-eyed, mad monk, he would make them wait until he positioned the stool, placed the box on the altar and supplicated God with his prayer. The rest of the day he would spend cultivating his herbs and made drawings of them in his journal, then wrote copious notes about their properties and uses for them.

'I wonder what's in the box?' I overheard Scand murmur to Wregan one evening.

'Priceless amongst glittering jewels, he said it was,' said Wregan.

'It's a waste, just sitting there in that box, whatever it is.'

'Whatever it is, it is none of our concern,' I said, interrupting their furtive conversation.

'There's no harm in wondering,' said Scand obviously startled by my sudden appearance.

'As long as it remains that way,' I said. 'Bald has been a good friend to us. If you offend him in any way, you will have me to answer to.'

'We meant nothing by it, lord, simply curious, that's all,' said Wregan as they skulked off muttering.

The snow lays thick and far, creating a barrier which keeps us in and our enemies out. With my new parchments and a scutch of sharpened goose quills, I will use these winter months wisely and continue with my account of the days when Edward, now seen by many as a saint, was king of all of Englaland.

ᛏᚻᛗ ᛚᚠᚱᚪᛗᚻ ᛒᚠᚤ

AD 1055

'**Mair** says you must meet her where the sacred tree stood.'

I awoke with a start the following morning, peering into the face of Fech who had crept unseen into my hall.

'I will go to her later,' I said, still half-a-sleep.

'You must go now, she is leaving.'

I rolled from under the wolf skin blanket and left without disturbing Astrid.

Mair stood by her small, copper cauldron hanging from a tripod of cut hazel rods over glowing embers. She held in her hand a small, golden-handled sickle which she used to cut thistle stalks into the pot, then she added calendula, coltsfoot and mugwort and bay.

'Fech tells me you are leaving.'

'Our lives are changing, Leofric, yours and mine. I have seen it in my dreams and the flight of birds. Our lives are entwined like twisted hemp strands. We have been chosen by the gods to help the poor wretches of the land, the downtrodden, the dispossessed, those unable to help themselves.'

'I have told you before, Mair, there is no you and me. I will go to Hereford tomorrow and clear my name with Earl Harold. I shall make peace with my father, then I shall return to Astrid and my son and I will breed war horses on this land and we will live a happy life. You are welcome to stay here, make potions, tend to your bees, and live in peace. I will instruct my men to protect you from those who wish you harm.'

'No one will dare harm the woman who can bring the dead back to life and conjure up warriors from nowhere. I cannot stay. My path is set, and I must follow the will of the gods. The churchmen will not allow me to live in peace, they are frightened of what they do not understand. I have known that since I was beaten in front of the cross at Æssefeld when I was a child. I learnt that day that their god is a cruel god. They speak of god's love yet threaten those who disagree with them with everlasting torment in a burning hell. They speak of god's love, yet it is their god who will unleash devils into this land to slaughter and maim and turn Britons and Saxons alike into all but slaves. I am leaving, Leofric, but we will meet again soon, and your eyes will be opened. There is trouble coming into your life, you will find hard to bear, but you will survive it, the gods have spoken.'

Before I could reply to her message of foreboding, she took a drinking horn from her girdle and dipped it in the cauldron and drank the liquid. Her body trembled, her eyes glazed, and she started

345

babbling words I did not understand. I left her in that trance, at one with her gods, or so she chose to believe.

I did not want to admit to myself that any of her nonsense disturbed me. It was just Mair with her wild imaginations and fanciful ideas.

Little did I know.

Goodbyes can be difficult. Leaving Astrid and my unborn son was the hardest I can remember.

'Be safe, my lord, and come home with your good name restored.'

'As soon as I have achieved that, I will back.'

With these words, we parted. I looked back over my shoulder frequently. Astrid waved until we lost sight of each other, and already I was longing for the day we would be reunited.

Mair had gone. She had left Fech and Kary, hanging a spell-woven amulet around each of their necks for protection. No one knew where she had gone, except she had ridden to the west.

'You need to take care of your alliance with Mair,' said Bishop Ealdred.

'We know of these cunning women and men, of course we do. Many in the Church want them whipped and banished, but why make martyrs of them? They will eventually be seen for the charlatans they are. Mind you, what Mair did last night was formidable. There are those who might use the fear and mystique she engenders for their own ends. Men would think twice opposing a warrior who rides with a sorceress. As long you remember it's all trickery and illusion, Leofric. You will find many who frown upon such an allegiance, though there are those in higher positions than you who turn to such ones for guidance, though they would be hard pressed to admit it.'

I wondered whether Ealdred was just confident in himself and the power of the Church or whether he underestimated Mair. I guessed a little of both. I also wondered if he was aware of King Edward's past interest in Nairn and her dreams.

We were a day into our journey, when we were approached by riders looking for the bishop. Their horses were hard ridden, thick with sweat and dust. Ealdred was given a sealed letter.

'We are to go to Lundene,' he said, 'Earl Siward has died and there is to be an assembly of the Witan. You are to accompany me, and the king wishes to speak with you about a pressing matter.'

I was saddened at the news of Earl Siward's death. In the short time I had known him I found him hard, but fair. I wondered about the chaos it might bring to Norðhymbraland and who would replace him as earl.

'I should return to Astrid,' I said, 'she could be in danger.'

The bishop drew his horse up close beside me.

'If there is one thing this king excels in, it's keeping a grudge. You turned your back on him once; a second time would be suicide. You have left those you trust to look after your wife, trust in your own judgement and know that they will see her safe.'

I knew he was right. If I was to fulfil my ambitions I needed to meet with the king and Harold, otherwise I would forever be looking over my shoulder in case the next stranger had come to kill me.

As we drew near to Lundene, we were joined by many thegns and their followers answering the call from their king; banners flapped, drums and pipes filled the air with noise. We passed through lush, green meadows and folk working in the fields gave us cursory glances as they busied themselves with their tasks. Young girls ran alongside the soldiers tossing meadow-picked flowers and blowing kisses at them. Young boys marched next to the men, pretending to be great warriors. The sun shone, the birds sang, and all seemed right with the world. Except, I was going to meet a king that I had once rejected and to face charges I could not yet disprove.

Once in Lundene we crossed the Flete, a long, narrow channel, and followed the Temes towards Thorney Island which was flanked by two channels of the Tiburne. This had once been a waste marshland, full of thorn and bramble until monks built a small church there. King Edward treasured it as a tranquil retreat away from the bustle of Lundene. He had made a vow that if he ever was to return to Englaland as king, he would make a pilgrimage to Rome. Circumstances made this unwise, so the Pope at the time, Leo, excused Edward from his vow, providing he restore an existing monastery or built a new church. Edward did this with an all-consuming passion.

First, he had built a new royal palace on the site; a great wooden hall with his own private quarters. Once this had been completed, he started on the church. The old one was demolished and the foundations of a much larger one was put in place. As we rode towards the royal palace, this imposing, growing structure of stone came into view. Masons and labourers were rushing back and forth with cart loads of stone. Buckets of mortar were being hauled up between the wooden scaffolding. Two slender, conical towers at one end, already tall but not yet complete, pointed to the heavens. It had vast, arched window openings and tall, fluted columns. I had never seen anything of its like before, the sheer size of it was overwhelming. Bishop Ealdred said it was being built in the same style as Norman churches and there was one just like it at Jumièges in Normandy, also under construction, and it would take years yet to complete both. It is called the West Minster to prevent confusion with Sancte Pauls, which is on the east side of Lundene.

We arrived only hours before the Witan was due to commence. After being given wine, cheese and bread, we were taken to the palace to be greeted at the carved oak doors by Earl Harold. He kissed the ring on Ealdred's hand and gripped my wrist with both hands.

'Welcome, Leofric, we have much to discuss. Once we have finished the matter of Siward's earldom, we will talk to the king. And you, Wulfgar, you and I will talk.'

We filed into the great hall. As is the custom, our weapons were taken at the entrance. The common place swords were stashed on trestles in the entrance and spears and shields were placed on racks next to them. The named swords, swords of fame and song, were kept in a small room under lock and key with a guard either side of the door. Even among these swords, men looked admiringly at Widewe Wyrhta with its patterned blade and bronze pommel.

King Edward had built his new palace next to the abbey, so he could personally supervise its progress. The main space of the hall consisted of a platform with thrones for the king and his queen and other grand seats for his earls and bishops. On either side of the platform, benches rose in tiers for the Witan to be seated. Tapestries adorned the walls and banners of all the great men of the kingdom hung from rafters in its lofty roof.

The men who entered the palace hall that day were from all over the kingdom. There were ones Wulfgar and I called the fat lords, like Fritjof Heironson; born into wealth, men of satin and silk, mean, dishonourable, rapacious men who employ others to do their fighting.

There were the warrior lords; hard fighting men, of leather and mail, such as Amund and Ravenswart. They were Earl Tostig's men who led their own followers into battle and fought for lords who could bring them the most success.

Then there were the war lords; fierce men, like Earl Harold and Earl Leofric of Mercia. Though the latter was of advancing years and battle weary, he had been formidable in his day. Now his son Ælfgar was set to take his place. Earl Siward had been one of those men; ring-givers and leaders, men of wealth and power either inherited or hard won, men others follow to the death. Now he was dead, another had to be chosen in his stead.

Finally, the men of God; the abbots and bishops. These were many of the wealthiest and most powerful men in the realm, who took their seats on the platform with the king, Earl Harold and Archbishop Cynesige of Eoferwic joined them. Earl Harold and Earl Leofric sat on either side of the two thrones as the king's most senior advisers. Stigand, the Archbishop of Contwaraburg sat next to Harold. He too had the king's ear.

Harold had left us under the watchful eye of his chaplain Leofgar. He wore the surplus of a chaplain, but instead of a cassock underneath, he wore a mail shirt. He was a tall man, large in stature and wore a long moustache as warriors do. He slapped me on the back with a hand like a barley shovel. 'So, you're the lad who Earl Harold thinks should be a priest but wants to be a warrior?' he roared.

'That could be me,' I said, 'and you must be the man who can't decide if he is a warrior or a priest.'

Leofgar bridled at that, then roared with laughter again. 'Harold said you had balls, lad, he was right about that. I am the chaplain to Harold's soldiers. I make sure they know God is on their side when they go to war. And I would never ask men to do what I wouldn't do myself. So, yes, I am both.'

'Can you be both?' I asked, 'a man of peace and a man of war?'

'Sometimes the only way to get peace is to have a war first,' he replied.

I agreed with what he said, but it was strange hearing it from a man of God. Most of them jabbered on about it being a sin to take life and that vengeance belongs to God, but then bless the soldiers as they go to take the lives of others in God's name when it suits them. At least Leofgar wasn't a hypocrite, although I guessed few churchmen agreed with him.

As if with one thought, all those seated stood. From rooms at the rear of the hall came a procession of choir boys, singing in Latin and priests swinging thuribles and chanting prayers. Amongst them were King Edward and his queen, dressed in satins and velvet, both with gold crowns adorning their heads. He was tall and slim, with swan white hair and beard and a sallow complexion. His tunic was red and gold. Draped over his shoulders was a white, woollen cloak trimmed with ermine and fastened about his neck with a diamond brooch. He carried the thin, golden rod given to him on his coronation.

Edyth, his queen, also slim, yet shorter than him, wore a long, pale blue silk dress embroidered with gold thread and many jewels. Under her crown was a silk cap, her hair worn short and braided. Her face was unsmiling and stern, her features, too thickset to be attractive, were proud and forceful. They were led to their thrones, where Edward was handed the golden orb and the short staff with the jewelled cross was laid at his feet. A myriad of blessings, prayers and hymns were said by Stigand and the other bishops, asking God to make their decisions wise and bring glory to God and benefit this great nation.

Earl Harold stood.

'Men of Englaland, a great warrior has left us to join God and use his sword and spear to fight evil from the heavens. Earl Siward was a mighty man who commanded respect throughout the land. Many will miss him, especially in his earldom of Norðhymbraland where, because of him, people could go about their daily affairs in safety. Earl Siward did not tolerate lawbreakers and was swift to act against those that would bring misery to others. So, who do we, as the men who must make such decisions, trust to continue to keep the peace in that sometimes-difficult part of our land?'

This brought murmurs from the assembly; those in agreement, others indignant.

'Unfortunately, as you all know, Siward has only one son living, three summers old Waltheof. We need a strong man to help Norðhymbraland and her people prosper and remain safe from those that would bring fear and ruin. The king is sure that you all have your own preference for who this shall be, so we invite anyone to take the floor in front of us, to state the case of each man you desire to be given this position. The king will listen to all who wish to speak and promises a fair and just decision will be made.'

One by one, men stood before the king, the earls and the bishops, and said why this one or that one should be the new earl. Some words spoken were true, many were clearly not. Men shouted, men cheered, a few scuffles broke out, but eventually, there were two names that stood above all others; Ælfgar, Earl of East Anglia, the son of Earl Leofric of Mercia; and Tostig Godwinson, brother of Earl Harold and queen Edyth. Both men acknowledged the desire and willingness to take on the office.

Separate groups huddled together to discuss the merits of both men. Several of the leading thegns spoke to the king and his closest advisors. More prayers were said. Finally, after long deliberations, the king stood and, in his soft, lilting voice, spoke to his subjects. 'We have listened to your wise council and guided by God through prayer, we have come to a decision. Through the power invested in me, by the will of my people and the authority of Almighty God, I appoint

Tostig Godwinson the new Earl of Norðhymbraland.'

Leofgar gasped, obviously astonished by the choice. Harold and Bishop Ealdred looked surprised but pleased.

Tostig knelt in front of the king and kissed the ring on his finger. Edward beckoned him to rise and hung the seal of Norðhymbraland around his neck. There was no speech from Tostig, only a smug smile that said the inevitable had just happened. There were many that day dismayed by the outcome, only four people looked unsurprised; the king, the queen, Archbishop Stigand and Tostig himself.

The queen embraced the new earl. It was well known, of all her brothers, Tostig was her favourite. Harold stood back as a host of men clamoured to congratulate his brother. All may not have wished him to be earl, but now he was, he was a man of power and could further their ambitions.

'You call this justice? You call this even handed? You call it honourable? I say it is a sham.'

Everybody turned to see who was shouting such claims. It was Ælfgar. He stood from his seat next to his father and forced his way towards the king, gesticulating, his face red and contorted, his eyes aflame with anger.

'How many of you wanted Tostig as earl of Norðhymbraland? Who has more experience than me? Certainly not this Godwinson. I have shown my worth in East Anglia. I have kept out our enemies from the sea. I have collected the taxes and fines. I have paid the dues owed to the king. I am Ælfgar, son of the mighty Leofric, Earl of Mercia. Norðhymbraland should be mine.'

The king's housecarles, the only armed men in the hall, gathered around Ælfgar and his man, Copsi.

Taking no heed of them, Ælfgar ranted on. 'Will these sons of Godwin not be content until they own all of Englaland? Will this king be forever under their yoke?' He turned to Earl Leofric, 'Father, will you also sit and allow your son to be humiliated and robbed of his destiny?'

Earl Leofric stayed seated. He gave a sigh, weary of this wild, impetuous son of his. 'Ælfgar, my son, the Witan has spoken. Our king has already shown his generosity to you when he gave you East Anglia. You will no doubt be given Mercia when I leave this world. Be patient, curb this angry nature of yours, or you will be in danger of losing what you have.'

'Patience! Patience! I have waited twice as long as this puppy,' Ælfgar said, pointing at Tostig, 'isn't that patience? Twice as long, only to be passed over for a Godwin yet again. You say the Witan has spoken, I say the king has spoken, driven by his Godwin wife and his Godwin brothers-in-law and an archbishop in the pay of the Godwins. I say, who rules this land, King Edward or the avaricious Godwins?'

At this, Earl Harold and Archbishop Stigand rose as one. Men shouted all about the hall, fights broke out between supporters of both men. King Edward rose slowly from his throne supported by the arm of his queen.

'My worthy counsellors,' he began, only to be drowned out by the furore of squabbling men. 'Wise men of Englaland, hear your king,' once again his words were lost in the uproar.

'Silence!' the giant voice of Gyrth Godwinson cut through the wall of noise. 'Heed the words of your sworn king.'

The noise stopped, and men fell to one knee to respect their sovereign. Only Ælfgar continued yelling abuse and insults to everyone he could see, until he was restrained by six housecarles.

'Wise and worthy councillors,' the king repeated, this time even his small, quiet voice was heard by all. 'I did indeed listen to you all and this decision was made in good faith and for good reasons, not, as is claimed, as an act of favouritism. The people of Norðhymbraland are proud of their Danish descent. Tostig is half Dane from his mother. Ælfgar is Saxon, born and raised. As his esteemed father Earl Leofric has stated, Ælfgar is likely to succeed to his father's lands in Mercia. It would be folly to disrupt Norðhymbraland once again when that happens. Perhaps it is Ælfgar's inability to grasp this, that shows he has not yet learnt all he needs for such an office. In this man,' he partially turned and placed his thin, bony hand upon Tostig's shoulder, 'I see no pup, but a strong and diligent leader who

353

will bring prosperity to the north of our realm. He is also a trusted friend of Malcolm, King of the Scotti, a troublesome nation, we know. Having their king as friend will be to our advantage. Therefore, the decision was made with reason, knowledge and foresight, nothing else.'

Many nodded in agreement.

Ælfgar wrenched himself free. 'Liars, sycophants, all of you. All my life I have lived in the shadow of these Godwins. No longer! Who is this Edward that he should be king? More Norman than English. More priest than king. More father or brother than husband. He can't even provide an heir to rule after him. His father was incompetent and he has surely inherited that trait. He talks of a decision made with reason, has he ever decided anything himself without the agreement of a Godwin? It is said any good ideas he does have come from his queen. Perhaps she should rule in his stead.'

Any support Ælfgar had at the start of his protest, evaporated swiftly at these words of treason. Men shouted him down. 'Traitor,' they shouted, 'Judas.' The housecarles drew their swords and physically restrained him.

King Edward held out his hands in a bid to quieten the situation.

'This outburst by Ælfgar has proved our decision was the correct one. A divinely appointed king cannot tolerate any man who questions his right to rule. He gives me no choice, other than to strip him of his earldom and any other titles he now possesses. He will forfeit all his lands in this realm and has two days to remove himself from these islands hence forth.'

The great chain and seal of East Anglia was removed from around his neck and he was forcibly taken from the hall, still shouting abuse and insults at the king and the entire Witan.

The king was handed the seal, and without hesitation, he hung it around the neck of Gyrth Godwinson. 'I, King Edward, King of all Englaland and its islands, proclaim this man, Gyrth Godwinson, Earl of East Anglia. If anyone doubts my legal right to make this decision, speak now.'

If any objected, they kept silent, and so the whole of Wessex, East

Anglia and Norðhymbraland lay in the power of the Godwins, and their nearest rival, Earl Leofric, was an old, spent force with an exiled son and decreasing authority.

Thirty-eight

The king, visibly shaken by the foregoing events, slumped back on his throne. His queen poured him a goblet of wine and mopped his brow from a bowl of perfumed water a servant brought. Archbishop Stigand addressed the Witan. 'We thank you for your attendance today and the wise counsel you have given and now the meeting is at an end. We ask that you leave the hall and enjoy the entertainment provided in the palace grounds. Those of you who have prior arrangements to address the king in private, please remain.'

The exodus from the hall was swift. A few mumbled to each other as they filed out into the sun, but most remained silent, stunned by the day's events. Wulfgar and I stood to leave when Leofgar stopped us. 'You are to remain.'

Most men had left the podium, only the king and queen, the earls, Archbishop Stigand and Bishop Ealdred remained. Leofgar stayed next to Wulfgar and me and we were aware of others behind us in the shadows.

The king sat staring at us for a while before he spoke. He had been passed several parchments by one of the scribes who were now busy writing up legal documents concerning the new earls and their earldoms. He beckoned me forward and held out his hand for me to kiss. I took his hand in mine, this king I despised. I bent my head to kiss the ring on his finger. Instead, I stared at it in disbelief. The blue stone reflected the flames of the torches and candles that lit the hall in a way that could not be mistaken. I had seen this stone many times before. Without a doubt it was the sapphire from my father's sceptre. I looked at the golden orb next to the king. At his feet lay the golden sceptre with a cross upon its top, also the sword of offering, and leaning against the throne was the golden staff. Many had puzzled where the money had come from to produce such magnificent pieces. I had often wondered why my father's sceptre had never been found even though many had searched for it. At that moment I wondered if the sceptre I longed to return to my father was no more. Was it possible it had been broken down and made into this new regalia? The sapphire had been turned into a ring and the ruby was the one I had seen in the priory. I had no proof of this, but it seemed to make the most sense. King Edward noticed my intense glare at the ring and withdrew his hand quickly.

He waved the pieces of parchment at me. 'Do you know what these are?' he asked in his soft, half French, half-stilted English wavering voice.

'No, Sire.'

'Complaints, complaints about you. Your father wants me to exile you. His right-hand man wants me to execute you. A leading northern thegn wants me to take lands from you. You are accused of being a coward, a thief, a murderer, a harbourer of a run-a-way slave, a blasphemer, and a conspirator with demons and sorceresses. Quite a list for one so young. How do you plead to these charges?'

'I admit to harbouring a run-a-way slave but...' I started to justify myself but was stopped by the king's raised hand.

'Bring the first witness.'

'Witness, Sire,' I said, 'is this a trial?'

'I am the king, it's whatever I want it to be. Come forward, man.'

Fritjof Heironson emerged from the shadows. He bowed before the king.

Keld stood just behind him, a bundle of papers and scrolls in his arms.

'You say this Leofric is a coward and he also stole your land?'

'Yes, sire, he let the great Earl Siward's son, Earl Osbeorn, known as Bulax, die when he was charged with protecting him. He came into Norðhymbraland and took land promised to me by its previous lord. He also took my intended bride for himself. Moreover, I most recently witnessed him participate in ungodly practices with a sorceress.'

The priest scribes stopped writing and crossed themselves so much I thought their hands would fall off. Picking up their quills once more they continued writing the words of Fritjof Heironson.

'Liar, liar.' Voices came from the back of the hall.

'Who shouts such things? Bring them here,' ordered the king. Three of Edward's housecarls ushered two men to the front. One was Iscariot, the other Ansgar.

My name is Iscariot, I am the man who brought the news of Earl Siward's death, sire. I trained the earl's soldiers for battle. This man, Leofric, accused of cowardice is anything but. He fought in the thick of the battle at Dunsinane and he did all he could to protect the young Earl Osbeorn. I was also present when Earl Siward gave the deeds of land to him. The accusations are false, my king.'

King Edward squinted at me from the dais. Queen Edyth, who now sat on the floor at his feet, spoke to him quietly.

'Did he steal the thegn's bride-to-be?' asked the king.

'No, Sire,' said Ansgar, 'she was never Fritjof's intended, she had rebuked him many times and Leofric stopped him from taking her by force. She is now a willing wife to Leofric. Heironson's men raped my daughter, Sire. It is he that should be on trial.'

'That is a serious accusation for a man such as you to make against a thegn of high standing. Why should I believe you over him?' said King Edward. He did not wait for an answer.

'What do you say to these men's claims, Fritjof?'

'They are his men, sire, they would say such things. I can produce a hundred men to each of his, who will support me in these matters. I possess written testaments to prove what I say is true. You yourself know I have always been loyal to you, my king, unlike others,' Fritjof said.

The king stared at me again.

'Just one of these charges is enough to condemn you,' he said. 'I am told your father believes you killed his steward and stole from him. Is he lying too? It appears all the evidence points to your guilt.'

'I did not do those things, sire, I was taken against my will, and held....'

'It is true, sire.'

I was interrupted by another man who emerged from the shadows. It was Thurstan.

He bowed before his king and kissed the ring.

'We found Leofric injured and bound up in the back of an abandoned cart outside the priory. We took care of him and restored him back to health. I have known him since he was a child, Sire, and I trust his word. I also knew of his talents with the quill. In return for our care, he willingly assisted us in the compiling of the holy work you are familiar with, my liege,' he said, lying.

King Edward turned his gaze to me again. 'Are you telling me, he was responsible for those words in your Psalter?'

'Most of them, sire.'

'Did you not tell me the scribe responsible for that work left the abbey without explanation?'

Wulfgar, who had remained silent up to now muttered, 'Lying bastard.'

'I did, sire. Leofric struggles with his spirituality. He is torn between the fight for heaven and earth. It seems he has a passion for violence as well as learning. I sincerely believe God nevertheless as a purpose for him, though he still fights against God's will. If you were to command him to return to the priory, Sire, our work could be completed, and you would possess an extraordinary artefact like no other, blessed by God's glory when your magnificent abbey is finished.'

For the first time that day King Edward smiled. I came to learn that since the Godwins had returned from exile, Edward's interest in all things political had waned. There was still a trace of resentment in the Godwin's power, but he was more at ease with Harold than he been with his father. He trusted him with what he felt were the tedious, worldly matters of running the country, which allowed him to concentrate on the far more important matters of spiritual advancement.

In contrast, Queen Edyth glared at me with a contempt that puzzled me. She turned to her husband once more and said something only he could hear. He tapped her hand consolingly.

'I read the work you produced at Filey, Leofric, and I believe it is inspired by God himself. Why He should choose one such as you is a mystery, yet God does often work in mysterious ways. It would be a crime against me, and indeed a crime against God, if you did not finish this godly undertaking. The only reason you are still alive is Earl Harold pleaded with me to spare you. He tells me you are more use to the realm alive than dead. Why or how I cannot guess. I find this whole thing tedious. I have an abbey to build. I am tired of father's rebellious sons. Thegn Fritjof, I suggest you take the matter up with the new Earl of Norðhymbraland if you still feel aggrieved.'

'I will, sire,' said Fritjof, 'I will.'

'Earl Harold, I entrust this, Leofric, to you for one year after which you will hand him over to the Abbott Thurstan. Leofric, if you want to live you will comply with these conditions. Once you complete your work on the Psalter you will be pardoned of all the crimes against you. Though if you should come to our attention again in the meantime, there will be no mercy.'

'I am certain he is a man of honour and trustworthy, Sire. If he proves to be otherwise, I will deal with him severely. You have my word,' said Harold.

'Yes, you will,' said the king. 'The other matter we talked about, you will deal with that also? My nephew, Earl Ralph, did not attend today as he was concerned about trouble on his Wealas' borders, he says he needs soldiers.' He hauled himself off the throne and Queen Edith helped him from the dais. 'See to it, Harold, but don't you be gone long, we need you here.'

'It will be done, Sire,' said Harold. 'I will return as soon as I am able.'

I felt lost. This had been my chance to plead my innocence and the king had refused to let me speak. I would still be seen by many as a guilty man. It seemed my fate was in the hands of Earl Harold and Thurstan yet again.

Once we were outside the hall, Earl Harold took me aside. 'You once defied your father and that king,' he said, pointing towards the hall, 'and supported my father and me. Why?'

'Because I believed the cause you stood for, defending the people of Doferum was the right one, and my father and the king were wrong.'

'And no other reason?'

'What other reason could there have been? It was the hardest decision I have ever had to make to go against my father. I understood why he had to take the action he did, but I couldn't. It was the Normans in the wrong that day, not the men of Doferum.'

'It is that honesty and sense of right that makes me sure you are innocent of the crimes held against you. There are many men willing to testify to your guilt. If you run from this, it will never go away. You will never become reconciled with your father. However great a warrior you become, whatever the reputation you gain, you will always be known as the man who stabbed an innocent steward in the back and fled from the scene like a coward. I have a task for you, Leofric. You help me with this, and I will do all I can to find out what happened back in Æssefeld.'

'Do I have a choice?' I said, already knowing the answer.

'We always have a choice, Leofric, sometimes not much of one, but we always have a choice.'

'What is it you want me to do?' I asked, resigned to my fate.

'Later, my friend,' he said. 'First, you must rest from your journey, and I must talk to Wulfgar.'

'Wulfgar did not kill your cousin Beorn, I am certain,' I said concerned.

'I will be the judge of that,' he said seriously, 'but I am sure you are right.'

I was taken to Harold's quarters and wondered what task Harold had in mind for me. I also thought of Astrid and my unborn son, and as thunder rumbled from the north, my tent was lit up as lightning ripped across the sky. I was glad I was not superstitious or believed in bad omens, and before long I fell into a deep sleep.

In the morning, I breakfasted with Harold and his hand-fast wife Edith. I liked Edith. She was kind and hospitable. She moved in a graceful, calming manner as she carried out her wifely duties making sure her husband's guests were well cared for. She brought fish, bread and eggs. Even though the name people called her by was a play on her family name Swannseshalls, it was easy to see why people named her Swan Neck, because of her pale, white skin and long, elegant neck. Even the way she walked was effortless as if she glided through water.

'Everything is prepared for your journey, my lord,' she said to Harold and they briefly touched hands as she passed by.

Bishop Ealdred came later that morning and after blessing our food and a short prayer of thanksgiving, he spoke to Harold. 'The king tells me when this business with the Wealas is finished I am to return to Hungary, this time at your side. The king has received word that the atheling, Edward, may now be prepared to come to Englaland as his heir apparent. It is the last chance for Englaland to appoint a king of royal Saxon blood. Our mission is to convince him his place is here by the side of the king, ready to take on this mantle.'

'A nation without an heir is a dangerous, precarious place,' said Harold, 'for I fear ambitious men of foreign nations are gathering like wolves and carrion prepared to bring this country to its knees to fulfil their desires to wear King Edward's crown. Who could be more fitting than the son of Edmund Ironsides to continue the Saxon line? The whole of the Witan prays for our success.'

Although men have said otherwise, I believe Harold said those words with all sincerity.

Thirty-nine

We arrived in Hereford three days later. Harold needed someone who could speak the tongues of the Wealas and Normans, someone who could read and write, someone he could trust. He had men that could do each of those things but not all three of them, therefore, he wanted me. Iscariot had approached Harold and offered his services as a warrior-maker, as his lord was now dead and he was vowed to no man. Harold accepted, and Iscariot accompanied us to Hereford.

It was a green, fertile land fed by the River Wæge. It had been in Saxon hands for hundreds of years but the Wealas, or as they call themselves, the Cymry, still claim it is theirs by birthright, as they do the whole of Englaland, which they call Britain.

It seemed peaceful enough as we rode through the tree-lined valley, but away in the distance loomed the dark outline of the Black Mountains from where hordes of screaming Wealas could swarm down at any time, bringing death and chaos before disappearing back to their rugged stronghold.

'The Wealas keep coming back, stealing cattle, raiding villages,' said Harold as we made our way towards the town. 'Recently, the situation has become somewhat calmer as Gruffydd-Ap-Llywelyn has been occupied fighting his closest rival, Gruffydd ap Rhydderch, to be king of all Wealas. If one or the other should be victorious and unite the country it could be hazardous for Englaland. We must prepare to prevent them from encroaching on English soil. Hereford is a strategic town right on the border, it would be a prime target for the Wealas to attack. There was once a strong wall and palisade around it, but it's been allowed to crumble and rot. That's what I want you to oversee, Leofric. Earl Ralph puts too much reliance on his castles, but they're not enough. He says he hasn't the men to maintain the walls, so I will leave you and a hundred men, five masons and six woodsmen. The earl already has three hundred of my soldiers with his own Norman force, that should be enough to keep the savages out.'

We were watched as we entered the town. Earl Harold was well known here, as his brother Sweyn was once the earl until he was exiled, and King Edward appointed his own nephew, the Norman, Ralph of Mantes, in his place.

We arrived at Ralph's castle; a big mound of earth, called a motte, with a pitched, tiled, wooden roof tower on top. A tall, wooden fence and an outer ditch surrounded it. At the side, encircled by another fence and ditch, was an enclosure called a bailey that housed the living quarters for the earl and his family.

Ralph rode out to greet us, accompanied by Ælfnoþ, the shire reeve and a retinue of ten armed horsemen. Ralph was slim, sat tall in the saddle, and wore his hair in the Norman fashion, thick on top, combed forward and shaved at the back, to an abrupt horizontal line, level with the ears. He was dressed in a mail shirt over a white linen ser coat. He was not yet thirty but had the demeanour of an older man with a dull, unsmiling face.

'Bienvenue,' he said.

'Earl Ralph is pleased you are here, the Wealas have increased their raids of late,' said Ælfnoþ, 'and the earl is committed to preventing them from possessing the king's lands.'

'Not committed enough to keep the walls from falling down,' said Harold brusquely, 'though I notice his castle appears in good repair.'

'It is the way of the Normans, lord,' said Ælfnoþ.

'We are not in Normandy, this is Englaland. King Edward commands that the walls must be repaired, and the town made secure,' said Harold. He placed his hand on my shoulder. 'This is

Leofric the Black, he will oversee that this work is carried out.' I nodded my agreement. I was surprised at Earl Harold's introduction. It was the first time anyone outside my circle of friends had called me by that name.

The soldiers joined the rest of Harold's men who had struck camp in the long meadow on the far side of the river. There was a large barn that had been set up as an armoury where all the shields and weapons were stored, and a smithy where they were busy making new and repairing old.

Harold went to see his cousin Agatha, Ralph's wife, and his godson, Harold, named after him.

Wulfgar and I were joined by Bishop Æthelstan. He was one of the oldest men I have met, round shouldered, crooked back, pinched face, and thin silver hair with the pink of his scalp showing through. He had been blind for thirteen years but had been able to carry on his ecclesiastical duties with the help of Tremerig, known as the Wealas Bishop. Tremerig said little but watched every step Æthelstan took and at times would take his arm to steady him.

'Stop fussing, Tremerig, I am blind not senile,' was the thanks he received.

'Most people here are talking about you and your friend as ruthless killers. Leofric, the Killer of Death no less, the companions of wizards and sorceresses.' Bishop Æthelstan smiled as he spoke and shook his head. 'People will believe anything if enough say it enough times, anything. I, on the other hand, Leofric, I have been told you are a lover of books, is that true?'

'About the books, yes,' I said.

'Follow me,' said the bishop.

Æthelstan carried a white staff, with which he prodded the ground, seeming to know every dip and divot that lay in front of him. The bishop took us across the town to a large, impressive, stone cathedral.

'It used to be a small building, been here for hundreds of years,' he explained, 'we have just finished working on it. Dedicated to Saint Ethelbert the King, his bones are still here to this day.'

He pushed open the big, oak door and we walked inside. Many priests and other religious men in white robes were busying themselves, scurrying here and there, especially when the bishop entered. We walked up the aisle to the altar and were amazed at the wealth of artefacts on show. All around the walls hung golden cherubs and angels, there were jewelled crosses and chalices and on either side of the altar, solid gold candle sticks, each the height of a tall man. On the altar itself was a golden bowl and a golden ladle with pearls set in the handle. Two carved oak tables were heaped with books; prayer books, bibles, records of the town, registers of all who had lived and died there, all with beautiful, bound, jewelled covers. The bishop ran his fingers over the books, carefully lifting one from the table. I was curious as to why he chose the one with the dullest, plain leather cover.

'This is the most precious of all our books, a copy of the Gospel of Saint John, it is over two hundred years old.'

He carefully turned the pages and I marvelled at the freshness of the colours and the skill of the scribe. Behind the altar was a large, glass case with human bones laid on red silk. Set behind all this were two tall, narrow windows, depicting Saint Ethelbert and the Virgin Mary, in hundreds of coloured glass pieces, the sunlight filtering through blues, greens and reds.

'I agree with Earl Harold. The town walls should be strengthened as soon as possible. We need to protect all this,' said the bishop.

'And the townsfolk,' I said.

'The poor are dispensable, Leofric, all this is irreplaceable, especially this,' he said, as he placed the gospel back onto the table.

'Perhaps if there wasn't all this, there wouldn't be so many poor,' I said.

'Even our Lord said the poor will always be with us, Leofric, always,' said Bishop Æthelstan, shaking his head and smiling again.

'I am certain the lords and the Church will make sure they always are,' I said.

Harold left the next day to attend to affairs on the far side of Englaland. He took Leofgar with him, though he left Iscariot to help train the soldiers. The Normans trained separately, mostly on horseback, charging back and forth, launching their throwing spears, stabbing with the longer shafted ones.

The Saxon soldiers and the local fyrd practised with shield and sword and the big, two-handed war axes they are famous for. Iscariot snarled and cursed and rapped knuckles.

On occasion, Earl Ralph would watch us training from a distance. When we were not training, we built. We felled trees and carted sandstone from a local quarry. We turned the trees into fence posts, planks and pointed stakes. The stone, we turned into blocks to repair the old walls on the town's perimeter. We worked through torrential rain that made the ground sodden and the wood difficult to cut.

Reports kept coming in from local scouts that a small army of Wealas were gathering in the valleys, but nobody came.

We had been there for over four months, when three Normans rode into Hereford. One of them was Reinald Levett. We had been told all the Normans who sided with Mac Bethad had been killed. Reinald Levett was very much alive, resplendent in a cloak of deep crimson and shining mail. He was sat astride a chestnut war horse. A red kite shield, with two golden lions painted on its face, the device of William, Duke of Normandy, hung down from his saddle. A fine sword, with an ornate pommel and hilt, was strapped to his waist in a scabbard with a snarling dragon motif etched into its hardened leather.

Wulfgar looked up. 'What's he doing here? Last time we saw him he was covered in Saxon blood.' Wulfgar was stripped to the waist and up to his knees in mud. He was helping men repair the collapsed banks of the moat in front of the palisade.

'I don't know, but it seems he's back in favour,' I said.

Levett nodded his head at us as they rode towards Ralph's castle.

I left Wulfgar in charge of the work party and joined Iscariot who was drilling the men in the shield wall.

'Come on, you shower of pig shit, we don't want Leofric thinking I haven't done my job properly now, do we? Shields!' he snarled, and as one, the mass of round shields were brought up in a defensive, solid wall. 'Weapons!' growled Iscariot and the wall bristled with swords and axes. 'Forward, as though your miserable lives depended on it,' he yelled, 'for soon they will.' In an unfaltering, straight line, forty men long, and roughly ten men deep, the wall moved forward ten paces. 'Hold!' barked Iscariot. Each man came to a sudden stop. 'Forward!' the order came again, once again the wall advanced relentlessly. They continued this for a hundred paces, stopping, starting, until Iscariot instructed, 'Turn!' Each man swivelled around so those that had been at the back were now at the front, and they repeated the whole process time after time.

'Impressive, I almost feel sorry for the Wealas,' I said, and although I sensed Iscariot did not care less if I was impressed or not, I could see that he was pleased the men had not let him down, though he would never admit it.

'Unless the Wealas are sending their women and children to fight they will squash you like dung beetles. Again! this time keep the wall tight. Forward!' he screamed once more.

I left them to it and rode slowly round the palisade checking on the progress of the rebuilding work. It was slow. It had been neglected for too long and we had too few men. Hopefully, the scout's reports were accurate and there was no attack imminent or one we could easily contend with.

Wherever I rode, the one thing that was always visible was Ralph's wooden castle. There were only three such structures in the whole of the land and they were all on this border between Englaland and Wealas. They had been erected when the Godwins had been exiled. Although they objected when they returned, King Edward insisted the castles remain as a deterrent to the Wealas. The other two castles were both held by Normans; Osbern Pentecost who had been killed at Dunsinane and Richard Fitz Scrob. The castle at Hereford stood tall on its manmade hill. An inner palisade, a deep moat, an outer palisade and the river at its back, formed formidable obstacles to thwart attack. Yet this was no refuge for the town's folk. This was purely for Earl Ralph and his close entourage in times of extreme danger. As I rode back to Wulfgar, I was approached by two of Earl Ralph's outriders. 'The earl wishes, speak you,' said one in stilted English. 'Follow.'

They led me across a wooden bridge over the moat and into the bailey to Ralph's living quarters. There were armed men at each gate and doorway. As I was about to enter, the door flew open and Iscariot came barging past me.

'Harold left you in charge, see if you can get through to the arrogant turds,' he snapped as he strode across the bailey courtyard.

Earl Ralph, Ælfnoþ and Reinald Levett were sat at a large table. They each had a goblet of wine and a serving boy offered one to me, which I declined.

It was Ælfnoþ who spoke first. 'Our scouts tell us Gruffydd-Ap-Llewellyn has gathered together a raiding party and they plan to attack the town. Earl Ralph has been watching your men train. He believes they fight in an old, static fashion which, against the mobile Wealas, will be useless. He wants your men to fight from their horses with lance and spear. Our combined forces will sweep them away and we will rid ourselves of this irritation for good.'

'So that's why Iscariot came storming out,' I said, 'I am sure he reminded you the Saxon fight in a shield wall, not from the saddle.'

Ælfnoþ translated my words to Ralph, though I guessed he had understood most of them.

'You have horses, no? We will supply the spears. This will be done. That man, Iscariot, you will replace him with Levett. He will help you train your men,' said the earl.

'Our horses are not warhorses. We ride them to battle but fight on foot. It is the Saxon way,' I protested.

'We have experience in the way the Wealas fight. They come as a storm, all at once, not in a shield wall. They would swarm over you like ants. Mounted soldiers are the way to defeat them. Your men will do this, with or without you or they will be executed for disobeying my orders. I will hear no more on the matter.'

Realising it was pointless to argue against his stubbornness I changed the subject. 'I noticed you have many men standing idle around the castle. We could do with help rebuilding the town walls,' I said.

The earl stared at me as though a cat had brought me in and dropped me at his feet.

'My men are not idle. They protect our stronghold. The castles are the main reason we have been able to resist the Wealas until now. Besides, our scouts ensure us there is only a small force preparing to come against us and we will sweep them away long before they reach the town walls.'

Reinald Levett leant over and spoke softly to the earl then addressed me.

'We were expecting Bishop Ealdred to be here. We are told there are arrangements in place to seek out Edward the Atheling as an heir to King Edward. Is this true?' said Levett.

I wondered why that would concern them and how they knew of such plans.

'I am not privy to the bishop's business, though I do believe he has returned to Lundene. To do what, I do not know.'

'If the rumour is true, it is a breach of King Edward's promise to Duke William of Normandy, that he would be the king's heir,' said Levett.

Who hasn't Edward promised the crown to? I thought, though did not say it.

'You would have to speak to either the king or the bishop, lord, I know nothing of such things.'

That was partly true. In my younger years, I had not been concerned with politics. My ambitions were personal, not political. Though I did know most men wanted a Saxon king not a Norman or a Dane. In truth, most men's lives were full of mud, sweat and near starvation whoever ruled over them, though they hoped a king of their own race would be more just and compassionate than a foreign ruler. The reality is, most noblemen, of any race, view the common man as little more than an animal to be worked and used to make their own lives more tolerable. A few, like Earl Harold, realised that if you treat a man fairly, he is more likely to show loyalty than one you treat badly, though men such as him are rare.

I took my leave and as I crossed the bailey, was nearly knocked over by the two local scouts, Bledig and Idwal, rushing towards the castle.

I rode back to the ramparts and sought out Iscariot and Wulfgar. Iscariot was still fuming. 'That Norman bastard's got no brains. I will not command the men to give up their shields, swords and axes,' he growled.

'Earl Ralph wants Levett and I to train them,' I said.

'He can go to hell. We fight in a shield wall, not on bloody horseback.'

'I agree,' I said, 'we will both go and tell him our men will fight in a shield wall or not at all.'

Wulfgar glanced across the meadow. 'You can tell him now.'

Earl Ralph, Levett and Ælfnoþ were riding quickly towards us. Bledig and Idwal rode with them. The sound of the cathedral bells rang loud. A group of Norman soldiers rode across the bridge carrying flaming torches. Folk working in the fields stopped, wondering what was happening.

It was Ælfnoþ who shouted first. 'Gruffydd and a small armed force of Wealas are moving towards the town. We must stop them now.'

Norman soldiers piled out of their tents, hurriedly pulling on mail. Wulfgar and Iscariot ran across the meadow to the Saxon camp. I followed as quickly as I could. As we arrived, a group of Norman horsemen, brandishing spears, rode between the men and the armoury, and the Normans with the torches flung them against its wooden walls and thatched roof setting it alight. At the same time, carts drew up full of spears for both throwing and stabbing. The men stood bewildered, called to battle but unable to get their shields and swords.

'The stupid Norman bastard,' screamed Iscariot, 'I'll kill him.'

Ansgar and Scalpi came running to our tent. Their swords were with ours, locked in an oak chest.

'What the hell is happening?' said Scalpi.

'The Wealas are attacking,' I said. 'Ralph wants the men to fight on horseback. We told him they wouldn't, so he's given them no option.'

Ralph and Levett rode amongst the men telling them to take up the spears and get on their horses. The men stepped back from the heat of the burning barn, black smoke billowing into the air. Realising their own weapons were lost, and that to disobey an earl would be mutiny, they reluctantly took up the spears and mounted their horses. The majority were small fell ponies, perfect for transportation, totally inadequate for charging at an enemy. I pulled on my black mail and helmet and strapped on Widewe Wyrhta. I clambered onto Stormbringer and Wulfgar leapt up onto Fleet. Ansgar and Scalpi also had bigger steeds than the regular army, and once re-united with their weapons, they pulled alongside Wulfgar and I at the front of our men. We four were the only Saxons with shields.

Levett rode up on his big warhorse. 'Our scouts tell us it's only a small force come against us. We will lead and crush them. You merely follow behind and finish off what is left. Throw the small one, stab with the big one,' he said, waving his spear above his head.

'We know how to use spears, your useless piece of Norman shit,' cracked one of our men.

'How about I shove one up his Norman arse,' said another to peals of laughter.

Levett ignored the remarks and as Earl Ralph swung his cavalry around and headed for the west, he spurred his horse onward to join him and we followed; four swordsmen and four hundred untrained, mounted spearmen. The townsfolk watched us leave, before carrying on as usual, confident that their army would stop the Wealas well before they reached their city.

I was puzzled at why Gruffydd would attack with a small army against what he must know was a substantial, mounted force. He was no fool. If the rumours were true and he had killed his main rival, Gruffydd ap Rhydderch, he was now king over the whole of Wealas. He had united the petty kingdoms and defeated all who got in his way. Why would he now risk defeat? It did not make sense.

As we rode through a narrow, shallow valley with ridges on either side, Gruffydd's army came into view in the distance and yes, the reports had been correct. I guessed we outnumbered them three to one. The spirit of our men lifted, and they quickened their pace. I drew Widewe Wyrhta from her scabbard and followed the Normans as they pushed on ahead towards the Wealas.

Without warning, from each side of the valley, countless arrows arched upwards then rained down, thumping into men and horses. This was followed by hordes of screaming men pouring over the ridges on either side. In front of the Normans, behind the small force we originally faced, from a dip at the valley's end, appeared thousands upon thousands of men following the banner of Ælfgar, the exiled earl. As soon as the Normans realised it was a trap, they split into two groups, turning left and right, riding back the way they had come, passing our men on the flanks. The four of us were now at the head of the charge. The only Norman not to flee was Reinald Levett. Realising Ralph had fled with his men, he slowed down until we caught him up and rode with us. I spurred Stormbringer onwards, our confident sense of victory now turned to horror and certain defeat. The Saxon horses, used to being left to graze when battles began, took fright. Many tried to turn and collided with those coming behind them. Others just stopped abruptly, causing their riders to be thrown to the ground. Before a Saxon or Norman spear had been thrown, our whole army was in disarray. Those that could, turned and fled with the Normans. We five rode headlong into the enemy forces. They parted either side of us, drawing us deep into their ranks. Wulfgar and I rode tight next to each other. He slashed his sword to his left and I hacked Widewe Wyrhta to my right. Ansgar and Scalpi were tucked in behind us and Levett, having launched his throwing spear, now took up the rear and stabbed with his lance. We rode right through that screaming, snarling mass of warriors. We could hear the slaughter behind us as the combined armies of Ælfgar and Gruffydd caught up with our fleeing men. We did not know it at the time, but it was a massacre. Five hundred Normans and Saxons were killed. Smoke hung over Hereford for days, as castle and cathedral were all burnt to the ground. The dean and his four sons were murdered on the cathedral steps. Ælfnoþ had ridden back into Hereford and had fought a hero's fight trying to defend the town. The Wealas took men and women as slaves and stripped the cathedral of all its treasures, leaving only the dull covered gospel of Saint John.

Fifty men turned back to confront us. They circled us, pressing inward like tightening the knot on a hangman's noose. We slashed and stabbed, killing ten before we were overpowered, but as Ansgar rammed his sword into a Wealas throat, he was pierced through his belly with a lance and lifted off his horse, then cut to pieces on the ground. We were dragged from our horses, our weapons taken, our wrists tied, and manacles placed on our ankles with a chain linking us together. It was obvious they would sooner have killed us, but for some reason they had been ordered not to. One of the Wealas came up close to me. He was a tall, lean man with tight, muscular arms and a sharp, mean face. His hair, brown and curly, his eyes were wild and seemed to flit constantly from side to side. A big, flat-bladed, broad sword swung at his side in a plain, leather scabbard. He pushed his face a hand's breadth from mine and spat, sending his vile phlegm onto my nose and beard.

'Mochyn Sacsonaidd,' he rasped, which meant, Saxon pig.

'You may live to regret that, Wealas,' said Scalpi.

'Not may, he will regret it,' I said.

The Wealas stared at both of us quizzically.

'Byddwch yn difaru hymy,' I repeated in his own tongue.

'I doubt it, you will all be dead in the morning,' he replied in Wealas and he spat again, this time into my eye. I did not flinch. The time would come for his regret, but it was not now.

Forty

The Wealas had set up camp amongst deserted farm buildings We were taken to a shack which had housed pigs, the troughs and their droppings still evident. It had been reinforced with extra timbers on the outside and two iron bars across the door. We were shackled to a gate of one of the pigsties on a short chain so we could not stand up. A young boy came with food for us. Five soldiers accompanied him, one of whom was the man who had spat at me. Two of the others were Bledig and Idwal the Hereford scouts. As the boy passed me the food, the spitter knocked it out of his hands on to the floor. Bledig squelched it with the heel of his boot into the dirty straw that was strewn about the shack.

'I'll get beaten for that, Madog,' the boy cried.

Madog struck the boy hard, knocking him to the floor. 'I'll beat you, boy, you scrawny piece of pig shit,' he yelled and kicked him in the stomach, winding the boy.

Two of the soldiers laughed. 'Go on, Madog, teach the little turd a lesson.' Madog moved to kick him a second time when the third soldier stepped between them.

'Leave the boy alone, Madog, he's only a child.'

Madog butted him in the face, causing blood to spurt from the soldier's nose. 'He's the bastard son of a Saxon shit, that's what he is, and if he brings any more food to waste on these other pieces of Saxon shit, I won't just beat him, I'll kill him. You any objections?' he growled at the soldier who was holding his hands to his nose to stop the flow of blood. He shook his head, the fight gone from him.

'I object to you kicking a child,' I said, ' and when I am released from here, we will see how brave you are.'

Madog came and stood over me.

'You thirsty, Saxon?'

'No,' I said.

'I'm sure you must be,' he said, as he undid the leather fastenings on his trews and taking his member in his hand, he pissed on us.

We tried to scramble out of the way, but the chains prevented us from doing so. This was a daily occurrence for the next four days. No food and Madog relieving himself on us. One of the soldiers did bring us water, but barely enough to keep us alive. On the fifth day, there was a scratching and scrambling at the back of the shack and a small hole appeared between the floor and one of the planks. Bread and hard cheese were slid through the hole. There was not a great deal, but it was better than nothing and the four of us shared it. The next day, the same thing happened. The day after we were ready and as the food came through the hole, I grabbed the hand holding it. There was a yelp and a whimper.

'Let me go!' It was the voice of a small boy.

'Who are you, why are you bringing us food?'

'My name is Bryn. I want you to live.'

'Why?'

'Because I want you to kill Madog. I promise to keep bringing you food if you promise to kill Madog.'

'Are you the boy he hit?'

'Yesterday, today and every day. He hurts my mother and he killed my father and if he finds out I bring you food, he will kill me. So, you must promise, when you are free, you will kill him.'

'How do you know I can kill him?' I asked.

'I know you are Leofric, Killer of Death, I have heard the stories. If you could kill Death, you can kill Madog. So, promise.'

'I promise, Bryn. As soon as I am able, I will kill Madog for you.' I let go of his hand and he was gone.

For two weeks Bryn continued to push food through the hole for us. He told us how Madog lusted after his mother for years, but she had spurned him for a half Wealas, half Saxon man. They eventually married and Bryn was born. One night in a drunken rage, Madog killed Bryn's father. He denied it, and no one dared speak against him. Most of the men hated Madog, but most were too afraid to stand up to him. He made Bryn's and his mother's lives a misery.

Madog seemed increasingly confused at why we seemed unaffected by not eating for weeks, but he still did not suspect Bryn, who he believed had done as he was told and stayed away.

Eventually, I was unshackled and taken to a thatched hut. They stripped me of my clothes and put me in a tub of hot water to rid me of the foul stench of sweat, faeces and piss. I was given a plain, brown hooded robe to wear and taken to a dilapidated barn, being used as a base for the Wealas king. The air was thick with smoke. Gruffydd and Ælfgar stood next to a crackling fire, talking in a lowered voice to whom I presumed was a monk, wearing his hooded habit. Around them were priests brandishing crosses and swinging thuribles, scenting the air with sweet smelling incense. They splashed holy water so vigorously it appeared as sparkling rain, catching the light from the fire's flames. One of the priests read repeatedly from a book of prayer in a high, shrill voice, another constantly crossed himself in a frantic manner. Another was naked from the waist up, his back bloodied from the small whip he thrashed across his back as he wailed and chuntered in Latin. Sat on the floor was a bishop, his eyes, huge white discs. Froth seeped out of his mouth and nostrils, abnormal sounds emanated from deep inside him as he rocked back and forth. His condition was obviously the reason for the priests' distress. It was the dead rabbits, cats and lambs spread in a circle around the bishop, with their entrails spilling onto the ground that told me the hooded man was no monk, but Mair.

'She wants you to go with her,' Ælfgar said to me.

'Go where?' I asked.

'I don't know or care, just get the weird bitch out of here,' Ælfgar's voice tremored, as he swept his hand across his sweat-beaded lip.

Fear is something a warrior learns to hide. All of us have it to a certain extent, but the best warriors conceal it in a veil of false bravado, swagger and brave words. The fear of the unknown dispels reason. Its power is not to make the knees shake, or bowels empty, as when faced by a mortal enemy or in a shield wall with hordes of screaming berserkers charging towards you. Its power is in the mind, the essence of the word unknown. Man's imagination can conjure up all kinds of horrors and abominations far worse than anything that ever walked the earth. I could sense the fear in Ælfgar. This man, who could slander kings and challenge warlords feared Mair. This young, slender girl, who he could kill in one effortless stroke of his sword, filled him with a dread he could not fathom.

'We want you back when she's finished with you,' said Gruffydd.

'And if I don't want to go with her?' I asked.

'She says she will kill the bishop and bring a curse upon my people. You will go with her and you will return, or your friends will die.'

'I give my word, I will return.' I held out my bound hands and was untied.

Gruffydd spoke to Mair. 'Mae'n rhaid I chi Swwynwraig ef yn awry n gadael fy Bishop ei ben ei hun.' Roughly meaning, you have him, now leave my bishop alone.

Mair, always one for the drama, snapped her fingers as she turned. The bishop sat upright, his eyes rolled and regained their pupils. The priests moved tentatively to help him, and I followed Mair out of the hall to where Stormbringer and Mair's white stallion, Wraith, were saddled and waiting.

We rode out of the Wealas camp and took a steep, winding track into the Black Mountains. 'Where are we going?' I asked Mair eventually.

'To Drust,' she replied.

'Where's that?'

'He's a warlock.'

'A warlock?' I said, 'What's that?'

'A shaman, a wizard, a necromancer, a descendant of the Druids, a keeper of the magic arts, whatever you want to call him.'

'Another trickster,' I said, bringing Stormbringer to a halt. 'Why would I want to go to him?'

'It's him that wants to see you. He told me he has something you need.'

She squeezed her knees into Wraith and carried on up the track. I was now curious and followed her further up the mountain. Rough moorland stretched out on either side. Deep valleys bathed in the mountain's shadows. Fathomless, dark pools nestled in the stillness, sheltered from the winds. Standing stones and huge earthworks, erected by the ancients, lingered from the past. Ravens, crows and birds of prey swooped and glided on the wind, their cries echoing across the heather. The sky turned heavy with thick cloud and the first snows of winter fluttered down to the earth and I pulled the hood of my cloak over my head.

Eventually, we came to a place where sheer cliffs clawed their way to the sky. We took a narrow, stony track between massive slabs of grey rock. Stormbringer just managed to squeeze through, my knees scraping the rock on either side. The track forked left to right and right to left. It became narrower and the rocks taller and shearer as we progressed. Mair knew each twist and turn as we came to them and I followed. Up ahead was the entrance to a cave. A small, semi-naked, hunched-back man with a hideously twisted face, his mouth sagging on one side, one eye higher than the other, his nose hooked and broken, skin pockmarked and grey as the stones, stood at the entrance.

'Is that Drust?' I asked Mair.

'His name is Lackland. They say he has lived in the mountains forever. He will take us to Drust.'

A young, black-haired boy came from the darkness of the cave and took our horses. Lackland took a lit rush light from the wall and a piece of meat from a stone ledge and led us out of the whiteness of the snow into the blackness of the cave and through a maze of tunnels, heavy with the acrid smell of bat droppings. There were many passages going in all directions, though Lackland never hesitated once. We came to two entrances side by side. One had a glowing, flickering light and thin wisps of smoke that smelt of damp embers and sulphur seeping up from a steep path going downwards. A huge, mud brown, smooth-skinned dog with jagged ears and what I could only describe as fangs, stood at the mouth of the other entrance, restrained by a chain that creaked and rattled as he strained to break free. Its chest was matted with blood and its bark bounced uncontrollably around the cave walls. Lackland tossed the meat to the far side of the entrance and the hound bounded after it, catching it in mid-flight before it hit the floor, and the chain tightened as it reached its full extent. Lackland rushed us through the first entrance before it could do us harm.

'Not much of a guard dog if we can get in so easily,' I said, relieved we had passed it.

'Its name is Ciouffern,' said Lackland, 'hound from hell, and it's not there to stop us coming in, but to stop unspeakable things coming out from below.'

I shuddered to think what.

That entrance led us through another narrow passage that meandered through damp moss and liverwort-lined walls until we arrived in a vast cavern. Children ran about the place carrying wooden pails of water, leather bags of herbs and wild plants. Others had bundles of kindle on their backs which they carried to a copper melting pot and stoked the fires beneath it. The smoke from the flames soared upwards like a pillar, drawn up through the cave to a sliver of daylight far above. Young girls in white dresses danced around the fire. They sang in a language I did not know. Their voices reminded me of the waves of the sea, rising and falling constantly.

Standing by the pot was a tall, slim man. He wore no moustache, though his beard was long to his waist and braided in an elaborate criss-cross pattern. He was clothed in a long habit, the colour of oxblood. His fingernails were long and painted gold. His head was bald except for a plait at the back, which was the same length as his beard and adorned with coloured beads, tiny bones and small bells which jingled as he moved. Next to the fire on a twisted, hazel rod perch, sat a raven, black as a moonless night, except for a glimmer of purple on its throat and chest and a splash of bright white on the nape of its neck. Mair told me later it was brought from a land where the sun shone constantly and the men had skin ten times darker than mine. It croaked huskily as we approached, a deep, throaty sound, whilst bobbing its head with its fat, white-tipped beak, watching us constantly through cold, black eyes. In front of them on a large, flat slab of stone, sat a thick, leather-bound book and a scruffy, hemp sack.

The man was talking to the raven, his lips hardly moving and the words soft and incomprehensible. He held a kid bag in one hand and with the other he sprinkled the contents of the bag into the pot, a pinch at a time.

'I presume this is Drust?' I asked Mair.

'This is Drust,' she replied.

'What is it you want, Leofric?' Drust spoke slowly, each word resonating in the vastness of the cave, his eyes staring alternatively between the bird and the simmering pot.

'Apparently, you wanted to see me,' I said.

'What is it you want most from this life?' he said, still watching the raven and feeding the pot from the bag.

I did not answer. I wanted to be a great warrior. I wanted to live a happy life with Astrid and our child. I wanted my father to be proud of me. These were the things I wanted but did not know which I wanted most.

'Most men want food in their stomachs and the means to provide for their families and to keep them from harm,' said Drust. 'Certain men want power and renown, others wealth and land. Others just drift through life never knowing what they want or achieving anything. Which are you, Leofric?'

I still did not answer his question. 'Why am I here?' I asked, irritated.

'Why are any of us here? Are we here simply to live and die, or is there a higher purpose? Is there a purpose mapped out for each of us guided by the moon and stars, or tossed around by the wind to confuse and distract us, with an end we cannot change or avoid? Or do we have choices? Are we in control of our own destinies? Which do you believe, Leofric?'

'He doesn't believe in anything,' said Mair dismissively.

'I believe in this,' I said gripping Widewe Wyrhta and lifting her slightly from her scabbard.

'I told you,' said Mair, 'all rage and no brains.'

Drust held up his hands to silence her. 'Mair, Mair, you of all people should trust in the wisdom of the gods. If they have decided to bring you and Leofric together, it is for a reason.'

'We are not together,' I said, 'she keeps coming to me with talk of gods and spells and I keep sending her and her nonsense away. Now, if you have nothing for me except idle chatter, I will be gone.'

As I turned to leave, the raven unfurled its wings and gave a piercing shriek that hurt my ears. A flash of blue and red came from within the copper pot, which now bubbled and hissed and vibrated on its hanging chain. Drust seemed to grow in stature, his shadow creeping higher and higher up the sides of the cave. The girls stopped singing and dancing. The children stood opened mouthed and wide-eyed. The torches on the walls dimmed and flickered. Lackland, who had been behind us, cowered in a corner. For the first time in that cave, a feeling of uncertainty, doubt and yes, fear came over me. Drust spoke again, this time his voice loud and dark.

'I am Drust, Seer of the Black Mountains, Keeper of the Book, Guardian of the knowledge of the ancients, adviser to the Kings of the Cymry, descendant of Myrddin. These people you call Wealas, are a proud people. They are the Cymry. This land, this island that the Romans stole and discarded like a broken sandal, will be engulfed with blood and fire. Christian will rise against Christian and the Saxon intruders will cease to rule over this land. Famine and disease will stretch their deathly fingers through village and town taking young and old, rich and poor.'

'Is this what you want to happen, Drust, not what will happen?' I said.

'What I want is of no consequence. The gods have decreed these things will take place and you, Leofric, will help it come to fruition.'

'Me! ' I spat. 'Even if I could, why would I act against my own

382

people?'

'Show him, Mair,' said Drust. A triumphant smirk crossed Mair's face. She undid the laces at the top of her outer garment and lifted out a leather cord on which was fastened an amulet.

'That's mine,' I said recognising the symbols.

'Look closer,' said Drust.

I took the amulet in my hand and even in the dim light I could see the symbols, though similar, were not quite the same.

'It is the other half of yours,' said Mair. 'The night before you were kidnapped, I saw the amulet around your neck. I didn't understand the meaning until I came to see Drust.'

'It belonged to a shaman, a man well versed in the magic arts,' said Drust, 'though he claimed he was descendant of Cadwallader, King of the Britons. He fell in love with a Saxon princess, herself a cunning woman. Her father, the king, spurning the shaman's claim to royal blood, forbade the union and locked his daughter away. She managed to escape and they ran away together. The king sent his soldiers to pursue them relentlessly. They were finally caught, and the princess once again held under lock and key. The shaman was banned forever from the kingdom. They never saw each other again. Before they were captured, the shaman pricked both their thumbs with the thorn of a black-budded rose and allowed the blood drops to fall on the amulet. They both spoke incantations and curses and cut the amulet in two and hung each half around the other's neck. They decreed, if they were forced to part by the king, one day the two halves would be united by each other's kin and the magic they had invoked would come to be and the Saxons would lose this land. All this is written here, Leofric, in this book, The Deep Book of the Fynyddoedd. I and mine, before and after, are its keepers. Many wish it destroyed to keep its message from the people. After the prophecy of the amulet, it is written:

'And in those last days of oppression and despair, the Mab Darogan, a son of destiny, born under a lighting sky, weak of limb yet strong of heart, will rise-up once more. An avenger in black, on a black steed, with a sword of justice and the helmet of death. The

Saxon thieves deprived of the land they stole.'

Just as the lovers had lost each other, the king's descendants would lose this land. The amulet, as well as the legend, was passed down through the generations, from mother to daughter. Mair's mother Nairn, was given it by her mother and passed it on to Mair. I have known of its existence for many years but not where the other half was until Mair came and said she had seen one just like it around your neck. That's when I knew for certain, you were the Mab Darogan, the Son of Destiny.'

'I have no idea what you are talking about,' I said, as I let go of Mair's half of the amulet.

'It was no accident that you received it, Leofric. It has been passed from your ancestors over hundreds of years to you, a living relative of that shaman and so a descendant of Cadwallader himself. Each piece parted through time and distance before being reunited. Likewise, Mair, a descendant of that Saxon princess, though very much a Briton now. I was with Nairn when she hung the amulet around Mair's neck when she was new-born. All this by accident? I think not. There is magic in this world, Leofric. Many deny it, but it exists. It is powerful and beyond most men's understanding, but it is there, and it affects our lives.'

I believed none of this nonsense.

'Tales children are told around a fire at night,' I said. 'Besides, I no longer have the amulet, it was stolen when I was kidnapped.'

'I know,' said Drust, 'it hangs around the neck of your half-brother Edgard.'

Surprised by this, I stalled for a moment. 'If you knew, why haven't you already got it?'

'Would you have us steal it?' asked Drust.

The raven, quiet for a while, gave another piercing screech and with a flap of its black wings flew high into the cave and circled us menacingly.

'It is yours by right, Leofric. For magic to take place it must be you and Mair who unite the two pieces and fulfil the prophecy.'

'I am a wolf's-head in Æssefeld. I am seen as a murderer. Men may

384

kill me with impunity and my father would never know his son is innocent,' I said, saddened at this reality.

'There was a witness,' Drust said abruptly.

'A witness?'

'Someone saw the whole incident of the murder and your kidnap, Leofric.'

I could not believe what I was hearing. Someone had seen what had happened that night. Someone else knew I had been telling the truth.

'Come forward,' said Drust, and out of the shadows walked Lugna.

My heart sank. For one moment, I thought the years of being accused as a murderer were at an end. At last, I could return to my father and prove my innocence, only to find that the one man that could make that happen was a simpleton who could hardly speak one whole sentence that made sense. Lugna, Nairn's dogsbody, stood next to Drust. One arm hung lower than the other, his shoulder drooped downwards, his back hunched, his forehead furrowed, his eyes narrow, the expression on his face as if his mind was elsewhere.

'That is my witness? He is the reason you brought me here? A man no one will believe or even listen to. It is a cruel jest you play on me, Drust.'

'It is no jest, Leofric. I told you before, not all things are as they seem. Lugna is my man. He is my ears and eyes. Men are not wary of an oaf. They say things around him they would not dream of saying in front of a man of sharper wit. Is that not so, Lugna?'

'It is, my lord.' As he spoke, Lugna stood upright, his hunched back melting away. He straightened his shoulders, his arms becoming equal length. His face brightened, losing its usual, vacant demeanour.

'As big as I am, I have become invisible at times because men see me as a fool of no consequence. But I watch, I listen, and I store it all in here,' he said tapping his head.

'I have taken an interest in you, Leofric, since the day Nairn told me of your birth,' said Drust. 'Lugna has been my ears and eyes in Æssefeld. He reports back to me, as do others from all over this land and I wait until it is the right time to act upon the information they bring me and what I am shown by the gods by means of the cauldron. Now, it is approaching your time, Leofric.'

'Time for what?' I said, still amazed that Lugna had been deceiving everyone all these years.

'Time to become the man you want to be. Time to become the man the gods know you are. Time to become someone that matters. There is further darkness to come into your life before that time, but it is fast approaching and whether you want it or not, whether you believe it or not, will count for nothing.'

I did not believe any of it, but I have learnt that what makes belief so powerful is that others do believe in it and that belief drives men to wild extremes. Maybe, just maybe, they would listen to Lugna and be fearful of a warrior dressed in black and a sorceress who raises the dead.

'What do you want me to do?' I said finally.

The raven shrieked again and flew down to its perch. The copper pot stopped vibrating and the rushlights regained their brightness. The girls returned to their dance and song and the children went back to their work. All trickery and prearranged skulduggery, I knew, but it was impressive, and I could see why many would fear and believe in this man's magic and perhaps I could use that fear too.

'You will go with Mair and Lugna to Æssefeld-Underbarroe. You will expose the real killers of your father's steward and you will give this to your father.'

Drust took a leather flask from his belt and scooped it into the copper pot, filling it with the liquid. 'He must drink this to dispel the malady that ails him. You will take the amulet from around your half-brother's neck. and you will bring it back to me and we will join the two halves. You and Mair will spill your blood on the whole-again amulet, I will speak the incantations and the spell will be complete.'

'What then?' I asked.

'The gods have many paths for you to tread, Leofric, which will be revealed when they wish it. You must learn to trust in them and fulfil your destiny. What I am about to give you will astound and bewilder you. Many things in this world, and the worlds above and below us, are beyond the grasp of mortal men, but they are true none the less.'

He lifted the sack from the stone slab and passed it to me. It was heavier than I expected. I opened the sack warily, peered inside and dropped it in shock. It was a war helmet. Though not just any war helmet. Its crest, peering back out at me, was the figure of a skeleton, the same as the one worn by the faded knight in the embroidery of the weeping lady that terrified me as a child.

'It is the helmet of Cadwallader, last King of the Britons, champion of the Cymry,' said Drust. 'Men will follow it, others will shrink back from it. No one will ignore it.'

I picked the sack up and took the helmet out. It was a wonderful, fearful thing, a magnificent, black war helmet with hinged cheek guards and a human skeleton in a crawling position, carved from whale bone, forming its crest.

He was right. I was astounded and bewildered.

How, why?

'I will do it,' I said, 'as soon as I am released by King Gruffydd, I will come for Mair and Lugna and we shall go to Æssefeld.'

'You will go to Æssefeld now, the gods have spoken,' said Drust.

'They haven't spoken to me,' I said, 'I have promised to return to the Wealas or my friends will die.'

'Many men will die, Leofric, one or two more are of no consequence,' said Mair, 'we must go now before the gods are offended.'

I decided to use their own reasoning.

'I am a man of honour,' I said, 'without that honour I am nothing. I will return to Gruffydd ap Llewelyn and stay there until Earl Harold comes to free us, which I am sure he will. If your gods are unhappy with that, I am sure they are powerful enough to stop me.'

Drust sprinkled more of the contents of the kid bag into the copper pot making it shake and bubble once again. He lent over its rim, peering intently.

'It appears the gods are more patient than you deserve, Leofric. You may return to the Wealas king, but beware, the gods are not to be mocked, there will be a price to pay. Mair will guide you back through the mountains. The raven will go with you and when you are free, you will say the words, 'mynd adref,' and the bird will return here and Mair and Lugna will meet you on the road to Æssefeld. The helmet is now yours if you have the courage to wear it. Show it to Gruffydd, he will understand its significance, though I doubt he will be pleased with the implication.'

He turned his back to us and clapped his hands. A flash, white smoke and he was gone. More trickery from Drust, though now I could see how I could use that to my advantage. I might not believe in supernatural powers, but others did.

Lackland led us out of the cave and I followed Mair to a ridge where I could see the Wealas camp.

When I rode towards the makeshift hall, I do not know what surprised the Wealas the most, the fact I had returned at all or the white-necked raven perched behind me on Stormbringer's back. I had left the camp reluctantly. I returned believing after all this time I could possibly clear my name and be reunited with my father. Now all I had to do was wait for Earl Harold to come and free us.

Forty-one

I was met by a group of Wealas soldiers. One of them grabbed Stormbringer's reigns and led me to Gruffydd's temporary hall.

I took the sack and followed him through the barn entrance. Gruffydd waved him out, leaving just us two and Ælfgar and a lone priest writing at a desk at the back of the tent.

'I see you are a man of honour and a man of his word,' Gruffydd said. 'You must be certain Earl Harold values you enough to come for you.'

'He will come, my lord, I am sure of that.'

'He is a Godwin, he will only come if it is in his interest to do so,' said Ælfgar.

'He will come because King Edward will demand it and Harold is loyal to his king,' I said, looking at Ælfgar.

I approached the Wealas king and held out the sack. 'Drust gave me this and said I was to show it to you, and you would understand.'

Gruffydd opened the sack. 'Duw an helpo!'

'God help you with what?' I could tell from his expression he was as confused as I was.

'What's in the sack?' said Ælfgar, discerning the king's discomfort.

'Drust gave you this?' Gruffydd said, without answering the question. 'Did he say anything to you?'

'He said he believed I am the Mab Darogan.'

'You, the Son of Destiny? It is true then, Drust has finally gone mad.'

389

'He also told me you would know what you should do, though he doubted you would do it.'

'What I should do is kill you and take that helmet for myself.'

'I think you are too mindful of its magic to do that,' I said, hoping I was right. 'If you were meant to have it, Drust would have given it to you, not me. He also said,' I lied, 'that you should free me and my men from that prison until Earl Harold Godwinson comes for us.'

The Wealas king pondered for a while on what I had told him. Then summoned a guard from the tent entrance to take me back to the pigsty.

I was taken back to the shack to Wulfgar, Scalpi and Levett. They stank worse than the pigs. I had caught sight of Bryn on my way through the village. His face was cut and bruised and Wulfgar told me no food had come, so I presumed Madog had found out the boy had been feeding us.

'I didn't think we would see you again, Saxon,' said Levett in his matter of fact way.

'I wasn't sure,' said Scalpi, 'but Wulfgar was certain you would come back.'

Wulfgar just shrugged his shoulders.

'What's in there, food?' pleaded Scalpi, grasping at the sack.

'No,' I said, yanking it away from him. 'Hopefully our way out of this mess.'

Later that day, we were moved to a clean tent, allowed to wash in a nearby stream and were given bread, cheese and weak ale. We were allowed to come out of the tent and move around, though there were always many guards nearby and if we strayed too far, we were encouraged to return.

We heard Earl Harold had returned to Hereford with a large army and was now erecting a new, wooden castle just beyond the River Dore. Gruffydd ordered the camp to be moved further up into the hills. Harold sent his forces in pursuit but didn't attack. Still, he did not come for us. The rain fell, the sun shone, still the English did not come.

'Harold is going to leave us here,' said Scalpi.

'If that is beneficial to Englaland, no doubt he will,' I said, ' but I do believe he will come.' And eventually, he came.

The first we knew about it was when we were dragged from our tent and roped together. We were taken, along with the combined armies of the Wealas, Irish, and English followers of Ælfgar, to a place called Bylgeslege. Harold was at the head of a huge force, which from the banners they carried was made up from all over Englaland. Except, I did not see the red and yellow of Norðhymbraland. I guessed Harold felt it prudent to leave Tostig out of it and not rile Ælfgar more than necessary. Also, the Earl of Mercia was absent, presumably reluctant to fight against his son. I also noticed there was no Earl Ralph.

Harold and his brother, Gyrth, were beneath two banners, the white dragon of Wessex and the pale blue with yellow birds of Edward. Although the king was not present, the banner showed they spoke on his behalf. Wulfgar, Scalpi, Levett and I were brought to the front but were kept to one side of Gruffydd and Ælfgar. Earl Harold was dressed in mail that had been polished until it gleamed like water-worn quartz. He wore a blue cloak trimmed with marten fur and an intricately patterned war helmet slung over the pommel of his saddle. He and Gyrth rode forward and stopped a few yards from the Wealas' lines. Gyrth wore a coat of wolf skin. He carried a blue shield with the three golden crowns of East Anglia and wore a helmet with a boar's crest.

Harold was the first to speak. 'King Edward, King of all the English and ruler of all these lands sends greetings to Gruffydd ap Llewelyn, King of the Britons and to you also, Earl Ælfgar. The king prays for peace for all men and has given me the authority to speak on his behalf.'

Gruffydd smiled. Mounted on a steel grey stallion, he wore an ancient, bronze helmet adorned with swan wings laid horizontally on each side. His red hair was long and a red bushy beard framed his ruddy face. Around him were standard bearers with the banners of red lions on gold of Powys and gold lions on red of Deheubath and directly next to him flew the red dragon of the Wealas.

'I too wish for peace,' he said, 'but you are on our land, the land of our forefathers, the land your forefathers stole, and we want it back.'

It was Harold's turn to smile. 'We both know that King Edward could never and will never allow that to happen. He is though, prepared to negotiate on land you have recently taken, to your advantage, providing you swear allegiance to him and recognise him as king over all this land. On his part and that of all his nobles, you will be free to be king of the Britons with no interference.'

Gruffydd wanted more, but knew he would be unlikely to get it, and faced with an army he probably could not defeat, he was ready to agree terms.

'And what of me?' said Ælfgar. It must have been galling for the Mercian to once again be in the Godwin's wake.

It was Gyrth who rode forward. Hands on both sides grasped sword hilts, in case one earl should attack the other. I wondered what would happen to Wulfgar, Levett, Scalpi and I, our hands tied and roped together, if fighting should begin. Gyrth rode hard up alongside Ælfgar. 'King Edward has commanded me to give you this shield and return to you the earldom of East Anglia as rightfully yours, on condition you swear your allegiance to him, and give up your desire for Norðhymbraland.'

Ælfgar gazed at the shield with the East Anglian arms and hesitated. I wondered what was going through his mind. He was in this position because he wanted Norðhymbraland. He was being offered only what he had before. Once more the Godwins were dictating events. He would know he and Gruffydd could not win the battle, but he could possibly rid himself of two powerful Godwins with two thrusts of his sword. Whether this was his thinking I am not sure, but he eventually nodded in agreement to Gyrth.

'I swear my allegiance to King Edward and revoke my claim to Norðhymbraland.'

And so, war was avoided. King Gruffydd and the earls, along with bishops from both sides, retired to thrash out the exact terms of their agreement. I imagined our release would be part of those discussions. I was right, but not how I had envisioned it.

When Gruffydd and Ælfgar returned they were accompanied by Ælfnoþ, the shire reeve of Hereford, together with men from Harold's personal guard.

We had been taken back to our tent but kept tied together. I managed to reach the bag and gave it to Wulfgar. 'Guard that with your life. Don't look inside it unless I shout, Wulfgar, sack! then and only then take out what is inside and pass it to me.'

After several hours, we were dragged out by Madog and his men. The brightness of the sun partially blinding us for a moment. Madog looked me in the face.

'When you are gone back to your English shits, I will beat the boy, rape his mother in front of him and kill them both and if I shall meet you in battle, I will take delight in ending your miserable Saxon life.' A few of his men laughed.

'It is easy for a man to threaten another whose hands are bound together,' I said, in his own tongue, 'and even easier to kill women and children. If ever we are on the same battlefield, no doubt I will have to come and seek you out, hiding with the other cowards and spineless bullies.'

The Wealas man bristled at that and hit me in the face with his fist, knocking me over. I spat blood from a cut lip.

'Take the Saxon shit to the king,' said Madog. I could see in his eyes he yearned to kill me but did not dare displease Gruffydd. We were half-pushed, half-dragged to where Gruffydd and Ælfgar and most of the Wealas army were waiting. Ælfnoþ and his men stood next to them, grim faced.

'It seems you are of value to Earl Harold after all, Saxon. You are to leave here and return to him,' Gruffydd said.

'I was led to believe your race were brave men and fearless fighters, not cowards who attack defenceless men and women and children,' I said, loud enough for all to hear.

There was uproar from the soldiers, just as I had hoped. I thought of Osbeorn Bulax and how he had reacted when I had accused his men of being cowards and hoped this king would react the same way.

Gruffydd held up his hand to halt the jeering and stared at me. 'I have been told you are rash and foolhardy. To bring into question my men's bravery when you are our prisoner seems to prove that fact. However, it would seem to defy the reason these men have come for you.'

Now it was my turn to be confused.

'I am not giving you your freedom, Leofric. These men have come to arrest you for cowardice.'

More uproar as the soldiers banged spears against shields and stamped their feet in disapproval. Warriors despise cowards.

'It is a lie!' shouted Wulfgar.

'A damn lie,' yelled Scalpi.

Ælfnoþ and his men started to move towards me.

Gruffydd was right, I was a rash, foolhardy young man. Without thinking of the possible outcome, I threw myself at Gruffydd's feet.

'Lord, I am nothing to you, I know, an irritation, perhaps nothing more, but I have been accused of being a coward in your presence. Let me prove to you and all these men I am no coward.' Ælfnoþ grabbed my arm to pull me up.

'Wait,' said the king. 'Let him speak.'

I stood, pulling my arm free from Alfnoþ's grip.

'I have slighted your men's bravery, lord,' more banging of shields and shouts from the soldiers, 'though it is one man I name. A man your soldiers seem to hold in esteem, a man who they seem to think is a brave man, a warrior. I call him a coward.' I turned and pointed at Madog. 'I call you, the one they call Madog, a coward.'

Madog spat on the floor. The soldiers around him were demanding my death. 'Madog' they shouted, 'Madog, Madog, Madog.'

I turned back to face Gruffydd. 'Lord, let two men accused of being cowards prove they are not, by fighting to the death. If he kills me, his men can hail him a hero. If I win, I will give myself up to Ælfnoþ and return to Earl Harold.' I could sense Gruffydd's reluctance to have to send a dead body back to Harold.

In a mass of screaming hate, one kindly face stared back at me. I saw not hatred but hope and faith in me. Bryn had pushed his way to the front and seeing the expectancy in his eyes I knew I must not fail in my promise.

'Of course, if Madog is too scared to face me, if he is indeed a coward, I cannot force him to fight. If the Cymry are too afraid a cowardly Saxon will beat their man.'

'Madog, Madog, Madog,' they chanted again. Although Madog was unpopular, he was still a Wealas man fighting a Saxon. Men slapped him on the back. 'Show him, Madog, kill him.'

There was no way out and nowhere to go. He knew he must fight me or be ridiculed and held in contempt thereafter. For a moment, I thought he might take that option and admit being the coward he was. Wulfgar came to my aid.

'Leofric, don't do this, I have seen him fight and he will beat you,' he said out loud.

'No, he wo....' Scalpi was silenced as Wulfgar's elbow slammed into his mouth. All this was unnoticed in the melee by all except Madog who heard Wulfgar loud and clear.

Madog slid his big sword from its scabbard and borrowed a helmet from one of the soldiers.

'Give the Saxon shit a sword,' he said. His name was chanted, repeatedly. Gruffydd nodded his acceptance and one of the soldiers handed me his sword. It was not Widewe Wyrhta, but it balanced well enough in my hand and it was sufficient to kill a bully and beater of small boys.

I was once again wearing my clothes of black but wore no helmet. Madog came at me full of confidence after hearing Wulfgar, but as he approached, I roared, 'I am Leofric the Black, Killer of Death.'

He lunged wildly at me and I stepped aside as he stumbled past. I hit him with the flat of my sword, sending him sprawling on to the ground. I did not want to just kill him, I wanted to humiliate him first. Four times he lunged at me and four times he ended up on his face in the dirt. His confidence was sapping away, and doubt showed on the lines of his brow each time he got back up to face me. Doubt changed to fear as he realised Wulfgar was grinning at him. He hung back, his sword up high defending his body and face. I moved towards him, my sword tip pointing towards the ground. I left an inviting, large target enticing him to attack me. His breathing was heavy, his eyes still shifting constantly like a nervous hare. I moved ever nearer, exaggerating my limp, averting my gaze away from his. He took the bait, sensing this was his moment. He lifted the big blade high above his head and brought it down towards me. I dropped to one knee and parried the blow, taking the full force on my sword. Sparks flew as the metals clashed. I swept my sword sideward forcing his blade to the right. I pushed my sword upwards, underneath his chin, through the soft skin and out the back of his neck. His gaping mouth filled with blood, his eyes still at last. His body twitched, and as I slid my sword out of his throat, he dropped dead to the floor.

The jeering stopped. The mood changed, first in disbelief that I had killed Madog so easily and then anger. Gruffydd was becoming increasingly alarmed. If this mob turned upon us, killing four hostages he had promised to return to the king's shire reeve, all he had achieved in his bargaining with Earl Harold would be in vain.

I used his hesitation to my advantage. 'Wulfgar, the sack.' Wulfgar reached in and pulled the helmet out of the sack. Even he was startled at the sight of the helmet of death. He passed it to me and I pulled it on to my head.

'This is the war helmet of Cadwallader, the last King of the Britons. Drust, the Seer of the Black Mountains claims I am the Mab Darogan, the Son of Destiny, come to vanquish the oppressor and free the down-trodden. You sons of the Cymry will step aside and let us pass.'

All the Cymry knew of Cadwallader. Most had heard of Drust. The Mab Darogan and the helmet of death were threaded through the verses of their bards. Confused as to why a Saxon spoke of such things and wore the legendary helmet, they did step back.

'Deliver him to Earl Harold immediately,' said Gruffydd to Ælfnoþ. 'Let them pass.'

Ælfnoþ instructed men to bind my hands again and the four of us were quickly led away to our horses and taken from the angry Wealas to an apparently angrier Earl Harold.

Forty-two

When we rode into Hereford we found a ruin. The castle had burnt to the ground; the cathedral, a smouldering, empty shell. Men and their families had drifted back slowly, sifting through the ashes for anything they might salvage. Bishop Æthelstan had taken to his bed and remained there, too ill to venture back into the world, and four weeks later his friend and guardian Tremerig died. Earl Ralph was a beaten man, forever more to be known as Ralph the Timid. Earl Harold had instructed the rebuilding of the town walls before he marched into Wealas, his soldiers helped bring timber and stone.

All that spring and summer we waited for Harold to send for us. We saw him when he rode out to inspect the building work but whenever we approached, he had always gone by the time we arrived. Desperate to see Astrid, and my son whom I knew must be born by now, I complained to Leofgar and Ælfnoþ and they promised they would intercede with the earl on our behalf, but still he refused to see us. We tried to leave several times but, on each occasion, mounted soldiers brought us back. We discovered Harold stayed away from Hereford, on the king's business or visiting his family, quite often. I am of the mind now, that Harold was testing me, testing my patience and perseverance. I wanted him to pardon me of crimes I did not commit but still, he kept me waiting. If we used force to leave Hereford, then we would be committing a crime against the king. I could not win, so I waited and with each day my love for Harold turned to resentment.

Eventually the waiting ended, and Ælfnoþ escorted us to Harold's hall. As we walked through the doorway, the white-necked raven flew over us and perched on a beam under the thatched roof. Harold sat at a large, oak table. Bishop Leofgar sat on his left and Leofwine, the earl's brother, five years younger than me, shorter and lithe of build with short, fair hair and a thin, wispy moustache, sat on his right. On either side of them sat numerous priests with quills and parchment to record the proceedings. Ælfnoþ stood at the front of the table.

'You are a fool, Leofric,' Harold said, 'I left you to fortify Hereford, not to lead my men into a futile battle. Yet you led those men in a manner they are unaccustomed to and ill-equipped to fight. When you saw the Normans retreat, you continued riding at your enemies with no hope of victory and by being captured, compromised our position of bargaining and left Hereford to the mercy of the Wealas. What's more, you went off with that sorceress who is an abomination in God's eyes.' The raven squawked, making everyone look upwards. 'The bishops demand you are punished for that alone. Next you go and kill one of the Wealas warriors after we had called a truce. King Edward has reminded me that if you came to his attention again for the wrong reasons there would be no mercy. What do you have to say?'

I was tired of trying to please other people. As a child, I had longed for my father's approval and never received it. I had pined for Turfrida, she abandoned me for another. I had been loyal to the Godwins and now Harold wanted me to beg for mercy.

'I have been arrested for being a coward, Ælfnoþ will tell you I am no coward. A fool I may be, but I have no knowledge of that being a crime. As for the sorceress, I no more believe her nonsense than the nonsense of the Church.' The priests looked up from their scribblings, shouting, 'Blasphemy, heathen.'

Harold held his hand up to stop them.

'If I had not continued to ride at the enemy, I would be no better

398

than those that turned and fled. Then coward would be my true name,' I said.

Harold talked quietly to Leofwine and Leofgar in turn. One of the priests shouted, 'He must be punished and made an example of, my lord, he blasphemed the holy Church.'

Earl Harold stood, his face stern. 'Leofric, Ælfnoþ confirms what I always knew to be true, cowardice is not one of your failings. It is also true you have shown loyalty in the past and because of that, I shall be lenient with you. However, you have behaved in a reckless manner. You have shown scant regard for the king or God's will. You have aligned yourself with a sorceress. You have blasphemed against the one true God. These are serious crimes, Leofric, that cannot go unpunished. King Edward says you must give up this notion of being a warrior. You must go to the priory at Filey and finish the sacred Psalter. It is his command. I suggest whilst you are there you search for enlightenment to rekindle your love for the one true God.'

'Amen,' shouted the priests in unison.

I can't rekindle any love for God, I thought to myself, because I never possessed it in the first place. Only perhaps as a small child when naively I prayed constantly for my leg to heal and to be able to run and play with the other children. I knew my mother prayed too and gave money and goods to the Church. Yet still, I limped. I was still the butt of everyone's jests and still ridiculed. The priests had told me it was God's will, that He worked in ways us mortals found impossible to understand, and everything He did had a purpose. I should be grateful that He had given me life, and not complain.

I thought of him as a cruel, unkind God. Why me? If He is all-powerful, why did He not cure all those who suffered from sickness or were deformed? I knew my father had prayed to the old gods in secret. He had paid Nairn to bury a corn-doll with a lock of my hair and dance around the sacred stone. Yet still, I limped. I had seen brave men call out to their god or gods on the battlefield and still they died, slow, painful deaths. I have listened to the stories about monks, slain at their altars by greed-frenzied Vikings. I have read of the Druids massacred by the Romans on their sacred isle. Where was their God as they bled to death? Why had my mother given birth to dead babies, what possible purpose could God have for that?

Eventually, I came to believe there are no gods. Things just happen. There is no purpose. We make our own way in life and deal with whatever comes to us. I, though, am like the solitary moon surrounded by myriads of stars. Men make images from wood and stone and pray to their gods that do not speak, yet I am the fool who does not believe.

I realized to try to explain these feelings to Earl Harold would be futile.

'I will return to the priory, lord, but not yet,' I said curtly. 'Though I am no man of God and never will be. I am certain the time is coming when you will need more warriors than priests, Lord Harold, and my sword will be yours to command. Other men have branded me a murderer and called into question my honour. This I vow to prove a falsehood and clear my name. I have made no oaths of allegiance to you, lord, so if you no longer deem me a coward, am I free to leave?'

'Unlike you, Leofric, I cannot disobey my king. You are free to leave this hall and when you are ready you will be escorted to Filey Priory. But if you try to leave Hereford for any other reason, I shall have you apprehended and brought back. Is that clear?'

'It is clear, lord. My companions are they prisoners, too?'

'Prisoner is a harsh word, Leofric, you are merely a guest here until you come to your senses and accept your true vocation in life. Your companions are free to leave at any time.'

'I have one more request my lord. My friend Rush, as earl you have the power to release him from slavery. I implore you to do so as he has been a loyal friend to me.'

'He is your father's slave, is he not? A runaway no less,' said Harold.

'Yes, on both counts,' I said, 'but he ran away to help me.'

'A run-away slave just the same, punishable by death. This is a matter you must take up with your father. He is his property.'

After those final words from Earl Harold I was dismissed from the hall.

I found Wulfgar and Scalpi at the Fat Ram, an inn on the edge of the town. Though it been partly burnt on its west side, the landlord had managed to resume brewing. Levett had gone. No one knew where, but Wulfgar guessed he had gone to Duke William over the British Sea.

'I have been ordered to stay here by Earl Harold until I agree to return to the priory at Filey,' I said, as I finished the ale Scalpi had passed to me.

'Are you going there?' asked Wulfgar.

'Yes, but not yet. I am going to Æssefeld-Underbarroe, to prove to my father my innocence. I need to go before winter sets in. You should both return to Horsdone and tell Astrid I will be home soon.'

'That is a message you must deliver, Scalpi,' said Wulfgar, 'I will stay with Leofric to make sure he can fulfil it.'

'And face Astrid's wrath when I tell her I abandoned you both and then you don't return home?' cried Scalpi.

'I go against Earl Harold's wishes and I will be joined by the sorceress,' I said. Scalpi crossed himself at the mention of Mair. 'The priests say my immortal soul is in peril as well as my life on earth. Although I do not believe, I respect that you both do. I can't ask you to risk offending your God.'

' I made an oath to serve you as my lord, you would not make me break such an oath, would you?' said Wulfgar.

'And I made that same oath, lord, to serve you with my sword and life,' said Scalpi. 'You didn't abandon us when you had the chance, so don't expect me to leave you now. Besides, you are the only man who has been able to take my sword from me, so who else would I follow?'

I placed a hand on each of their shoulders. No more words were necessary and none were spoken. We gathered what scant possessions we had and rode towards the east gate of the town. At the gate mounted soldiers barred our way. Ælfnoþ came forward, my hand went to the hilt of the sword I had purchased from the local smith with the last coins I had.

'You will give me your sword, Leofric,' Ælfnoþ said.

'And why would I do that?' I said, my hand gripping the hilt tighter, ready to slide the blade from the scabbard.

'Because you will want this one,' he said, as he drew Widewe Wyrhta from a long, hessian sack held by one of his men. Ælfnoþ passed me the sword, hilt towards me, and I took it from him.

Before I could ask how and why, he said, 'The boy, Bryn, his father was my friend. Many wanted Madog dead, this is their appreciation. Now my men and I must go to the west gate, where we believe three fugitives we are looking for have been seen. Godspeed.'

We were left to leave Hereford unhindered.

The white-necked raven followed us for a short while before swooping down and landing on Stormbringer's rump. It rolled its head from side to side as if listening for something. I said the words, 'mynd adref,' and, with a squawk, it flew off ahead of us and was soon just a speck in the sky before disappearing completely.

We rode for the rest of the day, stopping at dusk. We lit a small fire and spitted a lamb we had taken from the moor. The following day Mair and Lugna arrived. Lugna sat on a chestnut warhorse with stag antler headgear. He wore a jerkin of boiled hardened leather, a drab brown cloak of rough cloth and an undecorated helmet of burnished bronze. Slung across his back was a two-handed, double-edged sword.

Mair rode Wraith, her white stallion, and led a piebald pony carrying her small cauldron and iron standing rods and other equipment. She wore a blue dress with copper coloured, crescent moons sown into the skirts. Her thick black hair hung loose, her feet bare. Draped around her neck was a torc of coiled gold and her half of the amulet hung on the outside of her dress. A thin-bladed knife, her golden sickle and a small pouch of potions hung from a girdle around her waist. A cloak of wool, dyed blood red, fastened with a brooch of writhing snakes and a dragon's head, was draped around her shoulders. She carried a witch-hazel rod with a baby's skeleton tied to its top. She looked beautiful and terrifying at the same time.

Scalpi crossed himself on sight of them.

The sky, blue and light when we left Hereford, became heavy with dark, shifting clouds. Spots of rain soon turned into a downpour, turning the track to mud which slowed us down. In truth, I was in no haste to reach Æssefeld-Underbarroe, uncertain what we would find once we arrived. I had listened to the stories and rumours of my father being unwell and Grim running the estate in his stead. Folk whispered in dark corners of inns and taverns, that his wife's son was, in fact, Grim's, not my father's. Other folk said my father's illness was a curse by Nairn or God's punishment for invoking the old gods and inciting their anger over the toppling of the stone. The more cynical murmured it had been induced by Grim and my stepmother.

Through woods and valleys, we rode unchallenged; a giant with a huge sword, two formidable looking warriors, a sorceress and a warlord in black. We were seen, people talk, news travels quickly. When we arrived at Æssefeld-Underbarroe, the gates were closed.

Grim Ealdwulfson stood on the ramparts, surrounded by men from the village. My father was not there.

'Yer not welcome here, Leofric Wolf's-head,' shouted Grim. 'Yer accused of murdering our steward, Leofgar. Renweard, Thegn of Æssefeld-Underbarroe has disowned yer. He has only one heir, Edgard Renweardson.'

'I want to speak with my father, not his minder,' I said.

'Yer father is unwell. I am the authority here, by his order. Yer should leave and never return.'

Mair pressed her heels gently into Wraith's flank and rode slowly towards the village gates.

'Grim Ealdwulfson. I know your wrongdoings. Most people in Æssefeld know me, my mother, Nairn, helped to bring many of them into this world. I have the power to send all of them into the next. Open your gates and I will hold back my curses.'

'This is a godly place, Mair, you have no power here, you should take yourself and your friends away whilst you can.'

It was Crispin the priest, he held a wooden cross out in front of him. I sensed the fear in his voice. He had always been troubled by Nairn and her daughter.

Men scurried about on the village parapet, making sure each section was defended.

I knew exactly how far an arrow could reach and made sure we stayed beyond range. No one dared kill Mair as they believed she would be even more powerful in death than life and her mother would wreak vengeance and bring all kinds of evil curses upon them.

'What do we do now?' asked Scalpi.

'We wait until dark, then we go to find my father. I know a way in,' I said, 'a secret entrance used to escape in times of danger,' though I had no idea what we would do once we were in there.

Mair dismounted and took from her pony the small cauldron and setting up the fire rods, ignited the kindle. She poured liquid from her skin flasks into the cauldron and mixed in herbs from the pouch on her girdle. As the liquid became hot, it bubbled and spat, and she started to dance, hopping from one leg to another, her arms above her head, her hands turning in circles. She chanted as she danced, her voice shrill and piercing. Men scurried back and forth on the ramparts remonstrating with Crispin and Grim. Lugna stood behind Mair. His giant frame casting an ever-lengthening shadow as the sun slid lower in the sky.

As the dark came, Scalpi, Wulfgar and I slipped quietly away, through the trees and down to the river. The path, a well-trodden track, was rough and slippery from the rain. It no longer rained hard, just a miserable drizzle that slowly crept through your clothes to your skin. The path stopped at a small jetty at the river's edge. We entered rough scrub and brambles, keeping as close to the village walls as possible. Many years had passed since I last used this way into Æssefeld and it was difficult to find.

'Do you know where you're going?' asked Scalpi as impatient as ever.

'Just follow Leofric and think about what you're going to do when we get in there,' said Wulfgar.

'If we get in there,' said Scalpi, cursing as a bramble caught his tunic.

We could hear people talking as they patrolled the raised

walkways around the walls. Occasionally a flaming torch would be held out over the side giving a dim light, but we managed to keep concealed amongst the scrub. I nearly missed the entrance to the tunnel. The gnarled oak stump was smaller than I remembered and covered in ivy.

'This is it,' I whispered as I pulled ivy, fern and bramble away from the opening. Except there was no opening. Just stone and soil and twisted roots binding it all together.

'Shit!' said Scalpi.

'Shit indeed,' said Wulfgar, 'What now?'

'It's difficult to tell if it's been filled in deliberately or collapsed over time,' I said scrabbling at the debris. Whichever it was, after trying to pull the rubble away, we realised we were not going to get through.

'We will have to go back the way we came. Keep low and stay quiet.' Wulfgar led this time, pushing through the undergrowth. Another torch was held over the wall, its faint light flickering in front of us.

'Who's there?' someone shouted. An arrow, barely visible in the darkness, whisked passed us, landing harmlessly in the ferns, prompting a moor-hen to take flight.

'It's a bird, you fool, save your arrows.' The torch was withdrawn and once again we were hidden in darkness.

Mair was still cavorting around the cauldron when we came back through the coppice.

'You're supposed to be inside the gates, not here with me,' she said. 'Give men a simple task and they will prove how simple they are.'

'The passage is blocked,' I said, 'we will have to find another way.'

'Can't you just magic us in there?' asked Scalpi.

Mair gave him her withering stare.

'Magic is not a plaything. It is for the gods to determine when it is used, not men.'

She stared again into the cauldron, throwing more of the herbs from her bag into the bubbling liquid. 'It seems the gods want Leofric to find a way. To be a leader, you need to use cunning as well as force. The gods will help, but you must find a way in, Leofric. I will plead with them and they will help you. They will open your mind and the way will become clear.'

This was Mair's way of deflecting her lack of real magic, I thought, after all, it was just trickery and illusion. The gods would not help me because there are no gods.

Three days later, as if by magic, help came.

Forty-three

AD 1072
Spring

The glaring white of the snow has melted away to reveal a vibrant swathe of crocus, wood anemone and daffodil, and spread throughout the valley, celandine, appearing as though a myriad of stars have fallen from the sky to warm the hardened earth. Bald has been a good friend and provided us with shelter and food for little reward. 'It's no more than Saint Neot himself would have done,' the monk told me. But I fear we have overstayed our welcome.

Last evening, I was disturbed at my writing by shouting coming from outside our rooms. I tried to ignore it, engrossed as I was, but it continued, causing me to go and investigate. I found Scand on his knees outside Bald's cell. He clutched his face, blood pouring from his nose and eye. Moments later Bald appeared from inside wielding his staff. Blood, I presumed Scand's, dripped from Saint Neot's bronze face.

'Go anywhere near that box again and as God and all the saints are my witnesses, I will kill you,' Bald snarled at him. 'Little weasel must have seen me leave and sneaked in here. Luckily, I returned for herbs I'd forgotten and found him leaving with my box. You should be careful of the company you keep, Leofric.' He poked the staff towards Scand who cowered on the ground mewing like a weaning kitten.

Wulfgar, also alerted by the shouting, strode up to Scand and yanked him up by the cowl of his tunic.

'Scand will give you no more trouble Bald, will you Scand?'

Scand said nothing, just glared at Wulfgar. Wulfgar brought his fist hard into Scand's already bloodied face and brought his knee into his groin. Scand groaned in pain.

'Will you, Scand?'

'No, no more trouble, I swear it,' spluttered Scand. Wulfgar threw him to the ground and he slithered off empty handed.

Today we have received news from a man with stomach cramps who has come to Bald for a potion.

'The land is in terror once again,' he said, 'whole families heading west. There have been rumours that King Malcolm and Edgar Ætheling are planning to march into Englaland and take control of the north.'

He paused whilst he took a swig of the foul-smelling concoction Bald gave him. He screwed his face up, closing his eyes as the liquid slid down his throat, coughed violently four or five times, then continued. 'King William has been informed and is on his way with a huge army to crush this latest rebellion.'

On hearing this, we have decided to go to Malcolm's court and offer our support to Edgar, the rightful king of Englaland. We plan to leave the day after tomorrow.

It gives me an opportunity to continue my account of my return to Æssefeld all those years ago.

ᛏᚻᛗ ᚫᛁᛏᚷ ᛈᚻᚨᛃ ᛏᛗᚪᛗᚱ ᛈᚨᚻᛁ

AD 1057

We stayed outside Æssefeld for two days. Mair danced and sang to her gods and threw herbs into the small cauldron. Wulfgar and Scalpi chased hares and wood pigeons to keep us fed. Lugna alternated between sharpening his big war sword and practising whirling it around his head.

I tended to the horses and continually stared at the trees on the edge of the wood, particularly the big oak, whose leaves had turned from brown to a hint of gold and ochre. I knew it was around the time for the yearly slaughter when the livestock was brought to be butchered and salted for the winter. I remembered how Brokk and I had intervened when Leafwold was beating the swine-herd for trying to bring his pigs over the bridge and barred the steward's way. For those two whole days, nothing came out of the wood except for the odd pigeon or hare escaping from Wulfgar and Scalpi. The bridge remained empty and I started to fear the plan that had been forming in my head would come to nothing.

On the third day, as the first hint of light crept through the trees, Olaf, the swineherd's boy, now a young man, oblivious to the events happening in front of him, came out of the copse driving his pigs onto the bridge towards the village. He had grown since I last saw him, but I recognised him straight away, and he recognised me.

'Lord Leofric, you're back.'

'I am back, Olaf, but not welcome.'

'It's Grim, lord, he convinced your father, and many others besides, that you killed our steward in cold blood. I never believed it.'

'Why don't you believe it? I am told it was my knife he was killed with and they found my amulet by his body.'

'You might have killed him in a fair fight, lord, but a dagger in the back? You would never do that. Is that Mair?' he said, grimacing as he spoke.

'Yes,' I replied.

'She is the only reason they haven't come and taken you already. They are fearful of her magic.'

A pig bumped into my leg and another one squealed as Scalpi chased it out of the herd across the front of the copse. Olaf scowled but thought better of protesting.

'Are you taking the pigs around the village or inside?'

'Into the village, lord. They are to be slaughtered and salted for the winter.'

'I see you still wear the arm ring I gave you.'

'Always, lord, it even fits me now, look.' He showed me how it no longer slipped up and down as it had done when I gave it to him.

' I recognise that necklace too,' I said, 'it was your father's.'

'It was, it is of little worth, but it reminds me of him. He died a year ago.'

The necklace was made of green and yellow pebbles strung alternatively on a leather cord. Of no value, as Olaf said, but striking, memorable. He clutched at the beads, worried I would take them.

'Do you trust me, Olaf?' I asked.

'Of course, lord, ' he said removing his hand from the necklace. My plan was becoming clearer.

Scalpi finally caught the pig and dispatched it, and its burning flesh smelt delicious as it turned on a makeshift spit he'd rigged up over a fire using burning kindle he took from under Mair's cauldron. She spat and shrieked at him but even Mair needed to eat, so she allowed him to continue. Even Lugna, enticed by the aroma of cooking pig, moved towards the fire.

I beckoned Wulfgar and we took Olaf into the copse. I asked

Wulfgar to fetch water from the river in one of our leather flasks, and when he returned, I mixed in an extra-large dose of my pain-relieving herbs which Mair prepared for me.

It contained small traces of belladonna and henbane amongst others, and as well as relieving my pain it could also induce a deep sleep when used in greater quantities. It could also cause madness and ultimately, death, so it was to be used with great care. I offered the flask to Olaf, and Wulfgar and I drank from another flask which contained weak wine. Wulfgar looked puzzled but kept silent.

'I'm sure you could catch a pig quicker than Scalpi,' I said to Olaf.

'Of course, lord, they will just come to me.'

He placed his fingers in his mouth and gave a short, shrill whistle. One of the pigs came scurrying through the trees and straight to Olaf. He bent down to stroke the animal and as he stood back up his eyes glazed. His mouth fell open and his legs buckled. I caught him as he dropped, lowering him gently to the ground. I undid the cord around his waist and making a noose, slipped it over the pig's head. It squealed and tried to shake it off. We pulled the leather jerkin off Olaf, and his arm ring and the pebble necklace. We concealed Olaf under scrub and fallen branches.

'What are we doing?' said Wulfgar, still oblivious to my plan.

'We're going to dress the pig. Take hold of his back legs and try to keep him still.'

The pig struggled as Wulfgar grabbed it from behind. It tried to turn to bite him but Wulfgar hung on. I put the sleeveless jerkin over the pig's back and pushed its front legs through the armholes. I slipped the arm ring on to its right front leg and pushed it up as far as I could, so it became a tight fit. The necklace I draped around its neck just behind the ears.

'Hello, Olaf the pig. What has Mair done to you?' I said.

'You will never get away with it,' said Wulfgar shaking his head.

'We will soon find out,' and taking hold of the cord, I led the pig out of the copse.

Wulfgar took a white shirt from his saddlebag and tied it to the stick as a make-shift flag of truce. The rest of the pigs were scattered, one or two at the edge of the copse, several rooting in the long grass. With a few shrill calls and a prod of the stick from Wulfgar, we managed to get most of them moving towards Æssefeld. More joined in from curiosity and others, I guessed, from the herd instinct. I called to Scalpi to help us. He came reluctantly, still chewing on pig meat, his chin covered in grease.

'Where's the swineherd, they're his bloody pigs?' he grumbled.

'He's there, in front of you,' I said, 'can't you see him?'

'No, he's not there.'

'Look closer,' I said.

Scalpi scowled. 'There are only pigs.'

'And that one,' I said pointing out the pig in the leather jerkin. Scalpi moved closer to the animal, then noticed the beads and finally the arm ring.

'God's teeth,' he said, 'how did you do that?'

'Not me, it was Mair, the old gods have heeded her voice after all.'

'God's teeth,' he said again, crossing himself nervously. We continued toward the village gates, me with the pig on a cord and Wulfgar waving the white flag to signal we wanted to talk. There was much activity on the walls of Æssefeld.

'They have got the pigs!' someone shouted.

'Let the pigs in,' cried someone else. Three men with bows came to the fore on the wall. We stopped and Wulfgar waved the flag of truce.

'We are unarmed,' I shouted. 'We will come no further. The pigs are yours, you can let them in.'

The gates opened slowly, leaving a narrow entrance. A young lad came out carrying a bowl of swill and nervously threw a hand-full on the ground. The pigs quickened their pace and rushed to the food, the boy retreated backwards leaving a trail for them to follow. The pig with the arm ring strained on the cord wanting to join them. I kept tight hold until all the other pigs were inside. The gates were quickly closed once more. A man, I recognized as Gifre, appeared on the wall.

'What have you done with Olaf the swineherd?' he shouted. Before I could answer, Grim came next to him.

'If yer think you can use the swineherd as a hostage, Leofric, yer a bigger fool than I thought yer were. What do I care for a mere swineherd? Torture him, kill him if yer want, he is nothing to me.'

'He is no hostage, Grim. Here he is, let him in.'

I slipped the cord off the pig's head and it ran straight to the gates. They opened them up again, enough for the pig to squeeze through, and then shut them tight.

'Mair said to tell you if you do not let us in by the time the sun is over the old oak, she will turn the whole village, old and young alike, into a mass of snuffling swine. I have no quarrel with the good people of Æssefeld-Underbarroe. I just want to talk to you and my father.'

I could hear the yells and curses as people realised with horror what had become of their swineherd. Not everyone would be fooled, I guessed, but many would, and I hoped their fear would open the gates.

Mair had watched from afar and as she approached I wondered what her reaction would be. Mair was an expert of subterfuge, she realised exactly what I had done. She also knew how to turn each event to her advantage.

'Mighty are the gods that can give us wisdom and the ability to perform wondrous acts in the eyes of others,' she said to me.

With arms aloft, she strode purposefully towards Æssefeld, incantations flowing from her lips, and as if by magic, a black cloud blotted out the sun for an instant, causing a quick chill. As the cloud passed, the sun came over the oak tree and the gates of Æssefeld-Underbarroe were opened.

I strapped Widewe Wyrhta around my waist and put on the skeleton helmet. I dug my heels into Stormbringer's flanks and the four of us rode slowly behind the sorceress into my old home.

The whole village was gathered, the majority in a semi-circle around a group of village elders and younger men who had restrained Grim and his few followers by spear point.

Olaf's friend, Wiglaff, was crouched on the ground, his arm around the pig with the jerkin, consoling him. 'Don't worry, Olaf, Mair will restore you back to a man again soon. You can turn him back again, can't you?' he pleaded with Mair.

'He will be restored to himself as soon as our business is concluded,' I said. ' Where is my father?' I asked Grim.

'I told yer before, Renweard has only one son and heir, Edgard Renweardson,' he said pointing at my half-brother who stood next to my stepmother. When I last saw Edgard he was a babe in arms, now he was about five years old. His brown hair was cut short and in a straight fringe over his eyes and around his neck hung my amulet. His mother put a protective arm over his shoulder and pulled him close to her.

'I have no intention of harming your son,' I said, as I dismounted Stormbringer. Everyone stepped nervously backwards. 'All I want is justice. I have been wrongly accused of committing murder and I have come here to prove my innocence. Where is my father?'

'Your father is unwell, Leofric. He lies on his bed in his hall,' said one of the elder men.

'Mair will attend to him,' I said, and Mair was taken to see my father.

'And how will yer prove yer innocence?' said Grim. 'Yer dagger and that amulet,' he said, once again pointing at Edgard, 'were found next to the steward's body. A letter was taken from him that was of value only to you and yer left the village without a word to anyone. What more proof do we need of yer guilt?'

'There was a witness,' I said abruptly.

'A witness?' said Grim, sneering.

'Yes, someone watched the whole incident.'

'Who?' demanded one of the elders.

'Me,' said Lugna, who until now had stayed silent.

'And who are you?' said Grim, startled by this new development.

'I am Lugna, once the companion of Nairn the Dream Teller; a servant of Drust the High Seer of the Black Mountains.' He climbed down from his mount, still towering above everybody present.

'You are Lugna?' scoffed Grim.

Lugna took off his battle helmet, hunched his back, let his right arm hang low and contorted his face into the one familiar to the villagers.

'I am Lugna,' he said again, though this time the words were slow and slurred and barely distinguishable from a grunt.

There were gasps at the transformation and again as Lugna straightened and returned his features to that of a man of bearing and stature.

'On the night your steward was murdered, I was tending to a sick lamb in the barn over there. I was hidden in the shadows when Grim and two others, Eglaf and Gifre Idenson, came to the steward's home. Leafwold came out to see who called him and was greeted by Gifre. Grim came from behind and stabbed him in the back.

I followed them discreetly to Leofric's dwelling. They called his name, and when he came out Leofric was struck from behind and a sack put over his head. They bound him, removed his amulet and dagger, and loaded him on to a cart and he was taken from Æssefeld. Grim returned to the steward's house and stuck Leofric's dagger into the wound where the other had been. He took the letter from the steward's bag, dropped the amulet by the steward's body and left. I found out later that Leofric had been taken to a priory and held against his will.'

' Is this true, Grim?' Someone shouted.

Obviously taken aback by these revelations and the true account of my false accusation and abduction, Grim hesitated before answering.

'Lies, all lies. This man, Lugna, who lived amongst us as a dolt, by his own admission had been living a lie all those years. Why should you believe him now?'

Folk nodded their agreement.

'And why would I leave a dagger that all would know was mine in the steward's back?' I said.

Folk nodded at this too. The villagers were confused, they did not know who to believe. Arguments started amongst them about who was right and who was guilty.

'Just run the bastard through,' said Scalpi starting to draw his sword.

'No, Scalpi, we must send for the shire reeve from Wydeford, he must hear the evidence,' I said.

Grim looked agitated, he was no longer so sure of the outcome of this as he was before he learnt Lugna had witnessed the murder.

'I challenge you to Holmganga,' he blurted out, pointing to me. 'We have accused each other of a heinous crime. I call on the ancient way of settling disputes to decide this matter.'

I knew of such a thing, though I had never witnessed it in practice. Holmganga means, go to a small island. Originally, two men would row out to a small island and in that confined space would fight each other to the death. More recently, several cloaks or hides would be laid on the ground and a hazel rod would be stuck in the ground at each corner, and the fight would take place in that arena. There were rules to be decided by the two men before the fight began.

Wulfgar came beside me. 'Think carefully on this, Leofric. Grim is no Madog. He senses the fates are turning against him. He must think he has a better chance of beating you than being proven innocent by the reeve.'

Wulfgar was most likely right, but if I refused to do this, it would appear I was guilty after all and afraid to fight him.

'I accept your challenge, Grim,' I said.

'When?' said Grim, eager to get this done.

The crowd moved aside as Mair came from my father's hall.

'I have administered the potion Drust gave me for your father. It will nullify the so-called medicinal broth he has been receiving that has stolen his wits. In two or three days, he will start regaining his senses, though he will still be weak and unsteady.'

'Three days, and you will have your Holmganga, Grim, and whoever is the victor will be free from all blame or guilt for the other's death. Agreed?'

'Agreed,' said Grim, 'and as the challenger, you choose the weapons.'

'Swords and each man allowed three shields,' I said.

'Three blows each in turn, if both still stand, a free fight to the death. You will strike first, Leofric,' said Grim.

And so, it was decided.

That night, Wulfgar sneaked into Wiglaf's garden and grabbed the pig and took it behind the barn away from prying eyes and removed Olaf's possessions from it. Mair went to the copse with Wulfgar. They returned Olaf's possessions to his person. Mair gave him mug-wort to drink, which fuddled the mind and brought on a forgetfulness. They told him how Mair had turned him into a pig, which he said he had no recollection of and could not remember much of what had happened at all. He was so terrified of Mair that he believed anything she told him. Wiglaf had come rushing up to the steward to tell him that Olaf the pig had gone missing. He was so relieved when Olaf the swineherd turned up at dusk with Mair and Wulfgar, fully restored and none the worst for the experience, except for feeling sleepy. No more questions were asked.

Wulfgar and I walked around the village that evening. Even those that remembered me as a boy were reticent to speak with us. I had no fond memories of my past life in Æssefeld. Ridicule and pain were all I could remember. I was a weak, crippled boy back then whom they could mock and laugh at when bullied by others. Now, they saw a tall, muscular man in black with a war helmet of dread and a sword that gleamed strapped to his side and I could sense their fear. I thought of Horsdone and the life Astrid and I were building there. That's where my heart was, that's where I wanted to be, with my wife and child. As soon as this business was resolved, that is where I would return.

We entered my father's hall. Tallow candles burned in the corners of the room, giving off their fatty, rancid smell and faint light. The straw on the floor was old and stale. Renweard lay on the big bed I remembered him and my mother sharing. His hair and beard were greyer than when I last saw him. His eyes closed, face pale and drawn, yet he still bore that fierce, stern air about him. All I had ever wanted from this man was one word of fondness, one word of encourage-ment, just once to say, 'this is my son and I am proud of him.' Yet, even now, I doubted that would ever happen. I lifted his head and trickled the potion, Drust had sent for him, passed his lips. Wulfgar and I left him sleeping and made our way out through the main hall. Outside all was quiet. Lugna and Scalpi stood close to the house where Grim was being held, making sure he did not abscond. Mair had gone to the barrows to talk to the ancestors.

'Maybe Scalpi was right,' said Wulfgar, 'perhaps we should have run Grim through and put an end to it.'

'That would prove nothing,' I said, 'another murder and my guilt would seem more certain. This way most will believe the victor has God's approval and so is proved innocent.'

'And if he beats you?'

'That will prove there is no God,' I said, smiling.

'God will not aid a blasphemer, Leofric, innocent or not.' It was Crispin. 'You are aware Holmganga is banned?' he asked. 'It is illegal. If you kill him, it will be murder.'

'In who's eyes?'

'In God's all-seeing eye,' said Crispin.

'I will take my chance with God,' I said. 'As far as the law is concerned, I am led to believe it is a valid way of settling such disputes as long as both parties agree, and we do. I suppose you would rather I trusted my life to you and the other villagers, those who would profit from Grim living and my death. Grim must feel the same way, I am sure, there are many with a grudge against him. Better to trust in ourselves and our skill with a sword.'

Ever since I threatened to cut his balls off, Crispin had been wary of me. He knew I was aware of his preference for small boys and he was terrified I would reveal his sordid secret. The only reason I hadn't was because I made him swear on the altar that he would not do it again and if I found out he had reneged, I would kill him.

'I want only the truth of the matter, Leofric,' said Crispin.

I had known Crispin since I was a boy. His sincerity was without question, but he was a weak-willed man who succumbed easily to his desires and would always take the side of those who gave him the least pain and aggravation. He never understood why I stopped believing in God. The majority of those who lived in the towns and cities were Christians. A few, in the remote places like Æssefeld, although claiming to be Christian, still clung to the old ways; the lore of Odin and Thor, the power of Nertha, the earth's mother. Yet I saw no reason to put my faith in any of them.

'The wisdom of God is beyond the reproach of all men, Leofric, even a priest,' he said. 'Men whisper that Mair will use her magic on your behalf and the fight will not be fair.'

'There will be no help from Mair's magic,' I said, 'tell the whisperers they can be sure of that.'

The next day my father was sitting up in his bed. He still could not talk, but his eyes were open, and he drank hot broth. I stood in the shadows, not wanting to disturb him.

On the third day, I took Widewe Wyrhta to be sharpened by the smith. He marvelled at the blade. 'Any man who owns such a sword must be a mighty warrior,' he said, as moved the whetstone deftly across the blade.

'Just because a man has a fine sword doesn't mean he can use it.'

'True,' said the smith, 'but this one is so fine, if you couldn't use it, someone would have taken it from you by now.'

As I left the smithy, men were preparing the fighting area for the Holmganga. Cloaks of cow hides had been laid out on the ground. One of the old men of the village had recalled helping his father prepare the ritual when he was a young boy. He remembered that sticks were placed in a certain way, called Tjosnublot. He said they had made a sacrifice of a lamb and sprinkled the blood around the area, but he could not remember the words that were spoken. He vaguely recalled a narrow border was marked out around the cloak on three sides, and hazel staves were planted in the corners of the border. All this was carried out, a sheep was killed, the blood was sprinkled, and Crispin had been coerced to say a blessing to legitimise the proceedings.

Mair came to see me as I prepared to meet Grim.

'Renweard is well enough to be present as you wished,' she said. 'I have done as you asked. As soon as you kill Grim, you will retrieve the amulet from the boy and fulfil your part.'

'What if Grim kills me? What will you do?' I asked.

'He will not kill you, Leofric, if I thought that, we would have taken

419

the amulet already.'

'I want none of your tricks, Mair. I must beat Grim fairly and my father must see me do it.'

'I will not raise a finger to help you. Luckily, the gods have plans for you so they will not let you die,' she replied.

I finished cleaning my mail and leather tunic, wiping off the grime and dust of the last few days. I put on the helmet of death and gripping Widewe Wyrhta in my right hand, I went to kill Grim.

Forty-four

The whole village was gathered around the symbolic island of hide cloaks. Four young men carried out my father in a carved oak litter to watch me fight. He still looked weak, the colour gone from his face, though he had regained his voice.

Grim was already in the hazeled area. He was bare from the waist up. Both arms adorned with warrior rings. He wore a plain, conical helmet made from iron with a long, nasal guard.

As I walked to the Holmganga, I wondered if this is where it would all end. After years of false accusations of murder and betrayal from my father hanging over me, it had all come down to this moment. After Lugna's revelation of Grim's guilt, most men there believed I was innocent. My father thought me weak and unable to protect myself or others. Today, I would beat the man he entrusted to train his soldiers and enforce his rules. Today, I would show my father I was the son he longed for after all.

Three shields, prepared for each of us, stood in opposite corners of the hazeled area. Grim picked up a large, round shield made of linden wood with an iron rim and a sharp, pointed boss at its centre. It seemed to me unduly heavy, whereas the shields I was given were light and less cumbersome.

Gifre, who was now the steward of Æssefeld, was acting as Grim's second. As he had been implicated in the former stewards murder he had a vested interest in Grim's victory. 'You may use three shields during the contest. You will each strike three blows of your sword, Leofric striking first as Grim is the challenger. If both men are still standing after the sixth blow, you will commence fighting at will until only one man lives. If any part of either man comes outside of the border, either voluntary or otherwise, the contest will be over, and that man considered a nithing and banished from Æssefeld forever.'

Grim moved to the centre and banged his sword on his shield. 'You should go now, Leofric, whilst you still can. You are already banished and seen as a nithing, so why don't you simply walk away?'

'Because you and I both know I am innocent. You have turned my father against me and sullied my name and reputation.'

'Your father has always been against you, Leofric. He has always seen you as a weak, incomplete boy, unfit to be thegn of Æssefeld-Underbarroe. Now I am going to prove he was right. Strike your first blow, Dipper, then prepare to die.'

I walked slowly towards him, placed the shield on the ground and gripping Widewe Wyrhta with both hands, I swung the sword over my head with all my strength and smashed the entire length of the blade against Grim's shield. Splinters flew into the air and Grim stepped back slightly. I was taken aback by how insignificant the damage was to either Grim or his shield. The clash of metal on metal rang in my ears and I presumed it was the blade striking the shield rim or the edge of the shield boss.

'Now it is my turn,' said Grim.

I took up one of the shields, thinking once again how light it felt. With the sound of my heart pounding in my head, Grim discarded his shield and came towards me quickly. I stood with one leg slightly in front of the other, bracing myself for the impact. As the blade struck, the shield practically disintegrated, large pieces flying off in all directions. The sword hit me on the shoulder, my mail saving me from severe injury, though the impact sent me reeling backwards on to the floor, a hand's length from the edge of the skins. I stood up quickly. Grim took up his shield again and stared defiantly into my eyes.

'Come on, Dipper, yer disappoint me. I've heard the tales about yer fighting skills. Never once believed them. Yer on your own now. No Wulfgar or sorceress to hide behind, just you and me.'

I stepped forward for the second time and smashed my sword at Grim's shield. Again a few splinters and he did rock back a step further, but the shield stayed intact. He threw the shield to the ground. Gifre passed him the sword and he came at me a second time. I picked up a new shield which weighed even lighter than the last one. The straps for my arm felt loose, with no way to tighten them. I stretched my arm as fully as I could, pushing the shield in front of me as far as possible, hoping it would keep the sword away from my body. This time there was no resistance at all. The whole shield collapsed on impact, Grim's sword cutting deep into my shoulder and catching my forearm, drawing blood. There were gasps from the women and groans and jeers from the men. I looked across to where my father sat. His face was as blank parchment, revealing no emotion whatsoever. I looked to the corner for Wulfgar for encouragement, but he was not there.

As I lifted Widewe Wyrhta, I tried to grip with both hands, but had no strength, pain searing through my left arm.

'Last chance, Dipper,' said Grim grinning as he lifted a new shield which seemed even heavier than the last one.

I put all my effort into that stroke. Widewe Wyrhta's blade cutting deep into the wood and leather of Grim's shield, but the impact was not enough to move him backwards even slightly. I walked slowly to collect the last of the shields. Wulfgar reappeared and was stood just outside the border of the Holmganga. As I lifted the shield, I leant towards him. 'What are these pieces of shit supposed to protect?' I asked.

'They wouldn't let us near them,' said Wulfgar. 'Get ready to change that crap for this,' he said. He held a round shield, low down, partly concealed by his cloak.

'You miserable pieces of rotting horse dung.'

Everyone turned to see what the commotion was. It was Scalpi. He was standing, naked, on the roof of the big barn, a drinking horn in one hand, his sword in the other. 'If you want a proper fight come and fight me, you festering turds.' He took a swig from the horn, lost his footing and disappeared over the ridge. Everyone laughed at his antics. The distraction was enough for me to pass the flimsy shield to Wulfgar and to take the other from him. Straight away I noticed the difference. It was made of lime wood with four iron cross braces, two each side of the central boss. Boiled leather strips fastened around the rim gave it added strength. There were two straps on the inside which I fastened tightly onto my left arm, helping to stem the flow of blood from my wound. This time I kept Widewe Wyrhta in my right hand and moved to the middle of the fighting area. I stood square onto Grim, feet apart, my right foot slightly in front of the left giving me a good balance. Grim moved forward grinning, full of confidence. He dropped his shield on the ground and gripped the hilt of his sword with both hands. I fixed my eyes on his.

'This is your last chance, Grim, kill me now or you will die,' I said.

Grim lifted the sword above his head and turning slowly in a circle he shouted, 'I am Grim, master of Æssefeld and I will end this cripple's miserable life and prove his guilt.'

Spinning quicker at the last moment he slashed his blade down on my shield. The jolt sent me backwards, the pain searing through my cut arm, but I remained standing and the shield held intact except for a few splinters.

I could see the confusion on Grim's face as he looked over to Gifre.

It was my turn to raise my arms. Shield and sword aloft, I shouted, 'I am Leofric, son of Renweard, Thegn of Æssefeld-Underbarroe. I am Leofric the Black, Killer of Death. I have been falsely accused and I will be avenged.'

Grim seemed less confident now, he was no longer grinning, and staring into his eyes I could sense doubt. I knew that tricks and feints would not fool him, he was too experienced for that. To beat him, I must draw on all the training with Wulfgar and my experience in the shield wall.

Grim picked up his shield and we circled each other slowly. Grim struck first but I pushed his blade away with my shield and counterattacked driving my sword through a slight gap between his shield and his flailing sword, catching him on the shoulder. I drew back my blade and slashed it down towards his head. This time he managed to block it with his shield, but I struck blow after blow giving him no time to recover. Repeatedly, I pounded that shield, pushing him further back towards the edge of the hide cloaks. Each time he managed to recover moments before he stepped off the edge of the Holmganga.

I found out later, that Grim's shield was reinforced with wide metal bars and a double layer of wood. Perfect for when he was standing still to ward off my blows, but cumbersome and unwieldy in open combat.

I came at him repeatedly, forcing him ever backwards, slashing my sword constantly against his shield. The weight of it now a disadvantage, limiting his movement. Desperate to stay within the boundaries, he tripped over his own feet and landed flat on his back, the heavy shield's weight pinning him down. He pushed the shield off exposing his bare chest, one thrust of my sword and it would be over. Instead I stepped back allowing him to stand. I threw my shield to the ground. We both paused for an instant, our breathing heavy, our eyes locked. Grim came snarling, teeth bared, face contorted with deadly resolve. I let him come unhindered, watched him wield his sword towards me, convinced his blow would kill me. It was a risk, I knew, but as his blade, intended for my neck, almost connected, I leant my upper body swiftly to one side. The sword cut through the mail into my left shoulder as I plunged Widewe Wyrhta through flesh and ribs deep into his heart. His eyes, full of surprise, widened then glazed as he fell to his knees. I gave my blade a twist before pulling it from Grim's lifeless body which fell backwards in a crumpled heap.

Walking slowly to where my father sat, Grim's blood dripping from my sword, I took off my helmet. I turned slowly in a circle. 'If any man or woman still believes I murdered your steward, speak now.' There was silence. I singled out Gifre and picking up Grim's fallen sword, I thrust it towards him. 'Tell the truth of that night or fight me now.'

Gifre knelt before me. 'It is true, lord, Grim murdered the steward and left your dagger and amulet by his body. You were to be sent over the British sea and sold as a slave, but Grim was worried if you ever escaped you would come back and expose him, so he ordered that you were to be killed away from Æssefeld. Show mercy, lord,' he said, pushing my blade away from himself. 'We simply followed Grim's orders, he was doing it for someone else.'

'Who was he acting for?' I said, already knowing the answer but wanting others to hear it.

'I don't know, lord, someone of high status who promised him a position and land of his own. For some reason, that offer was withdrawn and Grim decided to carry out the deed himself.'

'With your help,' I said.

'Yes, lord. When Lord Renweard became ill, Grim arranged for a cure potion to be prepared for him but it was concocted to make him worse, not better. Slowly Grim took over the running of Æssefeld and aimed to take Renweard's place.'

'And was my stepmother involved with Grim?' I asked. Before he could answer, blood seeped from Gifre's mouth, his eyes swelled, he fell headlong to the ground, an arrow protruding from his back. Wulfgar and Scalpi, who was fully clothed again, ran towards the direction the arrow came from, but the assailant had fled.

Mair appeared next to me. 'The amulet, get the amulet.'

'All in good time, Mair,' I said dismissively.

'This is a good time, I demand you get it from the brat now,' she hissed.

'Who are you to demand anything of me,' I snapped and turned my back on the dream teller's daughter.

Once again, I faced my father.

'Renweard, Thegn of Æssefeld-Underbarroe, father, I did not murder your steward or steal the letter you gave him. I have produced a witness and slain the guilty man in combat and his man has admitted to their crime. Will you now acknowledge my innocence of these crimes?'

Renweard peered at me through watery eyes. 'I have only one son, Edgard,' he said, his voice rough and throaty.

'I am Leofric, your first-born son.'

'Firstborn, no, there were others, but they died. Edgard is my only son. Come here, boy,' he said in a half-whispered voice. 'Come here.' Edgard cautiously left his mother's side and stood next to Renweard. 'This is my only son and heir of Æssefeld-Underbarroe and all my estates,' he continued, putting an arm around the boy's shoulders and ruffling his hair with his ring-heavy fingers.

How many times had I craved for that? Yet we were further apart than ever. My father denying my very existence. My guts twisted, my heart despairing, my breathing short and quick. 'Why do you hate me so?' I said, the words cascading from my mouth like bitter ale.

'Why would I hate you, I do not know you. Do you know this man, Edgard?' asked Renweard.

'No, lord,' said Edgard truthfully. 'I don't know him, but I hate him.'

'Why do you hate him?'

'Because he has killed Grim and he was like a father to me.'

Renweard frowned at that. 'I am your father, boy, no other'.

'Why did you kill Grim?' said Renweard.

'Because he falsely accused me of crimes against you, father, and he has been poisoning you, prolonging your illness.'

'Why do you call me, father, I have told you, I have one son, Edgard?' Before I could answer him, he held up his hand to stop me. 'I am tired, I wish to return to my bed.'

At first, I thought my father was ignoring me out of stubbornness, unwilling to admit he had misjudged me for all those years. Now I believe the potions Grim had administered over time had permanently addled his mind and he genuinely did not remember me. I watched my father leave as the pain from my wounds, which I had been resisting, flared throughout my body, and overcome, I dropped to the floor.

Forty-five

I slept for two days. A restless, disturbed sleep where demons and all that is evil tried to drag me into dark, soulless realms, where limbless, headless warriors dwelt and six great white bears, with claws the length of a seax, pawed over my lifeless body. I would wake sporadically, sweat seeping from my brow, my shoulder throbbing with pain. At times Ulla would be mopping my forehead with wet cloths. Occasionally it would be Wulfgar or Olaf, or once even Scalpi, but before any words came from my lips, I would slip back into the senseless realms of nightmares.

On the third day, the fever had passed but the pain had not. I forced myself from the straw bed, stood gingerly and walked unsteadily to the door, adjusting my eyes to the bright sunlight.

'Lord, should you be up?' It was Olaf. 'Mair found traces of the poison devil's helmet and hemlock on Grim's blade and she has been giving you potions and applying poultices to your wound. She said you need rest.'

'I have rested long enough. Have you seen my father?' I asked.

'I believe he walks beside the river with his wife and son.'

'Then take me to the river.'

'Lord, is that wise?'

'Wise or not, take me to the river,' I said again.

Olaf took my arm and we slowly made our way to the small door in the ramparts at the back of my father's hall. Olaf lifted the bars off the latches and we passed through onto the river bank. I could see my father, Silfried and Edgard strolling on the far side of the river. I struggled to stay conscious as the pain ripped through my arm and shoulder, and I clung on to Olaf to stop myself falling.

'Father,' I tried to shout, but my voice strained to carry any distance. 'Father.' Whether he heard me, or just caught sight of me at that moment, my father stopped and stared at me across the water. Silfried put her arm around him and tried to keep him moving. He stood his ground.

'Father,' I called again.

'Leofric, Leofric, my son.'

Those were words I had craved to hear for so long. Silfried grabbed his arm, pulling him harder and he was too weak to resist. For him to acknowledge me as his son was what I'd wished for but I needed him to know I had committed no crime against him

'Olaf, we must cross the bridge and go to him.'

'Lord, you are too weak, you will never get that far.'

He was right, but my desire to be reconciled with my father defied all reason. And then they came. Out of the trees behind where my father, his wife and son walked on that glorious, sunny day; Mair on Wraith and Lugna on Myrddin, galloping at full speed.

It all happened so fast. Mair leant down from the saddle, sickle in one hand, grabbing the boy by his hood with the other, yanking him up towards her. Silfried desperately tried to cling to Edgard's flailing body, her fingers grasping at his woollen tunic. Mair slashed out with the sickle, cutting deep into Silfried's face. My stepmother screamed as her blood splattered across Mair's cloak and Wraith's white flank and she lost her grip on her son. Mair tore the amulet from Edgard's neck and as she released her hold on the hood, he spun through the air and bounced on the ground squealing like a kicked pig. My father, confused by the events unfolding around him, turned to see Lugna, hurtling towards him, his great war sword scything through the air, and shouting, 'There is always a price to pay!'

It was the last thing my father saw and heard on this earth, as the blade sliced through his neck so swiftly and cleanly, that his head remained in place before toppling sideways as a torrent of blood gushed skywards and Renweard's headless corpse fell backwards into a thicket of brambles.

Olaf and I stood motionless, aghast. Silfried, wailing uncontrollably,

429

sat cuddling a sobbing Edgard. Mair and Lugna rode off into the trees, out of sight, and before I managed to shout, 'Bring me my horse and sword,' I collapsed and lost consciousness.

Two days later Wulfgar and Scalpi stood next to me as the pyre under my father's dead body was lit. I watched in sadness as the flames devoured his corpse and all hope of being loved by my father drifted away in the rising smoke. Later, I helped dig into the small barrow where his ashes, having been placed in an earthen pot, were interred along with his sword and battle axe.

Two weeks passed before I had strength enough to ride Stormbringer and wield Widewe Wyrhta again. As soon as she realised I had risen from my sick bed, Silfried blustered into my hut brandishing a rolled scroll.

'These are the deeds to Æssefeld Underbarroe,' she declared, 'Renweard changed them, before witnesses, to name our son Edgard as the beneficiary of all his father's estates. If you contest it, Leofric, I shall raise an army against you and we will take it by force.'

I stared at this woman who had always hated me. Her beauty now marred by the savage cut across her face, which had begun to form a thick scab from her left eye to her right cheek.

'My lady, if I wished it, I could end your life and the life of my half-brother, if that is who he is, instantly. I doubt many would rise against me once your death became known. But fear not, all I have ever wanted was the love and acceptance of my father. This place has few happy memories. Edgard has suffered enough, he can keep Æssefeld as my father wished. I shall leave soon and will be out of your lives. I have a new life in Norðhymbraland with my wife and son.'

Silfried neither thanked or continued to berate me.

I met with the village elders and they chose three men to help run Æssefeld until Edgard came of age. I told them if anything untoward happened to the boy, I would return and burn the entire village to the ground. Their faces told me they believed me.

'So, what do we do now?' said Wulfgar, aimlessly twisting a stick between his fingers. 'Do you intend to return to Earl Harold?'

'If he wants me, he can come and find me. I have been away from Astrid too long and I have a son waiting for his father.'

'A peaceful life then, farming your lands and breeding horses, is that the future?' I could sense the question was directed at himself as much as me.

'If that life is too tame for you, Wulfgar, I would understand. Though how long a life of peace can last, I'm not sure. Mair has the amulet, but both her and Drust believe it is powerless without me. She will eventually seek me out and I did give my word to co-operate, however fanciful I believe their undertaking to be. Besides, I am honour bound to avenge my father. Eventually, I must kill Lugna, which will be no easy feat.'

Wulfgar nodded to everything I said. 'I suppose I can amuse myself thwarting Fritjof Heironson's plans until I can confront Hakon Sweynson about my old lord's murder,' he said snapping the stick in half and tossing it out of the open doorway.

'I want to come with you,' Olaf said, as he walked in to join us.

'We already have enough swineherds on the estates,' said Wulfgar, 'they would not thank us for another one.'

'You can teach me how to fight,' said Olaf, answering Wulfgar. 'You gave me this, my lord,' touching the ring on his arm, 'for my courage, not my pig herding skills.'

'That's true,' I said.

'I suppose it would keep me occupied while you're off canoodling,' said Wulfgar, grinning. And so it was agreed Olaf would come with us and learn the art of war.

Wulfgar, Scalpi, Olaf and I left Æssefeld the following day and I never looked back once. We took the Roman road known as Earninga Straete.

I would never have admitted it to the others, but my face became tear-stained often on that journey back home, so I wore my helmet of death to conceal it from them. My father had never been kind or loving to me, yet neither had he been physically cruel. His cruelty was his indifference, wishing I wasn't his son and not even caring enough to hide the fact. But however much he hurt me, however worthless and inadequate he made me feel, he was still my father and the loss I felt was acute. These feelings swept over me in great waves of melancholy and despondency. To break these dark moods, I thought of Astrid and my new son and how I would be the father to him I wished Renweard had been to me.

Eventually, we came home. A light breeze made the leaves of the willow sing, though her song seemed sadder then I remembered. A group of children playing by the river saw us, but instead of running to greet us ran back towards the village.

'What do you expect with that thing on your head, it scares me never mind them,' said Wulfgar only half jesting.

I removed my helmet and we continued towards Horsdone. As we approached the gates Tripp and Rush came out to meet us.

'My friends, it is good to see you, though I am the bearer of sad news,' I called.

'So are we,' Tripp said, and I became aware of their unsmiling, furrowed faces and heavy, slow footsteps, in no hurry to reach us. I also heard for the first time the church bell striking loud, before pausing, then a muffled subdued ring, a ponderous, solemn refrain, repeated constantly. Unmistakably the death knell.

'Who's died?' I asked.

Rush stopped, leaving Tripp to continue.

'I need to speak to you alone, Leofric,' Tripp said, coughing noisily then wiping the phlegm from his beard.

I dismounted, handing Stormbringer's reins to Wulfgar. 'Wait here.'

Tripp and I embraced. 'What is it old friend, what has happened?'

Tripp's lips moved but the words failed to come. He coughed again then took a deep breath.

'It's Astrid. There is no easy way to say this, Leofric, she is dead.'

'That cough of yours is getting worse, Tripp, for a moment I thought you said Astrid is dead. Where is she, Tripp, why is she not here to greet me?'

Tripp placed his hands on my shoulders, gripping me tightly.

'It is not my cough, Leofric. We buried her months since, next to the church. Riocus ordered the bells of mourning be rung once a day until your return.'

I knocked his arms from me and pushed him backwards.

'What jest is this old man?' I said, pushing him again. I could feel the veins in my neck pulsing, twitching. Wulfgar climbed down from Fleet and came to see what was happening. Tripp held his hand up as a signal stop him.

'We tried to get word to you but found out you were a prisoner of the Wealas. There was a feast, not long after you left. Folk came from all around. I still lay in my sick bed with the fever. I am told Astrid retired early with sickness. It was not until the morning, when most of the revellers had left, that she was found in your dwelling; naked, beaten about the head and body so severely, she never walked or spoke again.'

My whole body went numb. A noise in my head like the rushing tide made it difficult to understand what Tripp was saying. I found it difficult to breathe, my body still weak from my wounds.

Tripp continued, 'Miraculously, the baby lived inside her, until she could hold on to life no more and departed from this world. The old women cut her open and delivered your son from her belly. He is well and is with the smith and his wife. She had given birth a month earlier and was able to wet nurse your son.'

My whole body shook, partly from shock, partly from anger.

'Who was it Tripp, who did this to her?'

'That we do not know. Rush is devastated he was not there to protect her. He was drunk along with most of the other men. His guilt is the reason he holds back now.'

'Was Fritjof Heironson present?' I spat.

'He was, but he left early and has witnesses to verify the fact.'

'Someone must know,' I roared, and losing all reason I pushed past Tripp and stormed off towards the village. Rush tried to

433

intervene and was rewarded with a punch to the face, knocking him down. I slid Widewe Wyrhta from its scabbard and slicing the air with its lethal blade strode through the village scattering all before me in an inconsolable rage.

'All you worthless pieces of shit had to do was protect her,' I yelled at no one in particular. 'Just protect her.'

'Wasn't that your responsibility, my lord?'

I spun around ready to plunge Widewe Wyrhta into whoever dared question me. It was Torvald the smith, unarmed and undeterred.

'You insolent bastard,' I raged. And at that moment, I am ashamed to admit, I would have butchered a good, innocent man, except, before I struck, his wife came from behind him.

'This is your son, my lord.'

A small face appeared from behind the safety of her skirts and tottering on unsteady legs, the boy stood before me wide eyed. I thought for one moment I saw Astrid's eyes looking back at me. I dropped my sword and fell to my knees.

'Forgive me, Torvald, you're right, I should have been here. I and whoever attacked her are to blame, no one else.'

Torvald took my arm and helped me to stand. 'We loved her too, Leofric, and I will never forgive myself for not being there for her. But she has gone to a better place and now we must protect her son.'

Over the next month, I withdrew into myself. I would sit for hours beside Astrid's grave. I talked to no one but her. This village I had longed to return to filled me with grief. Everywhere I turned reminded me of her. I could not stay. Where would I go? I did not know or care. I visited my son once or twice, even he reminded me of my loss, and to my shame, I resented that he lived and his mother did not. He was a fragile child which was little wonder after the start in life he'd had. His hair was thin and wispy and I wondered if he would be fair like Astrid or dark like me.

I knew whatever path I decided to take would be no life for a child. I did not want him pining for a father who was never there. I watched how the smith and his wife cared for him and my decision was made. They would raise the boy as theirs. Torvald had a brother in the west. Where, I did not ask, and he did not tell me. They would move there and the boy would be accepted as theirs. I gave Torvald a bag of coins, which he refused, but I insisted he take. Before he left, he took me aside.

'A few weeks after she was attacked, Astrid pushed this into my hand.' Torvald gave me a small piece of red cloth. 'I was unclear of its meaning but presumed she tore it from her assailant's clothing. I searched the village but found nothing. I thought you should be aware of it, lord. Also, you should know Mair visited your wife on a number of occasions before and since the attack.'

I thanked him, and he and his wife left Horsdone for a new life with their daughter and their new son. Another piece of my heart broke but I believed it was the right thing for the boy. I folded the red cloth and placed it in my leather pouch. It was a slim piece of evidence, but it was all I had. What puzzled me more was Mair. She had known all along Astrid's fate yet never told me, why? Did she know who did this? One thing was certain, I would find out.

For two weeks I brooded around the village. Men eventually found the courage to approach me about the problems that were important to them, but I could not share the same concerns and directed them to Wulfgar, who more or less ran the estate along with Starcolf and Scalpi.

I spent most of my days sat by Astrid's grave begging her forgiveness. Riocus came to me on several occasions.

'It does seem unfair at times that God should spare you, the blasphemer, yet take your God-fearing, gentle wife. Yet He does nothing by chance, everything He does has a purpose. You know His purpose for you, lord. I was once resentful of your skill with the quill. Now I have come to see that you are just an instrument God uses so people will marvel at your letters and illustrations and through those will come to understand His magnificence, wisdom and power, that if He can enable even one such as you to accomplish such a work of beauty, then He can achieve anything. To resist His call now is to defame the name of your wife and everything she believed in.'

On each occasion, by the time Riocus left me, my spirit diminished, guilt overpowered me beyond all reason and I withdrew further and further into myself.

In those dark, joyless days, I hardly ate but drank too much ale. I would sit cross-legged, rocking, staring aimlessly. To those who witnessed this jabbering wreck, I must have seemed as far from a mighty warrior as a suckling lamb.

As I sat one grey, sunless morning, when it seemed my world could not become bleaker, Wulfgar stood before me. This man, who had believed in me when others did not, this man who could say to me things others dared not, seemed reticent to speak, yet knew he must. 'Leofric, my friend and my lord, I despise the fact that I have to be the bearer of more sad news. Our mutual friend, Tripp, has died.'

Those three words, 'Tripp has died,' were the culmination of all my grief. It was although my mind or heart could take no more sorrow. My ears filled with a loud, droning noise that deadened all other sound; my eyes blinded by a white, glowing light.

How long had passed since that moment or what occurred afterwards, I am unaware. The next memory I have is sitting on my horse, Stormbringer, dressed in my war gear surrounded by the monks at Filey priory.

'Welcome home, Brother Luke,' said a smiling Thurston. 'God does indeed work in ways that are a mystery to us mere mortals.'

I was helped down from my horse and led to a room at the end of the dormer.

I stripped off my clothes of black leather and placed them with my shield, my sword Widewe Wyrhta and the skeleton helmet of death, in a large, iron-studded chest. The heavy lid slammed shut and I locked away my old life and hung the key around my neck.

I put on the austere, woollen habit of a monk and went to the scriptorium, to bring glory with my quill to a God I did not believe in, unaware the threads of fate were not finished with me yet and were being woven to change my life forever.

Place Names

Three letters modern readers may not be familiar with which do appear in old English texts are;

The ash Æ; æ, pronounced a as in sat.

The thorn; þ, Þ used for th as in the.

The eth; Ð, ð, is said as in <u>leath</u>er.

*Denotes fictional places.

- **Ælmham**= **Elmham**... Norfolk.
- **Æsc** = **Ash River**... Hertfordshire.
- ***Æssefeld-Underbarroe**=**Ashfield-Under-Barrow**... Village on the border of south west Hertfordshire.
- **Alba** = **Kingdom of Scotland between AD 900 and 1286**
- **Ambell** = **Amble**...Small fishing port at the mouth of the River Coquet.
- **Bevere** = Island in the River Severn, north of Worcester.
- ***Branlei** = **Branley**... One of Leofric the Black's northern villages.
- **Brune** = **Bourne**...Lincolnshire.
- **Boseham**= **Bosham**...West Sussex.
- **Brycgstow**= **Bristol**...Town (in 11cen) west of England straddling River Avon.
- **Bylgeslege** = **Billingsley**...Shropshire.
- **Cocwud** = **River Coquet**... It flows from the Cheviot Hills on the

Scottish English border.

- **Contwaraburg = Canterbury**...Kent, seat of the Archbishop.
- **Cornwealum = Cornwall.**
- **Croyland = Crowland**... Near Peterborough, Lincolnshire.
- **Doferum = Dover**...Kent. The gateway to southern England.
- **Dertamuõa = Dartmouth**, Devon.
- **Dore = River Dore**... Herefordshire. It flows for twelve miles from the Black Mountains close to the border between England and Wales.
- **Dour = River Dour**... Flows through Dover down to the sea.
- ***Dunstede = Dunstead**... One of Leofric the Black's northern villages.
- **Eanulfesbyrig = Eynesbury,** part of present day St. Neots, Cambridgeshire.
- **Elig= Ely**... Cambridgeshire...Stronghold of the Saxon resistance against William the Conqueror.
- **Eoferwic...York**
- ***Falostunte = Fallowstones**... One of Leofric the Black's northern villages.
- ***Fenbrige = Fenbridge**... One of Leofric the Black's northern villages.
- **Filey= Filey**...Fishing village north Yorkshire coast. Site of fictious Priory in book.
- **Forth = River Forth**...Flows from west to east of Scotland to the sea, where it becomes the Firth of Forth.
- **Glæstingabyrig = Glastonbury**... Somerset. Wealthiest Abbey in England by 1066.
- **Glowecestre = Gloucestershire**...South west England.
- **Heorotford = Hertford**...Hertfordshire, has London on its southern border and was always on the cusp of the conflicts between

439

Saxon and Danes.

- **Hereford = Hereford...** Sitting on the River Wye it is sixteen miles east from the Welsh border.
- **Herefordscir = Herefordshire.**
- ***Horsdone = Horsdon...** One of Leofric the Black's northern villages.
- **Humbre = River Humber...** A tidal estuary on the east coast of northern England.
- **Lambhyo = Lambeth** (landing place for lambs) South bank of the River Thames.
- **Lemster = Leominster...** Herefordshire on the River Lugg.
- **Lindcylene = Lincoln...**West Lincolnshire on the River Witham.
- **Lincolnescire = Lincolnshire...** Has a long eastern coastline on the North Sea and borders Norfolk to the south east.
- **Lundene = London...** Over a thousand years ago a writer called it 'a trading place for many nations who visit by land and sea.'
- **Mældun = Maldon...** Ancient Essex town on the Blackwater Estuary.
- **Mercia =** An ancient earldom of England, an area now the Midlands.
- **Norðhymbraland =** Anglo Saxon kingdom north of the Humber. Later an English earldom, north east England.
- **Oxenaford = Oxford...** Central England.
- **Porland = Portland...** Dorset.
- **Sancte Eadmundes Byrig = Bury St. Edmunds...**Suffolk. By the time of the conquest boasted the fourth richest abbey in England.
- **Sandwic = Sandwich...**District of Dover on the south east coast of England.
- **Sæfern = Severn River...**longest river in Great Britain.

- **Streanæshealh = Hvitaby =** White Bay = Whitby, North Yorkshire.
- **Sture = Stour River...** Flowing past Sandwich.
- **Suþgeweorc** = Southwark... One of the oldest parts of London. Its name means southern defensive works.
- **Tese** = Tees River...Rises in the Pennines in northern England and flows east to the North Sea.
- **Temes = Thames River...**Longest river flowing entirely in England. The name means dark river.
- **Thorney Island =Westminster...**Originally bramble covered island in the middle of the Tyburn River, which still runs around it, though underground. Site of Westminster Abbey
- **Thorneley = Thorley...**Village in East Hertfordshire. Thorley manor was owned by Tostig Godwinson.
- ***Trogbyrne=Troughburn...** One of Leofric The Black's northern villages.
- **Wæge = River Wye**
- **Wealtham = Waltham...**Essex. Land owned by Tovi the Proud.
- **Wessex** = An ancient earldom in south west England, an area now Hampshire, Dorset, Wiltshire, Somerset.
- **Wigraceaster = Worcester**
- **Wintanceaster = Winchester**
- **Wydeford = Widford...**Neighbouring village to Ashfield-under-Barrow above the Ash valley in Hertfordshire.

Characters

As they are when first introduced in the story.
*Denotes entirely fictional. Those without an Asterix are my fictional interpretation of real historical characters.

- ÆLFGAR ... Son of the Earl of Mercia.
- ÆLFRIC PUTTOC ...Archbishop of York 1023-1051
- *ÆTHERIC... Astrid's maternal uncle.
- *ALBERIC... Key holding monk at Filey Priory.
- *AENOUD... Flemish steward of Wulfric Rabell.
- *AGATHA...Wulfric Rabell's daughter.
- *ALFLUNN THE RED... Skipper of the boat to St. Omer.
- ALFRED...Murdered brother of Edward the Confessor.
- *ASGER BLOOD SPILLER... One of Fritjof Heironson's henchmen.
- *ANSGAR... Miller.
- *ARAMOS... Old monk, watcher of the door.
- *ASTRID...Daughter of the Thegn of Horsdone.
- *BALD ... Albino monk, devotee of Saint Neot.
- BEORN ESTRITHSON...Nephew of Cnut, nephew of Godwin's wife Gytha.
- BERNARD of SAINT VALERY... Suitor of Turfrida.
- *BLEDIG... Hereford scout.
- *BROKK ... Orphaned companion of Leofric the Black.
- *BRUNI... Steward of Horsdone.
- *CEDRIC...Monk at Filey Priory.
- CNUT...Danish King of England, father of Harold

Harefoot and Harthecnut.

- *CRISPIN ... Priest at Æssefeld.
- CYNESIGE... Archbishop of York. 1051-1060
- *DAGFIN...Lord Gilbert's Steward.
- *DRUST...Welsh seer.
- EADSIGE...Archbishop of Canterbury.1038-1050
- *EALDAN IDENSON ... One of twin brothers, Æssefeld fyrd man.
- EALDRED...Bishop of Worcester.
- *EDGARD...Leofric the Black's half-brother.
- *EDMUND... Priest at Horsdone.
- EDWARD (The Confessor) Son of King Æthelred and Emma of Normandy.
- *EDWIN... Companion of Leofric the Black.
- EDYTH...Earl Godwin's daughter.
- *ELDRED...Thegn of Widford.
- EMMA...Queen of Æthelred and Cnut. Mother of two kings, Harthecnut and Edward. Mother of Alfred and step mother to Harold Harefoot.
- EUSTACE of BOULOGNE...Was married to Edward the Confessor's sister, Goda.
- *GIFRE IDENSON...The younger brother of Æssefeld's fyrd men.
- GILBERT of GHENT...Patron of a training camp in Northumbria, though his presence in England is disputed by some historians.
- *GLOM... One of Beorn's body-guards.
- *GODE... Hakon's mother, sister of Grim.
- GODWIN... Earl of Wessex. Father to Sweyn, Harold, Tostig, Gyth, Leofwine, Wulfnoth.

- *GRIM... Renweard, Thegn of Æssefeld's right-hand man.
- *GRINDAN IDENSON... One of twin brothers. Æssefeld fyrd man.
- GRUFFYDD AP LLYELYN...King of Gwynedd, South Wales.
- GRUFFYDD AP RHYDDERCH...King of Gwent and Deheubarth.
- *GUDBRAND...Harthecnut's henchman.
- *GUY BEAUFORT...Would-be knight.
- GYTH...Harold's brother, fourth Godwin son.
- HAKON... Bastard son of Sweyn Godwinson.
- HARALD HARDRADA...Norwegian adventurer, later King of Norway.
- HAROLD HAREFOOT... Deceased King of England.
- HAROLD GODWINSON... Second son of Earl Godwin.
- HARTHACNUT... King of Denmark, incoming King of England. Son of King Cnut and Emma of Normandy.
- HEREWARD...Head strong youth from Bourne.
- *IDWAL... Hereford scout.
- *INGVAR... Northern warrior.
- *ISCARIOT...Battle hardened warrior, trainer of men.
- *KELD...One of Fritjof Heironson's henchmen.
- *LAMONT... Bard.
- *LEAFWOLD...Renweard's steward at Æssefeld.
- LEAFGAR...Harold Godwinson's chaplain.
- LEOFRIC ... Earl of Mercia.
- LEOFRIC THE BLACK... Narrator.
- LEOFWINE...Earl Godwin's fifth son.

444

- LYFING...Bishop of Worcester, accused of involvement with Prince Alfred's murder.
- *MAIR...Strange daughter of Nairn the 'Dream Teller.'
- MARTIN LIGHTFOOT...Constant companion of Hereward of Bourne.
- *MILOSH...Leofric the Black's maternal grandfather.
- *MIRELA...Leofric the Black's mother.
- *MODRED... A captain of Renweard's fighting men.
- *NAIRN... 'Dream Teller,' 'Potion maker,' 'Cunning woman.'
- *OLAF...Pig-herder's son.
- OSBEORN BULLAX...Eldest son of Earl Siward.
- *OSWIN... Smith at Dover, old friend of Renweard.
- *OTTO... St. Omer sailor, Sophia's brother.
- *QUILLIAM...Old miserable monk at Filey Priory.
- *PETER... Young novice at Filey Priory.
- *REGNAR THE MEAN... One of Fritjof Heironson's henchmen.
- *REINALD LEVETT... Disgraced Norman knight.
- *RENWEARD SIGWEARDSON...Thegn of Ashfield-under-Barrow, Leofric the Black's father.
- *RIOCUS...Spiteful monk at Filey Priory.
- *RUNOLF... Messenger. Steward.
- *RUSH...A slave of Renweard...Leofric the Black's friend.
- *SIGEBERHT... Northern warrior.
- *SILFRIED...Renweard's second wife.
- SIWARD...Earl of Northumbria.
- SIWARD...Nephew of Earl Siward.

- *SCALPI...Ferocious hireling.
- *SCAND...Fugitive from Ely.
- *SOPHIA... Turfrida's hand maiden.
- SPEARHAFOC...Monk, artist and goldsmith.
- *STARCOLF... Fyrd man from Horsdone.
- STIGAND...Bishop of Elmham 1043
- SWEYN GODWINSON... Eldest son of Earl Godwin, father of Hakon.
- THURSTAN...Abbot at Ely.
- *TORVALD... The smith at Horsdone.
- TOSTIG GODWINSON...Third son of Earl Godwin.
- TOVI THE PROUD...Wealthy landowner in southern England.
- TURFRIDA... Leofric's first love.
- *TRIPP... Trader and old friend of Renweard.
- *ULF...Thegn of Widford's son.
- *ULIRIC ...One of Beorn's body-guards.
- *ULLA...Renweard's slave and mother of Rush.
- *WEALDHERE... Oswin the smith's son.
- WILLIAM THE BASTARD...Duke of Normandy and King of England.
- *WREGAN...Fugitive from Ely.
- *WULFGAR...Mysterious horseman.
- WULFRIC RABELL...The Castellan of St. Omer.
- WULFNOTH...Sixth and youngest son of Earl Godwin.

GLOSSARY

- CEORL...Pronounced Churl. Lowest of the classes in Anglo Saxon society.

- ELF-BOLT... Arrow head shaped flint (belemnite) said to be used by fairies and witches. Also used as a good luck charm to ward off such beings.

- HAUBERK... A long coat of chain mail.

- HANDFAST WIFE... The custom of binding the right hands of bride and groom with a cord. Accepted by the society of the time but not seen as a legal marriage by the church.

- HEORAWEROD...A personal body guard to a king or noble.

- JORMUNGAND... The world serpent who grew so large he encircled the earth and grasped his own tail in his mouth... When he spits it out Ragnarok will begin.

- MASLIN BREAD... A substandard bread mixture of rye, barley and wheat eaten by the poor and servants.

- MOOT... An assembly held for debate, especially in Anglo-Saxon and medieval times.

- RAGNAROK... The day of the death of Gods.

- SCOP...Anglo-Saxon poet.

- SEAX...Large Fighting knife.

- SKALD ...Norse poet.

- THEGN...Pronounced Thane. The majority of the aristocracy below an earl.

- WERGILD...Compensation, paid to the kin or lord of a slain man.

- WOLF'S HEAD...An outlaw, who if resisted capture could be killed with impunity and just his severed head be presented as proof. As if he were no better than a hunted wolf.

- YGGDRASIL...Mythical tree that connects the nine worlds, and where the norms thread the fates of men.

RUNE TRANSLATION

Historical observations

Even an event as famous as the battle of Hastings is shrouded in doubt and contradictions. The further back we look we realise why it is often called the Dark Ages. Learned historians (of which I am not) often disagree on dates of people's births, deaths, battles etc. Sometimes all we have are legends, changed and modified over the course of time. The Anglo-Saxon Chronicles, which is where a great deal of our knowledge of the period derives from, along with the Bayeux embroidery, often has three or four conflicting accounts of the same event.

That said, I have tried to stay as close to the historical facts as possible although if there are two or three alternative options, I have chosen the one that fits my story most.

In 973 Edgar the Peaceful was the first English king to wear an actual crown and he was given a sceptre at his coronation. However, the royal regalia, or crown jewels as we know them, are thought to have appeared in the reign of Edward the Confessor. Over the next thousand years they were sold, lost, melted down and eventually destroyed by the Puritans at the end of the civil war. The oldest piece is the anointing spoon. However, the sapphire from the ring of Edward the Confessor is now in the imperial state crown along with a large ruby, actually the largest, uncut spinel in the world, which belonged to the Black Prince and had been war booty. I have taken the liberty of supposing that ruby was once in England before, and after being stolen by Danes, ended up in the hands of Pedro the Cruel, King of Spain who gave it to the Black Prince.

Apparently, there were detailed plans and drawings of the regalia and what we have now are copies of the originals.

Throughout history there have been legends and myths about various artefacts concerning Jesus Christ; pieces of the true cross, the spear of destiny, the holy grail, the Turin shroud. So it took little imagination to conjure up the jewelled sceptre once owned by one of the 'three kings' who visited Christ in Bethlehem. The bible mentions neither the number nor nature of the men, simply stating, 'Wise men from the east came to Jerusalem.' However, that has not stopped the cult of the three wise men, or kings, from being perpetuated up to our day. The tomb of the three kings or magi is a gilded sarcophagus behind the high altar in Cologne Cathedral. It is the largest known reliquary in the western world. The relics, bones, were originally kept in Constantinople but later taken to Milan before ending up at Cologne, attracting many pilgrims to visit them up to this day.

Leofric the Black was an actual person, though as far as I can ascertain is mentioned only once in history as a companion of Hereward the Saxon, everything else about him in the novel is my invention.

Harthecnut did come in peace and also had his half-brother dug up and thrown into a bog, although not necessarily on the same occasion. He did die at Tovi the Proud's wedding, collapsing in front of the guests.

Sweyn Godwinson allegedly raped a nun, murdered his cousin and had an illegitimate son called Hakon. Some historians claim the nun was the child's mother, others that he was from an earlier liaison. Sweyn was forgiven for each of these crimes and died on a pilgrimage to Jerusalem.

Hakon is a shadowy figure in history only really noted as being the illegitimate son of Sweyn Godwinson and one of two hostages given by Earl Godwin at the time of his dispute with King Edward.

I have tried to keep the events at Dover and subsequent conflict between the Godwins and King Edward as near to the accounts we have of them as possible. The Godwins were exiled and returned the following year.

Hereward the Saxon was a real person but his life is clouded by half-truths and myth, making it difficult to separate the two. I have included both fact and myth in my interpretation of the hero of the fens.

451

Spearhafoc did become the king's goldsmith and did abscond with gold and jewels belonging to king and Church.

Bald's Leech Book is a three volume work of Anglo Saxon cures, remedies, medicines and salves. It was originally written in the ninth century for Bald, by a man called Cild. The Bald in the book is a fictitious descendent. There is only one copy in existence today, and that is an eleventh century copy of the work. The text survives in only one manuscript which is in The British Library.

Earl Siward of Northumberland supported Malcolm Canmore against Mac Bethad mac Findlaich, Shakespeare's Macbeth, and his son and nephew were killed in the battle. The traditional site of the battle was at Dunsinane Hill in Perthshire, Scotland. Many of the Normans, who fled England on the return of the Godwins, were given shelter by Mac Bethad in return for service in battle. Most of them were killed in this conflict.

Earl Ælfgar was banished when Tostig was made Earl of Northumberland, probably for treasonable talk against the king.

The Saxon soldiers at Hereford were forced to fight on horse-back in the Norman fashion and they and the Normans, under the command of Earl Ralph, turned and fled before a spear was thrown. He was known as Ralph the Timid forever after.

Y Mab Darogan or 'son of destiny' is a figure in the legends of the Welsh, who will come and liberate them from the English, driving them back across the sea and reclaiming Britain for the Celts. There have been numerous men believed to be the Mab Darogan; King Arthur, Llywelyn the Great, Owain Glyndwr, Henry Tudor and others.

I have used the nickname Hardrada for Harald Sigurdsson although some claim it was not used in his lifetime, yet others assert it was given to him whilst on various campaigns. As it is the name he is most associated with and means 'hard ruler', which contemporaries surely would have recognised him by, I have kept it if only to prevent confusion with Harold Godwinson.

Obviously, it is impossible to know the actual thoughts, desires and motives of people so far removed from us by time. To me, that is the challenge of the historical writer, to attempt to interpret the known facts into something more personal and relatable to ourselves, though keeping the essence of a past age, never forgetting that it is fiction and in my opinion our aim is not to instruct but to entertain. If in some way it stimulates readers to research further for an understanding of the past, to me that is a bonus. I hope readers enjoy reading this book as much as I have in writing it and encourage anyone who wishes to discuss any aspect of it to contact me.

e. mail edwardcbeard@yahoo.com

Or my website www.edwardcartwrightbeard.com